"Why should I trust you?" I snarled at Ash.

I was completely aware that I was being an idiot, that we needed to get out of there before anyone saw us, but it was like I'd eaten spill-your-guts, and words just kept pouring out. "You've been lying to me from the beginning. Everything you said, everything we did, that was all a ploy to bring me here. You set me up from the very start."

"Meghan—"

"Is this a game you like to play? Make the stupid human girl fall for you and then laugh as you rip her heart out? You knew what Rowan was doing, and you didn't do anything to stop it!"

"Of course not!" Ash snarled back, his vehemence startling me into silence. "I had to make everyone believe I didn't care, or they would've torn you apart. Emotions are a weakness here, Meghan. And the Winter Court preys on the weak. They would've hurt you to get to me. Now, come on." He reached for me again, and I let him take my hand without protest. "Let's get out of here before it's too late."

"I'm afraid it's already too late," drawled a snide, familiar voice, making my heart stop.

Also by Julie Kagawa
from Harlequin Teen

THE IRON KING (Book 1 of The Iron Fey)

and coming in February 2011, don't miss

THE IRON QUEEN (Book 3 of The Iron Fey)

LOVE & BETRAYAL.
A FAERY WORLD
GONE MAD.

THE IRON FEY

# IRON DAUGHTER

## JULIE KAGAWA

# HARLEQUIN®
# TEEN

# HARLEQUIN®
## TEEN

ISBN-13: 978-0-373-21013-8

THE IRON DAUGHTER

Copyright © 2010 by Julie Kagawa

Recycling programs
for this product may
not exist in your area.

This edition published by arrangement with Harlequin Books S.A.

For questions and comments about the quality of this book
please contact us at Customer_eCare@Harlequin.ca.

® and TM are trademarks of the publisher. Trademarks indicated with
® are registered in the United States Patent and Trademark Office,
the Canadian Trade Marks Office and in other countries.

www.HarlequinTEEN.com

**Printed in U.S.A.**

To Nick, my inspiration

PART ONE

# CHAPTER ONE

*The Winter Court*

The Iron King stood before me, magnificent in his beauty, silver hair whipping about like an unruly waterfall. His long black coat billowed behind him, accenting the pale, angular face and translucent skin, the blue-green veins glowing beneath the surface. Lightning flickered in the depths of his jet-black eyes, and the steel tentacles running the length of his spine and shoulders coiled around him like a cloak of wings, glinting in the light. Like an avenging angel, he floated toward me, hand outstretched, a sad, tender smile on his lips.

I stepped forward to meet him as the iron cables wrapped gently around me, drawing me close. "Meghan Chase," Machina murmured, running a hand through my hair. I shivered, keeping my hands at my sides as the tentacles caressed my skin. "You have come. What is it you want?"

I frowned. What did I want? What had I come for? "My

brother," I answered, remembering. "You kidnapped my
brother, Ethan, to draw me here. I want him back."

"No." Machina shook his head, moving closer. "You did not
come for your brother, Meghan Chase. Nor did you come for
the Unseelie prince you claim to love. You came here for one
thing only. Power."

My head throbbed and I tried backing away, but the cables
held me fast. "No," I muttered, struggling against the iron net.
"This…this is wrong. This isn't how it went."

"Show me, then." Machina opened his arms wide. "How
was it 'supposed' to go? What did you come here to do? Show
me, Meghan Chase."

"No!"

"Show me!"

Something throbbed in my hand: the beating pulse of the
Witchwood arrow. With a yell, I raised my arm and drove the
sharpened point through Machina's chest, sinking the arrow
into his heart.

Machina staggered back, giving me a look of shocked
horror. Only it wasn't Machina anymore but a faery prince with
midnight hair and bright silver eyes. Lean and dangerous, silhouetted all in black, his hand went to the sword at his belt
before he realized it was too late. He swayed, fighting to stay
on his feet, and I bit down a scream.

"Meghan," Ash whispered, a thin line of red trickling from
his mouth. His hands clutched at the arrow in his chest as he
fell to his knees, pale gaze beseeching mine. "Why?"

Shaking, I raised my hands and saw they were covered in glistening crimson, running rivulets down my arms, dripping to
the ground. Below the slick coating, things wiggled beneath
my skin, pushing up through the surface, like leeches in blood.
Somewhere in the back of my mind, I knew I should be terrified, appalled, majorly grossed out. I wasn't. I felt powerful,

powerful and strong, as if electricity surged beneath my skin, as if I could do anything I wanted and no one could stop me.

I looked down at the Unseelie prince and sneered at the pathetic figure. Could I really have loved such a weakling once upon a time?

"Meghan." Ash knelt there, the life fading from him bit by bit, even as he struggled to hold on. For a brief moment, I admired his stubborn tenacity, but it wouldn't save him in the end. "What about your brother?" he pleaded. "And your family? They're waiting for you to come home."

Iron cables unfurled from my back and shoulders, spreading around me like glittering wings. Gazing down at the Unseelie prince, helpless before me, I gave him a patient smile.

"I *am* home."

The cables slashed down in a silver blur, slamming into the faery's chest and staking him to the ground. Ash jerked, his mouth gaping silently, before his head lolled back and he shattered like crystal on concrete.

Surrounded by the glittering remains of the Unseelie prince, I threw back my head and laughed, and it turned into a ragged scream as I wrenched myself awake.

MY NAME IS Meghan Chase.

I've been in the palace of the Winter fey for a while now. How long exactly? I don't know. Time doesn't flow right in this place. While I've been stuck in the Nevernever, the outside world, the mortal world, has gone on without me. If I ever get out of here, if I ever make it home, I might find a hundred years have passed while I was gone, like Rip van Winkle, and all my family and friends are long dead.

I try not to think of that too often, but sometimes, I can't help but wonder.

My room was cold. It was always cold. *I* was always cold.

Not even the sapphire flames in the hearth were enough to drive out the incessant chill. The walls and ceiling were made of opaque, smoky ice; even the chandelier sparkled with a thousand icicles. Tonight, I wore sweatpants, gloves, a thick sweater and a wool hat, but it wasn't enough. Outside my window, the underground city of the Winter fey sparkled with icy radiance. Dark forms leaped and fluttered in the shadows, flashing claws, teeth and wings. I shivered and gazed up at the sky. The ceiling of the vast cavern was too far away to see through the darkness, but thousands of tiny lights, balls of faery fire or faeries themselves, twinkled like a blanket of stars.

There was a rap at my door.

I didn't call out *Come in.* I'd learned not to do so in the past. This was the Unseelie Court, and inviting them into your room was a very, very bad idea. I couldn't keep them out completely, but the fey follow rules above all else, and by order of their queen, I was not to be bothered unless I requested it.

Letting them into my room could almost sound like such a request.

I crossed the floor, my breath streaming around me, and cracked open the door.

A slinky black cat sat on the floor with its tail curled around itself, gazing up at me with unblinking yellow eyes. Before I could say anything, it hissed and darted through the crack like a streak of shadow.

"Hey!"

I spun around, but the cat was no longer a cat. Tiaothin the phouka stood there, grinning at me, canines glinting. Of course. It would be the phouka; they didn't follow social rules. In fact, they seemed to take great pleasure in breaking them. Furred ears peeked out of her dreadlocked hair, twitching sporadically. She wore a gaudy jacket that sparkled with fake gems and studs, ripped jeans and combat boots. Unlike the Seelie

Court, the Unseelie fey actually preferred "mortal" clothing. Whether it was in direct defiance of the Seelie Court, or because they wanted to blend in more with humans, I wasn't sure.

"What do you want?" I asked cautiously. Tiaothin had taken a keen interest in me when I was brought to court, the insatiable curiosity of a phouka, I suppose. We'd talked a few times, but she wasn't exactly what I'd call a friend. The way she stared at me, unblinking, like she was sizing me up for her next meal, always made me nervous.

The phouka hissed, running her tongue along her teeth. "You're not ready," she said in her sibilant voice, looking me over skeptically. "Hurry. Hurry and change. We should go, quickly."

I frowned. Tiaothin had always been difficult to understand, bouncing from one subject to the next so quickly it was hard to keep up. "Go where?" I asked, and she giggled.

"The queen," Tiaothin purred, flicking her ears back and forth. "The queen has called for you."

My stomach twisted into a tight ball. Ever since I'd come to the Winter Court with Ash, I'd been dreading this moment. When we'd first arrived at the palace, the queen regarded me with a predatory smile and dismissed me, saying that she wished to speak to her son alone and would call for me soon. Of course, "soon" was a relative term in Faery, and I'd been on pins and needles ever since, waiting for Mab to remember me.

That was also the last time I saw Ash.

Thinking of Ash sent a flutter through my stomach, reminding me how much had changed. When I first came to Faery, searching for my kidnapped brother, Ash had been the enemy, the cold, dangerous son of Mab, Queen of the Unseelie Court. When war threatened the courts, Mab sent Ash to capture me, hoping to use me as leverage against my father, King Oberon. But, frantic to save my brother, I made a bargain with the

Winter prince, instead: if he helped me rescue Ethan, I would return with him to the Unseelie Court without a fight. At that point, it was a desperate gamble; I needed all the help I could get to face down the Iron King and save my brother. But, somewhere in that blasted wasteland of dust and iron, watching Ash battle the realm that was poisoning his very essence, I realized I was in love with him.

Ash had gotten me there, but he almost didn't survive his brush with Machina. The King of the Iron fey was insanely strong, almost invincible. Against all odds, I managed to defeat Machina, rescue my brother, and take him home.

That night as per our contract, Ash came for me. It was time to honor my end of the bargain. Leaving my family behind once more, I followed Ash into Tir Na Nog, the land of Winter.

The journey through Tir Na Nog was cold, dark, and terrifying. Even with the Winter prince at my side, Faery was still savage and inhospitable, especially to humans. Ash was the perfect bodyguard, dangerous, alert and protective, but he seemed distant at times, distracted. And the farther we went into Winter, the more he drew away, sealing himself off from me and the world. And he wouldn't tell me why.

On the last night of our journey we were attacked. A monstrous wolf, sent by Oberon himself, tracked us down, intent on killing Ash and spiriting me back to the Summer Court. We managed to escape, but Ash was wounded fighting the creature, so we took refuge in an abandoned ice cave to rest and bind his wounds.

He was silent as I wrapped a makeshift bandage around his arm, but I could feel his eyes on me as I tied it off. Releasing his arm, I looked up to meet his silvery gaze. Ash blinked slowly, giving me that look that meant he was trying to figure me out. I waited, hoping I would finally glean some insight into his sudden aloofness.

"Why didn't you run?" he asked softly. "If that thing had killed me, you wouldn't have to come back to Tir Na Nog. You would've been free."

I scowled at him.

"I agreed to that contract, same as you," I muttered, tying off the bandage with a jerk, but Ash didn't even grunt. Angry now, I glared up at him, meeting his eyes. "What, you think just because I'm human I was going to back out? I knew what I was getting into, and I am going to uphold my end of the bargain, no matter what happens. And if you think I'd leave you just so I wouldn't have to meet Mab, then you don't know me at all."

"It's *because* you're human," Ash continued in that same quiet voice, holding my gaze, "that you missed a tactical opportunity. A Winter fey in your position wouldn't have come back. They wouldn't let their emotions get in the way. If you're going to survive in the Unseelie Court, you have to start thinking like them."

"Well, I'm *not* like them." I rose and took a step back, trying to ignore the feeling of hurt and betrayal, the stupid angry tears pressing at the corners of my eyes. "I'm not a Winter faery. I'm human, with human feelings and emotions. And if you want me to apologize for that, you can forget it. I can't just shut off my feelings like you can."

I whirled to stalk away in a huff, but Ash rose with blinding speed and gripped my upper arms. I stiffened, locking my knees and keeping my back straight, but struggling with him would have been useless. Even wounded and bleeding, he was much stronger than me.

"I'm not ungrateful," he murmured against my ear, making my stomach flutter despite itself. "I just want you to understand. The Winter Court preys on the weak. It's their nature. They will try to tear you apart, physically and emotionally, and I won't always be there to protect you."

I shivered, anger melting away, as my own doubts and fears came rushing back. Ash sighed, and I felt his forehead touch the back of my hair, his breath fanning my neck. "I don't want to do this," he admitted in a low, anguished voice. "I don't want to see what they'll try to do to you. A Summer fey in the Winter Court doesn't stand much of a chance. But I vowed that I would bring you back, and I'm bound to that promise." He raised his head, squeezing my shoulders in an almost painful grip as his voice dropped a few octaves, turning grim and cold. "So you have to be stronger than they are. You can't let down your guard, no matter what. They will lead you on, with games and pretty words, and they will take pleasure in your misery. Don't let them get to you. And don't trust anyone." He paused, and his voice went even lower. "Not even me."

"I'll always trust you," I whispered without thinking, and his hands tightened, turning me almost savagely to face him.

"No," he said, narrowing his eyes. "You won't. I'm your enemy, Meghan. Never forget that. If Mab tells me to kill you in front of the entire court, it's my duty to obey. If she orders Rowan or Sage to carve you up slowly, making sure you suffer every second of it, I'm expected to stand there and let them do it. Do you understand? My feelings for you don't matter in the Winter Court. Summer and Winter will always be on opposite sides, and nothing will change that."

I knew I should be afraid of him. He was an Unseelie prince, after all, and had in no uncertain terms admitted he would kill me if Mab ordered him to. But he also admitted to having feelings for me, feelings that didn't matter, but it still made my stomach squirm when I heard it. And maybe I was being naive, but I couldn't believe Ash would willingly hurt me, even in the Winter Court. Not with the way he was looking at me now, his silver eyes conflicted and angry.

He stared at me a moment longer, then sighed. "You didn't hear a word I said, did you?" he murmured, closing his eyes.

"I'm not afraid," I told him, which was a lie: I was terrified of Mab and the Unseelie Court that waited at the end of this journey. But if Ash was there, I would be all right.

"You are infuriatingly stubborn," Ash muttered, raking a hand through his hair. "I don't know how I'm going to protect you when you have no concept of self-preservation."

I stepped close to him, placing a hand on his chest, feeling his heart beat under his shirt. "I trust you," I said, rising so our faces were inches apart, trailing my fingers down his stomach. "I know you'll find a way."

His breath hitched, and he regarded me hungrily. "You're playing with fire, you know that?"

"That's weird, considering you're an ice prin—" I didn't get any further, as Ash leaned in and kissed me. I looped my arms around his neck as his snaked around my waist, and for a few moments the cold couldn't touch me.

THE NEXT MORNING, he was back to being distant and aloof, barely speaking to me no matter how much I prodded. That night, we reached the underground palace of the Winter Court, and Mab dismissed me almost immediately. A servant showed me to my quarters, and I sat in the small, chilly room waiting for Ash to find me again.

He never returned from his meeting with the queen, and after several hours of waiting, I finally ventured into the halls of the Winter Court, looking for him. That's when I found Tiaothin, or rather, she found me in the library, playing keep-away with a hulking Jack-in-Irons as he stalked me between the aisles. After getting rid of the giant, she informed me that Prince Ash was no longer in the palace, and no one had any idea when he would be back.

"But that's just Ash," she'd said, grinning at me from atop a bookcase. "He's hardly ever at court. You catch a glimpse of him and *poof!* He's gone for another few months."

*Why would Ash just leave like that?* I wondered for about the billionth time. *He could've at least told me where he was going, and when he'd be back. He didn't have to leave me hanging.*

Unless he was deliberately avoiding me. Unless everything he'd said, the kiss we'd shared, the emotions in his eyes and voice, meant nothing to him. Maybe everything he'd done was only to bring me to the Winter Court.

"You're going to be late," Tiaothin purred, jerking me back to the present, watching me with glowing cat eyes. "Mab doesn't like to be kept waiting."

"Right," I said faintly, shaken out of my dark mood. *Oops, that's right. I've got an audience with the Faery Queen of Winter.* "Just give me a minute to change." I waited, but when Tiaothin didn't move, I scowled at her. "Uh, a little privacy, please?"

Tiaothin giggled, and in one shivery motion, became a shaggy black goat, who bounced out of the room on all fours. I shut the door and leaned against it, feeling my heart thud in my chest. Mab wanted to see me. The Queen of the Unseelie Court was finally calling on me. I shivered and pushed away from the door, walking to my dresser and the icy mirror on top.

My reflection stared back at me, slightly distorted by the cracks in the ice. Sometimes, I still didn't recognize myself. My straight blond hair was almost silver in the darkness of the room, and my eyes seemed far too big for my face. And there were other things, a thousand little details I couldn't put my finger on, that told me I wasn't human, that I was something to be feared. And of course, there was the most obvious difference. Pointed ears knifed up from the sides of my head, a screaming reminder of how unnormal I was.

I broke eye contact with my reflection and looked down at my clothes. They were warm and comfortable, but I was pretty sure meeting the Queen of the Unseelie Court dressed in sweatpants and a baggy sweater was a bad idea.

*Great. I'm supposed to meet the Queen of the Winter fey in five minutes. What do I wear?*

Closing my eyes, I tried collecting the glamour around me and shaping it over my clothes. Nothing. The massive rush of power I'd drawn on while battling the Iron King seemed to have faded, so much that I couldn't craft even the simplest illusion anymore. And not for lack of trying. Recalling my lessons with Grimalkin, a faery cat I'd met on my first trip to the Nevernever, I'd tried to become invisible, make shoes levitate and create faery fire. All failures. I couldn't even feel the glamour anymore, though I knew it was all around me. Glamour is fueled by emotion, and the wilder and more passionate the emotion—rage, lust, love—the easier it is to draw on. Yet I couldn't access it like I used to. It seemed I was back to being plain, nonmagical Meghan Chase. With pointy ears.

It was strange; for years, I hadn't even known I was half-fey. It was just a few months ago, on my sixteenth birthday, that my best friend Robbie had revealed himself to be Robin Goodfellow, the infamous Puck from *A Midsummer Night's Dream.* My kid brother, Ethan, had been kidnapped by faeries and I needed to rescue him. Oh, and by the way, I was the half-human daughter of King Oberon, Lord of the Summer fey. It took some getting used to, both the knowledge that I was half-faery and that I could use the magic of the fey—faery glamour—to work my own spells. Not that I was very good at it—I sucked, much to Grimalkin's irritation—but that wasn't the point. I hadn't even believed in faeries back then, but now that my magic was gone, it felt like pieces of me were missing.

With a sigh, I opened the dresser and pulled out jeans, a

white shirt and a long black coat, shrugging into them as quickly as I could to avoid freezing to death. For a moment, I wondered if I should dress in something fancy, like an evening gown. After a moment I decided against it. The Unseelie spurned formal attire. I'd have a better chance of survival if I tried fitting in.

When I opened the door, Tiaothin, no longer a goat or cat, stared at me and broke into a toothy leer. "This way," she hissed, backing into the icy corridor. Her yellow eyes seemed to float in the darkness. "The queen awaits."

I FOLLOWED TIAOTHIN down the dark, twisted hallways, trying to keep my gaze straight ahead. Out of the corners of my eyes, however, I still caught glimpses of the nightmares lurking in the halls the Unseelie Court.

A spindly bogey crouched behind a door like a giant spider, the pale, emaciated face staring at me through the crack. An enormous black hound with glowing eyes trailed us down the hallways, making no noise at all, until Tiaothin hissed at it and it slunk away. Two goblins and a shark-toothed redcap huddled in a corner, rolling dice made of teeth and tiny bones. As I passed, an argument broke out, the goblins pointing to the redcap and crying "Cheat, cheat!" in high-pitched voices. I didn't look back, but a shriek rang out behind me, followed by the wet sound of snapping bones. I shuddered and followed Tiaothin around a corner.

The corridor ended, opening into a massive room with icicles dangling from the ceiling like glittering chandeliers. Will-o'-the-wisps and globes of faery fire drifted between them, sending shards of fractured light over the walls and floor. The floor was shrouded in ice and mist, and my breath steamed in the air as we entered. Icy columns held up the ceiling, sparkling like translucent crystal and adding to the dazzling, confusing array of light and colors swirling around the room. Dark, wild music echoed throughout the chamber, played by a group of humans on a corner stage. The musicians' eyes were glazed over as they sawed and beat at their instruments, their bodies frighteningly thin. Their hair hung long and lank, as if they hadn't cut it for years. Yet, they didn't seem to be distressed or unhappy, playing their instruments with zombielike fervor, seemingly blind to their inhuman audience.

Dozens of Unseelie fey milled about the chamber, each one a creature straight out of a nightmare. Ogres and redcaps, goblins and spriggans, kobolds, phoukas, hobs and faeries I didn't have a name for, all wandering to and fro in the shifting darkness.

I quickly scanned the room, searching for tousled black hair and bright silver eyes. My heart fell. He wasn't here.

On the far side of the room, a throne of ice hovered in the air, glowing with frigid brilliance. Sitting on that throne, poised with the power of a massive glacier, was Mab, Queen of the Unseelie Court.

The Winter Queen was stunning, plain and simple. When I was in Oberon's court I'd seen her beside her rival, Titania, the Summer Queen, who was also beautiful but in an evil socialite type of way. Titania also held a grudge against me for being Oberon's daughter, and had tried to turn me into a deer once, so she wasn't my favorite person. Though they were complete opposites, the two queens were insanely powerful. Titania was a summer storm, beautiful and deadly and prone to frying something with lightning if it pissed her off. Mab was the coldest day in winter, where everything lies still and dead, held in fear of the unforgiving ice that killed the world before and could again.

The queen lounged in her chair, surrounded by several fey gentry—the sidhe—dressed in expensive, modern-day clothes, crisp white business suits and pin-striped Armani. When I saw her last, in Oberon's court, Mab had worn a flowing black dress that writhed like living shadows. Today, she was dressed in white: a white pantsuit, opal-tinted nails and ivory heels, her dark hair styled elegantly atop her head. Depthless black eyes, like a night without stars, looked up and spotted me, and her pale mulberry lips curved in a slow smile.

A chill slithered up my back. Fey care little for mortals. Humans are merely playthings to be used up and discarded. Both the Seelie and Unseelie Courts are subject to this. Even if I was half-fey and Oberon's daughter, I was all alone in the court of my father's ancient enemies. If I irritated Mab, there was no telling what the queen would do. Maybe turn me into a white rabbit and sic the goblins on me, though that seemed more Titania's style. I had a feeling Mab could come up with something infinitely more awful and twisted, and that made me very afraid.

Tiaothin ambled through the crowds of Unseelie fey, who paid her little attention. Most of their interest was directed at me as I followed, my heart thudding against my ribs. I felt the hungry stares, the eager grins and the eyes on the back of my neck, and concentrated on keeping my head up and my step confident. Nothing attracts faeries more than fear. A sidhe noble with a face that was all sharp angles caught my gaze and smiled, and my heart contracted painfully. He reminded me of Ash, who wasn't here, who had left me alone in this court of monsters.

The Winter Queen's chill grew more pronounced the closer we got; soon it was so cold it hurt to breathe. Tiaothin reached the foot of the throne and bowed. I did the same, though it was hard to do so without my teeth chattering. The Unseelie fey crowded behind us, their breath and murmuring voices making my skin crawl.

"Meghan Chase." The queen's voice rasped over the assembly, making my hair stand on end. Tiaothin slunk away and disappeared into the crowd, leaving me truly alone. "How good of you to join us."

"It's an honor to be here, my lady," I replied, using every ounce of my willpower to keep my voice from shaking. A tremor slipped out anyway, and not just from the cold. Mab smiled, amused, and leaned back, observing me with emotionless black eyes. Silence fell for a few heartbeats.

"So." The queen tapped her nails with a rhythmic clicking sound, making me jump. "Here we are. You must think you are very clever, daughter of Oberon."

"I—I'm sorry?" I stammered, as an icy fist gripped my heart. This wasn't starting well, not at all.

"You're not," Mab continued, giving me a patient smile. "But you will be. Make no mistake about that." She leaned forward, looking utterly inhuman, and I fought the urge to run screaming from the throne room. "I have heard of your exploits, Meghan Chase," the queen rasped, narrowing her eyes. "Did you not think I would find out? You tricked a prince of the Unseelie Court into following you into the Iron Realm. You made him fight your enemies for you. You bound him to a contract that nearly killed him. My precious boy, almost lost to me forever, because of you. How do you think that makes me feel?" Mab's smile grew more predatory, as my stomach twisted in fear. What could she do to me? Encase me in ice? Freeze me from the inside out? Chill my blood so I would never be warm again, no matter what I wore or how hot it became? I shivered, but then noticed a faint shimmer, like heat waves, around me, and suddenly realized Mab was tinting the air with glamour, manipulating my emotions and letting me imagine the worst fate possible. She didn't have to threaten or say anything; I was terrifying myself quite well.

In a lucid moment of distraction, I wondered if Ash had done the same to my emotions, manipulating me into falling for him. If Mab could do it, I'm sure her sons had the same talent. Were my feelings for Ash real, or some sort of fabricated glamour?

*Now's not the time to wonder about that, Meghan!*

Mab stared at me, gauging my reaction. I still shook in fear, but a part of me knew what the queen was doing. If I lost it and begged for mercy, I would find myself trapped in a faery contract before I knew what was happening. Promises are deadly serious among the fey, and I wasn't going to let Mab strong-arm me into pledging something I would instantly regret.

I took a furtive breath to collect my thoughts, so that when I did answer the Queen of the Winter fey, I wouldn't start bawling like a two-year-old.

"Forgive me, Queen Mab," I said, choosing my words carefully. "I meant no harm to you or yours. I needed Ash's help to rescue my brother from the Iron King."

At the mention of the Iron King, the Unseelie fey behind me stirred and growled, glancing around warily. I felt hackles rise, teeth bare and claws unsheathe. For normal faeries, iron was deadly poison, draining their magic and burning their flesh. An entire kingdom made of iron was horrible and terrifying to them; a faery ruler called the Iron King was blasphemous. For a moment, I had the satisfying thought that the Iron fey had become the bogeys and bogeymen of the faery world, and bit down a vindictive smile.

"I would name you a liar, girl," Mab said calmly, as the growls and mutterings behind me died down, "if I had not heard the same from my son's own lips. Rest assured, the Iron King's minions are no threat to us. Even now, Ash and his brothers are scouring our territory for these Iron fey. If the abominations are within our borders, we will hunt them down and destroy them."

I felt a rush of relief, but not because of Mab's claim. Ash was out there. He had a reason not to be at court.

"And yet..." Mab regarded me with a look that made my stomach squirm. "I cannot help but wonder how you managed to survive. Perhaps Summer is in league with the Iron fey, plotting with them against the Winter Court. That would be terribly amusing, wouldn't it, Meghan Chase?"

"No," I said softly. In my mind's eye, I saw the Iron King, reeling back as I drove the arrow through his chest, and clenched my fists to stop them from shaking. I could still see Machina writhing in pain, felt something cold and serpentine slithering under my skin. "The Iron King was going to destroy Summer as well as Winter. He's dead, now. I killed him."

Mab narrowed her eyes to black slits. "And you would have me believe that you, a half-human with virtually no power, managed to kill the Iron King?"

"Believe her," a new voice rang out, making my stomach twist and my heart jump to my throat. "I was there. I saw what happened."

Voices rose around me as the ranks of Unseelie fey parted like waves. I couldn't move. I was rooted to the spot, my heart pounding in my chest as the lean, dangerous form of Prince Ash strode into the chamber.

I shivered, and my stomach began turning nervous backflips. Ash looked much as he always did, darkly beautiful in black and gray, his pale skin a sharp contrast to his hair and clothes. His sword hung at his side, the sheath a luminous blue-black, giving off a frozen aura.

I was so relieved to see him. I stepped toward him, smiling, only to be stopped dead by his cold glare. Confused, I stumbled to a halt. Maybe he didn't recognize me. I met his gaze, waiting for his expression to thaw, for him to give me the tiny smile I adored so much. It didn't happen. His frosty eyes swept over me in a brief, dismissive glance, before he stepped around me and continued toward the queen. I felt a stab of shock and hurt; maybe he was playing it cool in front of the queen, but he could've at least said *hi*. I made the mental note to scold him later when we were alone.

"Prince Ash," Mab purred, as Ash went down on one knee before the throne. "You have returned. Are your brothers with you?"

Ash raised his head, but before he could answer, another voice interrupted him.

"Our youngest brother practically fled our presence in his haste to get to you, Queen Mab," said a high, clear voice behind me. "If I didn't know better, I would think he didn't want to speak to you in front of us."

Ash rose, his face carefully blank, as two more figures strode into the chamber, scattering fey like birds. Like Ash, they wore long, thin blades at their hips, and carried themselves with the easy grace of royalty.

The first, the one who had spoken, resembled Ash in build and height: lean, graceful and dangerous. He had a thin, pointed face, and black hair that bristled like spines atop his head. A white trench coat billowed out behind him, and a gold stud sparkled in one pointed ear. His gaze met mine as he swept past, ice-blue eyes glittering like chips of diamond, and his lips curled in a lazy smirk.

The second brother was taller than his siblings, more willowy than lean, his long raven hair tied back in a ponytail that reached his waist. A great gray wolf trailed behind him, amber eyes slitted and wary. "Rowan," Mab smiled at the first prince as the two bowed to her as Ash had done. "Sage. All my boys, home at last. What news do you bring me? Have you found these Iron fey within our borders? Have you brought me their poisonous little hearts?"

"My queen." It was the tallest of the three that spoke, the oldest brother, Sage. "We have searched Tir Na Nog from border to border, from the Ice Plains to the Frozen Bog to the Broken Glass Sea. We have found nothing of the Iron fey our brother has spoken of."

"Makes you wonder if our dear brother Ash exaggerated a bit," Rowan spoke up, his voice matching the smirk on his face. "Seeing as these 'legions of Iron fey' seem to have vanished into thin air."

Ash glared at Rowan and looked bored, but I felt the blood rush to my face.

"He's telling the truth," I blurted out, and felt every eye in the court turn on me. "The Iron fey are real, and they're still out there. And if you don't take them seriously, you'll be dead before you know what's happening."

Rowan smiled at me, a slit-eyed, dangerous smile. "And why would the half-blood daughter of Oberon care if the Winter Court lives or dies?"

"Enough." Mab's voice rasped through the chamber. She stood and waved a hand at the fey assembled behind us. "Get out. Leave, all of you. I will speak with my sons alone."

The crowd dispersed, slinking, stomping or gliding from the throne room. I hesitated, trying to catch Ash's gaze, wondering if I was included in this conversation. After all, I knew about the Iron fey, too. I succeeded in capturing his attention, but the Winter prince gave me a bored, hostile glare and narrowed his eyes.

"Didn't you hear the queen, half-breed?" he asked coldly, and my heart contracted into a tiny ball. I stared at him, mouth open, unwilling to believe this was Ash speaking to me, but he continued with ruthless disdain. "You're not welcome here. Leave."

I felt the sting of angry tears, and took a step toward him. "Ash—"

His eyes glittered as he shot me a glare of pure loathing. "It's *Master* Ash, or *Your Highness* to you, half-breed. And I don't recall giving you permission to speak to me. Remember that, because the next time you forget your place, I'll remind you with my blade." He turned away, dismissing me in one cold, callous gesture. Rowan snickered, and Mab watched me from atop her throne with a cool, amused gaze.

My throat tightened and a deluge pressed behind my eyes, ready to burst. I trembled and bit my lip to keep the flood in check. I would *not* cry. Not now, in front of Mab and Rowan and Sage. They were waiting for it; I could see it on their faces as they watched me expectantly. I could not show any weakness in front of the Unseelie Court if I wanted to survive.

Especially now that Ash had become one of the monsters.

With as much dignity as I could muster, I bowed to Queen Mab. "Excuse me then, Your Majesty," I said, in a voice that trembled only slightly. "I will leave you and your sons in peace."

Mab nodded, and Rowan gave me a mocking, exaggerated bow. Ash and Sage ignored me completely. I spun on my heel and walked from the throne room with my head held high, my heart breaking with every step.

# CHAPTER TWO

*A Declaration*

When I woke up, the room was light, cold beams streaming in the window. My face felt sticky and hot, and my pillow was damp. For one blissful moment, I didn't recall the events of the past night. Then, like a black wave, memory came rushing back.

Tears threatened again, and I buried my head under the covers. I'd spent most of the night sobbing into my pillow, my face muffled so that my cries wouldn't be overheard by some fey in the hall.

Ash's cruel words stabbed me through the heart. Even now, I could hardly believe the way he'd acted in the throne room, like I was scum beneath his boots, like he truly despised me. I'd been hoping for him, longing for him, to come back, and now those feelings were a twisted nail inside. I felt betrayed, as if what we shared on our journey to the Iron King was only a farce, a tactic the cunning Ice prince had used to get me to come to the Unseelie Court. Or perhaps he had just grown tired of me and moved on. Just another reminder of how capricious and insensitive the fey could be.

In that moment of utter loneliness and confusion, I wished Puck were here. Puck, with his carefree attitude and infectious smile, who always knew what to say to make me laugh again. As a human, Robbie Goodfell had been my neighbor and best friend; we shared everything, did everything, together. Of course, Robbie Goodfell turned out to be Robin Goodfellow, the infamous Puck of *A Midsummer Night's Dream,* and he was following Oberon's orders to protect me from the faery world. He'd disobeyed his king when he brought me into the Nevernever in search of Ethan, and again when I fled the Seelie Court and Oberon sent Puck to bring me back. His loyalty cost him dear when he was finally shot in a battle with one of Machina's lieutenants, Virus, and nearly killed. We were forced to leave him behind, deep within a dryad's tree, to heal from his wounds, and guilt from that decision still ate at me. My eyes filled with fresh tears, remembering. Puck couldn't be dead. I missed him too much for that.

A tapping came at my door, startling me. "Meghaaaan" came the singsong voice of Tiaothin the phouka. "Wake uuuup. I know you're in there. Open the doooor."

"Go away," I yelled, wiping my eyes. "I'm not coming out, okay? I don't feel good."

Of course, this only encouraged her further. The tapping turned to scratching, setting my teeth on edge, and her voice grew louder, more insistent. Knowing she'd sit there all day, scratching and whining, I leaped off the bed, stomped across the room and wrenched open the door.

"What?" I snarled. The phouka blinked, taking in my rumpled appearance, tear-streaked face and swollen, runny nose. A knowing grin came to her lips, and my anger flared; if she was here just to taunt me, I was so not in the mood.

Stepping back, I was about to slam the door in her face when she darted into the room and leaped gracefully onto my bed.

"Hey! Dammit, Tiaothin! Get out of here!" My protests went ignored, as the phouka bounced gleefully on the mattress, shredding holes in the blankets with her sharp claws.

"Meghan's in lo-ove," sang the phouka, making my heart stop. "Meghan's in lo-ove. Meghan and Ash, sitting in a tree—"

"Tiaothin, shut up!" I slammed the door and stalked toward her, glaring. The phouka giggled and came to a bouncing stop on my bed, sitting cross-legged on the pillow. Her gold-green eyes gleamed with mischief.

"I am not in love with Ash," I told her, crossing my arms over my chest. "Didn't you see the way he spoke to me, like I was dirt? Ash is a heartless, arrogant bastard. I hate him."

"Liar," the phouka retorted. "Liar liar, lying human. I saw the way you stared at him when he appeared. I know that look. You're smitten." Tiaothin snickered, flicking an ear back and forth as I squirmed. She grinned, showing all her teeth. "Not your fault, really. Ash just does that to people. No silly mortal can look at him and *not* fall head over heels. How many hearts do you think he's already broken?"

My spirits sank even lower. I'd thought I was special. I thought Ash cared for me, if only a little. Now, I realized I was probably just another girl in a long line of humans who'd been foolish enough to fall for him.

Tiaothin yawned, settling back against my pillows. "I'm telling you this so you won't waste your time chasing after the impossible," she purred, slitting her eyes at me. "Besides," she continued, "Ash is already is love with someone else. Has been for a long, long time. He's never forgotten her."

"Ariella," I whispered.

She looked surprised. "He told you about her? Huh. Well then, you should already know Ash would never fall for a plain, half-human girl, not when Ariella was the most beautiful sidhe in the Winter Court. He'd never betray her memory, even if the law wasn't an issue. You know about the law, don't you?"

I didn't know about any law, and I really didn't care. I got the feeling the phouka wanted me to ask about it, but I wasn't going to oblige. But Tiaothin seemed determined to tell me anyway, and went on with a sniff.

"You're Summer," she said disdainfully. "We're Winter. It's against the law that the two should ever be involved. Not that we have many incidents, but occasionally some star-struck Summer fey will fall in love with a Winter, or vice versa. *All* sorts of problems there—Summer and Winter are not meant to be together. If they're found out, the high lords will demand they renounce their love at once. If they refuse, they're banished to the human world forever, so they can continue their blasphemous relationship out of sight of the courts...if they're not executed right then.

"So, you see," she finished, fixing me with a piercing stare, "Ash would never betray his queen and court for a *human*. It's best to forget about him. Maybe find a silly human boy in the mortal world, if Mab ever lets you go."

By now I was so miserable I couldn't open my mouth without screaming or crying. Bile burned my throat, and my eyes swelled up. I had to get out of here, away from Tiaothin's brutal truths, before I fell to pieces.

Biting my lip to keep the tears at bay, I turned and fled into the halls of the Unseelie Court.

I nearly tripped over a goblin, who hissed and gnashed his teeth at me, jagged fangs gleaming in the darkness. Muttering an apology, I hurried away. A tall woman in a ghostly white dress floated down the corridor, eyes red and swollen, and I ducked down another hall to avoid her.

I needed to get out. Outside, into the clear, cold air, to be alone for just a few minutes, before I went crazy. The dark corridors and crowded halls were making me claustrophobic. Tiaothin had showed me the way out once; a pair of great double doors, one carved to resemble a laughing face, the other curled in a terrible snarl. I had searched for them on my own but could never find them. I suspected Mab put a spell on the doors to hide them from me, or maybe the doors themselves were playing a twisted game of hide-and-seek—doors did that sometimes in Faeryland. It was infuriating: I could see the sparkling, snow-covered city from my bedroom window, but could never get there.

I heard a clatter behind me and turned to see a group of redcaps coming down the hall, mad yellow eyes bright with hunger and greed. They hadn't seen me yet, but when they did, I'd be alone and unprotected, far from the safety of my room, and redcaps were *always* hungry. Fear gripped my heart. I hurried around a corner…

And there they stood, across an ice-slick foyer. The double doors, with their laughing face and snarling face, seeming to mock and threaten at the same time. Now that I'd finally found them, I hesitated. Would I be able to get back in, once I was out? Beyond the palace was the twisted, frightening city of the Winter fey. If I couldn't get back in, I'd freeze to death, or worse.

An excited whoop rang out. The redcaps had seen me.

I hurried across the floor, trying not to slip, as the tiles appeared to be made of colored ice. A pencil-thin butler in a black suit watched me impassively as I approached, his lank gray hair falling to his shoulders. Huge round eyes, like shiny mirrors, stared at me unblinking. Ignoring him, I grabbed the door with the laughing face and pulled, but it didn't budge.

"Going outside, Miss Chase?" the butler asked, tilting his smooth, egg-shaped head.

"Just for a while," I snapped, straining at the door, which, infuriatingly, started laughing at me. I didn't jump or scream, having experienced far stranger, but it did make me mad. "I'll be right back, I promise." I heard the jeering laughter of the redcaps, mingling with the howling of the door, and gave it a resounding kick. "Dammit, open up, you stupid thing!"

The butler sighed. "You are assaulting the wrong door, Miss Chase." He reached over and pulled open the snarling door, which scowled at me as it creaked on its hinges. "Please be careful in your excursion outside," the butler said primly. "Her Majesty would be most displeased if you…ahem…ran away. Not that you would, I'm sure. Her protection is all that keeps you from being frozen, or devoured."

A blast of frigid air blew into the foyer. The land beyond was dark and cold. Glancing behind at the redcaps, who watched me from the shadows with bright, pointy grins, I shivered and stepped out into the snow.

I almost went back inside, it was so cold. My breath hung on the air, and ice eddies stung my exposed flesh, making it tingle and burn. A pristine, frozen courtyard stretched before me, trees, flowers, statues and fountains encased in the clearest ice. Great jagged crystals, some taller than my head, jutted out of the ground at random intervals, spearing into the sky. A group of fey dressed in glittering white sat on the lip of a fountain, long azure hair rippling down their backs. They saw me, snickered behind their hands and rose. The nails on their fingertips glimmered blue in the half-light.

I went the other way, my boots crunching through the snow, leaving deep prints behind. A while ago, I might've wondered how it could snow underground, but I'd long accepted that things never made sense in Faeryland. I didn't really know where I was going, but moving seemed better than standing still.

"Where do you think you're going, half-breed?"

Snow swirled, stinging my face and blinding me. When the blizzard receded, I was surrounded by the four fey girls who had been sitting at the fountain. Tall, elegant and beautiful, with their pale skin and shimmering cobalt hair, they hemmed me in like a pack of wolves, full frosted lips twisted into ugly sneers.

"Ooh, Snowberry, you were right," one of them said, wrinkling her nose like she smelled something foul. "She *does* reek of a dead pig in the summer. I don't know how Mab can stand it."

Clenching my fists, I tried to keep my cool. I was *so* not in the mood for this now. *God, it's like high school all over again. Will it never end? These are ancient faeries, for Pete's sake, and they're acting like my high school pom squad.*

The tallest of the pack, a willowy fey with poison green streaked through her azure hair, regarded me with cold blue eyes and stepped close, crowding me. I stood my ground, and her gaze narrowed. A year ago, I might have grinned benignly and nodded and agreed with everything they said, just to get them to leave me alone. Things were different now. These girls weren't the scariest things I'd seen. Not by a long shot.

"Can I help you?" I asked in the calmest voice I could manage.

She smiled. It was not a nice smile. "I'm just curious to see how a half-breed like you gets off on speaking to Prince Ash like an equal." She sniffed, curling her lip in disgust. "If I were Mab, I would've frozen your throat shut just for looking at him."

"Well, you're not," I said, meeting her gaze. "And since I'm a guest here, I don't think she'd approve of whatever you're planning to do to me. So, why don't we do each other a favor and pretend we don't exist? That would solve a lot of problems."

"You don't get it, do you, half-breed?" Snowberry pulled herself up, staring down her perfect nose at me. "Looking at my prince constitutes an act of war. That you actually *spoke* to him makes my stomach turn. You don't seem to understand that you disgust him, as well you should, with your tainted Summer blood and human stench. We'll have to do something about that, won't we?"

*My prince?* Was she talking about Ash? I stared at her, tempted to say something stupid like, *Funny, he never mentioned you.* She might act like a spoiled, rich, mean girl from my old school, but the way her eyes darkened until there were no pupils left reminded me that she was still fey.

"So." Snowberry stepped back and gave me a patronizing smile. "This is what we're going to do. You, half-breed, are going to promise me that you won't so much as glance at my sweet Ash, ever again. Breaking this promise means I get to pluck out your wandering eyes and make a necklace with them. I think that's a fair bargain, don't you?"

The rest of the girls giggled, and there was a hungry, eager edge to the sound, like they wanted to eat me alive. I could have told her not to worry. I could have told her that Ash hated me and she didn't have to threaten to get me to stay away. I didn't. I drew myself up, looked her in the eye, and asked, "And what if I don't?"

Silence fell. I felt the air get colder and braced myself for the explosion. A part of me knew this was stupid, picking a fight with a faery. I would probably get my butt kicked, or cursed, or something nasty. I didn't care. I was tired of being bullied, tired of running into the bathroom to sob my eyes out. If this faery bitch wanted a fight, bring it on. I'd do my fair share of clawing, too.

"Well, isn't this fun." A smooth, confident voice cut through the silence, a second before all hell would have broken loose. We jumped as a lean figure dressed entirely in white materialized from the snow, his coat flapping behind him. The look on his pointed face glowed with haughty amusement.

"Prince Rowan!"

The prince grinned, his ice-blue eyes narrowed to slits. "Pardon me, girls," he said, slipping up beside me, making the pack fall back a few steps. "I don't mean to ruin your little party, but I need to borrow the half-breed for a moment."

Snowberry smiled at Rowan, all traces of hatefulness gone in an instant. "Of course, Your Highness," she cooed, as if she'd just been offered a wonderful gift. "Whatever you command. We were just keeping her company."

I wanted to gag, but Rowan smiled back as if he believed her, and the pack drifted away without a backward glance.

The prince's smile turned to a smirk as soon as they'd gone, and he gave me a sideways leer that made me instantly cautious. He might have saved me from Snowberry and her harpies, but I didn't think he'd done it to be chivalrous. "So, you're Oberon's half-blood," he purred, confirming my suspicion. His eyes raked me up and down, and I felt horribly exposed, as though he was undressing me with his gaze. "I saw you at Elysium last spring. Somehow I thought you were…taller."

"Sorry to disappoint you," I said frostily.

"Oh, you're not disappointing." Rowan smiled, his gaze lingering on my chest. "Not a bit." He snickered again and stepped back, gesturing for me to follow. "Come on, Princess. Let's take a walk. I want to show you something."

I really didn't want to, but I saw no way of politely refusing a prince of the Unseelie Court, especially since he'd just done me a favor by getting rid of the pack. So I followed him to another part of the courtyard, where frozen statues littered the snowy landscape, making it eerie and surreal. Some stood straight and proud, some were twisted in abject fear, arms and limbs thrown up to protect themselves. Looking at some of their features, so real and lifelike, made me shudder. *The Queen of Winter has a creepy sense of style.*

Rowan paused in front of one statue, covered in a layer of smoky ice, its features barely distinguishable through the opaque seal. With a start, I realized this wasn't a statue at all. A human stared out of his ice prison, mouth open in a scream of terror, one hand flung out before him. His blue eyes, wide and staring, gazed down at me.

Then he blinked.

I stumbled back, a shriek lodging in my throat. The human blinked again, his terrified gaze beseeching mine. I saw his lips tremble, as if he wanted to say something but the ice rendered him immobile, frozen and helpless. I wondered how he could breathe.

"Brilliant, isn't it?" said Rowan, gazing at the statue in admiration. "Mab's punishment for those who disappoint her. They can see, feel and hear everything that goes on around them, so they're fully aware of what's happened to them. Their hearts beat, their brains function, but they don't age. They're suspended in time forever."

"How do they breathe?" I whispered, staring back at the gaping human.

"They don't." Rowan smirked. "They can't, of course. Their noses and mouths are full of ice. But they still keep trying. It's like they're suffocating for eternity."

"That's horrible!"

The sidhe prince shrugged. "Don't piss off Mab, is all I can tell you." He turned the full brunt of his icy gaze on me. "So, Princess," he continued, making himself comfortable at the base of the statue. "Tell me something, if you would." Pulling an apple out of nowhere, he bit into it, smiling at me all the while. "I hear you and Ash traveled all the way to the Iron King's realm and back. Or so he claims. What do you think of my dear little brother?"

I smelled a hidden motive and crossed my arms. "Why do you want to know?"

"Just making conversation." Rowan produced another apple and tossed it at me. I fumbled to catch it, and Rowan grinned. "Don't be so uptight. You'd give a brownie a nervous break-down. So, was my brother a complete troll, or did he remember his manners?"

I was hungry. My stomach growled, and the apple felt cool and crisp in my hand. Before I knew it, I'd taken a bite. Sweet, tart juice flooded my mouth, with just a hint of bitter after-taste. "He was a perfect gentleman," I said with my mouth full, my voice sounding strange in my ears. "He helped me rescue my brother from the Iron King. I couldn't have done it without him."

Rowan reclined and gave me a lazy smile. "Do tell."

I frowned at his smirk. Something wasn't right. Why was I telling him this? I tried shutting up, clamping down on my tongue, but my mouth opened and the words rushed out of their own volition.

"My brother Ethan was stolen by the Iron King," I said, lis-tening to myself babble on in horror. "I came into the Nev-ernever to get him back. When Ash was sent by Mab to capture me, I tricked him into making a contract with me, instead. If he helped me rescue Ethan, I would go with him to the Unseelie Court. He agreed to help, but when we got to the Iron Kingdom, it made Ash horribly sick, and he was captured by Machina's Iron Knights. I snuck into the Iron King's tower, used a magic arrow to kill Machina, rescued my brother and Ash, and then we came here."

I clapped both hands over my mouth to stop the torrent of words, but the damage was already done. Rowan looked like the cat who just ate the canary.

"So," he crooned, slitting his eyes at me, "my little brother let himself be tricked—by a weakling half-blood—into rescuing a mortal child and nearly killing himself in the process. How very unlike Ash. Tell me more, Princess."

I kept my hands over my mouth, muffling my words, even as they began pouring out. Rowan laughed and hopped off the statue base, stalking toward me with an evil grin. "Oh, come now, Princess, you know it's useless to resist. No need to make this harder on yourself."

I wanted to punch him, but I was afraid if I took my hands from my mouth, I'd reveal something else. Rowan kept coming, his grin turning predatory. I backed away, but a wave of dizziness and nausea swept through me and I stumbled, fighting to stay on my feet. The prince snapped his fingers, and the snow around my feet turned to ice, covering my boots and freezing me in place. Horrified, I watched the ice crawl up past my knees, making sharp, crinkling noises as it inched toward my waist.

*It's cold!* I shivered violently, tiny needles of pain stabbing my flesh through my clothes. I gasped, wanting desperately to get away from it, but of course I couldn't move. My stomach cramped, and another bout of nausea made my head spin. Rowan smiled, leaning back and watching me struggle.

"I can make it stop, you know," he said, munching on the last of his apple. "All you have to do is answer a few innocent questions, that's all. I don't know why you're being so difficult, unless, of course, you have something to hide. Who are you trying to protect, half-breed?"

The temperature was becoming unbearable. My muscles

began to spasm from the awful, bone-numbing cold. My arms shook, and my hands dropped from my mouth.

"Ash," I whispered, but at that moment, the ice holding me in place shattered. With the sound of breaking china, it collapsed into thousands of crystalline shards, glinting in the weak light. I yelped and stumbled back, free of the icy embrace, as another lean, dark form melted out of the shadows.

"Ash." Rowan smiled as his brother stalked toward us, and my heart leaped. For a moment, I imagined Ash's gray eyes were narrowed in fury, but then he drew close and looked the same as he had the night before—cold, distant, slightly bored.

"What a coincidence," Rowan continued, still bearing that disgustingly smug grin. "Come and join us, little brother. We were just talking about you."

"What are you doing, Rowan?" Ash sighed, sounding more irritated than anything. "Mab told us not to bother the half-breed."

"Me? Bother her?" Rowan looked incredulous, blue eyes widening into the picture of innocence. "I'm never a bother. We were just having a scintillating conversation. Weren't we, Princess? Why don't you tell him what you just told me?"

Ash's silver gaze flicked to mine, a shadow of uncertainty crossing his face. My lips opened of their own accord, and I clapped my hands over my mouth again, stopping the words before they spilled out. Meeting his gaze, I shook my head, beseeching him with my eyes.

"Oh, come now, Princess, don't be shy," Rowan purred. "You seemed to have a lot to say about our dearest boy Ash, here. Go on and tell him."

I glared at Rowan, wishing I could tell him exactly what he could do with himself, but I was feeling so sick and light-headed now, it took all my concentration to stay upright. Ash's gaze hardened. Striding away from me, he bent and plucked something out of the snow, holding it up before him.

It was the fruit I'd dropped, a single bite taken out of the flesh, like Snow White's poisoned apple. Only it wasn't an apple now, but a big spotted toadstool, the fleshy insides white as bone. My stomach heaved, cramping violently, and I nearly lost the bite I'd taken.

Ash said nothing. Glaring at Rowan, he held up the mushroom and raised an eyebrow. Rowan sighed.

"Mab didn't specifically say we *couldn't* use spill-your-guts," Rowan said, shrugging his lean shoulders. "Besides, I think you'd be most interested in what our Summer princess has to say about you."

"Why should I be?" Ash tossed the mushroom away, looking bored again. "This conversation isn't important. I made the bargain to get her here, and now it's done. Anything I said or did was for the purpose of bringing her to court."

I gasped, my hands dropping away from my face, to stare at him. It was true, then. He'd been playing me all along. What he told me in the Iron Kingdom, everything we shared, none of that was real. I felt ice spreading through my stomach and shook my head, trying to erase what I just heard. "No," I muttered, too low for anyone to hear. "It's not true. It can't be. Ash, tell him you're lying."

"Mab doesn't care how I did it, as long as the goal was accomplished," Ash continued, oblivious to my torment. "Which is more than I can say for you." He crossed his arms and shrugged, the picture of indifference. "Now, if we're quite done here, the half-breed should return inside. The queen will not be pleased if she freezes to death."

"Ash," I whispered as he turned away. "Wait!" He didn't even glance at me. Tears pressed behind my eyes, and I stumbled after him, fighting a wave of dizziness. "Ash!"

"I love you!"

The words just tumbled out of me. I didn't mean to say them, but the moment I did, my stomach twisted with disbelief and utter horror. My hands flew back to my mouth, but it was far, far too late. Rowan grinned his biggest yet, a smile full of terrible glee, like he'd been given the best present in the world.

Ash froze, his back still to me. For just a moment, I saw his hands clench at his sides.

"That's unfortunate for you, isn't it?" he said, his voice dead of emotion. "But the Summer Court has always been weak. Why would I touch the half-breed daughter of Oberon? Don't make me sick, human."

It was like an icy hand plunged into my body, ripping my heart from my chest. I felt actual physical pain lance through me. My legs buckled, and I collapsed to the snow, ice crystals biting into my palms. I couldn't breathe, couldn't even cry. All I could do was kneel there, the cold seeping through my jeans, hearing Ash's words echo through my head.

"Oh, that was cruel, Ash," Rowan said, sounding delighted. "I do believe you broke our poor princess's heart."

Ash said something else, something I didn't catch, because the ground began to twirl beneath me, and another wave of dizziness made my head spin. I could have fought it off, but I was numb to all feeling, and I didn't care at the moment. *Let the darkness come,* I thought, *let it take me away,* before it pulled a heavy blanket over my eyes and I dropped into oblivion.

# CHAPTER THREE

*The Scepter of the Seasons*

I drifted for a while, neither awake nor asleep, caught somewhere between the two. Hazy, half-remembered dreams swam across my vision, mingling with reality until I didn't know which was which. I dreamed of my family, of Ethan and Mom and my stepdad, Luke. I dreamed of them going on without me, slowly forgetting who I was, that I ever existed. Shapes and voices floated in and out of my consciousness: Tiaothin telling me to snap out of it because she was bored, Rowan telling Queen Mab that he had no idea I would react so violently to a simple mushroom, another voice telling the queen that I might never wake up. Sometimes I dreamed that Ash was in the room, standing in a corner or beside my bed, just watching me with bright silver eyes. In my delirium, I might have heard him whisper that he was sorry.

"Humans are such fragile creatures, aren't they?" murmured a voice one night, as I drifted in and out of stupor. "One tiny nibble of spill-your-guts sends them into a coma. Pathetic." It snorted. "I heard this one was in love with Prince Ash. Makes you wonder what Mab will do to her, once she wakes up. She's none too pleased with the Summer whelp being all mushy-mushy with her favorite son."

"Well, she certainly picked an inconvenient time to go all Sleeping Beauty," added another voice, "what with the Exchange coming up and all." It snorted. "If she does wake up, Mab might kill her for the annoyance. Either way, it'll be entertaining." The sound of their laughter faded away, and I floated in darkness.

An eternity passed with few distractions. Voices slipping by me, unimportant. Tiaothin repeatedly poking me in the ribs, her sharp claws drawing blood, but the pain belonged to someone else. Scenes of my family: Mom on the porch with a police officer, explaining she didn't have a missing daughter; Ethan playing in my room, which was now an office, repainted and refurnished, all my personal items given away.

There was a dull throb in my chest as I watched him; in another life, it might have been sorrow, longing, but I was beyond feeling anything now and watched my half brother with detached curiosity. He was talking to a familiar stuffed rabbit, and that made me frown. Wasn't that rabbit destroyed…?

"They have forgotten you," murmured a voice in the darkness. A deep, familiar voice. I turned and found Machina, his cables folded behind him, watching me with a small smile on his lips. His silver hair glowed in the blackness.

My brow furrowed. "You're not here," I muttered, backing away. "I killed you. You aren't real."

"No, my love." Machina shook his head, his hair rippling softly. "You did kill me, but I am still with you. I will always be with you, now. There is no avoiding it. We are one."

I drew back, shivering. "Go away," I said, retreating into the black. The Iron King watched me intently, but did not follow. "You're not here," I repeated. "This is just a dream, and you're dead! Leave me alone." I turned and fled into the darkness, until the soft glow of the Iron King faded into the void.

ANOTHER ETERNITY PASSED, or perhaps only a few seconds, when through the confusion and darkness, I felt a presence near the bed. *Mom?* I wondered, a little girl once more. Or maybe Tiaothin, come to bother me again. *Go away,* I told them, retreating into my dreams. *I don't want to see you. I don't want to see anyone. Just leave me alone.*

"Meghan," whispered a voice, heart-wrenchingly familiar, drawing me out of the void. I recognized it immediately, just as I realized it was a figment of my desperate imagination, because the real owner of that voice would never be here, talking to me.

*Ash?*

"Wake up," he murmured, his deep voice cutting through the layers of the darkness. "Don't do this. If you don't come out of this soon, you'll fade away and drift forever. Fight it. Come back to us."

I didn't want to wake up. There was nothing but pain waiting for me in the real world. If I was asleep, I couldn't feel anything. If I was asleep, I didn't have to face Ash and the cold contempt on his face when he looked at me. Darkness was my retreat, my sanctuary. I drew back from Ash's voice, deeper into the comforting blackness. And, through the layer of dreams and delirium, I heard a quiet sob.

"Please." A hand gripped mine, real and solid, anchoring me to the present. "I know what you must think of me, but…" The voice broke off, took a ragged breath. "Don't leave," it whispered. "Meghan, don't go. Come back to me."

I sobbed in return, and opened my eyes.

The room was dark, empty. Faery light filtered through the window, casting everything in blue and silver. As usual, the air was icy cold. *A dream, then,* I thought, as the mist swirling around my head for so long finally cleared, leaving me devastatingly awake and aware. *It was a dream, after all.*

A sense of betrayal filled me. I'd come out of my lovely darkness for nothing. I wanted to retreat, to return to the oblivion where nothing could hurt me, but now that I was awake, I couldn't go back.

An ache filled my chest, so sharp that I gasped out loud. Was this what a broken heart felt like? Was it possible to die from the pain? I'd always thought the girls at school so dramatic; when they broke up with their boyfriends, they cried and carried on for weeks. I didn't think they needed to throw such a fuss. But I'd never been in love before.

What would I do now? Ash despised me. Everything he'd said and done was to bring me to his queen. He was a cheat. He'd *used* me, to further his own ends.

And the saddest part was, I still loved him.

*Stop it!* I told myself, as tears threatened once more. *Enough of this! Ash doesn't deserve it. He doesn't deserve anything. He's a soulless faery who played you every step of the way, and you fell for it like an idiot.* I took a deep breath, forcing back the tears, willing them to freeze inside me, to freeze everything inside me. Emotions, tears, memories, anything that made me weak. Because if I was going to play in the Unseelie Court, I had to be made of ice. No, not ice. Like iron. *Nothing will hurt me again,* I thought, as my tears dried and my emotions shriveled into a withered ball. *If the damned faeries want to play rough, so be it. I can play rough, too.*

I threw back the covers and stood tall, the cold air prickling my skin. *Let it freeze me, I don't care.* My hair was a mess, tangled and limp, my clothes rumpled and disgusting. I peeled them off and walked into the bathroom for a long soak in the tub—the only warm place in the entire court—before dressing in black jeans, a black halter top and a long black coat. As I was finishing lacing up my black boots, Tiaothin walked into the room.

She blinked, obviously astonished to see me on my feet, before breaking into a huge grin, fangs shining in the moonlight. "You're up!" she exclaimed, bouncing over and leaping onto my bed. "You're awake. That's a relief. Mab's been annoyed and cranky ever since you collapsed. She thought you were going to sleep forever, and then she'd have a devil of a time explaining your condition to the Seelie courtiers when they come for the Exchange."

I frowned at her, and for a moment, a tiny spark of hope flickered inside. "What Exchange?" I wondered. *Have they come for me? Has Oberon finally sent someone to rescue me from this hellhole?*

Tiaothin, in that guileless way of hers, seemed to know exactly what I was thinking. "Don't worry, half-breed," she sniffed, looking at me with slitted eyes. "They're not coming for *you*. They're here to pass on the Scepter of the Seasons. Summer is finally over, and winter is on the way."

I felt a pang of disappointment and quashed it. *No weakness. Show her nothing.* I shrugged and casually asked, "What's the Scepter of the Seasons?"

Tiaothin yawned and made herself comfortable on my bed. "It's a magical talisman that the courts pass between them with the changing of the seasons," she said, picking at a loose thread on my quilt. "Six months out of the year, Oberon holds it, when spring and summer are at their peak, and winter is at its weakest. Then, on the autumn equinox, it is passed to Queen Mab, to signify the shift in power between the courts. The Summer courtiers will be arriving soon, and we'll have a huge party to celebrate the start of winter. Everyone in Tir Na Nog is invited, and the party will last for days." She grinned and bounced in place, dreadlocks flying. "It's a good thing you woke up when you did, half-breed. This is one party you don't want to miss!"

"Will Lord Oberon and Lady Titania be there?"

"Lord Pointy Ears?" Tiaothin sniffed. "He's much too important to go slumming around with Unseelie lowlifes. Nah, Oberon and his bitch queen Titania will stay in Arcadia where they're comfortable. Lucky thing, too. Those two stiff necks can really ruin a good party."

So I'd be on my own after all. Fine with me.

THE SUMMER COURT ARRIVED in a hale of music and flowers, probably in direct defiance of Winter, whose traditions I was beginning to hate. I stood calf deep in snow, the collar of my fur coat turned up against cold, watching Unseelie fey mill about the courtyard. The event was to take place outside, in the courtyard full of ice and frozen statues. Will-o'-the-wisps and corpse candles floated through the air, casting everything in eternal twilight. Why couldn't the Winter fey hold their parties aboveground for once? I missed the sunlight so much it hurt.

I felt a presence behind me, then heard a quiet chuckle in my ear. "So glad you were able to make it to the party, Princess. It would've been terribly boring without you."

My skin prickled, and I squashed down my fear as Rowan's breath tickled the back of my neck. "Wouldn't miss it for the world," I replied, keeping my voice light and even. His eyes bored into my skull, but I didn't turn. "What can I do for you, Your Highness?"

"Oh ho, now we're playing the ice queen. Bravo, Princess, bravo. Such a brave comeback from your broken heart. Not what I expected from Summer at all." He shifted around me so that we were inches apart, so close I could see my reflection in his ice-blue eyes. "You know," he breathed, his breath cold on my cheek, "I can help you get over him."

I desperately wanted to back away, but I held my ground. *You are iron,* I reminded myself. *He can't hurt you. You're steel inside.* "The offer is appreciated," I said, locking gazes with the sidhe prince, "but I don't need your help. I'm already past him."

"Are you now?" Rowan didn't sound convinced. "You know he's right over there, don't you? Pretending not to watch us?" He smirked and took my hand, pressing it to his lips. My stomach fluttered before I could stop it. "Let's show dear Ash how much you're over him. Come on, Princess. You know you want to."

I did want to. I wanted to hurt Ash, make him jealous, put him through the same pain I had gone through. And Rowan was right there, offering. All I had to do was lean forward and meet his smirking mouth. I hesitated. Rowan *was* gorgeous; I could do worse in the casual make-out department.

"Kiss me," Rowan whispered.

A trumpet sounded, echoing over the courtyard, and the smell of roses filled the air. The Seelie Court was arriving, to the roars and shrieks of the Winter fey.

I started, wrenching myself out of the glamour-induced daze. "Dammit, stop doing that!" I snarled, yanking my hand from his grip and stumbling back. My heart slammed against my rib cage. God, I'd almost fallen for it this time; another half second and I would have been all over him. Shame colored my cheeks.

Rowan laughed. "You're almost attractive when you blush," he snickered, moving out of slapping range. "Until next time, Princess." With another mocking bow, he slipped away.

I glanced around furtively, wondering if Ash truly was

nearby and watching us, as Rowan claimed. Though I saw Sage and his enormous wolf lounging against a pillar near Mab's throne, Ash was nowhere in sight.

Two satyrs padded through the briar-covered gates of the courtyard, holding pale trumpets that looked made of bone. They raised the horns to their lips and blew a keening blast, one that set the Unseelie Court to howling. Atop her throne of ice, Mab watched the procedures with a faint smile.

"Gotcha!" hissed a voice, and something pinched me painfully on the rear. I yelped, whirling on Tiaothin, who laughed and danced away, dreadlocks flying. "You're an idiot, half-breed," she taunted, as I kicked snow at her. She dodged easily. "Rowan's too good for you, and he's experienced. Most everyone, fey and mortal boys included, would give their teeth to have him to themselves for a night. Try him. I guarantee you'll like it."

"Not interested," I snapped, glaring at her with narrowed eyes. My butt still stung, making my words sharp. "I'm done playing games with faery princes. They can go to hell, for all I care. I'd rather strip naked for a group of redcaps."

"Ooh, if you do, can I watch?"

I rolled my eyes and turned my back on her as the Seelie Court finally made its appearance. A line of white horses swept into the courtyard, their hooves floating over the ground, their eyes as blue as the summer sky. Atop saddles made of bark, twigs and flowering vines, elven knights peered down haughtily, elegant in their leafy armor. After the knights came the standard-bearers, satyrs and dwarfs bearing the colors of the Summer Court. Then, finally, an elegant carriage pulled up, wreathed in thorns and rosebushes and flanked by two grim-faced trolls who growled and bared their fangs at the crowds of Winter fey.

Tiaothin sniffed. "They're being highly paranoid this year," she muttered, as a troll took a swat at a goblin that edged too close. "Wonder who the high-and-mighty noble is, to warrant such security measures?"

I didn't answer, for my skin was prickling a warning, though I didn't know why until a moment later. The carriage rolled to a stop, the doors were opened...

And King Oberon, Lord of the Seelie Court, stepped out into the snow.

The Unseelie fey gasped and snarled, backing away from the carriage, as the Erlking swept his impassive gaze over the crowd. My heart hammered in my chest. Oberon looked as imposing as ever: slender, ancient and powerful, his silver hair falling to his waist and his eyes like pale leaves. He wore robes the color of the forest, brown and gold and green, and an antlered crown rested on his brow.

Beside me, Tiaothin gaped, flattening her ears. "Oberon?" she snarled, as I watched the Erlking's gaze sweep the crowd, searching meticulously. "What's Lord Pointy Ears doing here?"

I couldn't answer, for Oberon's piercing stare finally found me. His eyes narrowed, and I shivered under that look. The last time I'd seen the Erlking, I'd snuck away from the Seelie Court to find my brother. Oberon had sent Puck to fetch me back, and I'd convinced him to help me instead. After our re-bellion and direct disobedience, I imagined the Seelie king was none too happy with either of us.

My stomach twisted and a lump rose to my throat as I thought of Puck. I managed to swallow it down before any Unseelie noticed my bout of weakness, but the memories still haunted me. I desperately wished Puck were here. I stared at the carriage, hoping his lanky, red-haired form would come leaping out, flashing that defiant smirk, but he did not appear.

"Lord Oberon," Mab said in a neutral voice, but it was clear that she, too, was surprised to see her ancient rival. "This is a surprise. To what do we owe the honor of your visit?"

Oberon approached the throne, flanked by his two troll bodyguards. The crowd of Unseelie fey parted quickly before him, until he stood before the throne. "Lady Mab," the Erlking said, his powerful voice echoing over the courtyard, "I have come to request the return of my daughter, Meghan Chase, to the Seelie Court."

A murmur went through the ranks of Unseelie fey, and all eyes turned to me. *Iron,* I reminded myself. *You are like iron. Don't let them scare you.* I stepped out from behind Tiaothin and met the surprised, angry looks head-on.

Oberon gestured at the carriage, and the trolls reached inside, dragging out two pale Winter sidhe, their arms bound behind their backs with living, writhing vines. "I have brought an exchange, as the rules dictate," Oberon continued, as the trolls pushed the prisoners forward. "I will return to you your own, in exchange for my daughter's freedom—"

Mab interrupted. "I'm afraid you misunderstand, Lord Oberon," she rasped with the faintest of smiles. "Your daughter is not a prisoner of the Unseelie, but a willing guest. She came to us on her own, after making a bargain with my son to do so. The girl is bound by her contract to Prince Ash, and you have no power to demand her return. Once a bargain is made, it must be honored by all."

Oberon stiffened, then slowly turned to me again. I gulped as those ancient-as-the-forest eyes pierced right through me. "Is this true, daughter?" he asked, and though his voice was soft, it echoed in my ears and made the ground tremble.

I bit my lip and nodded. "It's true," I whispered. *I guess your wolf henchman didn't come back to tell you that part.*

The Erlking shook his head. "Then, I cannot help you. Foolish girl. You have doomed yourself to your fate. So be it."

He turned from me, a deserting gesture that spoke louder than any words, and I felt like he had punched me in the stomach. "My daughter has made her choice," he announced. "Let us be done with this."

*That's it?* I thought as Oberon walked back toward the carriage. *You're not going to fight to get me out, bargain with Mab for my freedom? Because of my stupid contract, you're just going to leave me here?*

Apparently so. The Erlking didn't look at me a second time as he reached the carriage and gestured to his trolls. One of them shoved the Unseelie prisoners back into the carriage, while the other opened the opposite door with a grunt.

A tall, regal faery stepped out into the snow. Despite her size, she looked so delicate it seemed she would break at the slightest puff of air. Her limbs were bundles of twigs, held together with woven grass. Fragile white buds grew from her scalp instead of hair. A magnificent mantle covered her shoulders, made of every flower under the sun: lilies, roses, tulips, daffodils, and plants I didn't have a name for. Bees and butterflies flitted around her, and the smell of roses was suddenly overpowering.

She stepped forward, and the hoards of Winter fey leaped back at her approach, as if she had a disease. However, it wasn't the flower woman all eyes were trained on, but what she held in her hands.

It was a scepter, like kings and queens used to carry, only this one wasn't just some decorated rod. It pulsed with a soft amber glow, as if sunlight clung to the living wood, melting the snow and ice where it touched. The long handle was wrapped in vines, and the carved head of the scepter continuously sprouted flowers, buds, and tiny plants. It left a trail of leaves and petals where the lady passed, and the Winter fey kept their distance, growling and hissing.

At the foot of the throne, the lady knelt and held out the scepter in both hands, bowing her head. For a moment, Mab did nothing, simply watching the faery with an unreadable expression on her face. The rest of the Winter Court seemed to hold their breath. Then, with deliberate slowness, Mab stood and plucked the scepter from the woman's hands. Holding it before her, the queen studied it, then raised it up for all to see.

The scepter flared, the golden aura swallowed up by icy blue. The leaves and flowers shriveled and fell away. Bees and butterflies spiraled lifelessly to the ground, their gossamer wings coated in frost. The scepter flared once more and turned to ice, sending sparkling prisms of light over the courtyard.

The faery kneeling before the queen jerked and then…she, too, shriveled away. Her gorgeous robe withered, the flowers turning black and falling to the ground. Her hair curled, becoming dry and brittle, before flaking off her scalp. I heard the snapping of twigs as her legs broke at the knees, unable to hold her up any longer. She pitched forward into the snow, twitched once, and was still. As I watched in horror, wondering why no one went forward to help, the smell of roses faded away, and the stench of rotting vegetation filled the courtyard.

"It is done," said Oberon, his voice weary. He raised his head and met Mab's gaze. "The Exchange is complete, until the summer equinox. Now, if you will excuse us, Queen Mab. We must return to Arcadia."

Mab shot him a look that was purely predatory. "You will not stay, Lord Oberon?" she crooned. "Celebrate with us?"

"I think not, Lady." If Oberon was disturbed by the way Mab looked at him, he didn't show it. "The ending of summer is not something we look forward to. I'm afraid we will have to decline. But, be warned, Queen Mab, this is not yet over. One way or another, I will have my daughter back."

I gave a start at those words. Maybe Oberon would come

through for me after all. But Mab's gaze narrowed, and she stroked the handle of the scepter.

"That sounds uncomfortably close to a threat, Erlking."

"Merely a promise, my lady." With Mab still glaring at him, Oberon deliberately turned his back on the Winter Queen and strode to the carriage. A troll opened the door for him, and the Erlking entered without a backward glance. The driver shook the reins, and the Summer entourage was off, growing smaller and smaller, until the darkness swallowed them up.

Mab smiled.

"Summer is over," she announced in her raspy voice, raising her other arm as if to embrace her waiting subjects. "Winter has come. Now, let the Revel begin!"

The Unseelie went berserk, howling, roaring and screaming into the night. Music started from somewhere, wild and dark, drums pounding out a fast, frenzied rhythm. The fey swarmed together in a chaotic, writhing mass, leaping, howling and twirling madly, rejoicing in the coming of winter.

I DIDN'T GET INTO the party. One, I wasn't in the mood, and two, dancing with the Winter fey didn't seem like such a great idea. Especially after I saw a group of drunk, glamour-high redcaps swarm a boggart and tear it limb from limb. It was like a mosh pit from hell. Mostly I hung back in the shadows, trying to avoid notice and wondering if Mab would think me rude if I retreated to my room. Looking at the frozen statues of humans and fey scattered throughout the courtyard, I decided not to risk it.

At least Rowan was absent from the celebrations, or lurking somewhere I couldn't see. I had been bracing myself to fend off his advances all night. Ash was also mysteriously absent, which was both a relief and a disappointment. I found myself searching for him, scouring the shadows and mobs of dancing fey, looking for a familiar tousled head or the glint of a silver eye.

*Stop that,* I thought, when I realized what I was doing. *He's not here. And even if he was, what would you do? Ask him to dance? He's made what he thinks of you perfectly clear.*

"Excuse me, Princess."

For a moment, my heart leaped at the soft, deep voice. The voice that could either be Rowan's or Ash's, they sounded so much alike. Bracing myself, I turned, but it wasn't Ash standing there. Thankfully, it wasn't Rowan, either. It was the other brother, the oldest of the three. Sage.

*Dammit, he's gorgeous also.* What was with this family, that all the sons were so freaking handsome it hurt to look at them? Sage had his brothers' pale face and high cheekbones, and his eyes were chips of green ice, peering out beneath slender brows. Long black hair rippled behind him, like a waterfall of ink. His wolf sat a few paces away, watching me with intelligent golden eyes.

"Prince Sage," I greeted warily, prepared to fend off another assault. "Can I help you with anything, Your Highness?" *Or did you just come to push yourself on me like Rowan, or mock me like Ash?*

"I want to speak with you," the prince said without preamble. "Alone. Will you walk with me a bit?"

This surprised me, though I still hesitated, wary. "Where are we going?" I asked.

"The throne room," Sage replied, sweeping his gaze back to the palace. "It is my duty to guard the scepter this night, as only those with royal blood are allowed to touch it. With all the chaos from the Revel, it is best to keep the scepter away from the masses. It could get messy otherwise." When I paused, thinking, he shrugged a lean shoulder. "I will not force you, Princess. Come with me or not, it makes no difference. I merely wanted to speak to you without Rowan, Ash, or some phouka trying to eavesdrop on the conversation."

He waited patiently as I struggled for an answer. I could refuse, but I wasn't sure I wanted to. Sage seemed straightforward, almost businesslike. Different from his brothers. He wasn't making any attempt to be charming, but he wasn't being condescending, either. And unlike Rowan, who oozed charm and malice, he wasn't using glamour, and I think that's finally what sold me.

"All right," I decided, motioning with my hand. "I'll talk with you. Lead the way."

He offered me his arm, which surprised me again. After a moment's hesitation, I took it, and we started off, his wolf trailing silently behind us.

He led me back into the palace, down empty halls swathed in ice and shadow. All the Unseelie fey were outside, dancing the night away. My footsteps echoed loudly against the hard floors; his and the wolf's made no sound at all.

"I've seen you," Sage murmured without looking at me. He turned a corner, so smoothly I stumbled to keep pace. "I've watched you with my brother. And I want to warn you, you mustn't trust him."

I almost laughed, the statement was so obvious. "Which one?" I asked bitterly.

"Either of them." He pulled me down another corridor, one I recognized. We were close to the throne room now. Sage pressed on without slowing. "You do not know the enmity between Ash and Rowan, how deep the rivalry goes. Especially on Rowan's part. The jealousy he feels for his youngest brother is a dark poison, eating him from the inside, making him bitter and vengeful. He has never forgiven Ash for Ariella's death."

We entered the throne room in all its frigid, icy beauty. Sage released me and walked toward the throne, his wolf padding behind him. I shivered, huddling deeper into my coat. It was colder in here than it was outside. "But Ash wasn't responsible for Ariella's death," I said, rubbing my forearms. "That—" I stopped, not wanting to say it out loud. *That was Puck, who led them into danger. Who was responsible for the death of Ash's love.*

Sage didn't answer. He had come to a stop a few feet beside Mab's icy throne, staring at something on the altar beside it. A moment later, I realized that was the source of the ungodly chill in the room. The Scepter of the Seasons hovered a few inches over the altar, washing the prince's face in icy blue light.

"Beautiful, isn't it?" he murmured, running his fingers over the frozen handle. "Every year, I see it, and yet it never ceases to amaze me." His eyes glittered; he seemed to be in some sort of trance. "Someday, if Mab ever gets tired of being queen, it will be mine to accept, to rule with. When that happens..."

I didn't get to hear the rest, for at that moment, the wolf let out a long, low growl and bared its teeth.

Sage whirled around. In one smooth motion, he drew the sword at his waist. I stared at it. It was much like Ash's, straight and slender, the blade throwing off an icy blue aura. I shivered, remembering what it was like to grasp that hilt, feel the awful cold bite into my skin. And for a moment, I was terrified. *He's going to kill me, that's why he brought me here alone. He was going to kill me all along.*

"How did you get in here?" Sage hissed.

I turned. There, against the back wall, several dark forms melted out of the shadows. Four were thin and lanky, almost emaciated, their frames nothing but wires twisted together to form limbs and a body, resembling huge puppets as they skittered over the ground on all fours. The wolf's growls turned into snarls.

My heart turned over as another form stepped into the light, dressed in segmented metal armor emblazoned with a barbed-wire crown. He wore a helmet, but the visor was up, showing a face as familiar to me as my own. There was no mistaking that pale skin, those intense gray eyes. Ash's face gazed out at me from under the helmet, his eyes as bleak as the winter sky.

# CHAPTER FOUR

*The Theft*

"Ash?" Sage muttered in disbelief. I shook my head mutely, but the prince wasn't looking at me.

The knight blinked, giving Sage a solemn look. "I'm afraid not, Prince Sage," he said, and I shivered at how much he sounded like his double. "Your brother was simply the blue-print for my creation."

"Tertius," I whispered, and Ash's doppelgänger gave me a pained smile. The last time I'd seen the Iron knight was in Machina's tower just before it came crashing down. I couldn't imagine how he'd survived. "What are you doing here?"

Tertius's gaze met mine, his eyes blank and dead, looking so much like Ash's it made my heart ache. "Forgive me, Princess," he murmured, and made a sweeping gesture with his arm.

With shrieks like knives scraping against each other, the Iron faeries rushed me.

They were appallingly fast, scuttling gray blurs across the

floor. I had the absurd image of being ambushed by a swarm of metallic spiders before they were upon me. The first attacker leaped up and slashed at my face with a twisted wire claw as sharp as any razor.

It met a gleaming blue sword instead, screeching off the blade in a volley of sparks, bringing tears to my eyes. Sage threw back one attacker and whirled to meet the next, ducking as wire talons slashed over his head. The Winter prince thrust out a palm, and a jagged ice spear surged out of the floor, stabbing toward the Iron fey. Lightning fast, they dodged, leaping back and giving us time to retreat. Grabbing my wrist, Sage yanked me behind the throne.

"Keep out of the way," he ordered, just as the faeries descended on us again, swarming over the chair and leaving deep gouges in the ice. Sage slashed at one, only to have it spring back. Another darted in from behind, lashing out with steel talons. The prince dodged, but he didn't move fast enough, and a bright splash of blood colored the floor.

My stomach twisted as the prince staggered, swinging his blade in a desperate circle to keep the assassins back. There were too many for him, and they were too quick. Frantically, I looked around for a weapon, but saw only the scepter, lying on the pedestal near the throne. Knowing I was probably breaking a dozen sacred rules, I lunged for the scepter and snatched it up by its frozen handle.

The cold seared my hands, burning them like acid. I gasped and nearly dropped it, gritting my teeth against the pain. Sage stood in the middle of a slashing whirlwind, desperately trying to keep them back. I saw lines of red on his face and chest. Trying to ignore the searing pain, I rushed up behind an Iron fey, raised the scepter over my head and smashed it down on the faery's spindly back.

It whirled with blinding speed. I didn't even see the blow

until it backhanded me across the face, making lights explode behind my eyes. I flew back into a corner, striking my head on something hard and slumping to the floor. The scepter dropped from my grasp and rolled away. Dazed, I watched the faery scuttle toward me but suddenly jerk to a stop, as if yanked by invisible strings. Ice covered its body, pushing up through the seams in the wire as the faery clawed at itself frantically. Wire-thin fingers snapped off, and the faery's struggles slowed before it curled in on itself like a giant insect and stopped moving altogether.

I didn't have the breath to scream. I tried pushing away from the wall, but everything spun violently and my stomach lurched. I heard footsteps coming toward me and opened my eyes to see Tertius bend down and take the Scepter of the Seasons.

"Don't," I managed, trying to struggle to my feet. The ground swayed, and I stumbled back. "What are you doing?"

He observed me with solemn gray eyes. "Following the orders of my king."

"King?" I struggled to focus. Everything seemed to be moving in slow motion. A few feet away, Sage and the assassins fought on. The wolf had its jaws clamped around a faery's leg, and Sage pressed it unmercifully with his sword. "You don't have a king anymore," I told Tertius, feeling light-headed and numb. "Machina is dead."

"Yes, but our realm endures. I follow the commands of the new Iron King," Tertius murmured, drawing his sword. I stared at the steel blade, hoping it would be quick. "I bear you no ill will, this time. My orders do not include killing you. But I must obey my lord."

And with that, Tertius spun on his heel and marched away, still holding the Scepter of the Seasons. It pulsed blue and white in his hands, coating his gauntlets with frost, but he did not fumble. His face was grim as he strode up behind Sage, still locked in battle with the assassins. The wolf thrashed on the ground in a pool of blood, and Sage's breaths came in ragged gasps as he fought on alone. In horror, I saw what Tertius was going to do and screamed out a warning.

Too late. As Sage cut viciously at one of the Iron fey, he didn't see Tertius looming behind him until the knight was right there. Aware of the danger at last, Sage whirled, swinging his sword, cutting at Tertius's head. The knight knocked the blade aside and, as Sage staggered back, took one step forward and plunged his own sword through the Winter prince's chest.

Time seemed to stop. Sage stood there a moment, a look of shock on his face, staring at the blade in his chest. His own sword hit the ground with a ringing clang.

Then Tertius yanked the blade free, and I gasped. Sage crumpled to the floor, blood pooling from his chest and streaming onto the ice. The assassins tensed to pounce on him, but Tertius blocked them with his sword.

"Enough. We have what we came for. Let's go." He flicked blood off the blade and sheathed it, his eyes moving to the corpse of the frozen assassin. "Fetch your brother, quickly. We can leave no evidence behind."

The Iron fey scrambled to comply, lifting the dead faery onto their shoulders, careful not to touch the ice piercing its skin. They even grabbed the pieces off the floor. Tertius turned to me, his gaze bleak, as darkness hovered on the edge of my vision. "Farewell, Meghan Chase. I hope we do not meet again." He spun quickly to follow the assassins, marching out of my line of sight. I turned my head to follow them, but they were already gone.

My head throbbed, and darkness threatened at the edges of my vision; I took several deep breaths to drive it back. I would *not* pass out now. Gradually, the churning blackness cleared, and I pulled myself upright, looking around. The throne room had fallen silent again, except for the slow thudding of my heart, which sounded unnaturally loud in my ears. Blood flecked the walls and pooled along the floor, horribly vivid against the pale ice. The altar that had held the Scepter of the Seasons lay empty and bare.

My gaze wandered to the two bodies still in the room with me. Sage lay on his back, his sword a few inches from his hand, gazing up at the ceiling, gasping. A few feet away, the furry body of the wolf, gray fur streaked with blood, lay crumpled on the ice.

Limping, I ran over to Sage, passing the body of the poor wolf, sprawled out next to him. The wolf's jaws gaped open, and a tongue lolled out between bloody teeth. It had died protecting its master, and I felt sick at the thought.

Just as I reached Sage, a shudder went through the prince's body. His head arced back, mouth gaping, and ice crawled up from his lips, spreading over his face, down his chest, and all the way to his feet. He stiffened as the air chilled around us, the ice making sharp crinkling sounds as it encased the prince in a crystal cocoon.

*No.* I looked closer, and realized Sage's *body* was turning to ice. His clawed fingers flexed, losing their color, becoming hard and clear. His thumb abruptly snapped off and shattered on the floor. I put both hands to my mouth to keep from screaming. Or vomiting. Sage gave a final jerk and was still, a cold, hard statue where a live body had been a moment before.

The oldest son of the Winter Court was dead.

And that's how Tiaothin found us a moment later.

Later, I didn't recall much of that moment, but I did remember the phouka's screech of horror and fury as she fled to tell the rest of the court. I heard her shrill voice echoing down the corridor, and knew I should probably move, but I was cold, numb to all feeling. I didn't leave the prince's side until Rowan swept in with a platoon of guards, who pounced on me with angry cries. Rough hands grabbed me by the arms and hair, dragging me away from Sage's body, oblivious to my protests and cries of pain. I shouted at Rowan to tell him what had happened, but he wasn't looking at me.

Behind him, Unseelie fey crowded into the room, and roars of fury and outrage filled the chamber when they saw the dead prince. Fey were screaming and crying, tearing at themselves and each other, demanding vengeance and blood. Dazed, I realized the Unseelie were outraged at the murder of a Winter prince in their own territory. That someone had dared slip in and kill one of their own, right under their noses. There was no sorrow or remorse for the prince himself, only fury and demands for revenge at the audacity of it. I wondered if anyone would truly miss the eldest prince of Winter.

Rowan stood over Sage's body, his expression eerily blank as he stared down at his brother. Amid the roars and cries of the fey around us, he regarded his sibling with the curiosity one might show a dead bird on the sidewalk. It made my skin crawl.

Silence fell over the room, and a chill descended like an icy blanket. I twisted in my captor's grasp and saw Mab standing in the doorway, her gaze locked on Sage's body. Everyone backed away as she entered the throne room. You could hear a pin drop as the queen walked up to Sage's body, bending down to touch his cold, frozen cheek. I shivered, for the temperature was still dropping. Even some of the Winter fey looked uncomfortable as new icicles formed on the ceiling and frost crept over skin and fur. Mab was still bent over Sage, her expression unreadable, but her mulberry lips parted and mouthed a single word. "Oberon."

Then she screamed, and the world shattered. Icicles exploded, flying outward like crystallized shrapnel, pelting everyone with glittering shards. The walls and floor cracked, and fey screeched as they disappeared into the gaping holes.

"Oberon!" Mab raged again, whirling around with a terrifying, crazy look in her eyes. "He did this! This is his revenge! Oh, Summer will pay! They will pay until they are screaming for mercy, but they will find no pity among the Winter Court! We will repay this heinous act in kind, my subjects! Prepare for war!"

"No!" My voice was drowned out in the roar that went up from the Unseelie fey. Twisting out of my captor's grip, I staggered into the middle of the room.

"Queen Mab," I gasped, as Mab swung the full brunt of her terrible gaze on me. Madness warred with the fury in her eyes, and I shrank back in terror. "Please, listen to me! Oberon didn't do this! The Summer Court didn't kill Sage, it was the Iron King. The Iron fey did this!"

"Be silent!" hissed the queen, baring her teeth. "I will not listen to your pathetic attempts to protect your wretched family, not when the Summer King threatened me in my own court. Your sire has murdered my son, and you will be silent, or I will forget myself and give him an eye for an eye!"

"But, it's true!" I insisted, though my brain was screaming at me to shut up. I glanced around desperately and spotted Rowan, looking on with a faint smile. Ash would back me up, but Ash, as usual, wasn't here when I needed him. "Rowan, please. Help me out. I'm not lying, you know I'm not."

He regarded me with a solemn expression, and for a moment I really thought he would come through, before a corner of his mouth curled nastily. "It isn't nice to deceive the queen, Princess," he said, looking grim apart from the sneer in his eyes. "If these Iron fey were a threat, we would have seen them by now, don't you think?"

"But they do exist!" I cried, on the verge of panic now. "*I've* seen them, and they *are* a threat!" I turned back to Mab. "What about the huge, fire-breathing iron horse that almost killed your son? You don't think that's a threat? Call Ash," I said. "He was there when we fought Ironhorse and Machina. He'll back me up."

"*Enough!*" Mab screeched, whirling on me. "Half-breed, you go too far! Your line has already robbed me of a son, and you will not touch another! I know you seek to turn my youngest against me with your blasphemous claims of love, and *I will not have it!*" She pointed a manicured nail at me, and a flare of blue-white shot between us as I stumbled back. "You will be silent, once and for all!"

Something gripped my feet, holding them fast. I looked down to see ice creeping up my legs, moving faster than I'd seen before. In the space of a blink, it had flowed up my waist and continued over my stomach and chest. Icy needles stabbed my skin as I wrapped my arms around myself, just before they were frozen to my chest. And still, the ice came on, creeping up my neck, burning my chin. Panic gripped me as it covered my lower jaw, and I screamed as ice flooded my mouth. Before I could suck in another breath, it covered my nose, my cheek-bones, my eyes, and finally reached the top of my head. I couldn't move. I couldn't breathe. My lungs burned for air, but my mouth and nose were filled with ice. I was drowning, suf-focating, and my skin felt like it was being peeled away by the cold. I wanted to pass out, I longed for darkness to take me, but though I couldn't breathe and my lungs screamed for oxygen, I didn't die.

Beyond the wall of ice, everything had fallen silent. Mab stood before me, her expression torn between triumph and hate. She turned back to her subjects, who watched her with wary eyes, as if she might lash out at them, too.

"Make ready, my subjects!" the queen rasped, raising her arms. "The war with Summer starts now!"

Another roar, and the minions of the Unseelie Court scattered, leaving the room with raucous battle cries. Mab spared me one more glance over her shoulder, her lips curling into a snarl before she walked out. Rowan stared at me a moment longer, snickered, and followed his queen from the room. Silence fell, and I was left alone, dying but unable to die.

When you can't breathe, each second feels like an eternity. My entire existence shrank into trying to draw air into my lungs. Though my head knew it was impossible, my body couldn't understand. I could feel my heart thudding laboriously against my ribs; I could feel the hideous chill of the ice, searing my skin. My body knew it was still alive and continued its fight to live.

I don't know how long I stood there, hours or only a few minutes, when a shadowy figure slipped into the room. Though I could still see out, the ice made everything cracked and distorted, so I couldn't tell who it was. The shadow hesitated in the doorway, watching me for a long moment. Then, quickly, it glided across the room until it stood next to my prison, laying a pale hand against the ice.

"Meghan," a voice whispered. "It's me."

Even through my air-starved delirium, my heart leaped. Ash's silvery eyes peered through the wall separating us, as bright and soulful as ever. The torment on his face shocked me, as if he were the one trapped and unable to breathe.

"Hang on," he murmured, pressing his forehead to mine through the wall. "I'm getting you out of there." He leaned back, both hands against the ice, and closed his eyes. The air began to vibrate; a tremor shook the walls around me, and tiny cracks spider-webbed through the ice.

With the sound of breaking glass, the prison shattered, shards flying outward but somehow leaving me unscathed. My legs buckled and I fell, choking and coughing, vomiting up water and ice shards. Ash knelt beside me and I clung to him, gasping air into my starved lungs, feeling the world spin around me.

Somehow, through the dizzying rush of air, the relief at being able to breathe again, I noticed that Ash was holding me, too. His arms were locked around my shoulders, pressing me to his chest, his cheek resting against my wet hair. I heard his rapid heartbeat, pounding against my ear, and strangely, that calmed me down a little.

The moment ended too soon. Ash pulled away, dropping his black coat around my shoulders. I clutched at it gratefully, shivering. "Can you walk?" he whispered, and his voice was urgent. "We have to get out of here, now."

"W-where are we g-going?" I asked, my teeth chattering. He didn't answer, only pulled me to my feet, his gaze darting about warily. Grabbing my wrist, he started leading me from the room.

"Ash," I panted, "wait!" He didn't slow down. My nerves jangled a warning. With all my strength, I stopped dead in the middle of the floor and yanked my hand out of his grip. He whirled, eyes narrowing to slits, and I remembered all the things he'd said to Rowan, that everything he'd done was in service to his queen. I quickly backed out of his reach. "Where are you taking me?" I demanded.

He looked impatient, stabbing his fingers through his hair in an uncharacteristically nervous gesture. "Back to Seelie territory," he snapped, reaching for me again. "You can't be here now, not when a war is about to start. I'll get you safely over to your side and then I'm done with this."

It felt as if he'd slapped me. Fear and anger flared, making me stupid, making me want to hurt him all over again. "Why should I trust you?" I snarled, throwing the words at him like stones. I was completely aware that I was being an idiot, that we needed to get out of there before anyone saw us, but it was like I'd eaten spill-your-guts again, and words just kept pouring out. "You've misled me from the beginning. Everything you said, everything we did, that was all a ploy to bring me here. You set me up from the very start."

"Meghan—"

"Shut up! I hate you!" I was on a roll now, and had the vindictive pleasure of seeing Ash flinch as if I'd struck him. "You're a real piece of work, you know? Is this a game you like to play? Make the stupid human girl fall for you and then laugh as you rip her heart out? You knew what Rowan was doing, and you didn't do anything to stop it!"

"Of course not!" Ash snarled back, his vehemence startling me into silence. "Do you know what Rowan would do if he found out…what we did? Do you know what *Mab* would do? I had to make them believe I didn't care, or they would've torn you apart." He sighed wearily, giving me a solemn look. "Emotions are a weakness here, Meghan. And the Winter Court preys on the weak. They would've hurt you to get to me. Now, come on." He reached for me again, and I let him take my hand without protest. "Let's get out of here before it's too late."

"I'm afraid it's already too late," drawled a snide, familiar voice, making my heart stop. Ash jerked to a halt, yanking me behind him, as Rowan stepped out of the hallway, grinning like a cat. "I'm afraid your time just ran out."

# CHAPTER FIVE

*Brothers*

"Hello, Ash." The older prince smiled gleefully as he sauntered into the room. His gaze met mine, and he raised a sardonic eyebrow. "And what, may I ask, are you doing with the half-breed? Could it be you're actually helping her escape? Oh dear, what a dreadfully treasonous idea you've come up with. I'm sure Mab will be quite disappointed in you."

Ash said nothing, but his hand on mine clenched tight. Rowan chuckled, circling us like a hungry shark. Ash moved with him, keeping his body between me and Rowan. "So, little brother," the older prince mused, adopting an inquisitive expression, "I'm curious. What made you risk everything for our wayward princess here?" Ash said nothing, and Rowan *tsked*. "Don't be stubborn, little brother. You might as well tell me, before Mab tears you limb from limb and banishes you from Tir Na Nog. What is the price of such loyal obedience? A contract? A promise? What is the little harlot giving you to betray your entire court?"

"Nothing." Ash's voice was cold, but I caught the faintest tremor below the surface. Rowan apparently did as well, for his eyebrows shot up and he gaped at his brother, before throwing back his head with a wild laugh.

"I can't believe it," Rowan gasped, staring at Ash in disbelief. "You're *in love* with the Summer whelp!" He paused and, when Ash didn't deny it, collapsed into shrieking laughter again. "Oh, this is rich. This is too perfect. I thought the half-breed was a fool, pining for the unattainable Ice prince, but it seems I was wrong. Ash, you've been holding out on us."

Ash trembled, but he didn't release my hand. "I'm taking her back to Arcadia. Get out of our way, Rowan."

Rowan sobered immediately. "Oh, I don't think so, little brother." He smiled, but it was a cruel thing, sharp as the edge of a blade. "When Mab finds out, you'll *both* be decorating the courtyard. If she's feeling merciful, maybe she'll freeze you two together. That would be tragically fitting, don't you think?"

I shuddered. The thought of returning to that cold, airless, living death was too much. I couldn't do it; I'd rather die first. And the thought of Ash having to endure it with me for hundreds of years was even more horrifying. I squeezed Ash's hand and pressed my face into his shoulder, glaring at Rowan for all I was worth.

"Of course," Rowan went on, scratching the side of his face, "you could always beg forgiveness, drag the half-breed to the queen, and still be in Mab's favor. In fact," he continued, snapping his fingers, "if you go to Mab right now and turn over the princess, I'll even keep my mouth shut about what I saw here. She won't hear a peep out of me, I swear."

Ash went rock still; I could feel muscles coiling beneath his skin, the tension lining his back.

"Come on, little brother." Rowan leaned against the door frame and crossed his arms. "You know it's for the best. There are only two choices here. Hand over the princess, or die with her."

Ash finally moved, as if coming out of a trance. "No," he whispered, and I heard the pain in his voice as he came to some terrible decision. "There is one more."

Releasing my hand, he took one deliberate step forward and drew his sword. Rowan's eyebrows shot up as Ash pointed his blade at him, a cold mist writhing along its edge. For a moment, there was absolute silence.

"Get out of the way, Rowan," Ash growled. "Move, or I'll kill you."

Rowan's face changed. In one instant, it went from arrogant, condescending and evilly smug, to something completely alien and terrifying. He pushed himself from the archway, his eyes gleaming with predatory hunger, and slowly drew his sword. It sent a raspy shiver echoing across the hall as it came into view, the blade thin and serrated like the edge of a shark's tooth.

"You sure about this, little brother?" Rowan crooned, flourishing his weapon as he stepped up to meet Ash. "Will you betray everything—your court, your queen, your own blood—for her? You can't change your mind once you start down this path."

"Meghan," Ash said, his voice so soft I nearly lost it. "Get back. Don't try to help me."

"Ash…" I wanted to say something. I knew I should stop this, this fight between brothers, but at the same time I knew Rowan would never let us go. Ash knew it, too, and I could see the reluctance in his eyes as he steeled himself for battle. He didn't want to fight his brother, but he would…for me.

They faced each other across the icy room, two statues each waiting for the other to make the first move. Ash had taken a battle stance, his sword out in front of him, his expression re-luctant but unwavering. Rowan held his blade casually at his side, tip pointing toward the floor, smirking at his opponent. Neither of them seemed to breathe.

Then Rowan grinned, a predator baring his fangs. "All right, then," he muttered, sweeping up his blade in a blindingly quick move. "I think I'm going to enjoy this."

He lunged at Ash, his sword a jagged blur through the air. Ash brought his weapon up, and icy sparks flew as the blades screeched against each other. Snarling, Rowan cut viciously at his brother, advancing with a series of savage head strikes. Ash blocked, ducked, and suddenly lunged, stabbing at Rowan's throat. But Rowan spun gracefully aside, his sword licking out and back again. Ash whirled with inhuman speed, and would've cut him in two if the older prince hadn't leaped back.

Smiling, Rowan raised his weapon, and I gasped. The gleaming point was smeared with crimson. "First blood to me, little brother," he taunted, as a trickle of red began to drip from Ash's sword arm, speckling the floor. "There's still time to stop this. Turn over the princess and beg for Mab's mercy. And mine."

"You have no mercy, Rowan," Ash growled, and lunged at him again.

This time, they both moved so quickly, twisting, jumping, spinning aside and slashing with their blades, it was hard to see it as anything but a beautifully timed dance. In fast-forward. Sparks flew, and the sound of blades clashing echoed off the walls. Blood appeared on both swords, and red splattered the floor around the combatants, but I couldn't see who had the advantage.

Rowan suddenly knocked Ash's blade aside, then thrust out his hand, sending a jagged spear of ice at his brother's face. Ash threw himself backward to avoid it, hitting the floor and rolling to his knees. As Rowan brought his sword down at his kneeling opponent and I screamed in fear, Ash ducked aside, letting the blade miss him by centimeters. Grabbing Rowan's arm, letting his brother's momentum carry him forward, Ash spun and threw him to the floor. Rowan's head struck the ice, and I heard the breath leave his body in a startled *whoof.* Quick as a snake, Rowan flipped over, sword in hand, but by that time, Ash had his blade at his throat.

Rowan glared at his brother, his face twisted into a mask of pain and hate. Both were panting, dripping blood from numerous wounds, yet Ash's grip was steady as he pressed the blade against Rowan's neck.

The older prince chuckled, raised his head and spit blood in Ash's face. "Go on then, little brother," he challenged, as Ash winced but didn't shy away. "Do it. You've betrayed your queen, sided with the enemy, drawn a sword against your own brother…you might as well add slaughtering your family to the list as well. Then you can run off with the half-breed and live out your sordid fantasy. I wonder how Ariella would feel, if she knew how easily she's been replaced."

"Don't talk about her!" Ash snarled, raising the hilt as if he really would thrust the sword through Rowan's throat. "Ariella is gone. Not a day goes by that I don't think of her, but she's gone, and there's nothing I can do about it." He took a deep breath to calm himself, the longing on his face plain to see. A lump caught in my throat, and I turned away, blinking back tears. No matter how much I loved this dark, beautiful prince, I could never match what he'd already lost.

Rowan sneered, narrowing his eyes. "Ariella was too good for you," he hissed, raising himself up on his elbows. "You failed her. If you'd really loved her, she would still be here."

Ash flinched, as if struck a physical blow, and Rowan pressed his advantage. "You never saw what a good thing you had," he continued, sitting up as Ash backed away a step. "She's dead because of you, because you couldn't protect her! And now you disgrace her memory with this half-breed abomination."

Pale, Ash glanced at me, and I saw Rowan's arm move a second too late. "Ash!" I cried, as the older prince leaped up and lunged with frightening speed. "Look out!"

Ash was already moving, the honed reflexes of a fighter kicking in even when his mind was elsewhere. Leaping back, his sword came up as Rowan slashed at him with a dagger that appeared from nowhere, and Rowan's lunge carried him right onto the point of Ash's blade.

Both brothers froze, and I bit down a scream. For a moment, everything ground to an abrupt halt, frozen in time. Rowan blinked and looked down at the blade in his stomach, his eyes wide and confused. Ash was staring at his hand in horror.

Then Rowan staggered back, dropping the knife and leaning against a wall, his arms around his gut. Blood streamed between his hands, staining the white fabric crimson.

"Congratulations…little brother." His voice came out choked, though his eyes were clear as he nodded at Ash, still frozen in shock. "You finally…managed to kill me."

Pounding footsteps echoed in the hall, and faint shouts carried into the throne room. I wrenched my eyes from Rowan's bloody form and ran to Ash, who was still staring at his brother in a horrified daze.

"Ash!" I grabbed his arm, snapping him out of his trance. "Someone's coming!"

"Yes, run away with…your half-breed, Ash." Rowan coughed, a line of blood trickling from his mouth. "Before Mab comes in…and sees that her last son is dead to her. I don't think you can do anything more…to betray your court."

The voices were getting louder. Ash shot Rowan one last guilty, agonized look, then grabbed my wrist and ran for the door.

I don't remember how we made it out. Ash pulled me along like a madman, running through hallways I didn't recognize. It was a miracle we didn't run into anyone, as footsteps and sounds of pursuit echoed all around us. Maybe it wasn't coincidence at all, as Ash seemed to know exactly where he was going. Twice, he yanked me into a corner and pressed his body up against mine, whispering at me to be silent and not move. I froze as a gang of redcaps skittered past, snarling and waving knives at one another, but they didn't notice us. The second time, a pale woman in a bloody dress floated by, and my heart thudded so loudly I was sure she would hear, but she drifted past without seeing.

We fled down a cold, empty corridor with icicles growing from the ceiling like chandeliers, flickering with a soft blue light. Ash finally pulled me through a door with the silhouette of a bone-white tree emblazoned on the front. The room beyond was rather small and sparsely decorated with a tall bookshelf, a dresser made of polished black wood, and an impressive knife collection on the far wall. A simple bed sat in the corner, the blankets pulled tight, looking as if it hadn't been used in decades. Everything looked exceptionally clean, neat and Spartan, not like a prince's bedroom at all.

Ash sighed and finally released me, leaning against the wall with his head back. Blood soaked his shirt, leaving dark stains against the black material, and my stomach turned.

"We should clean those," I said. "Where do you keep the bandages?" Ash looked right through me, his eyes glassy and blank. The shock was taking a toll on him. I bit down my fear and faced him, trying to sound calm and reasonable. "Ash, do you have any rags or towels lying around? Something to stop the bleeding?"

He stared at me a moment, then shook himself and nodded to the corner. "Dresser," he muttered, sounding more weary than I'd ever heard him. "There's a jar of salve in the top drawer. *She* kept it…for emergencies…"

I didn't know what he meant by that, but I walked over to the dresser and yanked open the top drawer. It held an assortment of weird things: dead flowers, a blue silk ribbon, a glass dagger with an intricately carved bone handle. I rummaged around and found a jar of herb-scented cream, nearly empty, sitting on an old, bloodstained cloth. In the corner sat a roll of what looked like gauze made of spiderwebs.

As I pulled them out, a thin silver chain came with the gauze and slithered to the floor. Bending down to pick it up, I saw two rings attached to the links, one large and one small, and what Ash said finally sank in.

This—this drawer full of odds and ends—was Ariella's, where Ash kept all his memories of her. The dagger was hers, the ribbon was hers. The rings, exquisitely designed with tiny leaves etched in silver and gold, were a matching set.

I replaced the chain and shut the drawer, a cold knot settling in my stomach. If I ever needed proof that Ash still loved Ariella, here it was.

My eyes stung, and I blinked them angrily. Now was not the time for a jealous tantrum. I turned and found Ash watching me, his eyes dull and bleak. I took a deep breath. "Um, I think you'll have to take off your shirt," I whispered.

He complied, pushing himself away from the wall, leaving a smear of red. Removing his tattered shirt, he tossed it on the floor and turned back to me. I tried hard not to stare at the lean, muscular chest, though my mouth went dry and my face burned crimson.

"Should I sit?" he muttered, helping me along. Gratefully, I nodded. He moved to the bed, easing himself down on the mattress with his back to me. The wounds on his shoulder and ribs seeped crimson against his pale skin.

*You can do this, Meghan*. Carefully, I moved up behind him, shuddering at the long, jagged cuts across his flesh. There was so much blood. I dabbed at it gingerly, not wanting to hurt him, but he didn't make a sound. When the blood was gone, I dipped two fingers in the salve and touched it lightly to the gash on his shoulder.

He made a small noise, like an exhalation of breath, and slumped forward, head down and hair covering his eyes. "Don't worry about hurting me," he muttered without looking up. "I'm…fairly used to this."

I nodded and applied more salve to the wound, liberally this time. He didn't flinch, though his shoulders were taut and rigid beneath my fingertips; I could feel the tight coil of muscles beneath my hands. I wondered if Ariella used to do this for him, in this very bedroom, patching him up whenever he was hurt. Judging from the pale scars across his back, this wasn't the first time he'd been wounded in a deadly fight. Had she felt the same as me, angry and terrified whenever Ash put himself in mortal danger?

My eyes grew blurry. I tried blinking, but it was no use. Retrieving the gauze, I wrapped it around his shoulder, biting my lip to keep silent as tears streamed down my face.

"I'm sorry."

He hadn't moved, and his voice was so soft I barely heard it, but I still almost dropped the gauze. Tying it off, I didn't answer as I went to work on his ribs, winding the bandages around his waist. Ash sat perfectly still, barely breathing. A teardrop fell from my chin to land on his back, and he flinched.

"Meghan?"

"Why are you apologizing?" My voice came out shakier than I wanted it to, and I swallowed hard. "You already told me why you were being a bastard. You had to protect me from your family and the Winter Court. They were perfectly good reasons." *Not that I'm bitter or anything.*

"I didn't want to hurt you." Ash's voice was still soft, hesitant. "I thought that if I could make you hate me, it would be easier when you returned to your world." He paused, and his next words were almost a whisper. "What I said in the courtyard… Rowan would have tormented you even more if he knew."

I finished binding his ribs and pulled the wrappings tight around his waist. My eyes still streamed, but they were different tears now. I didn't miss the subtle phrasing: when you return to your world. Not *if.* When. As though he knew I would go back someday, and we would never see each other again.

Still silent, I picked up the jar and returned it to the dresser. I didn't want to face him now. I didn't want to think that he could be gone from my life forever, vanishing back into a world where I couldn't follow.

"Meghan." Ash turned and grabbed my hand, sending tingles up my arm. Against my will, I looked down at him. His face was desolate, his eyes pleading for understanding. "I can't…have feelings for you," he murmured, tearing a hole right through my heart. "Not in the way you want. Whatever happens, Mab is still my queen, and the Winter Court is my home. What happened in Machina's realm…" His brow knitted, and his expression darkened with pain. "We have to forget that, and move on. Once I take you to Arcadia's borders and you're safe with Oberon, you won't see me again."

The pain in my heart became a sick and fiery gnawing. I stared at him, hoping he would take it back, tell me he was kidding. He withdrew his hand and stood, facing me with a deeply sorrowful expression. "I'm sorry," he murmured again, avoiding my eyes. "It's…better this way."

"No." I shook my head as he drew away, brushing past me.

I whirled to follow him, reaching for his arm, missing. "Ash, wait—"

"Don't make this harder." He opened his closet and pulled out a tight gray shirt, shrugging into it with barely a wince. "I...killed Rowan." He closed his eyes, struggling with the memory. "I'm a kinslayer. There's nothing left in my future now, so be glad you won't be around to see what happens."

"What will you do?"

He grimaced. "Return to court. Try to forget." Reaching into the closet, he pulled out a long black coat crossed with silver chains and drew it over his shoulders. "Throw myself on Mab's mercy and hope she doesn't kill me."

"You can't!"

He faced me fully, the coat swirling around him. Just like that, he became something cold and remote, a deadly beautiful faery, unearthly and unreachable. "Don't get involved in fey politics, Meghan," he said darkly, shutting the closet door. "Mab will find me, no matter what I do or how far I run. And with the war approaching, Winter will need every soldier it can get. Until Summer returns the scepter, Mab will be relentless."

He turned away, but mention of the war reminded me of something else. "The scepter. Ash, wait!" I grabbed his sleeve, ignoring the way he went perfectly still. "It wasn't the Summer Court!" I blurted before he could say anything. "It was the Iron fey. I saw them." He frowned, and I leaned forward, willing him to believe me. "It was Tertius, Ash. Tertius killed Sage."

He stared at me blankly for a moment, and I held my breath, watching his expression. Out of everyone in the Winter Court, Ash was the only one to actually see the Iron fey. If he didn't believe me, I didn't have a chance of convincing anyone else.

"Are you sure?" he murmured after a few seconds. Relief flooded me, and I nodded vigorously. "Why? Why would the Iron fey steal the scepter? How did they even get inside?"

"I don't know. Maybe they want its power? Or maybe they took it to start a war between the courts. They accomplished that much at least."

"I have to tell the queen."

"No!" I moved to block him, and he glared at me. "Ash, she won't believe you," I said desperately. "I tried to tell her, and she turned me into an icicle. She's convinced it's Oberon's doing."

"She'll listen to me."

"Are you sure? With everything you've done? Will she listen to you after you saved me and killed Rowan?" His expression darkened, and I ignored the guilt stabbing holes in my chest. "We have to go after them," I whispered, suddenly sure of what we had to do. "We have to find Tertius and get the scepter back. It's the only way to stop the war. Mab will have to believe us then, right?"

Ash hesitated. For a moment, he looked terribly unsure, balanced between me and duty to his queen. He raked a hand through his hair, and I saw the indecision in his eyes. But before he could reply, a sudden scratching on his door made us both jump.

We exchanged a glance. Drawing his sword and motioning me back, Ash strode to the door and warily cracked it open. There was a streak of dark fur, and a cat darted through the opening. I yelped in surprise.

Ash sheathed his blade. "Tiaothin," he muttered, as the phouka shed the feline form for her more human one. "What's happening out there? What's going on?"

The phouka grinned at him, slitted eyes bright and eager. "The soldiers are everywhere," she announced, twitching her tail. "They've sealed all doors into and out of the palace, and everyone is looking for you and the half-breed." She spared me a glance and chuckled. "Mab is *pissed*. You should go now, if you're going. The elite guard are on their way right now."

I looked to Ash, pleading. He glanced at me, then back to the door, his expression torn. Then, he shook his head as if he couldn't believe he was doing this. "This way," he snapped, yanking open the closet. "Inside, now."

I crossed the threshold into the small, dark space and looked back for Ash. He paused at the frame, glancing at the phouka dancing in the middle of the room. "Lie low after this, Tiaothin," he warned. "Stay out of Mab's way for a while. Got it?"

The phouka grinned, mischief written on every inch of her smile. "And what fun would that be?" she said, sticking out her tongue. Before Ash could argue, her ears twitched backward and she jerked her head up. "They're almost here. Go, I'll lead them away. No one does a wild-goose chase better than a phouka." And before we could stop her, she ran to the door, flung it open and leaned into the hall. "The prince!" she screeched, her shrill voice echoing down the corridor. "The prince and the half-breed! I saw them! Follow me!"

We ducked into the closet as the sound of booted feet thundered past the door, following Tiaothin as she led them away. Ash sighed, raking a hand through his hair. "Idiot phouka," he muttered.

"Will she be all right?"

Ash snorted. "Tiaothin can handle herself better than anyone I know. That's why I asked her to keep an eye on you."

So that's why the phouka was so interested. "I didn't need babysitting," I said, both annoyed and thrilled that he'd thought to look out for me when he couldn't be there.

Ash ignored me. Putting a hand to the wall, he closed his eyes and muttered several strange, unfamiliar words under his breath. A thin rectangle of light appeared, and Ash pulled open another door, bathing the room in pale light and revealing an icy staircase plunging into darkness.

"Come on." He turned to me and held out a hand. "This will take us out of the palace, but we have to hurry before it disappears."

Behind us, a roar of discovery echoed through the hall, as something poked its head in the room and bellowed for its friends. I grabbed Ash's hand, and we fled into the darkness.

# CHAPTER SIX

*The Goblin Market*

I followed Ash down the glittering staircase and through a narrow corridor studded with leering gargoyles and flickering blue torches. We didn't speak; the only sounds were our footsteps echoing off the stones and my ragged breathing. Several times, the tunnel split off in different directions, but Ash always chose a path without hesitation. I was glad for the long winter coat around my shoulders; the temperature here was frigid, and my breath clouded the air as we ran, listening for sounds of pursuit.

The passage abruptly dead-ended, a solid wall of ice blocking our path. I wondered if we'd taken a wrong turn, but Ash released me and walked forward, placing one hand against the ice. With sharp, crinkly sounds, it parted under his fingers, until another tunnel stretched away before us, ending in open air.

Ash turned to me.

"Stay close," he murmured, making a quick gesture with his

hand. I felt the tingle of glamour as it settled over me like a cloak. "Don't talk to anyone, don't make eye contact, and don't attract any attention. With that glamour, no one will notice you, but it will break if you make a noise or catch someone's eye. Just keep your head down and follow me."

I tried. The problem was, it was difficult *not* to notice anything beyond the castle walls. The beautiful, twisted city of the Unseelie fey rose up around me, towering spires of ice and stone, houses made of petrified roots, caves with icicles dangling from the openings like teeth. I followed Ash down narrow alleys with eyes peering out from under rocks and shadows, through tunnels that sparkled with millions of tiny crystals, and down streets lined with bone-white trees that glowed with sickly luminance.

And of course, the Unseelie were out in droves tonight. The streets were lit up with will-o'-the-wisps and corpse candles, and swarms of Winter fey danced, drank and howled at the top of their lungs, their voices echoing off the stones. I remembered the wild Revel in the courtyard, and realized the Unseelie were still celebrating the official arrival of winter.

We skirted the edges of the crowds, trying to avoid notice as the Winter fey whirled and spun around us. Music rang through the night, dark and seductive, stirring the mob into frenzies. More than once, the dancing turned into a bloodbath as some unfortunate faery vanished under a pile of shrieking revelers and was torn apart. Trembling, I kept my head down and my eyes on Ash's shoulders as we wove our way through the screaming throngs.

Ash grabbed me and pulled me into an alley, his glare warning me to be silent. A moment later, a pair of knights cantered into the crowd on huge black horses with glowing blue eyes, scattering the Winter fey like a flock of birds. The dancers snarled and hissed as they leaped aside, and a goblin screeched once as it was trampled beneath a charging horse, falling silent as a hoof cracked its skull open.

The knights yanked their mounts to a halt and faced the mob, ignoring the growls and hurled insults. They wore black leather armor with thorns bristling from the shoulders, and the faces beneath the open helms were sharp and cruel. Ash shifted beside me.

"Those are Rowan's knights," he muttered. "His elite Thornguards. They answer only to him and the queen."

"By orders of Her Majesty, Queen Mab," one knight shouted, his voice somehow rising over the cacophony of music and snarling voices, "the Winter Court has officially declared war on Oberon and the Summer Court! For the crime of killing Crown Prince Sage and the theft of the Scepter of the Seasons, all Summer fey will be hunted down and destroyed without mercy!"

The Winter fey roared, screeching and howling into the night. It was not a roar of rage, but rather one of ecstasy. I saw redcaps laughing, goblins dancing for joy, and spriggans grinning madly. My stomach heaved. They wanted blood. The Winter Court lived for violence, for the chance to rip into their ancient rivals without mercy. The knight let them howl and carry on a few moments before holding up his hand for silence.

"Also," he roared, bringing the chaos to a murmur, "be aware that Prince Ash is now considered a traitor and a fugitive! He has attacked his brother, Prince Rowan, gravely wounding him, and has fled the palace with the half-breed daughter of Oberon. Both are considered extremely dangerous, so it would do you well to be wary."

Ash sucked in a breath. I saw relief cross his face, as well as guilt and concern. Rowan was still alive, though our escape through the city had become much more dangerous.

"If you see them, by order of Queen Mab, they are not to

be harmed!" bellowed the knight. "Capture them, or report their whereabouts to any guard, and you will be greatly rewarded. Failure to do so invites the queen's wrath upon your head. Spread the word, for tomorrow we march to war!"

The knights spurred their mounts into action and galloped off, amid the roars of the Unseelie crowd. Ash looked deep in thought, his eyes narrowed to gray slits.

"Rowan isn't dead," he breathed, and I couldn't tell if he was pleased with this news or not. "At least, not yet. This will make things considerably more difficult."

"How will we get out?" I whispered.

Ash frowned. "The gates will be guarded," he muttered, looking past me into the street, "and I don't trust the regular trods if Rowan knows we're out here." He paused, thinking, then sighed. "There is one more place we can go."

"Where's that?"

He glanced at me, and I suddenly realized how close we were. Our faces were just inches apart and I felt his heartbeat quicken, matching my own. Quickly, he turned away, and I ducked my head, hiding my burning face.

"Come on," he whispered, and I thought I caught a tremor in his voice. "We're not going far, but we have to hurry. The Market keeps its own hours, and if we don't reach it in time, it will disappear."

A wild howl rang out of the darkness, and we looked back at the crowd. The Winter fey had gone back to their partying as if nothing had happened, but there was a meaner, desperate edge to their revels now, as if the promise of war had only whetted their appetite for blood. A pair of redcaps and a hag squabbled over the body of the dead goblin, and I turned away before I was sick. Ash took my hand and pulled me on, into the shadows.

WE FLED THROUGH the city, keeping to the shadows and darkness, somehow avoiding the mobs in the street. At one point, we very nearly tripped over a redcap exiting a hole in the wall. The creature snarled an insult, but then its beady eyes widened in recognition and it turned to shout a warning instead. Ash gestured sharply, and an ice dagger thunked into the creature's open mouth, silencing it forever.

We reached a circular courtyard on the banks of a huge underground lake, mist writhing off the water to drift along the ground. Colorful booths and tents stood empty as we passed through, flapping in the breeze like a dead, abandoned carnival. An enormous white tree stood in the very center, bearing fruit that looked like human heads. A narrow door was embedded in the thick trunk, and Ash quickened his pace as we approached.

"The Market is through here," he explained, pulling me behind the tree as an ogre lumbered past, its steps slow and ponderous. "Now, listen. Whatever you see in there, don't buy anything, don't offer anything, and don't accept anything, no matter how much you want it. The vendors will try to make a deal with you—ignore them. Keep silent, and keep your eyes on me. Got it?"

I nodded. Ash opened the narrow door with a creak and led me inside, shutting it behind him. The interior of the trunk glowed softly and had a putrid sweet smell, like decaying flowers. I looked around for another door or way out, but the trunk was empty except for the door we came in.

"Stay close," Ash whispered, and he pushed the door open again.

Noise exploded through the doorway. The circular courtyard now thronged with life; the booths overflowed with merchandise; music and faery fire drifted through the night, and fey milled about in huge numbers, buying, talking and haggling with the vendors. I shrank back against the trunk, and Ash gave me a reassuring smile.

"It's all right," he said, leading me forward again. "In the Market, no one questions why you're here or where you came from. The only thing they're concerned about is the deal."

"So, it's safe, then?" I asked, as a faery with a wolf's head stalked through the crowd, carrying a string of severed hands. Ash chuckled darkly.

"I wouldn't go that far."

We joined the throng who, despite the jostling, shoving and snarled insults, paid us little attention. Unearthly vendors stood beside their booths or tents, crying out their wares, beckoning to passersby with long fingers or claws. A warty goblin caught my eye and grinned, pointing to his display of necklaces made of fingers, teeth and bones. A hag waved a shrunken pig's head in my face, while a hulking troll tried handing me some kind of meat-on-a-stick. It smelled wonderful, until I noticed the crispy bird and rat heads stuck on the kebabs between other unidentifiable chunks, and hurried after Ash.

The oddities continued. Dream catchers made of spider silk and infant bones. Monkey Paws and Hands of Glory. One booth had a prominent display of still-beating hearts, while the tent beside it offered flowers of delicate spun glass. Everywhere I looked, I saw wonders, horrors, and the just plain weird. The vendors were incredibly persistent; if they caught you looking, they would leap in front of you, shouting the marvels of their wares and offering "a deal you can't refuse."

"A few locks of your hair," cried a rat-faced imp, holding out a golden apple. "Be young and beautiful forever." I shook my head and hurried on.

"A memory," crooned a doe-eyed woman, waving a glitter- ing amulet back and forth. "One tiny memory, and your greatest wish will be answered." Yeah right. I'd done the whole memory thing before, thank you. It wasn't pleasant.

"Your firstborn child," quite a few of them wanted. "Your name. A phial of your tears. A drop of blood." With every offer, I just shook my head and hurried after Ash, weaving my way through the crowds. Sometimes, a glare from the Ice prince would cower the more persistent vendors who followed us through the aisles or latched on to my sleeve, but mostly we just kept moving.

Near the lake, a row of wooden docks floated above the ink-black water. A weathered tavern crouched at the shoreline like a bloated toad. A goblin staggered out holding a tankard, puked all over the sidewalk, and collapsed in it with his face to the sky. Ash stepped over the groaning body and ducked through the swinging doors. Wrinkling my nose at the trashed goblin, I followed.

The interior was smoky and dim. Battered wooden tables were scattered about the room, hosting a variety of unsavory-looking fey, from the redcap gang in the corner to the single, goat-headed phouka who watched me with glowing yellow eyes.

Ash glided through the room, weaving his way to the bar, where a dwarf with a tangled black beard glared at him and spit into a glass. "You shouldn't be here, Prince," he growled in an undertone, wiping the tankard with a dirty rag. "Rowan's got half the city lookin' for you. Sooner or later, the Thorn-guards will show up an' tear the place apart if they think we're hidin' you."

"I'm looking for Sweetfinger," Ash said in an equally low voice, as I pulled myself onto a bar stool. "I need to get out of Tir Na Nog, tonight. Do you know where he is?"

The dwarf shot me a sidelong glance, his thick face pulled into a scowl. "If I didn't know you better, Prince," he muttered, polishing the glass again, "I would accuse you of goin' soft. Word is you're a traitor to the Winter Court, but I don't care about that." He plunked the tankard down and leaned across the counter. "Just answer me this. Is she worth it?"

Ash's face went blank and cold, like a door slamming shut. "Would this be considered payment for finding Sweetfinger?" he replied in a voice dead of emotion.

The dwarf snorted. "Yeah. Sure, whatever. But, I want a serious answer, Prince."

Ash was still for a moment. "Yes," he murmured, his voice so low I barely caught it. "She's worth it."

"You know Mab will tear you apart for this."

"I know."

The dwarf shook his head, giving Ash a look of pity. "You an' your lady problems," he sighed, putting the glass under the counter. "Worse than the satyrs, I tell you. At least *they're* smart enough not to get attached."

Ash's tone was icy. "Can you find me Sweetfinger or not?"

"Yeah, I know where he is." The dwarf scratched his nose, then flicked something away. "I'll send someone out to find him. You and the Summer whelp can stay upstairs until he shows up."

Ash pushed away from the counter. His face was still locked into that expressionless mask as he turned to me. "Let's go."

I hopped off the bar stool. "Who's Sweetfinger?" I ventured as we made our way across the room. No one stopped us. The other patrons either ignored us or gave us a very wide berth. Which wasn't surprising; the cold radiating from the Winter prince was palpable.

"He's a smuggler," Ash replied, motioning me up a set of stairs in the corner. "A goblin, to be specific. Instead of smuggling goods, he smuggles living creatures. He might be the only one who can get us out of the city. If we can pay his price."

Goblins. I shuddered. My own experience with goblins hadn't been pleasant. A pack of them tried to eat me once, when I first came to the Nevernever.

Upstairs, Ash led me down a creaky hallway, past several wooden doors with strange noises coming from beyond them, until we came to the last one. Inside, a tiny room greeted us, with two simple beds along opposite walls and a flickering lamp in the far corner. I noticed the lamp was actually a round cage atop a gilded stand, and the light made desperate squeaking noises as it flitted from side to side. Ash shut the door, and I heard the click of a lock before he leaned back against it, looking utterly exhausted.

I longed to hold him. I wanted to melt into him and feel his arms around me, but his last words hung between us like a barbed-wire fence. "Are you all right?" I whispered. He nodded and ran his fingers through his hair.

"Get some sleep," he murmured. "I don't know if we'll get another chance to stop after this. You should rest while you can."

"I'm not tired."

He didn't press the issue, but stood there watching me with a weary, sorrowful expression. I gazed back, wishing I could bridge the distance between us, not knowing how to reach him.

An awkward silence filled the room. Words hovered on the tip of my tongue, wanting to burst out, but I knew Ash didn't want to hear them. I teetered between silence and confession, knowing I would be spurned, still wanting to try. Ash stood quietly, his gaze wandering about the room. A couple times he, too, seemed about to say something, only to fall silent, stabbing his fingers through his hair. When words finally did come, we both spoke at the same time.

"Ash—"

"Meghan, I—"

Someone pounded on the door, making us both jump. "Prince Ash!" a squeaky voice shouted from the other side. "Are you there? Sweetfinger is downstairs, waiting for you."

"Tell him I'm on my way," Ash replied, and pushed himself off the door. "Wait here," he told me. "It should be safe. Lock the door and try to get some rest." He opened the door, revealing a leering goblin on the other side, and closed it softly behind him.

I sat down on one of the beds, which reeked of beer and dirty straw, and stared at the door for a long time.

THEN I WAS BEING shaken awake. I blinked in the darkness; someone had put a black cloth over the caged light and the room was swathed in shadow. Sleep made my eyelids heavy and awkward, but I cracked them open to focus on the blurred form above me. Ash sat on the edge of the mattress, silver eyes bright in the gloom, holding me gently by the shoulders.

"Meghan," he murmured, "wake up. It's time."

Exhaustion pulled at me. I'd been more tired than I thought, and my thoughts swirled muzzily. Seeing I was awake, Ash started to rise off the bed, but I slid forward and wrapped my arms around his waist.

"No," I murmured, my voice still groggy with sleep. "Stay."

He shivered, and his hands came to rest over mine. "You're not making this any easier," he whispered into the darkness.

"Don't care," I slurred, tightening my hold on him. He sighed and half turned in my arms, smoothing the hair from my cheek.

"Why am I so drawn to you?" he muttered, almost to himself. "Why is it so hard to let go? I thought...at first...it was Ariella, that you remind me of so much. But it's not." Though he didn't smile, his eyes lightened a shade. "You're far more stubborn than she ever was."

I sniffed. "That's like the pot calling the kettle black," I whispered, and a faint, tiny grin finally crossed his face, before his expression clouded and he lowered his head, touching his forehead to mine.

"What do you want of me, Meghan?" he asked, a low thread of anguish flickering below the surface. Tears blurred my vision, all the fear and heartache of the past few days rising to the surface.

"Just you," I whispered. "I just want you."

He closed his eyes. "I can't do that."

"Why not?" I demanded. His face swam above me, blurring with tears, but I refused to release him to wipe my eyes. My desperation grew. "Who cares what the courts say?" I challenged. "We could meet in secret. You could come to my world, no one will see us there."

He shook his head. "Mab already knows. Do you think she would let us get away with it? You saw how well she reacted in the throne room." I sniffled, burying my face in his side, as his fingers gently combed my hair. I didn't want to let him go. I wanted to curl into him and stay there forever.

"Please," I whispered desperately, not caring about pride anymore. "Don't do this. We can find a way around the courts. Please." I bit my lip as a shiver went through him, and I held him tighter. "I love you, Ash."

"Meghan." Ash's voice was tormented. "You don't…know me at all. You don't know what I've done…the blood on my hands, both faery and mortal." He stopped, taking a breath to compose himself. "When Ariella died, everything inside me froze. It was only through hunting—killing—that I could feel anything again. I cared for nothing, not even myself. I threw myself into fights I thought I would lose, if only to feel the pain of a sword blow, the claws tearing me apart."

I shivered and clung to him, remembering the scars across

his back and shoulders. I could imagine him fighting, his eyes dead and cold, hoping that something would finally get lucky and kill him.

"Then you came along," he muttered, touching my wet cheek, "and suddenly...I don't know. It was like I was seeing things for the first time again. When I saw you with Puck, the day you came to the Nevernever..."

"The day you tried to kill us," I reminded him.

He winced, nodding. "I thought fate was playing a cruel joke on me. That a girl, who could have been Ariella's shadow, was keeping company with my sworn enemy—it was too much. I wanted to kill you both." He sighed. "But, then I met you at Elysium, and..." He closed his eyes. "And everything I thought I'd lost forever came trickling back. It was maddening. I thought about killing you several times during Elysium, just to stop what I knew would be my downfall. I didn't want this, to feel anything, especially with a half-human girl who was the daughter of the Summer King." He snorted ruefully, shaking his head. "From the moment you stepped into the Nevernever, you've been my undoing. I should never have agreed to that contract."

I sucked in a breath. "Why?"

He brushed a strand of hair from my cheek, his voice gentler than before. "Because no matter what I feel, I can't fight centuries of rules and traditions, and neither can you."

"We could try—"

"You don't know the courts," Ash continued softly. "You haven't been in Faery long enough to know what could happen, but I do. I've seen it, centuries of it. Even if we get the scepter back, even if we manage to stop the war, we'll still be on opposite sides. Nothing will change that, no matter how much you wish it wasn't so. No matter how much *I* wish it was different."

I didn't answer, too miserable to comment. His voice, though filled with regret, was resolved. He had made up his mind, and I wouldn't be changing it.

A strange peace settled through me, or perhaps my despair finally gave in to resignation. *So, this is it,* I thought, as numbness spread through my body, easing the sharp pain in my chest. *This is what breaking up is like.* Although, I was sure "breaking up" was the wrong expression. It seemed much too common and trivial for what was happening.

"Come on." Ash pried my hands from his waist and stood up. "We should go. Sweetfinger and I made a deal. He'll get us out of the city through the goblin tunnels that run beneath it. We'll need to hurry—Rowan's Thornguards are still scouring the streets for us."

"Ash," I said, struggling upright. "Wait. Just one more thing, before we go."

He frowned warily. "What do you want?"

I rose from the bed, my heart thudding in my chest. "Kiss me," I whispered, and saw his eyebrows arc in surprise. "Just once more," I pleaded, "and I promise it will be the last time. I'll be able to forget you after that." A bald-faced lie. Even if I turned ninety, lost my mind and forgot everything else, the memory of the Winter prince would be a shining beacon that would never fade.

He hesitated, unsure, and I tried to make my tone light. "Last time, I swear." I met his gaze and tried for a smile. "It's the least you can do. I didn't get a proper breakup, you know."

Ash still wavered, looking torn. His eyes flicked to the door, and for a moment I thought he would walk away, leaving me to shrivel into a mortified heap. But then he let out a quiet sigh, and his shoulders slumped in resignation.

Meeting my gaze, he took one step forward, drew me into his arms, and brushed his lips to mine.

I think our last kiss was meant to be quick and chaste, but after the first touch of his lips fire leaped up and roared through my belly. My fingers yanked him close, digging into his back, and his arms crushed me to him as if wanting to meld us together. I knotted my fingers in his hair and bit down on his bottom lip, making him groan. His lips parted, and my tongue swept in to dance with his. There was nothing sweet or gentle in our last kiss; it was filled with sorrow and desperation, of the bitter knowledge that we could've had something perfect, but it just wasn't meant to be.

It ended much too soon. Ash pulled away, eyes bright, shaking with desire and passion. Both our hearts were thudding wildly, and Ash's fingers were digging painfully into my shoulders. "Don't ask me this again," he rasped, and I was too breathless to answer.

He released me and stalked through the door without looking back. I took a deep breath, halting the tears crawling up my throat, and followed.

A goblin waited for us at the foot of the stairs, his mouth pulled into a toothy grin that showed missing fangs and gold teeth. He was decked out in jewelry: rings, ear studs, necklaces, even a gold nose ring. A milky glass eye sparkled as he turned to me, rubbing his claws and grinning like a gleeful shark.

"Ah, this is princess that turned prince traitor," he hissed, eyeing me up and down. "And now they need goblin tunnels out of city, good, good." He gestured with a ring-encrusted hand. "No time to speak. We leave now, before guards show up, ask too many questions. Need anything before we go, traitor prince?"

Ash looked pained, but shook his head. The goblin cackled, gold teeth flashing in the dim light. "Yes, good! Follow me, then."

# CHAPTER SEVEN

*The Ring*

Sweetfinger led us out a back door of the tavern and along the edge of the lake. Past the docks, the ground dropped away sharply to a narrow coastline of jagged rock and stone. Hugging the breaker wall, we followed Sweetfinger to the water's edge, where two burlier goblins waited inside a small wooden boat.

"Quickly, quickly," Sweetfinger said, urging us inside. We took a cautious seat between the two hench-goblins, who picked up the oars as Sweetfinger shoved us into the water and leaped in. As they rowed us farther from shore, he turned to us with an apologetic smile.

"Goblin tunnels aren't far from here," he said, fingering one of his rings. "Only goblins know where they are, and only goblins are allowed to see them and live. Used to be, payment would be your lovely eyes, but times change. Point is, you not goblin, you cannot see our secret tunnels. Rules, you know. So sorry."

"Understood," Ash muttered as a goblin slid behind him and pulled a blindfold over his eyes. I jumped as a black cloth covered my eyes as well, plunging me into darkness.

We drifted for a long while, the only sounds being the rhythmic sloshing of the oars in the water and Sweetfinger's occasional comment to his thugs. Ash's body was tense against mine, muscles coiled bands under his skin. The air grew colder, and I heard the squeaking of bats somewhere above us. The boat bumped and scraped against rocks, and a foul stench crept into the air, smelling of dung and rotten meat. Snickers and cackling laughter echoed in the darkness, and clawed feet skittered over the rocks.

Then, the noises and smells faded, and we floated in silence for a time. I heard Sweetfinger and his guards muttering among themselves, and it made me very nervous. Finally, the boat bumped against solid ground, and someone pulled it ashore.

I pulled off the blindfold and blinked in the dim light. We were in a small cave with a pebbly floor, bones and trash scattered about the room. In the distance, a circle of light glimmered invitingly. I breathed a sigh of relief. We'd made it.

Sweetfinger leered at us as Ash helped me out of the boat. "As promised," he said, gesturing to the exit at the back of the room. "Safe passage out of city. Now, I believe traitor prince owes me something, yes?" He held out a jewel-encrusted claw, and Ash dropped a small leather pouch into his waiting hand.

"Tell no one you've seen us," Ash said as the two hench-goblins shoved the boat back into the water.

"I'm afraid it's too late for that, Your Highness," came a harsh, gravelly voice at the other end of the cave. We spun, Ash's hand on his sword, as four Thornguards stepped into view, their boots crunching over the stones.

"Very intelligent, not going through the regular trods, Ash," said one guard. His armor was thornier than the others', the barbs on his shoulders bristling like giant porcupine quills. "Mab has them all well guarded, but you knew that, didn't you? Unfortunately, Rowan already bribed every smuggler in the city by the time you found this one. Goblins are such disgusting opportunists, aren't they?"

Furious, I glared back at Sweetfinger, but the boat was already well out of reach, Sweetfinger grinning at me from the bow.

"Sorry, Princess," the goblin cackled. "Prince's offer was good. Other prince's offer was better. Nothing personal, yes?" He waved, and the boat drifted away into the dark. An icy stone settled in the pit of my stomach, and I turned back to the guards.

As one, the Thornguards drew their weapons. Their swords were spiky and black, with long thorns running the length of the blade, looking as sharp as razors.

"Stand down, Edgebriar," Ash commanded. He hadn't drawn his sword yet, but his posture was tense. "I don't want to fight you. You can walk away from this and Rowan would never know. We're not returning to the city."

"I'm afraid we weren't ordered to return you to the city, or Mab," Edgebriar said with the barest of smirks. "You see, Rowan knows you're going after the scepter, and he can't allow that. The new king wants the half-breed alive, but I'm afraid we're going to have to kill you, Prince. Like Sweetfinger said, it's nothing personal."

For a second, I didn't know who he was talking about. Then it hit me like a punch in the stomach. The new king. The new *Iron King*. They were working for the Iron Kingdom. Rowan must've let Tertius and the wiremen into the palace. He let them kill Sage and take the scepter, and convinced Mab that the Iron fey were not a threat!

Ash's face went blank with shock. "No," he said, as the

blood drained from his face. "No, Rowan wouldn't sell us out. Not to them. What have you done?"

"We can't stop the Iron Kingdom," Edgebriar continued, his voice earnest. "The old ways have become obsolete. Mab can't protect us any longer. It is time to ally ourselves with the stronger power, to become greater than we are. Rowan will lead us to a new era, one where we will fear nothing. Not the touch of iron, not the fading of human imagination, nothing! Let the oldbloods wallow in their ancient traditions. They will fall soon, and we will rise up to take their place."

"Rowan will destroy us," Ash said grimly. "This war only hastens our destruction. If Summer and Winter stood together, we could stop the Iron Kingdom."

"For how long?" Edgebriar demanded, punctuating his words with a savage swing of his blade. "The humans dream their technology, their grand sweeping visions, and forget us. We can't turn back the clock, but we *can* evolve to survive. I will show you what I mean." He ripped off his gauntlet, holding up his bare hand. On his third finger, an iron ring gleamed in the light. The entire digit was blackened and shriveled, and my stomach turned as he shook his fist triumphantly. "Look!" he demanded. "Look at me! I do not fear the touch of iron, of progress. It burns me now, but soon I will be able to use it freely, like the humans. Soon, I will be like them."

"You're dying, Edgebriar." Ash's voice was full of horror and pity. "It's killing you slowly, and you don't even realize it."

"No! After the war, when both sides are weak and open, the Iron fey will sweep in and destroy all traces of the old. There will be no more Summer or Winter. There will be no more courts. There will be only the Iron Kingdom, and those strong enough to stand with it."

I stared at him. "Rowan let the Iron fey into the palace, didn't he?" I whispered, and his fevered gaze turned on me.

"He sent them to steal the scepter, and he let them kill his own brother. How can you work for such a bastard? Can't you see he's using you?"

"Be silent, half-breed." Edgebriar glared at me. "Insult my prince again, and I will cut out your tongue and feed it to my hounds. Rowan is the only one who cares for the future of Tir Na Nog."

Ash shook his head. "Rowan wants power, and would sacrifice his entire court to achieve it. You don't have to be responsible for his insanity, Edgebriar. Let us pass. We can end this war, and if Summer stands with us, we can find a way to deal with the Iron Kingdom."

Edgebriar's face didn't change. "We have our orders, Prince Ash. We will be taking the half-breed with us, but I'm afraid your journey ends here. Rowan made it quite clear that he did not want you returning to Mab, for any reason." He gestured to the knights behind him, and they began to close in. "I apologize for the location. A prince's tomb should be a grander affair."

I backed away, knowing the violence that was coming next. For the millionth time, I tried desperately to do *something* with my glamour; pull up a root to trip the knights, throw a glowy ball of light to distract them, anything. It was like hitting a glass wall. I *knew* my power was on the other side, but I couldn't access it.

Ash faced the approaching knights calmly, though I could sense muscles coiling beneath his skin. "Rowan doesn't know me as well as he thinks," he murmured, seemingly unconcerned with the jagged blades closing in on him, "otherwise he never would've made such a mistake."

Edgebriar smiled, leering at Ash from behind the trio of knights, content to let his guards engage the Winter prince. "And what mistake would that be?"

"There's only four of you."

His arm whipped out, sending a flurry of ice shards at the oncoming Thornguards. The knights flinched, throwing up their arms to protect their faces, and Ash lunged into their midst.

The first one didn't stand a chance. Ash's blade sheared through his armor, and the faery crumpled before he could even raise his sword. Where he fell, his spiky armor seemed to unravel, flaring out into thick black briars, thorns curling into the air. In seconds, the faery's body had turned into a giant thornbush, growing right out of the rocks. A metal band glinted on one of the branches.

The screech of blades focused me on the current battle. I couldn't see Edgebriar, but the other two Thornguards had Ash pressed into a corner and were hounding him mercilessly. Ash parried and spun, blocking their attacks, his blade a blue-white streak through the air. I glanced around and picked up a fist-sized rock from the edge of the water. Maybe I couldn't throw fireballs, but that couldn't stop me from hurling other things.

*Please don't hit Ash,* I thought, winding back for the throw.

The first rock thumped off the back of a knight, doing nothing, but the second struck the side of his head, making him flinch for just a moment. It was enough. Ash's blade whipped out, ripping through his chest. The knight crumpled without a sound, and brambles erupted from his armor, covering the body in a cocoon of thorns.

I gave a shout of triumph, but a dark shape filled my vision. Edgebriar stepped out of invisibility and reached for me with taloned fingers. I tried to dodge, but the Thornguard latched on to my wrist and yanked me to him, twisting my arm behind my back. As I gasped in pain, his other arm came up to circle my throat. I squirmed and kicked at him, but only jabbed myself on his spiny armor as his arm tightened and cut off my air.

An explosion of brambles signaled the end of the last knight, and Ash came striding through the hedge toward us, a cold, murderous gleam in his eye.

"Stay where you are, Prince," Edgebriar spat, and pressed a cold black dagger against my cheek. "Not another step, or I will gouge out her pretty eyes. The Iron King doesn't care if she's a bit damaged when she comes to him."

Ash stopped, lowering his blade, his eyes never leaving the knight. Edgebriar's chokehold loosened just the tiniest bit, and I sucked in a much-needed breath, trying to be calm. This close, the knight smelled of sweat and leather, and something sharper, metallic. The ring on his hand glinted against his blackened finger as he held the knife point to my face.

"Now," Edgebriar panted, locking gazes with Ash, "I want you to put down your sword and swear you will not follow us." When Ash didn't move, Edgebriar stabbed the point of the knife into my cheek, just enough to draw blood. I gasped at the sudden pain, and Ash tensed. "I won't ask you again, Your Highness," Edgebriar growled. "You've lost this battle. Put down your sword, and promise you will not follow us."

"Edgebriar." Ash's voice was as cold as frozen steel. "Rowan has poisoned your mind, as surely as that iron is poisoning your insides. You can still walk away from this. Let me take the princess back to Arcadia, and then we can warn Mab about the Iron King and Rowan."

"It's too late." Edgebriar shook his head wildly. "They're already coming. You can't stop them, Ash. No one can." He chuckled, a note of madness coming to the surface, and tightened his stranglehold on my neck. *All the king's army and all the king's men,* he whispered, waving the knife in front of my eyes, *came to Faery on the day it would end.*

All right, enough was enough. Edgebriar had lost it; he had

taken a long walk off the short end. I had to do *something*. But without a weapon or glamour, what could I do?

Blood was trickling down my face, oozing a path over my skin like a giant red tear. My cheek throbbed, and pain brought everything into sharp focus. In my mind, I saw the metal ring glowing white, pulsing with energy. I felt the glamour around it, but it was different from anything I'd felt before—cold and colorless. Was this…iron glamour? Could I use it as the fey used the wilder magic of dreams and emotion? The ring shimmered, fluid and alive, eager to be worked upon. To be shaped into something new.

*Tighten,* I thought, and the metal band responded instantly, biting into the skin. Edgebriar jerked, looking startled, and I squeezed harder, twisting the ring so that it cut into his flesh, drawing blood. It hissed where it touched, and Edgebriar howled, jerking his arm from my neck as if burned. I twisted from his grasp and shoved him away.

Ash lunged for Edgebriar. The Thornguard saw him coming and at the last second went for his sword, too late. Ash stepped within his guard and plunged the blade through his chest, so hard that it erupted out the knight's back.

Edgebriar staggered and fell away, hitting the water with a loud splash. He stared at the blood on his chest, than gazed up at us, his eyes blank and confused. "You don't…understand," he gurgled, as Ash looked down on him sadly. "We were going to become…like them. Rowan…promised us. He promised…"

Then his eyes rolled up in his head, and thorny creepers slithered over his body, hiding him from view.

I shuddered, torn between throwing up and bursting into tears. Strange how all my time in the Winter Court still hadn't desensitized me to blood and death. I felt Ash's gaze on me, curious and wary, like a stranger's.

"What did you do to him?"

I shook my head. The strange glamour was already fading, like it had never been. My body trembled from the aftermath of shock and adrenaline. "I don't know."

Ash glanced once more at the thornbush, at the iron ring dangling from a twig, and shuddered. "Come here," he sighed, motioning me to a large rock. "Sit down. Let me see your face."

The cut wasn't deep, more of a puncture wound than a gash, though it still hurt like hell. Ash knelt and studied it, then tore a strip from his sleeve and dunked it in a nearby puddle. As he raised it to my cheek, I instinctively flinched and jerked away, grimacing. He shook his head, and a corner of his lip twitched.

"I haven't even touched it yet. Now hold still."

He lifted the rag, and our gazes met. Ash froze. I saw a dozen emotions cross his face before he took a quiet breath and very carefully pressed the cloth to my cheek.

I was tempted to close my eyes, but kept them open, watching his face. To have him here, to have him this close, was worth the pain. I studied his eyes, his lips, the tiny silver stud in his ear, almost hidden by his dark hair. I memorized those little details, searing his image into my brain, wanting to remember this moment. Though his expression was closed and businesslike after that first glance, his fingers were gentle.

"Why are you staring at me?"

His voice made me jump. "What? I'm not."

"Liar." Ash took my hand and pressed it to the cloth, holding it to my cheek. "Here. The bleeding's stopped, but keep pressure on it for a bit just to be sure." His hand lingered on mine, cool and smooth, though he wouldn't meet my eyes. "I'm sorry, Meghan."

"Why?"

"For Rowan. For all of this." He rose and walked to where Edgebriar had fallen. Now only a black thorny bush marked the place where he had died, and Ash glared at it as if it might come back to life.

"Rowan," I heard him mutter. "What are you thinking?"

Dropping the cloth, I walked up to him. "What now?"

He was quiet a moment, brooding. The shock of discovering that his brother was responsible for betraying all of Faery was still new, like a wound that wouldn't close. I could tell he didn't want to believe it. "Nothing's changed," he said at last, his voice cold and resolved. "The scepter is still out there, and if Rowan knows where it is, he isn't going to tell us. When this is over, Mab will decide what to do with Rowan, but the scepter comes first."

Very lightly, I touched his arm. "I'm sorry. He's a jerk, but I'm sorry it had to be him."

He nodded. "Let's get out of here."

Four horses stood waiting at the cave entrance; faery steeds with jet-black coats, lightning-colored manes, and glowing, white-blue eyes. Their slender hooves didn't quite touch the ground as they stamped and shifted, regarding us with eerie intelligence.

Ash helped me into one's saddle, and the fey-horse swished its tail and rolled its eyes at me, as if sensing my unease. I gave it a warning glare.

"Don't try anything, horse," I muttered, and it pinned back its ears, which was not a good sign. Ash approached another mount and swung easily into the saddle, as if he'd done it a thousand times.

"Where are we going?" I asked, fumbling with the reins, which made the horse prance sideways. Dammit, I'd never get used to this. "We know Tertius stole the scepter, Rowan helped him into the palace, and they're both working for a new Iron King." I frowned as I thought of the implications. "Ash, do you think we'll have to go back to the Iron Kingd—"

My horse suddenly let out a shrill whinny and half reared, nearly throwing me off. As I shrieked and grabbed its mane, the other mount tried to bolt, but Ash pulled one rein short, and the horse spun in frenzied circles until it calmed down. As our mounts quieted, still prancing and tossing their heads, we gazed around for the source of their fear. We didn't have to look far.

Through the trees, silhouetted against the cloudy sky, a lone figure on horseback watched us atop a snowy rise. The single tree standing over it had curled its branches as far away from the figure as possible, its limbs twisted and warped, but the rider didn't seem to care. As we stared at each other, the sun peeked out from behind the clouds, glinting off its steel armor.

A faint metallic rustling drifted over the wind, like thousands of knives scraping together, making my blood run cold. As the Iron knight stood motionless on the hill, an enormous pack of spindly legged creatures appeared around him. Claws flashing, limbs jerking sporadically, the wire-fey crowded the hilltop like huge spiders, gleaming in the sun.

Ash went pale, and my heart contracted in horror as the knight raised a hand toward us, sending the entire pack skittering down the hill.

We ran.

The faery steeds ate up the ground as they charged through the forest, their hooves making almost no noise in the snow. The trees flew by at a terrifying speed as the horses plunged between trunks and over logs, reminding me of my first wild ride through Faery, when I had been running *away* from Ash, ironically. At least I had a saddle this time. I clung to the horse's neck, unable to do anything else, steering or otherwise. Thankfully, Ash seemed to know where he was going, and my horse followed his as we flew over the ground.

Behind us, the metallic skittering of the wire-fey echoed on the wind, never fading or falling behind.

The trees fell away, and a steep incline soared above us, jagged rocks covered in ice as smooth as glass. My stomach turned, imagining my horse slipping and rolling on top of me, but the hooves of the Winter-born faery steeds charged up the hill without hesitation. It felt like they were running up a wall, and I clung to my horse until my arms burned with liquid fire.

At the top of the rise, Ash pulled his mount to a halt, and my horse stopped as well, prancing in place. Arms shaking from the strain of keeping my seat, I straightened cautiously.

Ash was staring down the slope, eyes narrowed to slits. I followed his gaze, and my stomach lurched. The edge of the rise fell away into a dizzying vertical drop, jagged rocks jutting up like spines. I suddenly wished I knew how to steer my horse, just to move it away from the edge.

"They're coming," Ash muttered.

The wiremen fey flowed from the trees in a glittering swarm. Scuttling to the rise, they began to climb, digging their claws into the ice as they edged upward. Steel limbs flashing, they crawled up the icy slope like ants, barely slowing down.

"What are these things?" Ash whispered. He raised his arm, and the air around him sparkled as a glittering ice spear formed overhead. With a flick of his hand, he hurled it down the slope, into the ranks of oncoming fey.

The spear hit one directly in the face, punching through the wires and tearing it from the hill. It clattered down the slope, arms and legs flailing, but the other fey leaped over the body or skittered aside, and kept coming.

My horse snorted and backed away. I grabbed for its mane as Ash whirled his steed around, his face grim.

"We can't outrun them," he announced, and I caught the faintest hint of fear in his voice, which only made me more terrified. "They're faster than us, and will overtake the horses long before we reach a trod. We have to make a stand."

I looked down at the approaching swarm, and my voice squeaked with terror. "Here? Now?"

"Not here." Ash shook his head and pointed down the other side of the slope. "There's an abandoned fort on the edge of the wyldwood. Ariella and I used it as a hunting lodge. If we can reach it, we might have a chance."

The other side of the slope fell away into the same breakneck drop. Far, far in the distance, I saw where the snow-covered treetops met the writhing gray mist of the wyldwood.

A raven circled us, giving a harsh cry as it passed overhead as the first of the wire-fey clawed its way to the top. Ash kicked his steed into motion, and mine followed, charging for the edge of the rise. I screamed as my horse gathered its legs underneath it and leaped into empty space.

We fell for what seemed like an eternity. When we finally hit the ground, the horses landed with barely a jolt and immediately plunged into the forest.

Behind us, the wiremen poured down the slope in a glittering flood.

My body ached and my arms burned from clinging to the horse for so long. Every bump sent a lance of pain through my side, and my breath came in short, agonizing gasps. Finally, we burst through the trees into a snow-covered clearing. In the center of the grove, a crumbling tower rose skyward in a precarious upside down *L,* as if it might collapse any moment.

"Come on!" Ash leaped off his mount, ignoring it as it raced away into the trees. My horse tried to follow, but the prince grabbed its reins, yanking it up short. I half slid, half fell out of the saddle, and I barely took a gasping breath before Ash was dragging me through the snow.

We ran for the fort, hearing the scraping of claws behind us. I didn't dare look back. Ahead, through the great wooden doors, I saw the darkened interior of the room. Sunlight slanted through holes in the roof, spilling over a strangely luminescent floor. As we drew closer, I gasped. The ground was completely carpeted in white, bell-like flowers, which glowed softly in the dim light. They grew on the walls and even covered the ancient furniture lying around the room: a wooden table, a cupboard, a few simple cots. Everything was also covered in snow and ice, as the roof was full of holes, but I supposed that hadn't mattered to Ash and Ariella. Freezing temperatures never bothered the Winter fey.

Ash pulled us through the opening, crushing flowers underfoot, and threw his weight against the doors. They groaned, reluctant to move. I joined him, and together, we strained at the stubborn gates. They closed slowly, creaking with age and time, and the wiremen were no more than twenty yards away when they finally banged shut. Ash threw down the bolt, then pressed both hands against it and sheathed the entire gate with ice. No sooner had he finished than the first blows rattled the wooden door, resounding through the chamber. The ice shivered and tiny cracks radiated through the surface as more blows shook the gate. It wouldn't hold them for long.

Ash drew his sword. "Get back," he told me as the door rattled again. More cracks shot through the ice. "Find a place to hide. There's an alcove behind that statue against the wall—you should be able to fit."

I shook my head frantically, seeing Sage surrounded by the hideous wire-fey, dying on the floor of the throne room. I couldn't watch Ash be torn apart like that before my eyes. Ash glanced back at me and frowned.

"Meghan, there's nothing you can do. Go! I'll hold them as long as I can. Go, now!"

A great chunk fell out of the door as a curved wire claw tore it away. The hole widened, as metal talons ripped and clawed at the wood. Fear got the better of me. I ran to the crumbling statue of some forgotten hero, darting behind it as the first of the wiremen squeezed through the crack like a giant spider.

Claws flashing, it lunged at Ash, who was waiting for it. His sword arced through the air, shearing the spindly fey in half. Another skittered toward him, and he whipped his blade around to slice off a flailing arm. The wireman collapsed, twitching, in the flowers, shredding the delicate blooms like paper.

I bit my cheek, trying not to be sick. More fey poured through the opening as they tore the gate to shreds. Ash was forced back, giving ground to prevent the wiremen from flanking him. Finally, he stood against a broken pillar, his back to the stones, as the Iron faeries swarmed around him, slashing and clawing.

I heard a noise above us, and a shower of stones and ice tumbled to the ground. A metallic form suddenly crawled through a hole in the roof and crawled along the ceiling, making my blood run cold. "Ash, above you!" I yelled, as more fey slithered through the cracks. "They're coming through the roof!"

The wiremen surrounded Ash in a chaotic blur. I could barely see him through the forest of slashing claws. Suddenly he leaped straight up, over the heads of the Iron fey, to land on the upright half of a broken pillar. His coat was in tatters, one side of his face was covered in crimson, and more blood dripped from numerous wounds to the flowers below.

The wiremen resumed their attack, crawling up the pillar or dropping from the ceiling. Fear hammered against my chest. I tried reaching for that strange, cold glamour I'd felt earlier with Edgebriar, but came up with nothing. I tried drawing in regular glamour, but hit the glass wall again. I wanted to scream. What was wrong with me? I had once taken down the Iron King; where was that power now? Ash was going to die in front of me, and I couldn't do anything to stop it.

Something big and black hurtled through the smashed door, diving toward the battle. It screeched as it slammed into a wireman, knocking it off the column, and the rest of the fey looked up, startled at this newest threat. It wheeled around to land on the pillar across from Ash—a giant black raven with emerald-green eyes. My heart leaped in my chest.

With a harsh, laughing cry, the bird disintegrated, vanishing in a swirling black cloud. A new form rose up from the explosion, shaking feathers from his fiery red hair, a wide, familiar grin spreading across his face.

"Hey, Princess," Puck called, brushing feathers from his clothes and gazing around at the carnage. "Looks like I got here just in time."

The wire-fey paused just a moment, blinking up at this newcomer, than scuttled forward once more. Puck drew a furry ball from his pocket, winked at me, and tossed it into the ranks of Iron fey swarming below him. It hit the ground, bounced once, and erupted into a large black boar, which charged into the fey with a maddened squeal.

Puck threw Ash a mocking smile. "You look like crap, Prince. Did you miss me?"

Ash frowned, stabbing a faery that was clawing at his feet. "What are you doing here, Goodfellow?" he asked coldly, which only caused Puck's grin to widen.

"Rescuing the princess from the Winter Court, of course." Puck looked down as the wire-fey piled on the squealing boar, ripping and slicing. It exploded into a pile of leaves, and they skittered back in confusion. "Though it appears I'm saving your sorry ass, as well."

"I could've handled it."

"Oh, I'm sure." Puck brandished a pair of curved daggers, the blades clear as glass. His grin turned predatory. "Well, then, shall we get on with it? Try to keep up, Your Highness."

"Just stay out of my way."

They leaped down from their pillars directly into the ranks of wiremen, who instantly swarmed around them. Back to back, Ash and Puck sliced into their opponents with renewed vigor, neither giving an inch now that the other was there. The mob of Iron fey thinned rapidly. Through the mass of writhing limbs, I caught glimpses of Ash's face, taut with concentration, and Puck's vicious smile.

Silently, the last few wiremen broke from the whirlwind of death in the middle of the floor. Without looking back, they scuttled up the walls, clawed their way through the holes in the roof and were gone.

Puck, his shirt now a tattered mess, sheathed his daggers and glanced around with a satisfied smirk. "Well, that was fun." His gaze found me, still frozen behind the statue, and he shook his head. "Wow, icy reception here. And to think I came back from the dead for this."

I squeezed from my hiding place, my heart pounding against my ribs, and ran to him. His arms opened, and I threw myself against his chest, hugging him fiercely. He was real. He was here, not dying in a tree somewhere, left behind and forgotten. "I missed you," I whispered against his neck.

He held me tighter. "I'll always come back for you," he murmured, sounding so unlike himself that I pulled back and looked at him. For a moment, his green eyes were intense, and I caught my breath at the emotion smoldering within. Then he smirked, and the effect was ruined.

I was suddenly aware of Ash leaning against a pillar, watching us with an unreadable expression. Blood streaked his face, splattering the white flowers beneath him, and his sword dangled limply from his grasp.

Puck followed my gaze, and his grin grew wider. "Hey, Prince," he greeted, "word is you're a traitor to the Winter

Court. You've got the entire wyldwood in an uproar—they say you tried to kill Rowan after he caught you escaping with the princess. Clearly, I've missed a few things."

"News travels fast," Ash replied wearily. He started to rake a bloody hand through his hair, then thought better of it, dropping it to his side. "It's been an interesting morning."

"To say the least." Puck gazed around at the bodies of the wiremen and wrinkled his nose. "What the hell are those things?"

"Iron fey," I said. "I've seen them before. They were in the throne room with Tertius when he stole the scepter."

"The Scepter of the Seasons?" Puck looked at me aghast. "Oh, man. So that's where the war rumors are coming from. Winter really *is* going to attack Summer." He glared at Ash. "So, we're at war. Perfect. Shall we save time and kill each other now, or did you want to wait until later?"

"Don't start, Goodfellow." Ash matched Puck's glare. "I didn't want this. And I have no time for a fight." He sighed, deliberately avoiding my gaze. "In fact, now that you're here, you can do us both a favor. I want you to take Meghan back to the Summer Court."

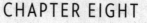

## CHAPTER EIGHT

*Partings and Memories*

"That's it?" Puck asked, as I stared at Ash, unable to believe what I'd just heard. He still wasn't looking and me, and Puck rattled on without noticing. "Take her back to Court? That's easy. I was going to do that anyway, whether you liked it or not. Comes with the whole rescue thing, you know—"

"What are you talking about?" I yelled, making Puck jump. "The hell with going back to Summer! We need to get the scepter back from the Iron fey! It's the only way to stop the war."

"I'm aware of that." Ash finally met my eyes, and his gaze was cold. "But this is Winter's problem. Retrieving the scepter is my responsibility. I want you to return to your own court, Meghan. You'll be safer there. You can't help me this time. Go home."

Hurt and betrayal stabbed me in the chest. "You were going

to dump me on Oberon all along, weren't you?" I spit at him. "You liar. I thought we were going after the scepter together."

"I never told you that."

Puck glanced from me to Ash and back again, looking confused. "Erm, so you're saying you don't want to go back home?" he asked me. I glared at him, and he shrugged. "Wow, so that totally makes the whole rescue plan a wash. You wanna throw me a bone here, Princess? I feel somewhat out of the loop."

"We have to go after the scepter," I told Puck, hoping he would back me on this. "Ash can't do it by himself. We can help—"

"No, you can't," Ash broke in. "Not this time. You'd be no use to me, Meghan, not with your magic sealed—" He caught himself, looking guilty, and Puck's eyes narrowed.

"Sealed?" Puck stepped forward threateningly. "You put a binding on her?"

"I didn't." Ash stared him down, defiant. "Mab did. When she first came to Winter. Mab was afraid her power would be too great, so she sealed her magic to protect the Court."

I remembered the wall I kept hitting whenever I tried using more than the simplest glamour, and my temper flared. How dare she! "And you knew," I accused Ash. "You knew about the seal, and you didn't bother telling me?"

Ash shrugged, unrepentant. "Mab ordered us not to. Besides, what difference would it make? I can't do anything about it."

I turned to Puck, who glowered at the prince as though he might attack him right then. "Can you break it?"

Puck shook his head. "Sorry, Princess. Only Mab, or someone of equal power, can remove a binding once it's been placed. That makes your choices Oberon, or Mab herself."

"All the more reason that you should return to Summer."

Ash pushed himself off the pillar, wincing. Behind him, the column was smeared with red.

"Where are you going?" I asked, suddenly afraid that he would walk out that door and not return.

He sheathed his sword without looking at me. "There's a spring a few yards behind this tower," he replied, walking slowly toward the door. I sensed he was trying hard not to limp. "Unless either of you object, I'm going to bathe."

"But you're coming back, right?"

He sighed. "I'm not going anywhere tonight," he promised, and swept a hand toward a far wall. "There's a trunk with blankets and supplies in that corner. Make yourselves comfortable. I think we're all going to be spending the night here."

The trunk held several quilts, a few canteens, a quiver of arrows, and a bottle of dark wine I didn't recognize and immediately left alone. Puck went hunting for firewood and came back with an armful, plus a branch bearing strange blue fruits he swore were safe to eat. Together, we cleared away flowers to make the campfire, though I felt a stab of guilt every time I yanked one up. They were quite beautiful, the petals so thin and delicate they were almost transparent.

"You're awfully quiet, Princess," Puck said as he arranged the firewood into a tepee. His slanted green eyes shot me a knowing look. "In fact, you haven't said a word since his royal iciness left. What's wrong?"

"Oh." I cast about for an excuse. No way was I telling Puck about my feelings for Ash. He'd probably challenge him to a duel the moment he walked through the door. "I...um...I'm just weirded out, you know, with all those wiremen bodies around. It's kinda creepy, like they might come to life and attack us while we're sleeping."

He rolled his eyes. "You and your zombie obsession. I've

never understood your fascination with horror movies, especially when they freak you out so much."

"They don't freak me out," I said, grateful for the change of subject.

"Riiiight, you just sleep with your light on to scare away roaches."

His comment made me smile. Not because he was right, but because it reminded me of another time, a simpler time, when all I had to worry about was homework and school and keeping up with the latest movie trends. When Robbie Goodfell and I could sit on the couch with a huge tub of popcorn and watch a marathon of *Friday the 13th* movies until the sun came up.

I wondered how much I'd missed in the time I'd been gone.

When I didn't answer, Puck snorted and shook his head. "Fine. Watch this." And he made a quick gesture with his hand. The air shimmered, and the twisted corpses lying around the room turned into piles of branches. "Better?"

I nodded, though I knew it was only an illusion. The dead fey were still there, beneath the faery glamour. Out of sight, out of mind didn't quite work for me, but at least it kept Puck from asking too many hard questions.

For a little while, anyway. "So, Princess," he began, once a cheerful fire crackled in the center of the room. I didn't know how he'd started it, but I'd learned not to question such things, in case it turned out to be an illusion and I only *thought* I was getting warm. "It seems I've missed a lot since I've been gone. Tell me everything."

I gulped. "Everything?"

"Sure!" He sat down on a quilt, leaning back comfortably. "Like, did you find Machina? Did you ever get your brother back?"

"Oh." I relaxed a bit and sat down beside him. "Yeah. Ethan is safe. He's home, and that stupid changeling is gone for good."

"What about Machina?"

I bit my lip. "He's dead."

Puck must've noticed the change in my voice, for he sat up and put his arm around my shoulders, pulling me close. I leaned into him, feeling his warmth, taking comfort in his nearness. "I'm sick of this place," I whispered, feeling like a little kid, as my eyes burned and the world went fuzzy. "I want to go home."

Puck was silent for a moment, just holding me as I leaned against him, fighting back tears. "You know," he said finally, "I don't have to take you back to the Summer Court. If you want, I can take you back to your world. If you really want to go home."

"Would Oberon let me go?"

"I don't see why not. Your magic has been sealed off. You'd be like an ordinary high school student again. Mab wouldn't consider you a threat anymore, so the Unseelie would probably leave you alone."

My heart leaped. Home. Could I really go home? Back to Mom and Luke and Ethan, back to school and summer jobs and a normal life? I missed that, more than I realized. I felt a bit guilty for ditching the plan to get the scepter back, but screw it. Ash didn't want me around. My contract with him was over, and I'd paid my dues to the Unseelie Court. Our deal said nothing about me *staying* in Winter.

"What about you?" I asked, looking up at Puck. "Weren't you ordered to bring me back to Summer? Won't you get in trouble?"

"Oh, I'm in hot water already." Puck grinned cheerfully. "I wasn't even supposed to let you go after the Iron King, remember? Oberon will skin me alive for that one, so I really can't dig myself any deeper."

His tone was light, but I closed my eyes, guilt tearing at me. It seemed everyone I cared about was getting hurt, risking so much, just to protect me. I was tired of it; I wished I had my magic back, so that I could protect them in return.

"Why?" I whispered. "Why do you hang around? You and Ash could've died today."

Puck's heartbeat sped up under my fingers. His voice, when it came, was very soft, almost a whisper. "I would've thought you'd've figured that out by now."

I looked up and found our faces inches apart. Twilight had deepened the room to shadow, though the carpet of flowers glowed brighter than ever. Firelight danced within Puck's eyes as we stared at each other. Though he still wore a tiny, lopsided smile, there was no mistaking the emotion on his face.

I stopped breathing. A tiny part of me, somewhere deep inside, was rejoicing at this newest revelation, though I think, deep down, I'd always suspected. *Puck loves me,* it whispered, thrilled. *He's in love with me. I knew it. I knew it all along.*

"You're kind of blind, you know?" Puck whispered, smiling to soften his words. "I wouldn't defy Oberon for just anyone. But, for you…" He leaned forward, touching his forehead to mine. "I'd come back from the dead for you."

My heart pounded. That tiny part of me wanted this. Puck had always been there: safe, reliable, protective. He was part of *my* Court, so there was no stupid law to get in the way. Ash was gone; he had already made up his mind. Why not try with Puck?

Puck moved closer, his lips hovering an inch from mine. And all I could see was Ash, the passion on his face, the look in his eyes when he kissed me. Guilt gnawed my insides. *No,* my mind whispered, as Puck's breath caressed my cheek. *I can't right now. I'm sorry, Puck.*

I drew back slightly, ready to apologize, to tell him I couldn't right now, when a shadow appeared in the doorway and Ash walked in.

He froze, silhouetted against the night sky, the flowers casting his features in a pale glow. His hair was slightly damp, and his clothes were mended, whether through glamour or something else I couldn't tell. For a moment, shock and hurt lay open on his face, and his hands fisted at his side. Then, his expression closed, his eyes turning blank and stony.

Puck blinked at my expression and turned as Ash walked in. "Oh, hey, Prince," he drawled, completely unconcerned. "I forgot you were here. Sorry 'bout that." I tried meeting Ash's gaze, to show him this wasn't what he thought, but he was studiously ignoring me.

"I want you gone by morning," Ash said in cold, clipped tones, sweeping around the campfire. "I want you out of my territory, you and the princess both. According to the law, I could kill you where you stand for trespassing. If I see either of you in Tir Na Nog again, I won't be so lenient."

"Jeez, don't get your panties in a twist, Your Highness." Puck sniffed. "We'll be happy to leave, right, Princess?"

I finally caught Ash's gaze, and my heart sank. He stared at me coldly, no traces of warmth or friendliness on his face. "Yeah," I whispered, my throat closing up. This was it, the last straw. I'd been in Faery long enough. It was time to go home.

Ash began moving the piles of branches, really the dead Iron fey, and dumping them outside. He worked quickly and silently, not looking at either of us, almost feverish in his desire to get them out. When the bodies were cleared away, he grabbed the bottle of wine from the trunk and retired to a far corner, brooding into the glass. His entire posture screamed *leave me the hell alone,* and even though I wanted to go to him, I kept my distance. Thankfully, Puck didn't try to kiss me again, but he was never far, giving me secret little smiles, letting me know he was still interested. I didn't know what to do. My mind was spinning, unable to settle on one thought. Later that evening, Ash stood abruptly and left, announcing he was going to "scout around" for more Iron fey. Watching him stalk out the door without a backward glance, I was torn between running after him and sobbing on Puck's shoulder. Instead, I pleaded exhaustion and climbed into one of the cots, pulling the blanket over my head so I wouldn't have to face either of them.

It was hard to sleep that night. Huddled beneath the quilts, I listened to the sound of Puck snoring and fought back tears.

I didn't know why I was so miserable. Tomorrow, I was going home, at last. I could see Mom and Luke and Ethan again; I missed them all so much, even Luke. Though I had no idea how much time had passed in the real world, just the thought of returning home should've filled me with relief. Even if Mom and Luke were old and gray, and my four-year-old kid brother was older than I was, even if it *had* been a hundred years, and everyone I knew was…

I gasped and veered my thoughts from that path, refusing to think about it. Home would be the same as it always was. I could finally go back to school, learn to drive, maybe even go to prom this year. *Maybe Puck can take me.* The thought was so ridiculous I almost laughed out loud, choking on unshed tears. No matter how much I wanted a normal life, there would be a part of me that longed for this world, for the magic and wonder of it. It had seeped into my soul and shown me things I'd never thought existed. I couldn't be normal and ignorant ever again, knowing what was out there. Faery was a part of me now. As long as I lived, I would always be watching for hidden doors and figures from the corner of my eyes. And for a certain dark prince who could never be mine.

I must've fallen asleep, for the next thing I knew, I was opening my eyes and the room was bathed in hazy starlight. The flowers had opened completely and were glowing as if tiny moons nestled between the petals, throwing back the darkness. Ethereal moths and ghostly butterflies flitted over the carpet, delicate wings reflecting the light as they floated between blooms. Careful not to wake Puck, I rose and wandered into the flowers, breathing in the heady scent, marveling as a feathery blue moth landed on my thumb, weighing nothing at all. I breathed out, and it fluttered off toward a dark figure in the center of the carpet.

Ash stood in the middle of the room, surrounded by glowing white flowers, eyes closed as tiny lights swirled around him. They shimmered and drew together, merging into a luminescent faery with long silver hair, her features so lovely and perfect that my throat ached. Ash opened his eyes as she reached for him, her hands stopping just shy of his face. Longing shone from his eyes, and I shivered as the spectral faery moved right through him, dissolving into tiny lights.

"Is that...Ariella?" I whispered, walking up behind him.

Ash whirled around, his eyes widening at the sudden interruption. Seeing me, several emotions crossed his face—shock, anger, shame—before he sighed in resignation and turned away.

"No," he murmured, as the ghostly faery appeared again, dancing among the flowers. "It isn't. Not in the way you think."

"Her ghost?"

He shook his head, his eyes never leaving the specter as she swayed and twirled over the glowing carpet, butterflies drifting around her. "Not even that. There is no afterlife for us. We have no souls with which to haunt the world. This is...just a memory." He sighed, and his voice went very soft. "She was always happy here. The flowers…remember."

I suddenly understood. This was Ash's memory of Ariella, perfect, happy and full of life, a yearning so great it was given form, if only for a moment. Ariella wasn't here. This was only a dream, an echo of a being long departed.

Tears filled my eyes and ran down my face. The gash on my cheek stung where they passed, but I didn't care. All I could see was Ash's pain, his loneliness, his yearning for someone who wasn't me. It was tearing me apart, and I couldn't say anything. Because I knew, somehow, that Ash was saying goodbye, to both of us.

We stood in silence for a while, watching Ariella's memory dance among the flowers, her gossamer hair floating on the breeze as bright motes swirled around her. I wondered if she really was that perfect, or if this was what Ash remembered her to be.

"I'm leaving," Ash said quietly, as I knew he would. He finally turned to face me, solemn, beautiful, and as distant as the stars. "Have Goodfellow take you home. It isn't safe here any longer."

My throat felt tight; my eyes burned, and I took a shaky breath to free my voice. And even though I already knew the answer, even though my head was telling me to shut up, I whispered, "I won't see you again, will I?"

He shook his head, once. "I wasn't fair to you," he murmured. "I knew the laws, better than anyone. I knew it would end…like this. I ignored my better judgment, and for that, I'm sorry." His voice didn't change. It was still calm and polite, but I felt an icy hand squeeze my heart as he continued. "But, after tonight, we'll be enemies. Your father and my queen will be at war. If I see you again, I might kill you." His eyes narrowed, and his voice turned cold. "For real this time, Meghan."

He half turned, as if to leave. The glow of the flowers made a halo of light around him, only accenting his unearthly beauty. In the distance, Ariella danced and twirled, free from sorrow and pain and the trials of the living. "Go home, Princess," murmured the Unseelie prince. "Go home, and forget. You don't belong here."

I couldn't remember much of the night afterward, though I think it involved a lot of sobbing into my quilt. In the morning, I woke up to snow drifting in through the roof, coating the floor with heavy white powder. The flowers had faded, and Ash was already gone.

PART TWO

# CHAPTER NINE

*The Summoning*

The evening following Ash's departure, Puck and I hit the
edge of the wyldwood.

"Not far now, Princess," Puck said, giving me an encouraging grin. A few yards from where we stood, the snow and
ice just…stopped. Beyond it, the wyldwood stretched before
us, dark, tangled, trapped in perpetual twilight. "Just gotta
cross the wyldwood to get you home. You'll be back to your
old boring life before you can say 'summer school.'"

I tried smiling back, but couldn't manage it. Even though
my heart soared at the thought of home and family and even
summer school, I felt I was leaving a part of me behind.
Throughout our hike, I'd kept turning around, hoping to see
Ash's dark form striding through the snow after us, gruffly embarrassed and taciturn, but there. It didn't happen. Tir Na Nog
remained eerily empty and quiet as Puck and I continued our
journey alone. And as the sun sank lower in the sky and the

shadows lengthened around us, I slowly came to realize that Ash wasn't coming back. He was truly gone.

I quivered on the verge of tears but held them back. I did not want to have to explain to Puck why I was crying. He already knew I was upset, and kept trying to distract me with jokes and a constant string of questions. What happened after we left him to confront Machina? How did we find the Iron Realm? What was it like? I answered as best I could, leaving out the parts between me and Ash, of course. Puck didn't need yet another reason to hate the Winter prince, and hopefully he would never find out.

As we approached the colorless murk of the wyldwood, something moved in the shadows to our left. Puck spun with blinding speed, whipping out his dagger, as a spindly form stumbled through the trees and collapsed a few feet away. It was a girl, slender and graceful, with moss-green skin and hair like withered vines. A dryad.

The tree woman shuddered and gasped, clawing herself upright. One long-fingered hand clutched her throat as if she were being strangled. "Help…me," she gasped at Puck, her brown eyes wide with terror. "My tree…"

"What's happened to it?" Puck said, and caught her as she fell. She sagged against him, her head lolling back on her shoulders. "Hey," he said, shaking her a little. "Stay with me now. Where's your tree? Did someone cut it down?"

The dryad gasped for air. "P-poisoned," she whispered, before her eyes rolled up and her body turned to wood in his arms. With the sound of snapping twigs, the dryad curled in on herself until she resembled little more than a bundle of dry branches. I watched the faery's life fade away, remembered what Ash had said about the fey and death, and felt terribly, terribly sad. That was it for her, then. She'd simply ceased to exist.

Puck sighed, bowing his head, and gathered the lifeless dryad into his arms. She was thin and brittle now, fragile as spun glass, but not one twig snapped or broke off as he carried her away. With utmost care, he laid the body at the foot of a giant tree, murmured a few words and stepped back.

For a moment, nothing happened. Then, huge roots unfurled from the ground, wrapping around the dryad to draw her down into the earth. In seconds, she had disappeared.

We stood quietly for a moment, unwilling to break the somber mood. "What did she mean by poisoned?" I finally murmured.

Puck shook himself, giving me a humorless grin. "Let's find out."

WE DIDN'T HAVE to search far. Only a few minutes into the wyldwood, the trees curled away, and we stumbled onto a familiar patch of dead ground in the middle of the forest. An entire swath of forest was sickened and dying, trees twisted into strange metal parodies. Metal lampposts grew out of the ground, bent over and flickering erratically. Wires crawled over roots and trunks, choking trees and vegetation like red and black creeper vines. The air smelled of copper and decay.

"It's spreading," Puck muttered, holding his sleeve to his face as the metallic breeze ruffled my hair and clothes. "This wasn't here a few months ago." He turned to me. "I thought you said you killed the Iron King."

"I did. I mean, yes, he's dead." I gazed out over the poisoned forest, shuddering. "But that doesn't mean the Iron Realm is gone. Tertius told me he served a new Iron King."

Puck's eyes narrowed. "*Another* one? You sort of failed to mention that before, Princess." Shaking his head, he scanned the wasted area and sighed. "Another Iron King. Dammit, how many of them are we going to have to kill? Are they going to keep popping up like rats?"

I squirmed at the thought of yet another killing. A sharp wind hissed over the wasteland, scraping the branches of the metal trees, making me shiver. Puck coughed and staggered away.

"Well, come on, Princess. We can't do anything about it now. Let's get you home."

Home. I thought about my family, about my normal life, so tantalizingly close. I thought of the Nevernever, dying and fading away bit by bit. And I made my decision. "No."

Puck blinked and looked back. "What?"

"I can't go home yet, Puck." I gazed around at the poisoned Nevernever, seeing echoes of Machina's realm looming over everything. "Look at this. People are dying. I can't close my eyes and pretend it isn't happening."

"Why not?" I blinked at him, stunned by his cavalier attitude. He just grinned. "You've done enough, Princess. I think you deserve to go home after everything you went through. Hell, you already took care of one Iron King. The Nevernever will be fine, trust me."

"What about the scepter?" I persisted. "And the war? Oberon should know Mab is planning to attack him."

Puck shrugged, looking uncomfortable. "I was already planning on telling him, Princess, provided he doesn't turn me into a rat as soon as he sees me. As for the scepter, the Ice prince is already looking for it. Not a lot we can do, there." At my protest, he waved a hand airily. "The war is going to start with or without us, Princess. It's nothing new. Winter and Summer have always been at odds. Not a century goes by that there isn't some kind of fighting going on. This will pass, like it always does. Somehow, the scepter will be returned, and things will go back to normal."

I frowned, remembering something Mab had said to Oberon at the ceremony. "What about my world?" I demanded. "Mab said there would be a catastrophe if Summer held the scepter longer than it was supposed to. What will happen if the Iron King gets it? Things will get really screwed up, right?"

Puck scratched the back of his neck. "Erm…maybe."

"Maybe, like how?"

"Ever wanted to go sledding in the Mojave Desert?"

I stared at him. "We can't let that happen, Puck! What's wrong with you? I can't believe you'd think I'd just ignore this!" He shrugged, still infuriatingly nonchalant, and I went for the cheap shot. "You're just afraid, aren't you? You're scared of the Iron fey and you don't want to get involved. I didn't think you'd be such a coward."

"I'm trying to keep you safe!" Puck exploded, whirling on me. His eyes glowed feverishly, and I shrank back. "This isn't a game, Meghan! The shit is about to hit the fan, and you're right in the middle of it without knowing enough to duck!"

Righteous indignation flared; I was sick of being told what to do, that I should be afraid. "I'm not helpless, Puck!" I shot back. "I'm not some squealing cheerleader you have to babysit. I've got blood on my hands now, too. I killed the Iron King, and I still have nightmares about it. I *killed* something! And I'd do it again, if I had to!"

"I know that," Puck snapped, throwing up his hands. "I know you'd risk everything to protect us, and that's what worries me. You still don't know enough about this world to be properly terrified. Things are going to get screwed eight ways from Sunday, and you're making goo-goo eyes at the enemy! I heard what happened in Machina's realm and yes, it scared the hell out of me. I love you, dammit. I'm not going to watch you get torn apart when everything goes bad."

My stomach twisted, both from his confession, and what he'd said about me and Ash. "You…you knew?" I stammered.

He gave me a scornful look. "I've been around a long time, Princess. Give me a little credit. Even a blind man would see the way you looked at him. I'm guessing something happened in Machina's realm, but once you came out, our boy remembered he wasn't supposed to fall in love with Summer." I blushed, and Puck shook his head. "I didn't say anything because he'd already made up his mind to leave. You might not know the consequences, Princess, but Ash does. He did the right thing, much as I hate to speak well of him."

My lip trembled. Puck snorted, but saw me teetering on the brink of tears. His expression softened. "Forget about him, Meghan," he said gently. "Ash is bad news. Even if the law wasn't an issue, I've fought him enough times to know he would break your heart."

The tears finally spilled over. "I can't," I whispered, giving in to the despair that had followed me all morning. This wasn't fair to Puck, after he'd finally confessed that he loved me, but I couldn't seem to stop. My soul cried out for Ash, for his courage and determination; for the way his eyes thawed when he looked at me, as if I were the only person in the world; for that beautiful, wounded spirit I saw beneath the cold exterior he showed the world. "I can't forget. I miss him. I know he's the enemy, and we broke all kinds of rules, but I don't care. I miss him so much, Puck."

Puck sighed, either in sympathy or aggravation, and pulled me close. I sobbed into his chest, releasing all the pent-up emotions that had been building since I first saw Ash in the throne room. Puck held me and stroked my hair like old times, saying nothing, until the tears finally slowed and I sniffled against his shirt.

"Better?" he murmured.

I nodded and broke away, wiping my eyes. The ache was still there, but it was bearable now. I knew it would be a long time before the hurt went away, if ever, but I knew in my heart that I had said my last goodbyes to Ash. Now, maybe I could let him go.

Puck moved behind me and put his hands on my shoulders, leaning close. "I know it's too soon right now," he muttered into my hair, "but, just so you know, I'll wait. When you're ready, I'll be right here. Don't forget, Princess."

I could only nod. Puck squeezed my shoulders and stepped back, waiting quietly while I composed myself. When I turned around again, he was back to being normal Puck, perpetual grin plastered to his face, leaning against a tree.

"Well," he sighed, "I don't suppose I'll be changing that stubborn mind of yours, will I?"

"No, you won't."

"I was afraid of that." He leaped onto an old stump, crossing his arms and cocking his head. "Well then, my scheming princess, what's the plan?"

I wanted to smile at him, but something was wrong. My legs felt all tingly, and a strange pull tugged at my stomach. I felt restless, like ants crawled beneath my skin, and I couldn't hold still if my life depended on it. Without meaning to, I began edging away from Puck, toward the forest.

"Princess?" Puck hopped down, frowning. "You all right? Got ants in your pants or something?"

I had just opened my mouth to reply when some invisible force nearly yanked me off my feet, and I shrieked instead. Puck reached for me, but I leaped away without meaning to. "What is this?" I cried, as the strange force yanked on me again, urging me into the trees. "I can't...stop. What's going on?"

Puck grabbed my arm, holding me back, and my stomach felt like it was being pulled in two. I screamed, and Puck let go, his face white with shock.

"It's a Summoning," he said, hurrying after me as I walked away. "Something is calling you. Did you make a bargain or give anything personal away recently? Hair? Blood? A piece of clothing?"

"No!" I cried, grabbing a vine to stop myself. Pain shot up my arms, and I let go with a yelp. "I haven't given anything away! How do I stop it?"

"You can't." Puck jogged at my side, his gaze intense and worried, but he made no move to touch me. "If something is Calling, you have to go. It only gets more painful if you resist. Don't worry, though." He attempted a cheerful grin. "I'll be right behind you."

"Don't worry?" I tried to scowl at him over my shoulder. "This is like *Invasion of the Body Snatchers;* of course I'm worried!" Once more, I tried latching on to a tree to stop my feet from waltzing away without my say-so. No use. My arms wouldn't even obey me anymore. With a final glance at Puck, I gave in to the strange compulsion and let my body take me away.

I strode through the forest like I was on a mission, ignoring all but the greatest obstacles. I scrambled over rocks and fallen trees, charged headlong down gullies, and walked through brambles and briar patches, gasping as they tore at my skin and clothes. Puck followed close behind, his worried gaze at my back, but he didn't stop me a second time. My legs burned, my breath came in short gasps, and my arms bled from dozens of cuts and scratches, but I could no sooner make myself stop than fly. And so we continued our mad rush through the forest, getting farther away from Tir Na Nog and deeper into unknown territory.

Night was falling when the weird spell faded at last, and my feet stopped so abruptly that I fell, pitching forward and rolling in the dirt. Puck was beside me instantly, helping me up, asking whether I was okay. I couldn't answer him at first. My legs burned, and all I could do was suck air into my starving lungs and feel relieved that my body was finally my own again.

"Where are we?" I gasped as soon as I was able.

It seemed we had stumbled onto some sort of village. Simple mud and thatch huts lay in a loose semicircle around a fire pit, which was empty and cold. Bones, animal skins, and half-eaten carcasses lay scattered about, buzzing with flies.

"Looks like an abandoned goblin village," Puck muttered as I leaned against him, still gasping. He looked down at me, smirking. "Piss off any goblins lately, Princess?"

"What? No." I wiped sweat from my eyes and stumbled over to a log, collapsing on it with a groan. "At least, I don't think so."

"There you are," came a disembodied voice, from somewhere near the edge of the trees. I jumped up and looked around, but couldn't see the speaker. "You are late. I was afraid you had gotten lost, or eaten. But, I suppose it is only human failing that is to blame for the loss of punctuality."

My heart leaped. I knew that voice! I gazed around eagerly, but of course I couldn't see anything until Puck grabbed my arm and pointed me toward the edge of the trees. An old log lay in the shadows just outside the village border, dappled by moonlight. One moment, it was empty. Then, I blinked, or the moonlight shifted, and a large gray cat sat there, bottlebrush tail curled around his legs, regarding me with lazy golden eyes.

"Grimalkin!"

Grimalkin blinked at me, looking much as he always did, long gray fur blending perfectly into the moonlight and shadows. He ignored me as I rushed up, completely absorbed in washing his front paw. I might have swooped him up and given him a squeeze, if I didn't know his sharp claws would turn my face into hamburger and he would never forgive me.

Puck grinned. "Hey, cat," he greeted with an airy wave. "Long time no see. I guess you're the one responsible for our little Death March?"

The feline yawned. "That is the last time I put a Summoning on a human," he mused, raising a hind leg to scratch his ear. "I could have taken a nap instead of waiting for you to finally show up. What took you so long, human? Did you *walk?*"

I finally remembered: Grimalkin had helped me in the search for my brother, and in return, we had agreed that he could call on me, once, at a time of his choosing, though I'd had no idea what that entailed at the time. That was our bargain. Seems he'd finally gotten around to calling it in.

"What are you doing here, Grim?" I asked, torn between delight and aggravation. I was happy to see him, of course, but I wasn't thrilled about the forced march through goblin-infested woodlands, just to say hi. "This better be good, cat. Your stupid Summoning spell could've killed me. What is it you want?"

Grimalkin turned to groom his hindquarters. "*I* do not want anything from you, human," he said between licks. "I brought you here as a favor for someone else. You will have to take your business up with him. And, if you would, remind him that he now owes me a boon, since I wasted a perfectly good Summoning on you."

"What are you talking about?"

"HE MEANS ME, MEGHAN CHASE." The thunderous voice shook the ground, and the smell of burning coal drifted over the breeze. "I ASKED HIM TO CALL YOU HERE."

Something stepped out from behind a hut, a monstrous horse of blackened iron, with burning red eyes and flames smoldering through the chinks in its belly. Steam billowed from its nostrils as it swung to face me, huge and imposing and terrifyingly familiar.

Ironhorse.

# CHAPTER TEN

*Truth and Lies*

"STOP!" Ironhorse bellowed as Puck immediately pulled out his dagger, shoving me behind him. "I DID NOT COME HERE TO FIGHT, ROBIN GOODFELLOW. PUT YOUR WEAPON DOWN AND LISTEN TO ME."

"Oh, I don't think so, Rusty," Puck sneered, as we began backing toward the edge of the village. "I have a better idea. You stay there until we get to Oberon, who will rip you apart and bury your pieces so far apart you'll never get put back together."

My heart pounded, both from fear and a sudden fury. Ironhorse was one of Machina's lieutenants, sent to capture me and bring me to the Iron King. We'd escaped him twice before, once in Tir Na Nog and once in the Iron Kingdom, but Ironhorse had a bad habit of popping up when we least expected it. I certainly hadn't expected to run into him *here*.

"Dammit, Grim!" I raged, shooting the cat a furious glare

as we backed up. He blinked at me calmly. "You sold us out to *them?* That's low, even for you."

Grimalkin sighed and gave Ironhorse a chiding look. "I thought you were to stay hidden until I could explain things," he said with an exasperated flick of his tail. "I told you they would overreact."

Ironhorse stamped a hoof, sending an explosion of dirt into the air. "TIME IS PRESSING," he boomed, tossing his head. "WE DO NOT HAVE THE LUXURY OF WAITING MUCH LONGER. MEGHAN CHASE, I MUST SPEAK WITH YOU. WILL YOU HEAR ME OUT?"

I hesitated. This was new. Normally, about this time, we'd be fighting for our lives. Ironhorse wasn't usually polite. And Grimalkin still watched calmly from the log, gauging our reaction. Curiosity got the better of me. I put a hand on Puck's arm to stop him from backing up farther.

"I want to talk to him," I whispered, ignoring his frown. "He came here for a reason, and maybe he knows about the scepter. Keep an eye on him, will you?"

Puck glared at me, then shrugged. "Fine, Princess. But the second he makes a move, he'll be upside down in a tree before he can blink."

I squeezed his arm and stepped around him to face Ironhorse. The huge Iron fey loomed over me, steam writhing from his mouth and nostrils. "What do you want?"

I'd forgotten how *big* Ironhorse was. Not just tall, but massive. He shifted his weight, gears clanking and groaning, and I took a wary step back. He might not be attacking, but I trusted him about as far as I could throw him, which was not at all. I also hadn't forgiven him for nearly killing Ash the last time we'd met.

Ironhorse lowered his head in what was almost a bow. "THANK YOU, MEGHAN CHASE. I CALLED YOU

HERE BECAUSE WE HAVE A MUTUAL PROBLEM.
YOU SEEK THE SCEPTER OF THE SEASONS, IS THAT
NOT CORRECT?"

I crossed my arms. "What do you know about that?"

"I KNOW WHERE IT IS," Ironhorse continued, swishing
his tail with a clanking sound. "I CAN HELP YOU RETRIEVE
IT."

Puck laughed. "Sure you can," he mocked, as Ironhorse
snorted and pinned his ears. "And all we have to do is follow
you like eager little puppy dogs, all the way into the trap. Sorry,
tin can, we're not that naive."

Ironhorse snorted. "DO NOT MOCK ME, ROBIN
GOODFELLOW," he said with a blast of flame from his
nostrils. "MY OFFER IS GENUINE. I DO NOT SEEK TO
MISLEAD YOU."

"Bull," I snapped, crossing my arms. Ironhorse blinked at me,
astonished. "Tertius and a bunch of creepy metal assassins stole
the scepter and killed Sage, knowing Mab would blame Oberon
for it. The new Iron King designed this war. He plans to
slaughter everyone when the courts are at their weakest. Why
would you want to help us stop it?"

"BECAUSE—" Ironhorse stamped a hoof. "—THE NEW
IRON KING IS A FRAUD."

It was my turn to blink at him. "A fraud? What do you
mean?"

The lieutenant tossed his head disdainfully. "EXACTLY
WHAT I SAID. THE KING CURRENTLY SITTING THE
THRONE IS AN INTRUDER AND A FAKE. I FEEL NO
LOYALTY TOWARD HIM." He swished his tail and raised
his head imperiously. "I AM NOT LIKE THE IRON
BROTHERHOOD. THE KNIGHTS WERE CREATED
TO OBEY WHOEVER SITS UPON THE THRONE.

THEIR SENSE OF DUTY IS WARPED. I KNOW THE TRUTH. AND I WILL NOT SERVE HIM."

I glanced at Puck. "What do you think of all this?"

"Me?" Puck smirked and crossed his arms. "I think all Iron fey should be melted down into scrap metal. I wouldn't follow Rusty here if my life depended on it."

"How very predictable." Grimalkin's voice drifted up from near my feet. I hadn't even heard him move. "Your prejudice blinds you to what is really happening."

"Oh, really?" I glared at him. "Then why don't you tell us what's going on, Grim."

Grimalkin yawned. "Is it not obvious? When you killed Machina, the Iron fey lost their ruler. They needed someone to sit upon the throne, give them direction. A false monarch claiming to be the Iron King answered them, but not everyone accepted him. Now, the Iron fey are split into two camps, one siding with the false king, and one that wishes to bring him down. Ironhorse is part of the second. Is that not true?"

"THAT IS CORRECT."

"If the false king gets the scepter, he will become even more powerful," Grimalkin continued, gazing at me with unblinking golden eyes. "If he is to be stopped, it must happen before he receives it. Ironhorse claims to know its location. You would be foolish not to listen to him."

"What if he's lying?"

Ironhorse threw up his head with an indignant blast of flame. "I DO NOT LIE," he boomed, and I shrank back from the heat. "DESPITE WHAT YOU THINK OF ME, I AM STILL FEY, AND NO FEY CAN TELL AN UNTRUTH."

Blinking, I looked at Puck. I hadn't heard that before, except in vague mentions of faery lore. "Really?"

Puck nodded. "Pretty much, Princess." He shot an evil look

at Ironhorse. "Though comparing Rusty to one of us is a bit of a stretch."

"But…you told lies all the time, when you were Robbie. Your entire life was a lie."

Grimalkin snorted. "Just because he cannot lie does not mean he cannot deceive, human. Robin Goodfellow is an expert at dancing around the truth."

"Oh, look who's talking. If you're not an expert at screwing people over, I'll eat my head."

Ironhorse snorted and shook his mane. "ENOUGH. TIME IS PRESSING. WE DO NOT HAVE TIME TO ARGUE. MEGHAN CHASE, WILL YOU ACCEPT MY HELP OR NOT?"

I looked him in the eye. His blank, rigid mask gazed back at me, expressionless and impassive. "Are you really here to help us?" I asked. "You really want to get the scepter back and stop the war?"

"YES."

"And, you aren't going to lead us into some kind of trap?"

"NO."

I took a deep breath and let it out again. "That seems to be all the questions I can think of right now."

"Here's an important one," Puck added. "Where *is* the scepter anyway, Rusty?"

Ironhorse blew a puff of steam at him. "I DO NOT ANSWER TO YOU, OLDBLOOD. MY BARGAIN IS WITH THE GIRL."

"Yeah?" Puck's grin grew dangerous. "What if I take you apart and turn you into a toaster oven? How'd you like that, tin can?"

"I WOULD LIKE TO SEE YOU TRY."

"Guys, please!" This was as bad as refereeing the frequent threat-fests between Puck and Ash. "Enough with the posturing and testosterone. Ironhorse, if we're going to do this, we need to know where the scepter is. We can't follow you blindly into wherever."

Ironhorse bobbed his head. "OF COURSE, MEGHAN CHASE." I frowned at his compliancy, but he went on without pause. "THE SCEPTER OF THE SEASONS HAS BEEN TAKEN INTO THE MORTAL REALM. IT IS BEING HELD IN A PLACE CALLED SILICON VALLEY."

"Silicon Valley? That's in California."

"YES."

"Why there?"

"SILICON VALLEY WAS THE BIRTHPLACE OF LORD MACHINA," Ironhorse said gravely. "MANY OF HIS LIEUTENANTS, LIKE VIRUS AND GLITCH, ALSO HAIL FROM THAT AREA. IT IS A REGION OF IRON FEY, ONE THAT THE OLDBLOODS—" he shot a glance at Puck "—AVOID COMPLETELY. IT IS THE IDEAL PLACE TO HIDE THE SCEPTER."

"You can say that again," I mused. Silicon Valley wasn't just one city, it was every city in that area. "Finding the scepter will be like looking for a needle in a haystack—in a field of haystacks."

"I CAN FIND IT." Ironhorse raised his head, looking down his long nose at us. "I SWEAR IT. DO YOU WANT ME TO SAY THE WORDS? MEGHAN CHASE, I, IRONHORSE, LAST LIEUTENANT OF LORD MACHINA, WILL TAKE YOU TO THE SCEPTER OF THE SEASONS, AND I VOW TO PROTECT YOU UNTIL IT IS IN YOUR HANDS. THIS I SWEAR, ON MY HONOR AND MY DUTY TO THE TRUE MONARCH OF THE IRON COURT."

I drew in a breath, and even Puck looked surprised. An oath like that meant the speaker was bound to fulfill it. Ironhorse wasn't playing around. As I stood there gaping at him, Puck took my arm and turned me aside.

"What about Oberon?" he murmured. "He's the only one who can remove the seal. If we go gallivanting off to California, you won't have your magic to protect you."

"We can't worry about that now." I shook off his hand. "The scepter is more important. Besides, that's what I have *you* for." I smiled at him, and turned to Ironhorse. "All right, Ironhorse. We have a deal. Take us to the scepter."

"Finally." Grimalkin stood and stretched, bottlebrush tail curling over his back. "You make decisions as slowly as you answer Summonings, human. I do hope this will not become a habit."

"Wait. You're coming, too? Why?"

"I am bored." Grimalkin waved his tail languidly. "And you are always entertaining…except when I am waiting for you to arrive, of course. Besides, the lieutenant and I have business, as well."

"You do?" I waited, but he didn't elaborate. "What is it?"

He sniffed and half slitted his eyes. "None of your concern, human. And you will need my guidance, if you want to get the scepter as quickly as possible. I believe the closest trod to Silicon Valley is through the Briars."

Puck's eyebrows shot up. "The Briars? You're risking an awful lot, cat. Why don't we try a trod a little less, oh I don't know…lethal? If we double back, we can use the trod through the Frost Meadows. That will bring us close to San Francisco, and we can easily hitch a ride from there."

Grimalkin shook his head. "If we want to reach Silicon Valley, we must go through the thorns. Do not worry, I will not get you lost. The trod past the Frost Meadows has become inaccessible. It sits too close to Tir Na Nog."

"Still don't see the problem, cat."

Ironhorse snorted. "THE FROST MEADOWS HAVE BECOME A BATTLEFIELD, ROBIN GOODFELLOW," he said, making my stomach clench. "WINTER HAS ALREADY CUT A SWATH OF DESTRUCTION THROUGH THE WYLDWOOD, AND THEY ARE ADVANCING ON SUMMER AS WE SPEAK. THERE IS A HUGE ARMY OF UNSEELIE BETWEEN US AND THAT TROD. THE CAITH SITH IS RIGHT—WE CANNOT TURN BACK."

"Of course I am," Grimalkin agreed. "We go through the Briars."

"I don't get it," I said, as Grim trotted off with his tail in the air, confident in his victory. "What are the Briars? Grimalkin? Hey!"

Grimalkin looked back, his eyes bright floating orbs in the gloom.

"I am not here to chitchat, human. If you truly want your question answered, ask your Puck. Perhaps he will be able to soften the reality for you. I would not." He twitched his tail, and continued into the trees without looking back.

I looked at Puck. He grimaced and shot me a humorless smile.

"Right. The Briars. Just a second, Princess. Hey, Rusty," he called, motioning to Ironhorse, who pinned back his ears, "why don't you walk ahead of us, huh? I want your big ugly ass where I can see it."

Ironhorse glared at him balefully, tossed his head, and strode after the quickly vanishing Grimalkin. The Iron faery left a faint path of destruction in his wake; branches curled away from him, plants withered and grass shriveled under his feet, leaving burned-out hoofprints on the trail. Shaking his head, Puck muttered something very rude under his breath and followed, leading us deeper into the wyldwood.

# CHAPTER ELEVEN

*The Briars*

Later, after a night of following Grimalkin through increasingly thick forest, I decided that some questions are better left unanswered.

"The Briars," Puck began, keeping a wary eye on Ironhorse walking in front of us, "or Brambles or Thorns, or whatever you want to call it, is a maze. No one knows how big it really is, but it's huge. Some say it encircles the entire Nevernever. There are rumors that if you're in the wyldwood and start walking in any direction, you'll eventually hit the Briars. You can find patches growing most anywhere, from the Greatwood and the Venom Swamps, to the courts of Arcadia and Tir Na Nog."

"Like the Hedge," I murmured, remembering the tunnel of thorns in Oberon's court and the brambly escape route Grimalkin had used to get us out of Faery. The bramble wall surrounding the Seelie Court had opened for the cat, revealing a maze of tunnels in the thorns, and I'd followed him as he led me back to the mortal world.

Puck nodded. "That's another name for it. Though the Hedge is a tamer version of the real Briars. In Arcadia, the Hedge responds fairly consistently, taking you wherever you want to go within the court. Out here, in the wyldwood, the Briars are rather…sadistic."

"You make it sound like they're alive."

Puck gave me a very eerie stare. "They *are* alive, Princess," he warned in a low voice. "Not in the way that we're accustomed to, but do not take them lightly. The Briars are a force, one that cannot be tamed or understood, even by Oberon or Mab. And they're always hungry. It's easy to get in—getting out is the tricky part. Not only that, but the things that live in the Briars are always hungry, too."

I felt a chill run all the way down my spine. "And we're going through the Briars…why?"

"Because the Briars have the greatest concentration of trods in all the Nevernever," Puck replied. "There are doors hidden throughout the Briars, some constantly shifting, some only appearing at a special time under special circumstances. Rumors are that, within the Briars, there is a trod to every doorway in the mortal realm, from an L.A. strip club to some kid's bedroom closet. Find the right door, and you're home free." The grin grew wider, and he shook his head. "But you have to get to it first."

RAIN HISSED through the branches of the trees, a cold, gray rain that leeched color from everything it touched. Even Puck's bright auburn hair turned dull and colorless in the misty deluge. He'd rake his fingers through it, streaking his hair with red, only to have the rain soak through it once more, bleaching away the color. Grimalkin was nearly invisible; not even his eyes glimmered in the gloom.

Above us, the massive wall of black thorns rose into the air, tendrils creaking and curling about. Some of the thorns were longer than me, waving about like the spines of a sea urchin, and the whole thing bristled with eerie menace.

I shivered, even standing close to Ironhorse and the smoldering heat radiating from him. The Iron faery steamed in the rain, surrounded by writhing smoke, as water struck his hot metal skin and sizzled away. Ironhorse gazed up at the wall of thorns, craning his neck to stare at it, billowing like a small geyser in the storm.

"How do we get through?" I wondered.

No sooner were the words out of my mouth than the wall shifted. Branches creaked and moaned as they peeled away to reveal a narrow, spiky corridor through the thorns. Mist curled out of the hallway, and the space beyond was choked in shadow.

Puck crossed his arms. "Looks like we're expected." He looked down at Grimalkin, a gray ghost in the mist, calmly washing his front paws. "You sure you can get us through, cat?"

Grimalkin gave one paw a few more licks before standing up. Shaking himself so that water flew everywhere, he yawned, stretched and trotted forward without looking back. "Follow me and find out" were his last words before he vanished into the tunnel.

Puck rolled his eyes. Holding out his hand, he gave me an encouraging smile. "Come on, Princess. Don't want to get separated in here." I clasped his hand, and he curled his fingers tight around mine. "Let's go, then. Rusty can bring up the rear. That way, if we're jumped from behind, we won't lose anything important."

I felt Ironhorse's indignant snort as we entered the tunnel, and I pressed closer to Puck as the shadows closed in on us like grasping fingers. Around us, the corridor pulsed with life, slithering, creaking, unfurling with faint hissing sounds. Whispers and strange voices drifted down the hallway, murmuring words I couldn't quite understand. As we stepped in farther, the hole behind us shut with a quiet hiss, trapping us within the Briars.

"This way," came Grimalkin's disembodied voice up ahead. "Try to stay close."

The bristly walls of the corridor seemed to press in on us. Puck didn't release my hand, but we had to walk single file through the tunnel to avoid behind scratched. A couple times, I thought I saw a thorn or creeper actually move toward me, as if to prick my skin or catch my clothes. Once, I glanced back at Ironhorse to see how he was faring, but the thorns, much like the rest of the Nevernever, seemed loath to touch the great Iron fey, curling back from him as he passed.

The tunnel finally opened up into a small hollow with tunnels and paths twisting off in all directions. Overhead, the canopy of bramble shut out the light, so thick you couldn't see the sky through the cracks. Bones lay here and there among the thorns, bleached white and gleaming in the darkness. A skull grinned at me from a tangle of brambles, empty eye sockets crawling with worms. I shuddered and turned my face into Puck's shoulder.

"Where's Grim?" I whispered.

"Here," Grimalkin said, appearing out of nowhere. The cat leaped atop a large skull and regarded each of us in turn. "We are going deep into the Briars now," he stated in a calm, very soft voice. "I would tell you what we might face, but perhaps it is better that I do not. Try to be silent. Do not separate. Do not go down another path. And stay away from any doors you come across. Many of the gates here are a one-way trip; go through one and you might not be able to go back. Are you ready?"

I raised my hand. "How do you know your way around this place, Grim?"

Grimalkin blinked. "I am a cat," he said, and vanished down one of the tunnels.

WHEN I WAS TWELVE, my school took a field trip to a "haunted" corn maze on the outskirts of town, a week or so before Halloween. Sitting on the bus, listening to the boys brag about who would find his way out first, and the girls giggling in their own little groups, I made my own vow that I would do just as well. I remember walking down the rows of corn all by myself, feeling a thrill of both fear and excitement as I tried finding my way to the center and back again. And I remembered the sinking feeling in my gut when I knew I was lost, when I realized no one would help me, that I was alone.

This was ten thousand times worse.

The Briars were never still. They were always moving, slithering, reaching for you out of the corner of your eye. Sometimes, if you listened just right, you could almost hear them whisper your name. Deep within the tangled darkness, twigs snapped and branches rustled as *things* moved through the brambles. I never got a clear look, just glimpsed dark shapes shuffling away into the undergrowth. It creeped me out. Bigtime.

The Briars went on, an endless maze of twisted thorns and gnarled branches, shifting, creaking and reaching out for us. As we ventured ever deeper, doors, frames and archways began appearing at odd intervals in completely random places. A faded red door hung perilously from an overhead branch, a tarnished *216* glimmering in the dim light. A filthy restroom stall, cracked and shedding green paint, stood near the edge of the path, so wrapped in thorns that it would be impossible to push the door open. Something lean and black slithered across our path and vanished through an open closet. As it creaked shut, I caught a glimpse of a child's bedroom through the frame, and a crib outlined in moonlight, before thorny vines curled around the door and pulled it back into the Briars.

Grimalkin never hesitated, leading us on without a backward glance, passing gates and doors and strange, random things stuck in the tangled web of thorns. A mirror, a doll and an empty golf bag dangled from the branches as we walked by, as well as the countless bones and sometimes full skeletons that littered the trail. Strange creatures watched us from the shadows, mostly unseen, just their eyes glowing in the dark. Black birds with human faces perched in the branches, observing us silently as we passed, like waiting vultures. At one point, Grimalkin pulled us all into a side tunnel, hissing at us to be quiet and not move. Moments later, a massive spider, easily the size of a car, crawled over the brambles directly overhead, and I bit my lip so hard that I tasted blood. Huge and shiny, with a splash of red across its bloated abdomen, it paused a moment, as if sensing warm blood and fluids were very close, waiting for the slightest tremor to betray its quarry.

We held our breath and pretended to be stone.

For several heart-pounding seconds, we crouched in the tunnel, feeling our muscles cramp and our hearts thud too loud in our chests. Above us, the spider sat perfectly still as well, patiently waiting for its prey to grow bored, to assume it was safe and make the first move that would be its last. Eventually, something rustled in the branches ahead, and it darted away, frighteningly quick for something that huge. The scream of some unfortunate creature pierced the air, and then silence.

For a few moments after the spider left, no one dared to move. Eventually, Grimalkin crept forward, poking his head out warily, scanning the thorns.

"Wait here," he told us. "I will see if it is safe." Slipping into the shadows like a ghost, he disappeared.

I sagged to my knees as the adrenaline wore off and my muscles started to shake, leaving me weak and nearly hyperventilating. I could handle goblins and bogeymen and evil, flesh-eating horses, but giant freaking spiders? That's where I drew the line.

Puck knelt and put a hand on my shoulder. "You okay, Princess?"

I nodded, ready to make some snarky comment about the pest problem around here. But then, one of the thorns moved.

Frowning, I bent closer, squinting my eyes. For a moment, nothing happened. Then, the three-inch barb shivered and unfurled into a pair of pointed black wings, attached to a tiny faery with glittering eyes that glared with insectlike menace. Its spindly body was covered by a shiny black carapace. Spikes grew from its elbows and shoulders, and it clutched a thorn-tipped spear in one tiny claw. As we stared at each other, the faery curled its lip, revealing teeth as sharp as needles, and flew at my face.

I jerked back, swatting wildly, and hit Puck, causing us both to tumble back. The faery dodged my flailing hands, buzzing around us like an angry wasp. I saw it pause, hovering in the air like an evil hummingbird, then streak forward with a raspy cry.

A gout of flame seared the air in front of me. I felt the blast of heat on my face, bringing tears to my eyes, and the faery disappeared into the fire. Its tiny, charred body dropped like a stone to the earth, curling in on itself, the delicate black wings seared away. It gave an insectlike twitch, then was still.

Ironhorse tossed his head and snorted, looking pleased as smoke curled from his nostrils. Puck grimaced as he pushed himself to his feet, holding out a hand to help me up.

"You know, I'm really starting to hate the insect life around here," he muttered. "Next time, remind me to bring a can of Off!"

"You didn't have to kill it," I told Ironhorse, dusting off my pants. "It was like three inches tall!"

"IT ATTACKED YOU." Ironhorse sounded puzzled, cocking his head at me. "IT CLEARLY HAD AGGRESSIVE INTENT. MY MISSION IS TO PROTECT YOU UNTIL WE RETRIEVE THE SCEPTER. I WILL ALLOW NOTHING TO BRING YOU HARM. THAT IS MY SOLEMN VOW."

"Yeah, but you don't need a machine gun to kill a fly."

"Human!" Grimalkin appeared, bounding up with his ears flattened to his head. "You are making too much noise. All of you are. We must leave this area, quickly." He glanced about, and the fur on his back started to rise. "It might already be too late."

"Ironhorse killed this teensy little faery—" I began, but Grimalkin hissed at me.

"Idiot human! Do you think that was the only one? Look around you!"

I did, and my heart nearly stopped. The thorns around us were moving, hundreds upon hundreds of them, unfurling into tiny faeries with pointed, gnashing teeth. The air filled with the sound of buzzing, and thousands of tiny black eyes glimmered through the thorns.

"Oh, this isn't good," Puck murmured as the buzz grew louder, more frantic. "I really, really wish I had that Off!"

"Run!" spit Grimalkin, and we ran.

The faeries swarmed around us, the hum of their wings vibrating the air, their high-pitched voices shrieking in my ears. I felt the weight of their tiny bodies on my skin, an instant before the stings, and flailed wildly, trying to dislodge them.

Puck snarled something unintelligible, swiping at them with his knives, and Ironhorse blasted flame from his mouth and nostrils, roaring. Charred, dismembered faeries dropped shrieking from the air, but dozens more buzzed in to take their place. Grimalkin, of course, had vanished. We charged blindly down a tunnel of thorns, through swarms of furious killer wasp-fey, with no clue of where we were going.

As I rounded a corner, a body appeared right in front of me. I had no time to react before I crashed into it, and we both went sprawling.

"Ow! What the hell!" someone yelped.

Swatting faeries, I looked into the face of a girl a year or two younger than me. She was tiny and Asian, with hair that looked as if she'd taken a machete to it, wearing a ratty sweater two sizes too big. For a second, my mind went blank with the shock at seeing another human, until I saw the furry ears peeking out of her hair.

We blinked at each other for a second, before the sting from a killer-wasp faerie snapped me out of my daze. Flailing, I scrambled to my feet as the swarm buzzed around the strange girl as well. She yelped and swatted wildly, backing away.

"What is this?" she hissed, as Puck came up behind me and Ironhorse charged in, blowing flame. "Who the hell are you people? Oh, never mind! Run!" She darted past us, looking back once to shout "Hurry up, Nelson!" over her shoulder. I barely had time to wonder who Nelson was when a kid built like a linebacker barreled through us, somehow dodging Puck and Ironhorse, and pounded after the girl. I caught a glimpse of gorillalike shoulders, muddy blond hair, and skin as green as swamp water. He clutched a backpack in his arms like a football and charged down the trail without a backward glance.

"Who were they?" I asked, over the buzzing of the swarm and my own frantic flailing.

"No time," Puck said, slapping at a faery on his neck. "Ow! Dammit, we have to get out of here! Come on!"

We had started down the path again when a roar shook the air ahead of us, causing the swarm of killer fey to freeze in mid-air. It came again, guttural and savage, as something rattled the wall of thorns, coming toward us with the sound of snapping wood. I sensed hundreds of creatures in the brambles fleeing for their lives.

The faeries scattered. Buzzing in terror, they vanished into the hedge, through cracks and tiny spaces between the thorns. In seconds, the whole swarm had disappeared. I peered through the branches and saw something coming down the trail, ripping through the wall of thorns like it wasn't there. Something black and scaly, and much, much bigger than the spider.

*Is that what I think it is?*

"Thiiiief!" roared a deep, inhuman voice, before a gout of flame burst through the hedge, setting an entire section on fire, making the air explode with heat. Ironhorse bugled, rearing up in alarm. Puck cursed, grabbed my arm, and yanked me back the way we came.

We fled down the trail after the strange girl and her muscle-necked companion, feeling the heat from the monster's fire at our backs. *"Thieves!"* the terrible voice snarled, staying right on our heels. *"I can smell you! I can feel your breath and hear your hearts. Give me back what is mine!"*

"Great," Puck panted, as Ironhorse cantered beside us, bellowing that he would shield me from the flames. "Just great. I hate spiders. I hate wasps. But, you know what I hate even more than that?"

The thing behind us roared, and another blast of flame seared the branches overhead. I winced as we ran beneath a rain of cinders and flaming twigs. "Dragons?" I gasped.

"Remind me to kill Grimalkin next time we see him."

The trail narrowed, then shrank down to a tight, thorny tunnel that twisted off into the darkness. Bending down and peering into it, I could just make out a door at the end of the burrow. And, I couldn't be sure, but I thought I saw the door shut.

"I think I see a door!" I called, looking over my shoulder. Puck nodded impatiently.

"Well, what are you waiting for, Princess! Go!"

"What about Ironhorse?"

"He'll have to squeeze!" Puck pushed me toward the mouth, but I resisted. "Come on, Princess. We don't want to be in the middle of that if Deathbreath decides to sneeze on us."

"We can't leave him behind!"

"WORRY NOT, PRINCESS," Ironhorse said, and I gaped at him, not believing my eyes. Where a horse had been, now a man stood before me, dark and massive, with a square jaw and fists the size of hams. He wore jeans and a black shirt that bulged with all the muscles underneath, the skin stretched tight over steely tendons. Dreadlocks spilled from his scalp like a mane, and his eyes still burned with that intense red glow. "YOU ARE NOT THE ONLY ONE WITH A FEW TRICKS UP YOUR SLEEVE, GOODFELLOW," he said, a faint smirk beneath his voice. "NOW, GO. I WILL BE RIGHT BEHIND YOU."

With a horrible cracking sound, the dragon's head rose above the briars on a long, snaking neck, looming to an impossible height. It was bigger than I'd imagined, a long toothy maw covered in black-green scales, ivory horns curling back from its skull to frame the sky. Alien, red-gold eyes scanned the ground impassively, gleaming with cunning and intelligence. *I see you, little thieves.*

Puck gave me a shove, and I tumbled into the burrow,

scratching my hands and knees and jabbing myself on the thorns. Cursing, I looked up and saw two familiar golden eyes floating before me in the dark.

"Hurry, human," Grimalkin hissed, and fled down the burrow.

The tunnel seemed to shrink the farther I went, scraping my back and catching my hair and clothes as I followed Grimalkin, bent over like a crab. I heard Puck and Ironhorse behind me, felt the glare of the dragon's eye at my back, and cursed as my sleeve caught on a thorn. We were going too slow! The red door loomed at the end of the tunnel, a beacon of light and safety, so far away. But as I got closer, I saw Grimalkin standing in front of it, ears flattened against his skull, hissing and baring his teeth.

"Saint-John's-wort," he snarled, and I saw a cluster of dried yellow flowers hanging on the door like tiny sunbursts. "The fey cannot enter with that on the door. Take it down, quickly, human!"

*"Burn, little thieves!"*

Fire exploded down the tunnel, writhing and twisting in a maelstrom of heat and fury, shooting toward us. I ripped the flowers off the door and dove through, Puck and Ironhorse toppling in after me. Flames shot over my head, singeing my back as I lay gasping on a cold cement floor. Then, the door slammed shut, cutting off the fire, and we were plunged into darkness.

# CHAPTER TWELVE

*Leanansidhe*

For a few moments, I lay there on the concrete, my body curiously hot and cold at the same time. My neck, my shoulders, and the backs of my legs burned from the fire that had come way too close for comfort. But my cheek and stomach pressed into the cold cement, making me shiver. To either side of me, Puck and Ironhorse struggled to their feet with muffled curses and groans.

"Well, that was fun," Puck muttered, helping me stand. "I swear, if I ever see those two kids again, we're going to have a little chat. If you're going to steal from a fifty-foot, fire-breathing lizard with the memory of an elephant, you'd better have a damn impressive riddle, or you wait until it isn't home. And who the hell put Saint-John's-wort over the door? I'm feeling very unwelcome right now."

A flashlight clicked on in the shadows, blinding me. Shielding my eyes, I counted three silhouettes at the end of the beam. Two I recognized; the tiny girl with furry ears and the green-skinned boy we'd met in the Briars. The last, the one holding the flashlight, was tall and skinny, with thick dark hair, a scraggly goatee, and two ridged horns curling up from his brow. He held a cross in the other hand, raised in front of his face like he was warding off a vampire.

Puck laughed. "Hate to break it to you, kid, but unless you're a priest, that isn't going to work. Neither is the salt you have poured across the floor. I'm not your average bogey."

"Damn faeries," spit goatee boy, looking pale. "How did you get in here? You'd better leave right now, if you know what's good for you. *She'll* tear your guts out and make harp strings with them."

"Well, there's a problem with that," Puck continued with mock regret. "See, right outside that door is a very pissed off reptile who is eager to turn us into shish kebab, because *you three* were stupid enough to steal from a dragon." He sighed and shook his head in a disappointed manner. "You know dragons never forget a thief, don't you? So, what'd you take?"

"None of your business, faery," goat boy shot back. "And maybe I wasn't clear when I said you're not welcome here." He reached into his pocket and pulled out three iron nails, holding them between white, shaking knuckles. "Maybe a faceful of iron will convince you otherwise."

I stepped forward, shooting Puck a warning glare before he could rise to the challenge. "Take it easy," I soothed, holding up my hands. "We don't want any trouble. We're just trying to get through the Briars, that's all."

"Warren!" gasped the girl, staring at me wide-eyed. "It's her!"

All eyes flashed to me.

"It *is* you," Warren breathed. "You're her, aren't you? Oberon's half-blood. The Summer princess."

Ironhorse growled and pressed closer, causing the trio to shrink back. I put a hand on his chest. "How do you know me?"

"*She's* looking for you, you know. Got half the exiles looking for you—"

"Whoa, slow down, goat-boy." Puck held up a hand. "Who is this remarkable *she* you keep talking about?"

Warren shot him a look that was half fearful, half awe. "*Her,* of course. The boss of this place. So…if this is Oberon's daughter, you must be him, aren't you? Robin Goodfellow? The Puck?" Puck smiled, which caused Warren to swallow noisily. His Adam's apple bobbed in his throat. "But—" he glanced at Ironhorse "—she didn't say anything about him. Who's he?"

"Stinks," rumbled the green-skinned boy, curling his lip to reveal blunt, uneven teeth. "Smells like coal. Like iron."

Warren's eyebrows shot up. "Aw, crap. He's one of *them,* isn't he? One of those Iron faeries! She won't be happy about this."

"He's with me," I said quickly, as Ironhorse drew himself up. "He's safe, I promise you. And who do you keep talking about? Who is this *she?*"

"Her name is Leanansidhe," Warren stated, as if I were an idiot for not figuring it out. "Leanansidhe the Dark Muse. Queen of the Exiles."

Puck's eyebrows arched into his hair.

"You're kidding," he said, his face caught between a grimace and a smirk. "So, Leanansidhe fancies herself a queen, now? Oh, Titania will love that."

"Who's Leanansidhe?" I asked.

The grimace won out. He shook his head and turned to me, his face grim. "Bad news, Princess. At one time, Leanansidhe was one of the most powerful beings in all the Nevernever. The Dark Muse, they called her, because she inspired many great artists, helping them produce their most brilliant works. You might recognize some of the mortals she's helped—James Dean, Jimi Hendrix, Kurt Cobain."

"No way."

Puck shrugged. "But, as you should know, such help always comes with a price. None whom Leanansidhe inspires lives very long, ever. Their lives are brilliant, colorful, and very brief. Sometimes, if the artist was particularly special, she'd take him back to the Nevernever to entertain her for eternity. Or until she got bored. Of course, this was before…" He trailed off, giving me a sideways look.

"Before what?"

"Titania banished her to the mortal realm," Puck said quickly, as if he was really going to say something else. "According to some, Leanansidhe was growing too powerful, had too many mortals worshipping her, and there was talk that she wanted to make herself queen. Naturally, this made our good Summer Queen more than a little jealous, so she exiled the self-proclaimed Queen of Muse and sealed off all trods to her, so that Leanansidhe could never return to Faery. That was several years ago, and no one has seen or heard from her since.

"But, apparently," Puck continued, glancing at the three teenagers listening in rapt fascination, "Leanansidhe has a new following. A new little mortal cult ready to throw themselves at her feet." He smothered a laugh. "Pickings must be pretty slim nowadays."

"Hey," said the girl, narrowing her eyes at him. "What's that supposed to mean?"

"Why is Leanansidhe looking for me?" I asked, before an unpleasant thought drifted to mind. "You…you don't think she wants revenge, for what Titania did to her?" Great. That was all I needed, another faery queen who was out to get me. I must hold some sort of record.

We glared at Warren, who stepped back and raised his hands.

"Hey, man. Don't look at me. I don't know what she wants. Just that she's been looking for you."

"WE CANNOT GO TO THIS LEANANSIDHE NOW," Ironhorse boomed, making the teens jump and the ceiling rattle. God, he couldn't speak quietly if his life depended on it. "OUR MISSION IS URGENT. WE MUST GET TO CALIFORNIA AS SOON AS POSSIBLE."

"Well, we're not going anywhere now, not with ol' Death-breath guarding the only way out."

"Come with us."

I looked up. Warren had spoken and was staring at me intently. The eager look in his eyes made me uncomfortable, as did his sudden change in mood. "Come with us to Leanan-sidhe's," he urged. "She could help. You want to go to California? She can get you there, easy—"

"Warren," said the girl, grabbing his sleeve and pulling him aside. "Come here a second, would you? 'Scuse us a sec, people." Surprisingly strong for her size, she dragged him into a far corner. Huddled against the wall, they whispered furiously to each other, casting suspicious glances at Ironhorse over their shoulders.

"What are we going to do?" I wondered. "Should we wait until the dragon leaves to find our way back through the Briars? Or should we find out what Leanansidhe wants?"

"NO," thundered Ironhorse, his voice bouncing off the walls. "I DO NOT TRUST THIS LEANANSIDHE. IT IS TOO DANGEROUS."

"Puck?"

He shrugged. "Under normal circumstances, I'd agree with the toaster oven," he said, earning a hard glare from Ironhorse. "Leanansidhe has always been unpredictable, and she has enough power to make that dragon look like a cranky Gila monster. But…I always say the enemy you know is better than the enemy you can't see."

I nodded. "I agree. If Leanansidhe is looking for us, I think we should meet her on our own terms. Otherwise, I'd just worry about what she's sending after us."

"Besides…" Puck rolled his eyes. "I think we have another problem."

"What's that?"

"Our trusty guide has gone AWOL."

I looked around, but Grimalkin had vanished, and he didn't respond to my hissed calls for him to show himself. The street kids were watching us now, eager and hesitant at the same time. I sighed. There was no telling where Grimalkin was, or when he'd return. Really, there was just one option.

"So." I gave them a hopeful smile. "How far is Leanansidhe's?"

TURNS OUT, we were in the basement of her mansion.

"So, Leanansidhe has you guys steal from dragons?" I asked the girl as we walked down the dimly lit corridors, torchlight flickering over the damp stone walls. Whatever the house looked like, the basement was huge. It reminded me of a medieval dungeon, complete with heavy doors, wooden portcullises, and gargoyles leering at us from the walls. Mice scurried over the floor, and other things moved in the shadows, just out of sight.

The girl, Kimi, grinned at me. "Leanansidhe has lots of clients with very unusual tastes," she explained. "Most of them are exiles, like her, who can't go back into the Nevernever for some reason. She uses us—" she gestured to herself and Nelson "—to fetch things she can't get herself, like that thing with the dragon. Apparently, a banished Winter sidhe in New York is paying a fortune for real dragon eggs."

"You stole its *eggs?*"

"Only one." Kimi giggled at my stunned expression. "Then the stupid lizard woke up and we had to book it." She giggled again, smoothing down her ears. "Don't worry, we're not going to decimate the dragon population. Leanansidhe told us to leave a couple behind."

Puck made a noise that might've been appreciation. "And what do you guys get out of this?"

"Free room and board. And the rep that goes with it. We'd be out on the streets, otherwise." Kimi and Nelson shared a secret glance, but Warren was staring at me. He'd been doing that since we left to meet Leanansidhe, and it was making me very uncomfortable.

"The pay's not bad, either," Kimi went on, oblivious to Warren's scrutiny. "At least, it's better than the alternative— being hunted down for what we are, getting stepped on by the exiles and the fey who just like it better in the mortal realm. Leanansidhe's made it safer for us—you don't screw around with the queen's pets. Even the redcap gangs know to leave you alone. For the most part, anyway."

"Why?" I asked. "You're exiles, too, right? Why should it be different for you?" I looked at her furry, tufted ears, at Nelson's swamp-water skin and Warren's horns. They weren't human, that much was certain. But then I remembered Warren holding out the iron cross, his fearful *damned faeries,* how they could get through the door when Grimalkin couldn't. And I knew what they were even before Kimi said it.

"Because," she said cheerfully, twitching her ears, "we're half-breeds. I'm half-phouka, Nelson's half-troll, and Warren is part-satyr. And if there's one thing an exile hates more than the fey who banished him, its half-breeds like us."

I hadn't thought of that before, though it made sense. I sus-pected half-breeds like Kimi, Nelson and Warren had it pretty tough. Without Oberon's protection, they would've been left to the whims of the true fey, who probably made life very difficult for them. It wasn't surprising they would make a deal with this Queen of the Exiles, in exchange for some degree of protection. Even if it meant stealing dragon eggs right out from under the dragon.

"Oh, and by the way," Kimi went on, with a quick glance at Ironhorse, clanking along behind me. "Leanansidhe knows about…um…*his kind*. They've been killing off lots of exiles lately, and it's making her mad. Your 'friend' should be really careful around her. I don't know how she'll take an Iron faery in her living room. I've seen her throw a fit for less."

"Shut up, Kimi," Warren said abruptly. We had reached the end of the hall, where a bright red door waited for us atop a flight of stairs. "I told you, it's not a big deal."

I frowned at him, but something caught my attention. Strains of music drifted down the steps, the low, shivery chords of a piano or organ. The music was dark and haunting, reminding me of a play I'd seen a long time ago, *The Phantom of the Opera*. I remembered Mom dragging me to the theater when the play came through our little town, shortly before Ethan was born. I remembered thinking I'd have to sit through three hours of absolute boredom and torture, but from the first booming organ chords, I was completely entranced.

I also remembered Mom crying through several of the scenes, something she never did, even with the saddest movies. I didn't think anything of it then, but it seemed a little odd, now.

We stepped up and through the doorway into a magnificent foyer, with a double grand staircase sweeping toward a high vaulted ceiling and a roaring fireplace surrounded by plush black sofas. The hardwood floor gleamed red, the walls were patterned in red and black, and gauzy black curtains covered the high arched windows near the back of the room. Nearly every clear space on the wall was taken up by paintings—oil paintings, watercolors, black-and-white sketches. The Mona Lisa smiled her odd little smile on the far wall, next to a weird, disjointed painting that was probably Picasso.

Music echoed through the room, dark and haunting piano chords played with such force that they made the air vibrate and my teeth buzz. An enormous grand piano stood in the corner near the fireplace, the flames dancing in the reflection of the polished wood. Hunched over the keys, a figure in a rumpled white shirt beat and pounded the ivory bars, fingers flying.

"Who—?"

"Shh!" Kimi shushed me with a light smack on the arm. "Don't talk. *She* doesn't like it when someone's playing."

I fell silent, studying the pianist again. Brown hair hung limp and shaggy on his shoulders, looking as if it hadn't been washed in days. His shoulders were broad, though his shirt hung loose on a lean, bony frame that was so thin his spine pressed tightly against his skin.

The song ended with one last, vibrating chord. As the notes faded and silence descended on the room, the man remained hunched over the keys. I couldn't see his face, but I thought his eyes were closed, and his muscles trembled as if from exertion. He seemed to be waiting for something. I looked to the others, wondering if we should applaud.

A slow clapping came from the top of the stairs. I looked up and saw none other than Grimalkin, sitting on the railing with his tail around his feet, looking perfectly at home. Any annoyance I felt with him disappeared at the sight of his companion.

A woman stood on the balcony, her gold and crimson gown billowing around her, though I was sure there'd been no one there a second ago. Her wavy, waist-length hair shimmered like strands of copper, almost too bright to look at, floating around her face as if it weighed nothing at all. She was pale and tall and magnificent, every inch a queen, and I felt my stomach contract. Forget Arcadia or Tir Na Nog; we were in her court now, playing by her rules. I wondered if she expected us to bow.

"Bravo, Charles." Her voice was pure song, made of poetry given sound, of every creative notion you've ever had. Hearing it, I felt I could sweep onto a stage and bring the masses roaring and screaming to their feet. "That was quite magnificent. You can go now."

The man rose shakily to his feet, grinning like a little kid whose finger painting had been praised by the teacher. He was younger than my stepdad, but not by much, the hint of a beard shadowing his mouth and jaw. When he turned and spotted us, I shivered. His face and hazel eyes were blank of reason, as empty as the sky.

"Poor bastard," I heard Puck mutter. "He's been here awhile, hasn't he?"

The man blinked at me, dazed for a moment, but then his eyes grew wide. "You," he muttered, shambling forward, jabbing at me with a finger. I frowned. "I know you. Don't I? Don't I? Who are you? Who?" He frowned, an anguished expression crossing his face. "The rats whisper in the darkness," he said, clutching at his hair. "They whisper. I can't remember their names. They tell me…" His eyes narrowed and he panted, glaring at me. "Rag girl, flying round my bed. Who are you? *Who?*" This last was a shout, and he lurched forward.

Ironhorse stepped between us with a rumbling growl, and the man leaped back, hands flying to his face. "No," he whimpered, cringing on the floor, arms cradling his head. "No one in here. Empty empty empty. Who am I? I don't know. The rats tell me, but I forget."

"That is enough." Leanansidhe floated down the staircase, her gown trailing behind her. Sweeping up to the human, she touched him lightly on the head. "Charles, darling, I have guests now," she murmured, as he gazed up at her with teary eyes. "Why don't you take a bath, and then you can play for us at dinner?"

Charles sniffled. "Girl," he whimpered, clutching at his hair. "In my head."

"Yes, I know, darling. But if you don't leave, I'll have to turn you into a harp. Go on, now. Shoo, shoo." She made little fluttery motions with her hands, and with one final glance at me, the man scuttled away.

Leanansidhe sighed and turned to us, then seemed to notice the trio for the first time. "Ah, there you are." She smiled, and their faces lit up in the glow of her attention. "Did you manage to get the eggs, darlings?"

Warren snatched the backpack from Nelson's arm and held it out. "We found the nest, Leanansidhe. It was just where you said. But the dragon woke up then, and…" He unzipped the pack, revealing a yellow-green egg the size of a basketball. "We were only able to get one."

"One?" Leanansidhe frowned, and shadows fell over the room. "Only one? I need at least two, pets, or the deal is off. The former Duke of Frostfell specifically said a pair of eggs. How many is in a pair, darling?"

"T-two," Warren stammered.

"Well, then. I'd say you still have work to do. Go on, now. Chop-chop. And don't come back without those eggs!"

The trio fled without hesitation, following the human out the same door. Leanansidhe watched them go, then whirled on us with a bright, feral smile. "Well! Here we are at last. When Grimalkin told me you were coming, I was ever so pleased. It's so *good* to finally meet you."

Grimalkin descended the stairs with his typical indifference, completely unfazed by the Death Glares coming from me and Puck. Leaping onto a sofa, he sat down and began grooming his tail.

"And Puck!" Leanansidhe turned to him, clasping her hands in delight. "I haven't seen you in forever, darling. How is Oberon these days? Still being henpecked by that basilisk of a wife?"

"Don't insult the basilisks," Puck replied, smiling. Crossing his arms, he gazed around the room, moving ever so slightly in front of me. "So, Lea, looks like you've been busy. What's up with the crazies and the half-bloods? Building an army of misfits?"

"Don't be silly, darling." Leanansidhe sniffed, plucking a cigarette holder from a lamp stand. She took a puff and blew a hazy green cloud over our heads. It writhed and twisted into a smoky dragon before dissipating in the air. "My coup days are behind me, now. I've made a nice little realm for myself here, and overthrowing a court is so tedious. However, I'd ask you not to tell Titania that you found me, darling. If you went and blabbed, I might have to rip out your tongue." She smiled, examining a bloodred nail, as Puck inched closer to me. "Also, Robin dear, you needn't worry about protecting the girl. I mean her no harm. The Iron faery I might have to dismember and send its remains to Asia—" Ironhorse tensed and took a step forward "—but I have no intention of hurting the daughter of Oberon. So relax, pet. That's not why I called her here."

"Ironhorse is with me," I said quickly, putting a hand on his arm before he did something stupid. "He won't hurt anything, I promise."

Leanansidhe turned the full brunt of her glittering sapphire gaze on me. "You're so *cute,* did you know that? You look just like your father. No wonder Titania can't stand to look at you. What's your name, darling?"

"Meghan."

She smiled, vicious and challenging, appraising me. "And what's a cutie like you going to do if I want that abomination out of my home? That's quite the binding you've got there, dove. I doubt you can scrape up the glamour to light my cigarette."

I swallowed. This was a test. If I was going to save Ironhorse, I couldn't falter. Steeling myself, I looked into those cold blue eyes, ancient and remorseless, and held her gaze. "Ironhorse is one of my companions," I said softly. "I need him, so I can't let you hurt him. I'll make a deal with you, if that's what it takes, but he stays here. He's not your enemy, and he won't hurt you or anyone under your protection. You have my word."

"I know that, darling." Leanansidhe continued to hold my stare, smiling all the while. "I'm not worried about the Iron faery harming me. I'm worried I won't be able to get his stink out of my carpets. But, no matter." She straightened, releasing me from her gaze. "You've given your word, and I'll hold you to that. Now, come darling. Dinner first, then we can talk. Oh, and please tell your iron pet not to touch anything while he's here. I don't want him melting the glamour."

WE FOLLOWED Leanansidhe down several long corridors carpeted in red and black velvet, past portraits whose eyes seemed to follow us as we walked by. Leanansidhe didn't stop talking, a mindless, bubbly stream, as she led us through her home, spouting names, places and creatures I didn't recognize. But I couldn't stop listening to the sound of her voice, even if all I heard was chipmunk chatter. In my peripheral vision, I caught glimpses of rooms through half-opened doors, drenched in shadow or strange, flickering lights. Sometimes, I thought the rooms looked weird, as if there were trees growing out of the floor, or schools of fish swimming through the air. But Leanansidhe's voice cut through my curiosity, and I couldn't take my eyes from her, even for a closer look.

We entered a vast dining hall, where a long table took up most of the left wall, surrounded by chairs of glass and wood. Candelabra floated down the length of the surface, hovering over a feast that could feed an army. Platters of meat and fish, raw fruits and vegetables, tiny cakes, candies, bottles of wine, and a huge roast pig with an apple in its mouth as the center-piece. Except for the flickering candlelight, the room was pitch-black, and I could hear things scurrying about, mutter-ing in the darkness.

Leanansidhe breezed into the room, trailing smoke from her cigarette, and stood at the head of the table. "Come, darlings," she called, beckoning us with the back of her gloved hand. "You look famished. Sit. Eat. And please don't be so rude as to think the food glamoured or enchanted. What kind of host do you think I am?" She sniffed, as though the very thought annoyed her, and looked away into the shadows. "Excuse me," she called, as we cautiously moved toward the table. "Minions? I have guests, and you are making me look impolite. I will not be pleased if my reputation is soured, darlings."

Movement in the shadows, muttering and low shuffles, as a group of little men edged into the light. I had to bite my lip to keep from laughing. They were redcaps, evil-eyed and shark-toothed, with their hats dipped in the blood of their victims, but they were also dressed in matching butler suits with pink bow ties. Sullen and scowling, they emerged from the darkness, glaring for all they were worth. *Laugh and die,* their eyes warned, but Puck took one look at them and started cracking up. The redcaps glared at him like they were going to bite his head off.

One of them caught sight of Ironhorse and let out a piercing hiss that sent all of them scrambling back. "Iron!" he screeched, baring his jagged fangs. "That's one of them stinking Iron faeries! Kill it! Kill it now!"

Ironhorse roared, and Puck's dagger flashed out, a devilish grin stretching his face at the thought of violence. The redcaps surged forward, snarling and gnashing their teeth, just as eager. I grabbed a silver knife from the table and held it ready as the redcaps lunged forward. One of them leaped onto the table, gathering his short legs under him to launch himself at us, fangs gleaming.

"That is *enough!*"

We froze. It was impossible not to. Even the redcap on the table locked up, then fell into a bowl of fruit salad.

Leanansidhe stood at the end of the table, glowering at us all. Her eyes glowed amber, her hair whipped away from her face, and the candelabra flames danced wildly. For a heart-stopping moment, she stood there, alien and terrifying. Then she sighed, smoothed back her hair and reached for her cigarette holder, taking a long drag. As she blew out the smoke, things returned to normal, including our ability to move, but no one, least of all the redcaps, had any aggressive thoughts left.

"Well?" she finally said, looking to the redcaps as if nothing had happened. "What are you minions standing about for? My seat isn't going to move itself."

The largest redcap, a burly fellow with a bone fishhook through his nose, shook himself and crept forward, pulling Leanansidhe's chair away from the table. The others followed suit, looking like they'd rather beat us to death with our own arms, but wordlessly drew out our chairs. The one attending Ironhorse growled and bared his teeth at the Iron faery, then darted away as quickly as he could.

"I apologize for the minions," Leanansidhe said when we

were all seated. She touched her fingers to her temple, as if she had a headache. "It's so hard to find good help these days, darlings. You have no idea."

"I thought I recognized them," Puck said, casually reaching for a pear near the center of the table. "Isn't the leader Razor Dan, or something like that? Caused a bit of a stir during the Goblin Wars, when they tried selling information to both sides?"

"Nasty business, darling." Leanansidhe snapped her fingers twice, and a brownie melted out of the darkness with a wine flute and a bottle, scrambling onto a stool to fill her glass. "Everyone knows you don't cheat the goblin tribes if you know what's good for you. Like poking a stick down an ant nest." She sipped the wine the brownie poured her and sighed. "They came to me for asylum, after pissing off every goblin tribe in the wyldwood, so I put them to work. That's the rule here, darling. You stay, you work."

I glanced in the direction the redcaps left, feeling their hateful gaze staring out from the darkness. "But aren't you afraid they'll get mad and eat someone?"

"Not if they know what's good for them, darling. And you're not eating anything. Eat." She gestured at the food, and I suddenly realized how hungry I was. I reached for a platter of tiny frosted cakes, too hungry to care about glamours or enchantments anymore. If I was munching on a toadstool or a grasshopper, so be it. Ignorance is bliss.

"While you're here," Leanansidhe continued, smiling as we ate, "you leave all personal vendettas behind. That's my other rule. I can easily deny them sanctuary, and then where will they be? Back in the mortal realm, dying slowly or fighting it out with the Iron fey who are gradually infesting every town and city in the world. No offense, darling," she added, smiling at Ironhorse, implying the exact opposite. Staring blindly at the table, Ironhorse didn't respond. He wasn't eating anything, and I figured he either didn't want to be indebted to Leanansidhe, or he didn't eat regular food. Thankfully, Leanansidhe didn't seem to notice. "Most choose not to take the risk," she went on, stabbing her cigarette holder in the direction the redcaps had fled. "Take the minions, for example. Every so often, one will poke his nose back in the mortal realm, get it hacked off by some goblin mercenary, and come crawling back to me. Exiles, half-breeds and outcasts alike. I'm their only safe haven between the Nevernever and the mortal world."

"Which begs the question," Puck asked, almost too casually. "Where *are* we, anyway?"

"Ah, pet." Leanansidhe smiled at him, but it was a frightening thing, cold and vicious. "I was wondering when you would ask that. And if you think you should run and tattle on me to your masters, don't bother. I've done nothing wrong. I haven't broken my exile. This is my realm, yes, but Titania can relax. It doesn't intrude upon hers in any way."

"Okay, totally not the question I asked." Puck paused with an apple in hand, raising an eyebrow. "And I think I'm even more alarmed now. Where are we, Lea?"

"The Between, darling." Leanansidhe leaned back, sipping her wine. "The veil between the Nevernever and the mortal realm. Surely you've realized that by now."

Both Puck's eyebrows shot up into his hair. "The Between? The Between is full of nothing, or so I was led to believe. Those who get stuck Between usually go insane in very short order."

"Yes, I'll admit, it was difficult to work with at first." Leanansidhe waved her hand airily. "But, enough about me, darlings. Let's talk about you." She took a drag on her cigarette and blew a smoky fish over the table. "Why were you tromping around the Briars when my streetrats found you? I thought you were looking for the Scepter of the Seasons, and you certainly won't find it down there, darlings. Unless you think Bellatoral-lix is sitting on it."

I started. Ironhorse jerked up, sending a bowl of grapes clattering to the floor. Brownies appeared from nowhere, scurrying to recover the lost fruit as it rolled about the tile. Leanansidhe raised a slender eyebrow and took another drag on her cigarette as we recovered.

"You knew?" I stared at her, as the brownies set the bowl on the table again and scampered off. "You knew about the scepter?"

"Darling, please." Leanansidhe gave me a half scornful, half patronizing look. "I know everything that happens within the courts. I find it unforgivable to be so out of the loop, and it's terribly boring here otherwise. My informants clue me in on all the important details."

"Spies, you mean," Puck said.

"Such a dirty word, darling." Leanansidhe *tsked* at him. "And it doesn't matter now. What matters is what I can tell you. I know the scepter was stolen from under Mab's nose, I know Summer and Winter are about to go to a bloody war over it, and I know that the scepter is not in the Nevernever but in the mortal realm. And—" she took a long drag on her cigarette and sent a hawk soaring over our heads "—I can help you find it."

I was instantly suspicious, and I could tell Ironhorse and Puck felt the same. "Why?" I demanded. "What's in it for you?"

Leanansidhe looked at me, and a shadow crept into her voice, making it dark and ominous. "Darling, I've seen what's been happening in the mortal realm. Unlike Oberon and Mab, who hide in their safe little courts, I know the reality pressing in on us from every side. The Iron fey are getting stronger. They're everywhere: in computers, crawling out of television screens, massing in factories. I have more exiles under my roof now than I've had in the past century. They're terrified, unwilling to walk in the mortal realm any longer, because the Iron fey are tearing them apart."

I shuddered, and Ironhorse had gone very still. Leanansidhe paused, and nothing could be heard except the faint skittering of things unseen in the pressing darkness.

"If Summer and Winter go to war, and the Iron fey attack, there will be nothing left. If the Iron fey win, the Nevernever will become uninhabitable. I don't know what that will do to the Between, but I'm sure it will be quite fatal for me. So you see, darling," Leanansidhe said, taking a sip of wine, "it would be advantageous for me to help you. And since I have eyes and ears everywhere within the mortal realm, it would be prudent of you to accept."

Ironhorse shifted, then spoke for the first time. To his credit, he tried to keep his voice down, but even then it echoed around the room. "YOUR OFFER IS APPRECIATED," he rumbled, "BUT WE ALREADY KNOW WHERE THE SCEPTER IS LOCATED."

"Do you now?" Leanansidhe shot him a vicious smile. "Where?"

"SILICON VALLEY."

"Lovely. *Where* in Silicon Valley, pet?"

A pause. "I DO NOT—"

"And how do you plan on getting to the scepter once you find it, darling? Walk in the front door?"

Ironhorse glowered at her. "I WILL FIND A WAY."

"I see." Leanansidhe gave him a scornful look. "Well, let me tell you what *I* know about Silicon Valley, pet, so the princess has an idea of what she's up against. It's the gremlins' spawning ground. You know, those nasty little things that crawl out of computers and other machines. There are literally thousands of them down there, perhaps hundreds of thousands, as well as some very powerful Iron fey who would turn you into bloody strips as soon as look at you. You go down there without a plan, darling, and you're walking into a death trap. Besides, you're already too late." Leanansidhe snapped her fingers, holding out her glass for more wine. "I've been keeping tabs on the scepter's movements ever since I heard it was stolen. It was being held in a large office building in San Jose, but my spies tell me it's been moved. Apparently, someone already tried to get in and steal it back, but didn't quite succeed. Now, the building has been cleared out, and the scepter is gone."

"Ash," I whispered, glancing at Puck. "It had to be Ash." Puck looked doubtful, so I turned back to Leanansidhe, a cold desperation spreading through my stomach. "What happened to him, the one who tried to take the scepter? Where is he now?"

"I've no idea, pet. Ash, you say? Am I right in assuming this is Mab's Ash, the darling of the Unseelie Court?"

"We have to find him!" I stood up, causing Puck and Iron-horse to blink at me. "He could be in trouble. He needs our help." I turned to Leanansidhe. "Could you get your spies to look for him?"

"I could, dove." Leanansidhe twiddled her cigarette lighter. "But I'm afraid I have more important things to find. We're after the scepter, remember, darling? The prince of the Winter Court, scrumptious though he is, will have to wait."

"Ash is fine, Princess," Puck added, dismissing the idea immediately. "He can take care of himself."

I sat back down, anger and worry flooding my brain. What if Ash wasn't fine? What if he'd been captured, and they were torturing him, like they had in Machina's realm? What if he was hurt, lying in a gutter somewhere, waiting for me? I became so worked up over Ash, I barely heard what Puck and Leanansidhe were discussing, and a small part of me didn't care.

"What do you suggest, Lea?" This from Puck.

"Let my people search the valley. I know a sluah who is simply fabulous at finding things that don't want to be found. I've sent for him today. In the meantime, I have all my minions scouring the streets, keeping their heads down and their ears to the ground. They'll turn up something, eventually."

"Eventually?" I glared at her. "What are we supposed to do until then?"

Leanansidhe smiled and blew me a smoke rabbit. "I suggest you get comfortable, darling."

It wasn't a request.

# CHAPTER THIRTEEN

*Charles and the Redcaps*

I hate waiting. I hate standing around with nothing to do, cooling my heels until someone gives me the go-ahead to move. I hated it while I was at the Winter Court, and I certainly didn't like it now, in Leanansidhe's mansion, waiting for complete strangers to bring word of the missing scepter. To make things worse, there were no clocks anywhere in the mansion and, even weirder, no windows to see the outside world. Also, as most faeries did, Leanansidhe hated technology, so that of course meant no television, computers, phones, video games, *anything* to make time pass more quickly. Not even a radio, although the crazy humans wandering the mansion would often spontaneously burst into song, or start playing some kind of instrument, so the house was never without noise. The few exiled fey I saw either fled my presence or nervously told me that I was not to be bothered, Leanansidhe's orders. I felt like a mouse trapped in some kind of bizarro labyrinth. Add in my constant worry for Ash, and it started to drive me as crazy as Leanansidhe's collection of gifted but insane mortals.

Apparently, I wasn't the only one going nuts.

"THIS IS UNACCEPTABLE," Ironhorse announced one day—night?—as we lounged in the library, a red-carpeted room with a stone fireplace and bookshelves that soared to the ceiling. With an impressive collection of novels and mostly fashion magazines at my fingertips, I managed to keep myself entertained during the long hours that we waited for Leanansidhe's spies to turn something up. Today, I was curled on the couch with King's *The Dark Tower* series, but it was difficult to concentrate with a restless, impatient Iron faery in the same room. Puck had vanished earlier, probably tormenting the staff or getting into some kind of trouble, and Grimalkin was with Leanansidhe, swapping favors and gossip, which left me alone with Ironhorse, who was getting on my last nerve. He was never still. Even in a human body, he acted like a flighty racehorse, pacing the room and tossing his head so that his dreadlocks clanked against his shoulders. I noticed that even though he wore boots, he still left hoof-shaped burn marks in the carpet, before the glamour of the mansion could smooth it out again.

"PRINCESS," he said, coming around the couch to kneel in front of me, "WE MUST ACT SOON. THE SCEPTER IS GETTING FARTHER AND FARTHER AWAY, WHILE WE SIT HERE AND DO NOTHING. HOW CAN WE TRUST THIS LEANANSIDHE? WHAT IF SHE IS KEEPING US HERE BECAUSE SHE WANTS THE SCEPTER FOR HERSEL—?"

"Shh! Ironhorse, be quiet," I hissed, and he immediately fell silent, looking as contrite as his expressionless face would allow. "You can't say those things out loud. She could hear you, or her spies could rat us out. I'm pretty sure she has them watching our every move." A quick glance around the library revealed nothing, but I could still feel eyes on me, peering unseen from cracks and shadows. "She already has it in for all Iron fey. Don't add to it."

"MY APOLOGIES, PRINCESS." Ironhorse bowed his head. "I CANNOT ABIDE THIS WAITING. I FEEL AS IF I SHOULD BE DOING SOMETHING, BUT I AM USELESS TO YOU HERE."

"I know how you feel," I told him, placing a hand on his bulky arm. His skin was hot to the touch, and the tendons beneath were like solid steel. "I want to get out of here, too. But we have to be patient. Puck and Grim are out there— they'll let us know if anything turns up or if we have to leave."

He looked unhappy, but nodded. I sighed with relief and hoped Leanansidhe's spies found something soon, before Iron-horse started tearing down the walls.

The door banged open, and we both jumped, but it was only a human, the scruffy piano player we'd seen when we first came to the mansion. He ambled into the room, blank eyes scanning the floor, until they spotted me. With an empty smile, he stumbled forward, but stopped when he saw the huge Iron faery kneeling in front of me.

Ironhorse rose with a growl, but I smacked his arm, wincing as the rock-hard bicep bruised my knuckles. "It's all right," I told him when he gave me a puzzled look. "I don't think he'll hurt me. He looks pretty harmless."

Ironhorse gave the human a suspicious glare and snorted. "IF YOU NEED ME…"

"I'll yell."

He nodded, shot the man one last dark look, and retreated to the other side of the room to glower at us.

With Ironhorse at a distance, the man seemed to relax. He

inched up to the couch and perched on the edge, staring at me curiously. I smiled at him over my book. He seemed much calmer now, not so crazy. His eyes were clear, though the way he stared at me, unblinking, was making me a bit uncomfortable.

"Hi," I greeted, squirming a bit under that unrelenting gaze. "You're Charles, aren't you? I heard your playing earlier. You're really good."

He gave me a confused frown, tilting his head. "You heard me…play?" he murmured, his voice surprisingly clear and deep. "I don't…remember that."

I nodded. "In the foyer. When we first came here. You were playing for Leanansidhe and we heard the end of it."

"I don't remember," he said again, scratching his head. "I don't remember a lot of things." He blinked and looked up at me, suddenly contemplative. "But…I remember you. Isn't that strange?"

I glanced at Ironhorse, hovering in the corner and pretending not to listen to us. "How long have you been here, Charles?"

He frowned, scrunching his forehead. His face, though lined and worn, was curiously childlike. "I…I've always been here."

"They can't remember anything." Grimalkin popped into existence on the back of the couch, waving his tail. I started and dropped my book, but Charles simply looked at the cat, as if he had seen far stranger. "He's been here too long," Grimalkin continued, sitting down and curling his tail around his legs. "That's what being in Faery does to mortals. This one's forgotten everything about his life before. Same as all the other mortals wandering around this place."

"Hi, kitty," muttered Charles, reaching a hand toward Grimalkin. Grimalkin bristled and stalked to the other end of the couch.

"How many of them are there?" I asked.

"Humans?" Grimalkin licked a paw, still keeping a wary eye on Charles. "Not so many. A dozen or so, I'd guess. All great artists—poets or painters or other such nonsense." He sniffed and scrubbed the paw over his face. "That's what keeps this place alive, all that creative energy and glamour. Not even the redcaps will lay a finger on them."

"How can she keep them here?" I asked, but Grimalkin yawned and settled down on the couch back, burying his nose in his tail and closing his eyes. Apparently, he was done answering questions. I'd poke him, but he would just swat me or disappear.

"Here you are, darlings." Leanansidhe breezed into the room, trailing a gauzy black dress and shawl behind her. "I'm so glad I caught you before I left. Charles, darling, I must speak with my guests now. Shoo shoo." She fluttered her hands, and with a last glance at me Charles slipped off the couch and out the door.

"You're leaving?" I eyed her dress and purse. "Why?"

"Have you seen Puck, darling?" Leanansidhe gazed around the library, ignoring my question. "We need to have a little chitchat. Cook has been complaining that certain dinner items keep going missing, the head maid is mysteriously in love with a coatrack, and my butler has been chasing mice around the foyer all evening." She sighed and pinched the bridge of her nose, closing her eyes. "Anyway, darling. If you see Puck, be a dear and tell him to reverse the glamour on my poor maid, and to please stop stealing cakes from the oven before Cook has a meltdown. I shudder to think of what I might return to, but I simply cannot stay."

"Where are you going?"

"Me? I'm off to Nashville, darling. Some brilliant young songwriter is in need of inspiration. It's horrible to be so blocked, but not to worry. Soon, everyone will be in love with his muuuusic." She sang the last word, and I bit my lip to kill the urge to dance. Leanansidhe went on without notice. "Also, I need to pay a visit to a night hag, see if she has any information for us. I'll be back in a day or two, human time. Ciao, darling."

She waggled her fingers at me and vanished in a swirl of glitter.

I blinked and fought the urge to sneeze.

"Show-off," Puck muttered, appearing from behind one of the bookshelves, as if he'd been waiting for her to leave. He crossed the room to perch on the armrest, rolling his eyes. "She could've left without all the sparkly. But then, Lea always knew how to make an exit."

"BUT SHE IS GONE." Ironhorse hurried over, looking around as if he feared Leanansidhe was really hiding behind one of the chairs in the room, listening to him. "SHE IS GONE, AND WE CAN FIND A WAY OUT OF HERE."

"And do what, exactly?" Grimalkin raised his head and gave him a scornful look. "We still do not know where the scepter is. We would only be announcing our presence to the enemy and lowering our chances of finding it."

"Furball's right, unfortunately," Puck sighed. "Lea's not the easiest fey to deal with, but she's true to her word, and she has the best chance of finding the scepter. We should stay put until we actually know where it is."

"SO." Ironhorse crossed his massive arms, his eyes smoldering heat and fury. "THAT IS THE PLAN FROM THE GREAT ROBIN GOODFELLOW. WE SIT HERE AND DO NOTHING."

"And what's your brilliant plan, Rusty? Go clomping off to the city and poke our noses into every major corporation until the scepter falls on our heads?"

"PRINCESS." Ironhorse turned to me. "THIS IS FOOLISH. WHY WAIT HERE ANY LONGER? DON'T YOU WANT TO FIND THE SCEPTER? DON'T YOU WANT TO FIND PRINCE ASH—"

"Stop right there." My voice dropped a few degrees, and maybe Ironhorse heard the warning in it because he quickly shut up. I stood, clenching my fists. "Don't you dare bring Ash into this," I hissed, making him take a step back. "Yes, I want to find him—he's on my mind every single day. But I can't, because we have to find the scepter first. And even if the scepter wasn't an issue, I still couldn't do anything about Ash because he doesn't *want* to be found. Not by me. He made that perfectly clear last I saw him." My throat started to close up, and I took a shaky breath to fight it. "So, the answer to your question is, yes, I want to find Ash. But I can't. Because the damn scepter is more important. And I'm not gonna screw up just because you can't sit still for two damn minutes." Tears welled, and I blinked angrily, aware that all three were staring like my head was on fire. I couldn't tell what Ironhorse was thinking behind that expressionless mask, but Grimalkin looked bored, and Puck's face was balanced between jealousy and pity.

Which pissed me off even more.

"Meghan," Puck began, but I spun around and stormed out before I really started bawling. He called after me, but I ignored him, swearing that if he grabbed me or got in my way he would get an earful.

"Let her go," I heard Grimalkin say as I bashed the door open. "She would not hear you now, Goodfellow. She wants only him."

The door swung shut behind me, and I stomped down the hall, fighting angry tears.

It wasn't fair. I was tired of being responsible, tired of making the hard decisions because it was the right thing to do. I wanted nothing more than to find Ash and beg him to reconsider. We could be together; we could find a way to make it work if we tried hard enough, screw the consequences. And the scepter.

The hallways stretched on, each one similar to the last: narrow, dark and red. I didn't know where I was going, and I didn't really care. I just wanted to get away from Puck and Iron-horse, to be alone with my selfish wishes for a while. Statues, paintings and musical instruments lined the corridors; some of them vibrated softly as I passed, faint shivers of music hanging on the air.

Finally, I sank down beside a harp, ignoring a piskie that watched from the end of the hall, and buried my face in my hands.

*Ash. I miss you.*

My eyes stung. I swiped at them angrily, determined not to cry. The harp thrummed in my ear, sounding curious and sympathetic. Idly, I drew my finger across the strings, and it released a mournful, shivery note that echoed down the hall.

Another chord answered it, and another. I raised my head and listened as the low, faint strains of piano music drifted into the corridor. The song was dark, haunting and strangely familiar. Wiping my eyes, I stood and followed it, down the twisted hallways, past instruments that hummed and added their voices to the melody.

The song led me to pair of dark red doors with gilded handles. Beyond the wood, it sounded like a symphony was in full swing. Cautiously, I pushed the doors open and stepped into a large, circular red room.

Waves of music flowed over me. The room was full of instruments: harps and cellos and violins, along with a few guitars and even a ukulele. In the middle of the room, Charles sat hunched over the keys of a baby grand piano, eyes closed as his fingers flew over the instrument. Along the walls, the other instruments thrummed and trilled and lent their strains to the melody, turning the cacophony into something pure and wondrous. The music was a living thing, swirling around the room, dark and eerie and haunted, bringing new tears to my eyes. I sank onto a red velvet couch and gave in to my churning emotions.

*I know this song.*

But try as I might, I couldn't remember from where. The memory taunted me, keeping just out of reach, a gaping hole where the image should be. But the melody, mysterious and devastatingly familiar, pulled at my insides, filling me with sadness and a gaping sense of loss.

Tears flowing freely down my skin, I watched Charles's lean shoulders rise and fall with the chords, his head so low it almost touched the keys. I couldn't be sure, but I thought his cheeks were wet, too.

When the last note died away, neither of us moved for several heartbeats. Charles sat there, his fingers resting on the final keys, breathing hard. My mind was still spinning in circles, trying to remember the tune. But the longer I sat there, trying to recall it, the farther it slipped away, vanishing into the walls and carpet, until only the instruments remembered it at all.

Charles finally pushed the seat back and rose, and I stood with him, feeling faintly guilty for eavesdropping.

"That was beautiful," I said as he turned. He blinked, obviously surprised to see me there, but he didn't startle or jump. "What was the name of the song?"

The question seemed to confuse him. He frowned and cocked his head, furrowing his brow as if trying to understand me. Then a sorrowful expression crossed his face, and he shrugged. "I don't remember."

I felt a pang of disappointment. "Oh."

"But…" He paused, running his fingers along the ivory

keys, a faraway look in his eyes. "I seem to recall it was a favorite of mine. Long ago. I think." He blinked, and his eyes focused on me again. "Do you know what it's called?"

I shook my head.

"Oh. That's too bad." He sighed, pouting a bit. "The rats said you might remember."

Okay, now it was time to leave. I stood, but before I could make my escape, the door creaked open, and Warren entered the room.

"Oh, hey, Meghan." He licked his lips, eyes darting about in a nervous fashion. One hand was tucked into his jacket, hiding it from view. "I…um…I'm looking for Puck. Is he here?"

Something about him put me off. I shifted uncomfortably and crossed my arms. "No. I think he's in the library with Iron-horse."

"Good." He stepped in farther, pulling his hand out of his jacket. The lights gleamed along the black barrel of a gun as he raised the muzzle and pointed it at me. I went stiff with shock, and Warren glanced over his shoulder. "Okay," he called, "coast is clear."

The door swung open, and a half-dozen redcaps poured into the room behind him. The one with the fishhook in his nose, Razor Dan, stepped forward and leered at me with a mouthful of jagged teeth.

"You sure this is the one, half-breed?"

Warren smirked. "I'm sure," he replied, never taking the gun, or his eyes, off me. "The Iron King will reward us handsomely for this, you have my word."

"Bastard," I hissed at Warren, making the redcaps snicker. "Traitor. Why are you doing this? Leanansidhe gives you everything."

"Oh, come on." Warren sneered and shook his head. "You

act like it's a total shock that I want something better than this."
He gestured around the foyer with his free hand. "Being a
minion in Leanansidhe's sorry refugee cult hasn't exactly been
my life goal, Princess. So I'm a little bitter, yeah. But the new
Iron King is offering half-breeds and exiles part of the Nevernever and a chance to kick the pure-blooded asses of all the
dicks who stomped on us if we just do him a teensy favor and
find you. And you were nice enough to drop into my lap."

"You'll never get away with it," I told him desperately. "Puck
and Ironhorse will come looking for me. And Leanansidhe—"

"By the time Leanansidhe gets back, we'll be long gone,"
Warren interrupted. "And the rest of Dan's crew is taking care
of Goodfellow and the iron monster, so they're a little busy at
the moment. I'm afraid that no one is coming to your rescue,
Princess."

"Warren," snapped Razor Dan with an impatient glare. "We
don't have time to gloat, you idiot. Shoot the crazy and let's
get out of here before Leanansidhe comes back."

My stomach clenched tight. Warren rolled his eyes, swinging
the barrel of the gun around to Charles. Charles stiffened,
seeming to grasp what was happening as Warren gave him a
crooked leer.

"Sorry, Charles," he muttered, and the gun filled my vision,
cold, black and steely. I saw the opening of the barrel like
Edgebriar's iron ring, and felt a buzzing beneath my skin. "It's
nothing personal. You just got in the way."

*Tighten,* I thought at the pistol barrel, just as Warren pulled
the trigger.

A roar shattered the air as the gun exploded in Warren's hand,
sending the half-satyr stumbling back. Screaming, he dropped the
mangled remains of the weapon and clutched his hand to his chest
as the smell of smoke and burning flesh filled the room.

The redcaps stared wide-eyed at Warren as he collapsed to

his knees, wailing and shaking his charred hand. "What are you waiting for?" he screamed at them, his voice half shout and half sob. "Kill the crazy and get the girl!"

The redcap closest to me snarled and lunged. I shrank back, but Charles suddenly stepped between us. Before the redcap could dodge, he grabbed a cello off the wall and smashed it down over its head. The instrument let out a shriek, as if in pain, and the redcap crumpled the floor.

Razor Dan sighed.

"All right, lads," he growled, as I grabbed Charles's hand and pulled him back behind the piano. "All together now. Get them!"

"PRINCESS!"

Behind them, the door burst open with a furious roar, and two redcaps were hurled through the air, landing face-first into the wall. The pack spun around, their eyes going wide as Ironhorse barreled into them, swinging his huge fists and bellowing at the top of his lungs. Several redcaps went flying and the rest swarmed him with bloodthirsty cries, biting at his arms and legs. They fell back, shrieking in pain, teeth shattered, mouths blackened and raw. Ironhorse continued to hurl them away like he'd gone berserk.

"Hey, Princess." Puck appeared beside me, grinning from ear to ear. "Grimalkin said you were having redcap trouble. We're here to help, although I must say Rusty is doing fine on his own." He ducked as a redcap flew overhead, landing with a crunch against the wall. "I'll have to remember to keep him around. He'd be great fun at parties, don't you think?"

The redcap Ironhorse had thrown into the wall staggered to his feet, looking dazed. Seeing us, he bared a mouthful of broken teeth and tensed to lunge. Puck grinned and pulled out his dagger, but there was an explosion of light between them, and a ringing voice filled the hallway.

*"Everyone freeze!"*

We froze.

"Well," Leanansidhe said, striding over to me and Puck. "Turns out this game was a rousing success. Although, I must say, I was hoping to be surprised. It gets rather boring when you're right about everything."

"L-Leanansidhe," Razor Dan stammered, all the blood draining from his face as she regarded him with her fearsome smile. "H-how…? You're supposed to be in Nashville."

"Dan, darling." Leanansidhe shook her head and *tsked*. "Did you really think I was blind to what was going on? In my own house? I know the rumors circulating the streets, pet. I know the Iron King has been offering rewards for the girl. I had the feeling there was a traitor in my house, a so-called agent of the Iron King. What better way to flush him out than to leave him alone with the princess and wait for him to make his move? Your kind is so very predictable, darling."

"We…" Dan glanced around at his crew, clearly looking for someone else to blame. "This wasn't our idea, Leanansidhe."

"Oh, I know, darling. You're too dull to organize something like this. Which is why I'm not going to punish you."

"Really?" Dan relaxed a bit.

"Really?" I blurted, looking up at her. "But they attacked me! And they were going to kill Charles! You're not going to do anything about that?"

"They were only following their base instincts, pet." Leanansidhe smiled at me. "I expected nothing less of them. What I really want is the mastermind. Why don't you stick around… *Warren*."

We all turned to where Warren was trying to sneak down the corridor without being seen. He froze, wincing at the sound of his name, and gave Leanansidhe a feeble smile.

"Leanansidhe, I…I can explain."

"Oh, I'm sure you can, darling." Leanansidhe's voice made my stomach curl. "And you will. We're going to have a little chitchat, and you're going to tell me everything you know about the Iron King and the scepter. You're going to sing, darling. Sing as you've never sung before, I promise."

"Come on," Puck told me, taking my elbow. "You don't want to hear this, Princess, trust me. Lea will give us the information when she has it."

"Charles," I said, and he turned from Leanansidhe to me, his eyes blank and empty once more. "Come on. Let's get out of here."

"Pretty lady's sparkly," Charles muttered. I sighed.

"Yeah," I said sadly, taking his hand. "She is."

With Ironhorse glowering and Puck leading the way, we fled the music room and Leanansidhe's presence, leaving Warren to his fate.

# CHAPTER FOURTEEN

*Royal Treatment*

"A software corporation?" Puck repeated, brow furrowing. "Really. That's where they've been hiding it all this time?"

"Apparently, darling." Leanansidhe leaned back in her chair, crossing her long legs. "Remember, the Iron fey aren't like us. They're not going to be hanging around parks and museums, singing to flowers. They like high-tech places that attract the cold, calculating mortals we care so little for."

I shared a glance with Puck. We'd been talking about that strange, cold glamour I'd used on the gun before Leanansidhe came in. Though we were only guessing, we'd both come to the conclusion that it had indeed been iron glamour that I'd used on Warren, and that Leanansidhe, with her obvious hate and contempt for the Iron fey, definitely should not know about it yet.

I wished *I* knew more about it. I had the feeling this had never happened in the faery world before, that I was a first, and there was no expert to talk to. Why did I have iron glamour? Why could I use it sometimes and not others? Too many questions, and no answers. I sighed and decided to focus on the problem at hand, instead of the one I had no hope of unraveling yet.

"What's the name of this place?" I asked Leanansidhe, not pointing out that I was one of those cold, calculating mortals who liked gadgets and computers and high-tech. I still missed my poor drowned iPod, the victim of a river crossing the first time I came to Faery, and this was the longest I'd ever gone without television. If I ever got back to having a normal life, I'd have a lot to catch up on.

Leanansidhe tapped her fingers against the armrest, pursing her lips in thought. "Oh, what did they call it? They all sound the same to me, darling." She snapped her fingers. "SciCorp, I believe it was. Yes, in downtown San Jose. The heart of Silicon Valley."

"Big place," I muttered. "I don't think we can just walk in. There's sure to be cameras and security guards and everything."

"Yes, a frontal assault is doomed to fail," Leanansidhe agreed, glancing at Ironhorse, who stood in the corner with his arms crossed. "And remember, it's not only mortals you have to worry about. There's sure to be Iron fey as well. You're going to have to be…sneakier."

In the corner, Ironhorse raised his head. "WHAT ABOUT A DISTRACTION?" he offered. "I COULD KEEP THEIR ATTENTION ON ME, WHILE SOMEONE GOES IN THROUGH THE BACK."

"Or I could glamour Meghan invisible," Puck added.

Grimalkin yawned from where he lay the couch. "It will be risky holding a glamour with all the iron and steel inside," he said, blinking sleepily. "And we all know how horribly incompetent the human is when it comes to magic, even without her glamour sealed off."

I threw a pillow at him. He gave me a disdainful look and went back to sleep.

"Do we know anything about the building?" I asked Leanansidhe. "Blueprints, security, that kind of thing?" I suddenly felt like a spy in an action movie. The image of me dangling over a net of trip wires, *Mission Impossible* style, sprang to mind, and I bit down a nervous giggle.

"Unfortunately, Warren didn't have much to say about the building, though he really wanted to at the end, poor boy." Leanansidhe smiled, as if reliving a fond memory, and I shivered. "Thankfully, my spies found out all we needed to know. They said they're holding the scepter on floor twenty-nine point five."

"Twenty-nine point five?" I frowned. "How's that work?"

"I've no idea, darling. That's just what they said. However—" and she produced a slip of paper with a flourish "—they were able to come up with this. Apparently, it's some sort of code, used to get into the Iron faeries' lair. They couldn't solve it, but perhaps you will have better luck. I've no head for numbers at all, I'm afraid."

She handed the paper to me. Puck and Ironhorse crowded around, and we stared at it for several moments. Leanansidhe was right—it was definitely part of a code.

3
13
1113
3113
132113
1…

"Okay," I mused, after several moments of racking my brain and not coming up with anything. "So, we just have to figure this out and then we're home free. Doesn't sound too hard."

"I'm afraid it's a bit more complicated, darling." Leanansidhe accepted a glass of wine from a brownie. "As you said before, SciCorp is not a place you can just walk into. Visitors are not allowed past the front desk, and security is fairly tight. You have to be an employee to get off the first floor."

"Well, what if we pretended to be the janitor or cleaning service, or something like that?"

Grimalkin snorted and shifted position on the couch. "Would you not need an ID card for that?" he said, settling comfortably on the pillow I'd thrown at him. "If the building is so well guarded, I doubt they let in common riffraff off the street."

I slumped, frowning. "He's right. We would need a fake ID, or the ID of one of the workers, to make it inside. I don't know anyone who can get us something like that."

Leanansidhe smiled. "I do," she said, and snapped her fingers twice. "Skrae, darling," she called, "would you come here a moment? I need you to find something."

A piskie spiraled into view, gossamer wings buzzing. Three inches tall, he had indigo skin and dandelion hair, and wore nothing but a razor-toothed grin as he fluttered by. His eyes, enormous white orbs in his pointed face, regarded me curiously, until Leanansidhe clapped her hands.

"Skrae, pet, I'm over here. Focus, darling." The piskie gave me a wink and a suggestive hip wiggle before turning his attention to Leanansidhe. "Good. Now, pay attention. I have a mission for you. I want you to find the streetrats. The half-phouka and the troll boy, I forget their names. Tell them to leave off the eggs for now, I have another job for them. Now go, darling.

Buzz buzz." She fluttered her hand, and the piskie zipped away out of sight.

"Kimi and Nelson," I said softly.

"What, darling?"

"That's their names. Kimi and Nelson. They were with... with Warren, when we first met." I remembered Kimi's impish grin, Nelson's stoic expression. "You don't think they're involved with the Iron fey, too?"

"No." Leanansidhe leaned back, snapping at a brownie for wine. "They knew nothing of Warren's betrayal or plot to kidnap you. He made that very clear."

"Oh. That's a relief."

"Although," Leanansidhe mused with a faraway look, "the girl would make a lovely violin. Or maybe a lyre. The troll is more of a bass, I believe. What do you think, darling?"

I shuddered and hoped she was kidding.

KIMI AND NELSON showed up a few hours later. When they walked into the foyer, Leanansidhe wasted no time in telling them what had happened to Warren, which left them shocked and angry but not disbelieving. No tears were shed, no furious accusations were hurled at anyone. Kimi sniffled a bit, but when Leanansidhe informed them they had a job, both perked up instantly. They struck me as very pragmatic kids, used to the school of hard knocks, which left little room for self-pity or wallowing.

"So," Kimi said, flopping back on the sofa, which almost swallowed her whole, "what do you want us to do?"

Leanansidhe smiled and gestured for me to take over. "This is your plan, dove. You tell them what you need."

"Um...right." The two half-breeds looked at me expectantly. I swallowed. "Um, well, have you heard of a company called SciCorp?"

Kimi nodded, kicking her feet. "Sure. Big corporation that makes software, or something like that. Why?"

I looked at Leanansidhe, and she waved her cigarette at me encouragingly. "Well, we need to get inside the building and steal something. Unnoticed."

Kimi's eyes widened. "You serious?"

I nodded. "Yes. But, we need your help to get past the guards and the security. Specifically, we need an ID card from one of the workers, and Leanansidhe said you might be able to get us one. Could you do that?"

Kimi and Nelson shared a glance, and the half-phouka turned to me with a mischievous smile. "No problem." Her eyes gleamed, relishing the encounter. "When do you want it?"

"As soon as possible."

"Right, then." Kimi squirmed off the couch and tapped Nelson's huge bicep. "Come on, big guy. Let's go terrorize a human. Back before you know it."

As the two left the foyer, Puck glanced at Leanansidhe. "You sure those two can handle it?" he asked, and grinned mischievously. "Want me to help them out?"

"No, darling. It's best that you do not." Leanansidhe stood, green smoke swirling about her. "Half-breeds have it easier in Silicon Valley—they won't attract as much attention as normal fey, and they haven't our allergies to all the iron and steel. Those two will be fine, trust me. Now, then." She walked toward me, smiling. "Come with me, my pet. We have a big day ahead of us."

I stared at her nervously. "Where are we going?"

"Shopping, darling!"

"What? Now? Why?"

Leanansidhe *tsked*. "Darling, you can't expect to waltz into SciCorp looking like *that*." She regarded my jeans and sweater imperiously, and sniffed. "It doesn't exactly scream 'I'm a business professional.' More like, 'I'm a Goodwill junkie.' If we're going to get you into SciCorp, you'll need more than luck and glamour. You'll need an entire makeover."

"But we're running out of time. Why can't Puck just glamour me some clothes—"

"Darling, darling, darling." Leanansidhe waved her hand. "You *never* turn down a chance to go shopping, pet. Besides, didn't you hear Grimalkin? Even the most powerful glamour has the tendency to unravel if surrounded by steel and iron. We don't want you to *look* like a corporate worker, dove, we want you to *be* a corporate worker. And we're going shopping, no buts about it." She gave me an indulgent smile I didn't like at all. "Think of me as your temporary faery godmother, darling. Just let me get my magic wand."

I FOLLOWED Leanansidhe down another long corridor that dumped us out onto a sunny sidewalk bustling with people, who didn't notice our sudden appearance from a previously empty alleyway. Even though the sun was shining and the sky was clear, there was a frigid bite to the air, and people hurried down the street in thick sweaters and coats, a sign that winter was on its way or had already arrived. As we passed a newspaper machine, I quickly scanned the date in the corner and breathed in a sigh of relief. Five months. I'd been stuck in Faery five months; a long time to be sure, but better than five years, or five centuries. At least my parents were still alive.

I spent the rest of the afternoon being dragged from shop to shop, following Leanansidhe as she plucked clothes from racks and shoved them at me, demanding I try them on. When I balked at the ungodly prices, she laughed and reminded me that she was my temporary faery godmother today, and that price was not an issue.

I tried on women's suits first, sleek jackets and tight, knee-length skirts that made me look five years older, at least to Leanansidhe's reckoning. I must've tried on two dozen different styles, colors and combinations before Leanansidhe finally announced that she liked a simple black outfit that looked like every other black outfit I had tried on.

"So, we're done now?" I ventured hopefully, as Leanansidhe had the store clerk take the suit away to be wrapped. The faery looked down at me in genuine surprise and laughed.

"Oh, no, darling. That was just a suit. You still need shoes, makeup, a purse, a few accessories…no pet, we've only just begun."

"I didn't think faeries liked shopping and buying stuff. Isn't that a bit…unnatural?"

"Of course not, darling. Shopping is just another form of hunting. *All* fey are hunters, whether they admit it or not. It's in our nature, pet, nothing unnatural about it."

That made a strange sort of sense.

MORE STORES. I lost track of all the places we visited, the aisles we stalked, the racks we pored over. Leanansidhe was a faery on a mission; the second she swept through the doors, all salespeople would drop what they were doing and flock to her side, asking if they could help, if they could be of service. I was invisible beside her; even when Leanansidhe announced we were shopping for *me,* the clerks would forget I existed the second they turned away. Still, they were eager to please, bringing out their best shoes in my size, showing us a staggering variety of purses I would never use, and suggesting earrings that would accent the color of my eyes. (This was also the time Leanansidhe discovered I didn't pierce my ears. Thirty minutes later, I sat with my earlobes throbbing as a bubbly clerk pressed cotton to my ears and cheerfully told me the swelling would go down in a day or two.)

Finally, as the sun was setting over the buildings, the Queen of Shopping decided we were finished. Relieved that the long day was over, I sat on a chair, staring at the stupid code, annoyed that I still couldn't solve it. I watched Leanansidhe chat up the clerk as she wrapped and bagged the merchandise. When she announced the grand total, I nearly fell out of my seat, but Leanansidhe smiled and handed her a credit card without blinking once. For just a moment, when the clerk handed it back, the card looked more like a piece of bark, but Leanansidhe dropped it into her purse before I could get a closer look.

"Well," my temporary faery godmother said brightly as we departed the store, "we have your clothes, your shoes, and your accessories. Now, the real fun begins."

"What?" I asked wearily.

"Your hair, my dove. It's just…not good." Leanansidhe made as if to pluck my bangs, but couldn't quite bring herself to touch them. "And your nails. They need help. Fortunately, it's almost time for the spa to open."

"Spa?" I looked at the glowing orange ball disappearing over the horizon, wishing we could go home. "But it must be six o'clock. Aren't most places like that closed?"

"Of course, darling. That's when all the humans leave. Don't ask such silly questions." Leanansidhe shook her head at my naïveté. "Come now. I know Ben will be dying to meet you."

Natural Earth Salon and Spa was crowded tonight. We passed a pair of giggling sylphs on the pebbled path to the salon. Petite and delicate, their razor-edged wings buzzing softly, they grinned at us as we walked by, teeth glinting like knives. A Winter sidhe, tall and cold and beautiful, brushed by us as we stepped through the door into the waiting area, leaving a trail of frost on my skin and a chill in my lungs. A trio of piskies landed in my hair, laughing and tugging, until Leanansidhe gave them a look and they buzzed out the door.

Inside, the lighting was dim, the walls hewn of natural stone, giving it a cavelike feel. A marble fountain with fish and mermaids bubbled in the center of the foyer, filling the room with the cheerful sound of running water. Orchids and bamboo flourished in natural planters, and the air was warm and damp.

"Why are there so many fey here?" I asked softly, as a huge black dog loped across the doorway in the back. "Is this a place for exiles? A salon and spa? That's kind of weird."

"Can't you feel it, dove? The glamour of this place?" Leanansidhe leaned down, gesturing to the walls and fountain. "Some places in the mortal world are more magical than others, hot spots for glamour, if you will. It draws us like a moth to a flame—exiles, solitary and court fey alike. Besides, darling—" Leanansidhe straightened with a sniff. "Even our kind appreciates a bit of pampering now and then."

A blond, well-dressed satyr welcomed Leanansidhe with a kiss on both cheeks, before turning to me with a dazzling smile.

"Ah, so this is the princess I've heard so much about," he gushed, taking my hand to press it to his lips. "She's absolutely adorable. But—" and he glanced at Leanansidhe "—I can see what you mean about her hair. And her *nails.*" He shuddered and shook his head before I could say anything. "Well, leave it to me. We'll have her looking fabulous in no time."

"Work your magic, Ben," Leanansidhe said, wandering away toward a back door. "I'll be with Miguel if you need me, darling. Meghan dear, just do what Ben says and you'll be fine." She waved her hand airily as she sauntered through the door, and was gone.

Ben turned to me and clasped his furry hands. "Well, sweetcakes, you're in luck. We have the rest of the evening booked for you."

"Really?" I couldn't help sounding dubious. I had never

been to one of these places before, let alone one run completely by the fey, and didn't know what to expect. "How long can it take to do hair?"

Ben laughed. "Oh, sweet pea, you're killing me. Come, now. We've got a lot to do."

THE NEXT FEW HOURS flew by in a confused blur. The fey staff, mostly satyrs and a few brownies, were alarmingly attentive. They took my clothes away and wrapped me in a very white bathrobe. I was made to lie on my back while brownies in white suits slathered cream on my face and put cucumbers over my eyes, telling me to lie still. After maybe an hour of this, they sat me up, and a cute satyr named Miroku soaked my hands in a warm bath that smelled like cocoa and coffee beans. He massaged my hands with lotion before meticulously filing, polishing, and painting my nails. Then the whole procedure was done to my feet. After that, they whisked me away to the stylist, who shampooed, trimmed and styled my hair—with bronze scissors, I noted—chatting at me all the while. It was odd. I won't say I didn't enjoy all the attention and pampering, but I did feel a bit dazed through the whole process, and a little out of place. This wasn't me. I wasn't a princess or a superstar or anything special. I was a poor pig-farmer girl from Louisiana, and I didn't belong here.

They were adding the final touches of makeup to my eyes and lips when Leanansidhe sauntered back into the room, looking so smug and relaxed that her skin glowed. She had dropped her more human glamour, and her ethereal beauty filled the room, red-gold hair nearly blinding under the artificial lights. Ben trailed behind her, gushing about how radiant she looked.

"Mmm yes, I swear that Miguel is a virtual musician with his fingers," Leanansidhe murmured with a catlike stretch, raising too-slender arms over her head. "If you didn't need him so badly, love, I'd kidnap him myself and take him home. That kind of talent is hard to find, believe me. Well now," she exclaimed when she saw me. "Look at you, darling. You're a completely different person. I barely recognize you."

"Isn't she cute?" Ben added, beaming at me. "Don't you love what they did with her hair? I adore the highlights, and Patricia does layering so well."

"It's perfect," Leanansidhe nodded, studying me with a half smile that made me very uncomfortable. "If I don't recognize her, no one in SciCorp will, either."

I wanted to say something, but at that moment, a strange odor cut through the smell of perfume, makeup and moisturizers, stopping me mid-breath. Leanansidhe and Ben stiffened, as did every faery in the room. A couple brownies went scurrying away in terror, and the faery patrons began to murmur and shift restlessly as the foreign smell grew stronger. I recognized it, and my heart sped up, beating against my ribs. Metal. There was an Iron faery on the premises.

And then, it walked through the door.

My stomach turned over, and some of the patrons gasped. The Iron faery was dressed in a dove-gray business suit, and an expressive-looking one at that. Short black hair didn't conceal the long pointed ears, or the Bluetooth phone near his jaw. His skin, green as circuit board, glinted with hundreds of blinking lights, wires and computer chips. Behind thick, wire-rimmed glasses, his eyes shimmered green, blue and red.

Smooth as glass, Ben sidled in front of me, blocking my view but also shielding me from the faery's gaze. I froze and tried to be as invisible as possible.

"Well." The Iron faery's voice, thick with mockery, cut through the room. "Isn't anyone going to invite me in? Give me a pamphlet? Tell me your services? For such a high-ranking business, the customer service leaves much to be desired."

For a moment, nobody moved. Then one of the satyrs edged forward, shaking but furious at the same time. "We don't serve your kind here."

"Really?" The faery put a hand to his chest, feigning astonishment. "Well, I must say, I'm rather embarrassed. Then again, I could probably kill you all without even thinking about it, so I suppose a little prejudice is acceptable."

Leanansidhe stepped forward, her hair coiling behind her like snakes. "What do you want, abomination?"

"Leanansidhe." The Iron faery smiled. "You are Leanansidhe, aren't you? We've heard of you, you and your little network of spies. Word is, you know the location of Oberon's daughter, the Summer princess."

"I know a lot, darling." Leanansidhe sounded utterly bored and disinterested. "It's my business to be informed, for my own amusement and safety. I don't make a habit of involving myself. Nor do I make a habit of conversing with iron abominations. So, if we're quite done here, I think you should leave."

"Oh, I'll be gone soon enough." The Iron faery didn't seem the least bit perturbed. "But, my boss has a message for you, and an offer. Give us the location of Oberon's daughter, and all your crimes will be abolished when we take the Nevernever. You can go home. Don't you want to go home, Leanansidhe?" He raised his voice, addressing the rest of the assembled fey. "And that goes for every half-breed and exile, pure-blooded or not. Help us find the Summer princess, and your place in the Nevernever will be assured. The Iron King welcomes all who want to serve him."

He paused after this announcement, waiting for someone to step forward. No one moved. Probably because Leanansidhe, standing in the middle of the room, was throwing off some seriously scary vibes, flickering the lamps with her power. Which was a good thing, because everyone was looking at her and not me.

The Iron faery waited a moment longer, and when no one volunteered to piss off the Queen of the Exiles, he stepped back with a smile. "Well. If anyone changes his mind, just call us. We're everywhere. And we will come for you, in the end."

He spun on a heel and left, footsteps clicking over the tile. Everyone watched him go. Leanansidhe glowered at the door until the last traces of iron faded away, then spun on me.

"Party's over, darling. Let's go. Ben, you're a doll and your assistance today is much appreciated, but we really must dash."

"Of course, girl." Ben waved to us as we hurried out. "You bring that cutie back to see me soon, okay? And good luck infiltrating the megacorporation!"

WHEN WE RETURNED to the mansion, we found Puck and Ironhorse discussing strategy with Kimi and Nelson, who had returned from their mission. All four were huddled around the library table, heads bent close together, muttering in low voices. When we came in, followed by several redcaps carrying our bags, they straightened quickly, and their eyes went wide. Even Ironhorse's glowing eyes got big and round when we swept through the door.

"Wow, Meghan!" Kimi bounced in place, clapping her hands. "You look awesome! I love what you did with your hair."

"PRINCESS." Ironhorse looked me up and down, nodding in approval. "TRULY, YOU ARE A VISION."

I glanced at Puck, who was staring at me in a daze. "Um…" he stammered, while I nearly went into shock with the novelty of actually rendering Puck speechless. "You look…nice," he muttered at last.

I blushed, suddenly self-conscious.

"Children." Leanansidhe clapped her hands, bringing our attention back to her. "If we are going to retrieve the scepter, we need to move quickly. You, streetrats." She snapped her fingers at Kimi and Nelson. "Did you get what I sent you for, darlings?"

Kimi nodded at Nelson, who dug in his pocket and held up a plastic ID card. The face of a bespectacled blond woman glared out from the right corner, lips pursed as if trying to kill the camera with a look. Nelson tossed the card to Leanansidhe, who studied it disdainfully.

"Rosalyn Smith. A bit old, but she'll have to do. Well, then." She turned to the rest of us. "Tomorrow is a big day, darlings. Don't stay up too late. I'll meet you in the foyer tomorrow morning. Meghan, dove, you really need to figure out that code before tomorrow. Operation Scepter begins at dawn. Ta!" She gestured dramatically and vanished in a swirl of glitter.

THAT NIGHT, I was too nervous to sleep. I lay on my bed, Grimalkin dozing beside me on the pillow, trying to figure out the code but really just staring at the numbers until my eyes glazed over. I kept visualizing everything that could go wrong during the mission, which was a rather lengthy list. In a few hours, we were going to sneak into SciCorp using some woman's badge, grab the scepter, and book out before anyone realized we were there. As if it would be that easy, like a walk on the beach. As if they wouldn't have the scepter guarded day and night.

There was a soft rap on my door, and Puck peeked his head inside.

"Hey, Princess. Thought you could use something to eat. Mind if I come in?"

I shook my head, and Puck entered with a plate bearing

sandwiches and apple slices. "Here," he announced, setting it down on the bed. "You should eat something. I tried making something better, but Cook chased me out of the kitchen with a rolling pin. I don't think she's very fond of me." He snickered and fell across the bed, helping himself to an apple slice as he got comfortable.

"Appreciate it," I murmured, picking up a sandwich. Cheese and…more cheese; better than nothing, I guessed. "Where's Ironhorse?"

"Off with the two streetrats, discussing strategy," Puck replied, stuffing the whole apple wedge into his mouth. "You should hear them—they think they're in a James Bond movie or something." He noticed me fiddling with a corner of the paper square and sat up. "How's it going, Princess?"

I crumpled the paper into a wad and threw it across the room. Puck blinked. "Um, not well, I assume?"

"I don't get it," I sighed, drawing my hand across my eyes. "I've tried everything I can think of to make heads or tails of it—addition, multiplying the lines, division—and I still don't get it. And if I can't decrypt the stupid code, we won't get up to the right floor, which means we won't get the scepter, which means everyone will die because of me!"

"Hey." Puck sat up and put an arm around me. "Why are you freaking out? This is nothing, Princess. This should be cake for you. You're the one who took down the Iron King. You marched into the heart of enemy territory and kicked ass. This isn't any different."

"Yes, it is!" I put my sandwich down and stared at him. "This is worlds apart! Puck, when I faced Machina, it was to rescue Ethan, just Ethan. I'm not saying he wasn't important—I would've died to save him in a heartbeat. But it was only one person." I closed my eyes and leaned into Puck's chest, listening to his heartbeat for a few seconds. "If I screw this up," I muttered, "if I don't get the scepter back, *everyone* will die. Not just you and Ironhorse and the others, but everyone. Faery will be wiped out. No Summer, no Winter, nothing. Nothing but the Iron fey will be left. Now do you see why I'm a little jumpy?"

I didn't mention that I wished Ash was here. That he was the main reason I'd been brave in the Iron Kingdom. I missed him, his calm, unflinching determination, his quiet self-confidence.

Puck shifted so that he was facing me, tilting my chin to look at me square. I met his eyes and saw a hundred churning emotions in his emerald gaze.

"I'm here," he murmured, running long fingers through my hair. "Don't forget that. No matter what happens, I'll protect you." He leaned in, resting his forehead to mine. I smelled apples on his breath, saw my own reflection in his eyes. "I'll never leave your side, no matter what comes at us. Count on it."

My heart thumped in my ears. I knew I was standing on the edge of a vast precipice, looking down. I knew I should pull away, that if I stayed here, a line would be crossed, and we could never go back.

I closed my eyes instead. And Puck kissed me.

His lips were hesitant at first, brushing lightly against mine, giving me room to pull away. When I pressed into him, he cupped the back of my head and kissed me in earnest. I wrapped my arms around his neck and pulled him close, wanting to forget everything that was happening, to drown myself in feeling. Maybe now the gaping hurt and loneliness would go away for a little while. Puck shoved the plate off the bed and leaned back, pulling me down with him, his lips suddenly at my neck, tracing a line of fire down my skin.

"If you are going to do that, would you mind not jostling

the bed so much?" came a sarcastic voice near the headboard. "Perhaps you could roll around on the floor."

Blushing furiously, I looked up. Grimalkin lay on the pillow, watching us with a bemused, half-lidded stare. Puck followed my gaze and let out an explosive sigh.

"Did I ever mention how much I hate cats?"

"Do not blame me, Goodfellow." Grimalkin blinked, managing to sound bored and indignant at the same time. "I was minding my own business long before you and the princess started humping like rabbits."

Puck snorted. Rolling to his stomach, he pushed himself off the bed and pulled me up with him, wrapping me in his arms. My face flamed, but whether it was from Grimalkin's ill-timed comments or something else, I couldn't tell.

"I'd better go," Puck sighed, sounding reluctant. "I told Ironhorse I'd look at some blueprints Kimi managed to swipe from somewhere." His gaze strayed to the scattered food on the floor, sandwiches and apple slices everywhere, and he bit down a sheepish grin. "Erm, sorry about the mess, Princess. And don't worry about the code, we'll figure something out. Try to get some sleep, okay? We'll be right outside."

He bent down, as if to kiss me, but I couldn't meet his eyes and looked away. He paused, then placed a light kiss on my forehead and left, shutting the door behind him.

I collapsed to the bed, burying my face in a pillow. What had I done? I kissed Puck, because he was there. Because I was scared and lonely for someone else. Puck loved me, and I had kissed him for all the wrong reasons. I'd kissed him thinking of Ash. And…I liked it.

Guilt gnawed at me. I missed Ash, and the longing was ripping my stomach to pieces, but I also wanted Puck to come back and kiss me some more.

"I am so screwed up," I muttered, flopping back on the bed.

The cracks in the ceiling smirked at me, and I groaned. "What am I going to do?"

"Hopefully obsess in silence so I can get to sleep," Grimalkin said without opening his eyes. He flexed his claws, yawned, and burrowed deeper into the pillow. "Perhaps you can work on deciphering the code so that we can retrieve the scepter. I would hate to put in all this work for nothing."

I glared at him, but he was right. And, maybe it would take my mind off Puck for a while. "I mean, it's not like I'm cheating on Ash or anything," I reasoned, retrieving the crumpled ball of paper and climbing back onto the bed. "He was the one who dumped me and said to forget about him. We're over. Actually, I'm not sure we had anything in the first place."

Grimalkin didn't answer. I stared at the code and sighed again, heavily, as the numbers seemed to crawl across the paper like ants. "I'm never going to get this, Grim," I muttered. "This is hopeless. You'd have to be a mathematical genius or something."

Grimalkin thumped his tail and shifted around so that his back was to me. "Try looking at the code as a riddle, instead of a mathematical equation," he muttered. "Perhaps you are trying too hard to fit it to a formula. The Iron fey are still fey, after all, and riddles are in our blood."

A riddle, huh? I looked down at the paper again and frowned. I still couldn't make heads or tails of the stupid code, no matter how much I looked at it.

3
13
1113
3113
132113
1...

"Grim, I don't—"

"Read it out loud, human." Grim sounded annoyed but resigned, as if he knew he wasn't going to get any sleep until he helped me. "If you must make noise, at least try to be useful."

"Fine," I muttered. "But it's not going to help." Grim didn't reply, so I started reading it from the top. "Three. One-three. One-one-one-three. Three-one-one-three." I stopped, frowning. It sounded different, reading it out loud. I tried the third line again. "One-one, one-three."

One 1. One 3.

I blinked. Could it really be that simple? I ran through the rest of the lines, just to be sure, and my eyes widened as it all clicked into place. "I...I got it! I think. Wait a minute." I scanned the paper again. "Yes, that's right! It's not just a number riddle, it's a language riddle, too! You were right, Grim! Look!" I shoved the paper at Grimalkin, who continued to ignore me, but I went on anyway. "Each of the lines describes the line before it. The first number is a three, so the second line goes, One 3. The next line is One 1, One 3, and so on. So, if that's the case, the last line of the riddle, and the answer to the code would have to be..." I counted the numbers in my head. "1-1-1-3-1-2-2-1-1-3." I felt a thrill of pride and excitement, somehow knowing I was right, and couldn't help the huge grin spreading over my face. "I figured it out, Grim! We can get the scepter after all."

Grimalkin didn't answer. His eyes were closed, and I couldn't tell if he was asleep or faking it. I considered tracking down Puck and Ironhorse to share in my victory, but on reflection I wasn't sure I wanted to face Puck just then. So I lay on the bed, listening to the brownies scurry back and forth, cleaning up apple slices, while my mind replayed Puck's kiss until the memory was seared into my brain. Guilt and excitement assaulted me by turns. One moment, I was ready to drag Puck back here to finish what we'd started, the next, I missed Ash so much my chest hurt. I stayed awake, too hyped up to sleep, until a brownie poked his head in to tell me it was dawn and Leanansidhe was waiting for me.

# CHAPTER FIFTEEN

*Operation Scepter*

The woman stared at me over the gold rim of her glasses, lips pursed in a disdainful expression. She wore a black business suit that clung to her body, and her hair was pulled into a tight yet elegant bun, giving her a stern demeanor. Her makeup was perfect, and the towering black heels made her seem taller and even more imposing.

"What do you think, darling?" Leanansidhe asked, sounding pleased. "The glasses might be a bit much, but we don't want to take any chances today."

I stuck out my tongue at the woman, who did the same in the mirror's reflection. "It's perfect," I said, amazed. "I don't even recognize myself. I look like a lawyer or something."

"Hopefully enough to get you into SciCorp this afternoon," Leanansidhe murmured, and all the dread and fear I'd managed to suppress all morning rose up like a black tide. I swallowed hard to keep the nausea down, wishing I hadn't eaten that box of powdered doughnuts Kimi brought in for breakfast. I wouldn't look very professional if I puked all over my expensive shoes.

Puck, Kimi, Nelson and Ironhorse were in the foyer, huddled around a blueprint when we came in, me wobbling behind Leanansidhe in my flimsy heels. Grimalkin dozed on the top of the piano, his tail brushing the keys, ignoring us all. I saw Leanansidhe glance his way and wince, as if imagining scratch marks on the polished wood.

Puck glanced up at me and smiled. He held out a hand, and I tottered up to him, grabbing his arm for support. My toes throbbed, and I leaned into him, trying to take the weight off my feet. How did women do it, walking around in these things every day without snapping their ankles?

"How's that walking thing coming?" Puck murmured so that only I could hear.

"Shut up." I smacked his arm. "I'm still learning, okay? This is like walking around on toothpicks." He snickered, and I shifted my attention to the map spread out between them. "What are we looking at?"

"The plan," Kimi answered, standing on tiptoes to bend over the table. "This is the SciCorp entrance," the half-phouka continued, pointing to an obscure line near the bottom of the paper. I squinted, but I couldn't make it out from all the other lines spread over the blueprint. "According to Warren," Kimi went on, tracing a finger up to another line, "the scepter is being held here, between floors twenty-nine and thirty."

"I still don't know how that's possible," I muttered. "How can a building have a floor between floors?"

"The same way I can have a mansion between the mortal world and the Nevernever, darling," Leanansidhe answered, looking at Grimalkin as if she really wanted to shoo him off the piano. "The Iron fey have their horrible glamour, just as we have ours. We turn into rabbits, they eat bank accounts. Grim, darling, do you *have* to sleep there?"

"You, Puck and Ironhorse will come in here," Kimi continued, tapping the bottom of the blueprint. "Past the doors will be the security checkpoint, which will scan your ID card. Puck and Ironhorse will be invisible to mortal eyes, so we don't have to worry about them being seen."

"What if there are Iron fey on the first floor?" Puck asked.

"There aren't," Kimi replied, glancing at him. "Nelson and I checked it out. If the Iron fey are going into the building, they're not using the front doors."

That sounded ominous, like the Iron fey could have hidden doors or trods we didn't know about, but there was nothing for it now.

"Once you're past the checkpoint, the elevators are here," Kimi went on, tracing the path with her finger before giving us a grave look. "And this is where things get dicey. I don't know how you're getting up to floor twenty-nine and a half. They might have a certain button only those with Sight can see, or there might be a password, or you might have to press buttons in a certain sequence. I have no idea. Alternatively, you can take the stairs, here, but that will mean climbing up thirty floors from ground level, with no guarantee there will be an entrance to floor twenty-nine and a half."

"We'll burn that bridge when we come to it," Puck said, waving it away. "So, what about the floor with the scepter? What can we expect?"

"Wait a minute," I warned, putting a hand on his chest. "This sounds awfully risky. We don't know if we can even get up to the twenty-ninth floor? How is this good planning?"

"Twenty-nine point five," Puck corrected me. "And it's not. Good planning, I mean. But, look at it this way." He grinned. "We either go with our gut, or we don't go at all. Not a lot of choices, Princess. But, don't worry." He put an arm around my shoulders and squeezed. "You don't need a plan. You have the Puck with you, remember? I'm an expert at this. And I've never needed an elaborate plan to pull anything off."

There was a loud clank from the piano, as Leanansidhe finally convinced Grimalkin to sleep elsewhere. Annoyed, the cat had slid from his perch and landed with his full weight on the keys, then leaped to the bench. "Worry not, human," the cat sighed, giving himself a thorough shake. "I am going with you as well. With Goodfellow's exemplary planning, someone has to make sure you go through the right door."

"Huh." Puck snorted and glared at the feline. "That's awfully helpful of you, cat. What's in it for you?"

"Grimalkin and I worked something out, darling, don't worry about it." Leanansidhe gave the blueprint a cursory glance over Puck's shoulder before dismissing it with a sniff. "Remember, pets, when you get to the floor where the scepter is being held, you must be prepared for anything. Robin, it will be up to you and the iron thing to protect the princess. I'm quite sure they won't have the scepter lying around where anyone can snatch it. There will most likely be guards, wards, nasty things like that."

"I WILL PROTECT THE PRINCESS WITH MY LIFE," Ironhorse boomed, making Puck grimace and Kimi pin back her ears. "I SWEAR, WHILE I STILL LIVE AND BREATHE, NO HARM WILL BEFALL HER. WE WILL RETRIEVE THE SCEPTER, OR WE WILL DIE TRYING."

"And personally, I'd like *not* to do the dying thing," Puck added.

I was about to agree, when there was a commotion in the hall, and a moment later a human rushed into the room. It was Charles, the crazy piano player, looking as wild and panicked as I'd ever seen, even more than when we'd faced the redcaps. His anguished brown eyes met mine and he lurched forward, only to be stopped by Ironhorse stepping in front of me with a warning growl.

"She…she's leaving?" Charles looked utterly despondent, wringing his hands and biting his bottom lip. "No no no. Can't leave again. Can't disappear. Stay."

"Charles." Leanansidhe's voice made the air tremble, and the poor man gave her a terrified look. "What are you doing here? Go back to your room."

"It's all right, Charles," I said quickly, as he looked on the verge of tears. "I'm not leaving for good. I'm coming back, don't worry."

He stopped wringing his hands, straightened, and looked at me dead on. And for just a moment, I saw him without the crazy light to his eyes. The way he must have been…before. Young. Tall. Handsome, with laugh lines around his mouth and jaw. A kind yet weary face. One that was vaguely familiar.

"You'll come back?" he murmured. "Promise?"

I nodded. "Promise."

Then Leanansidhe clapped her hands, the sharp rap making us jump. "Charles, darling," she said, and was it my imagination, or did she sound a bit nervous? "You heard the girl. She'll be back. Now, why don't you find the other Charles and find something to play tonight? Go on, now. Shoo." She waved her hand, and Charles, with one last look at me, stumbled from the room.

I frowned at Leanansidhe. "Other Charles? There's more than one?"

"I call them all Charles, darling." Leanansidhe shrugged. "I'm horrible with names, as you've no doubt seen, and human males look virtually the same to me. So they're all Charles, for simplicity's sake."

Grimalkin sighed and leaped from the bench. "We are wasting time," he announced, bottlebrush tail held straight up as he trotted past. "If we are going to get this circus started, we should leave now."

"Good luck, darlings," Leanansidhe called as we followed Grim out of the room. "When you return, you must tell me *all* about it. Meghan, dove, don't do anything I wouldn't do."

KIMI AND NELSON LED the way back to the outside world. We followed them through several rooms, where groups of fey and humans watched us leave, down a red carpeted hallway, then up a long spiral staircase that finally stopped at a trapdoor in the ceiling. The trapdoor was oddly shaped: round, gray and heavy looking. I peered closer and saw that it was the bottom of a manhole cover. When Nelson pushed it up to peek through, bright sunlight spilled through the crack, and the smell of asphalt, tar and exhaust fumes assaulted my nose. While the half-troll scanned the road overhead, waiting for a clear spot, Kimi turned to me.

"This is as far as we go, I'm afraid." The little half-phouka looked disappointed as she handed me a plastic ID card on a string.

"You're not coming?"

She gave me an apologetic smile, nodding to Puck and Ironhorse. "Nah, you have your champions. Those two are purebloods. They'll be invisible to humans just by virtue of being fey. Nelson and I can't work glamour as well, and it would look suspicious if you were seen with a couple of streetrats in tow. Don't worry, though. We're really close to SciCorp, and from here you can take a taxi or something. Here." She handed me a slip of paper, scrawled on with bright green ink. "That's the address you're looking for. The trod back will be on Fourteenth and Maple, and you want the second manhole from the left. Got it?"

I nodded, as my stomach fluttered nervously. "Got it."

"Clear," Nelson grunted, and shoved the manhole cover out of the way. Puck scrambled out first, then pulled me up after him. As Ironhorse and Grimalkin crawled out, I gazed around the middle of a busy street,

A horn blared, and a bright red Mustang screeched to a stop a few feet away. "Get out of the road, you crazy bitch!" the driver yelled from the window, and I scrambled to the edge of the curb. The driver roared off, oblivious to the massive Iron faery who swung a huge fist at the hood, barely missing.

"You ran a light anyway, dickhead!" I yelled after him, as Puck and Ironhorse joined me on the sidewalk. People stared at me, shaking their heads or chuckling under their breath. I scowled, trying to calm my racing heart. They wouldn't laugh if they could see Ironhorse looming over me like a protective bodyguard, glaring at anyone who got too close.

"Are you all right?" Puck asked anxiously, standing so close that his breath tickled my cheek. I nodded, and he kissed the top of my head, making butterflies swarm through my stomach. "Don't scare me like that, Princess."

"Well, that was amusing." Grimalkin hopped lightly onto the sidewalk, making a show of taking his sweet time. "Are we quite ready to go, now? Human, you know where we are headed, correct?"

I looked down at the paper, still clutched in my hand. It trembled only a little. "You guys okay with taking a taxi?"

Puck made a face. "Now see, anyone else would have a few qualms about riding in a big metal box, but I've learned to deal." He smirked. "All those years I took the bus with you was good practice. Still, keep the windows open, Princess."

We found a pay phone, and I called for a taxi. Ten minutes

later, a bright yellow cab pulled up, driven by a bearded man chewing a thick cigar. He kept glancing at me in the rearview window and smiling, oblivious to the two faeries pressed on either side of me, one glaring, one hanging his head out the window. I sat squashed between Puck and Ironhorse, with Grim on my lap and both windows rolled down, as we tore through the city streets. The smoke from the cabby's cigar stung my nose and made my eyes water, and Puck looked positively green.

At last, we pulled up in front of a gleaming tower, the sunlight reflecting off the mirrored walls as they rose into the sky. I paid the cab fare, and we piled out of the car. As soon as we were free of the cab, Puck started coughing. He looked pale and sweaty, and my heart lurched, remembering Ash in the wasteland of the Iron fey. Ironhorse watched him curiously, as though fascinated, and Grimalkin sat down to wash his tail.

"Ugh, that was unpleasant," Puck muttered when the harsh explosions finally stopped. He spit on the sidewalk and wiped his mouth with the back of his hand. "I don't know what was worse, the cab or the stench coming from the guy's cigar."

"Will you be all right?" I gave him a worried look, but he just grinned.

"Never better, Princess. So, here we are." He craned his neck, gazing up at the looming expanse of SciCorp towers. His eyes gleamed with familiar mischief. "Let's get this party started."

MY HEART BEHAVED ITSELF until we passed through the large glass doors. Then it started beating my ribs so forcefully I thought they would break.

"Oh, wow," I whispered, stopping to gape at the enormous lobby. A great vaulted ceiling soared above us, maybe eight or ten stories, with strange metallic designs dangling from wires, glittering in the sun. People in expensive suits rushed by us, designer shoes clicking over the sterile gray floor. I saw cameras in every corner, armed guards hovering by a turnstile security gate, and I locked my knees together to keep them from shaking.

"Steady, Princess." As I stood there, gawking like an idiot, Puck's firm hands came to rest on my shoulders. "You can do this. Keep your head up, your back straight, and it wouldn't hurt to sneer at anyone who makes eye contact." He squeezed my shoulders and bent close, his breath warm on my ear. "We're right behind you."

I gave my head a jerky bob. Puck squeezed my shoulders one last time and released me. Raising my chin, I took a deep breath, squared my shoulders and marched toward the security desk.

A guard in a slate-gray uniform eyed me with disinterest as I approached, looking the way I felt in algebra class, eyes glazed over and bored. The man in front of me muttered a quick, "Mornin', Ed," before passing his ID card under a scanner. The red light blipped to green, and the man swept through the turn-stile.

My turn. Adopting what I hoped was an imperious expres-sion, I sauntered up to the gate. "Good morning, Edward," I greeted, slipping Rosalyn Smith's badge under the flickering red scanner light. The guard bobbed his head with a polite smile, not even looking at me. *Ha,* I thought, triumphant. *That was easy. We're home free.*

Then the scanner let out a shrill warning beep, and my heart stood still.

Ed stood up, frowning. "Sorry, miss," he said, as ice water began creeping up my spine. "But I'll have to see your badge."

Puck, Grim and Ironhorse, already on the other side of the gate, looked back fearfully. I swallowed my terror, wondering if we should abandon the plan now and get the hell out. The guard held out his hand, waiting, and I forced myself to be calm.

"Of course." Thankfully, my voice didn't crack as I looped the badge from my neck and held it out. The guard took it and held it up to his face, squinting his eyes. I felt a dozen gazes on the back of my neck, and crossed my arms, trying to appear bored and irritated.

"Sorry, Ms. Smith." Ed finally looked up at me. "But did you know your card expired yesterday? You'll have to get a new one before tomorrow."

"Oh." Relief bloomed through my stomach. Maybe I could pull this off after all. "Of course," I muttered, trying to sound embarrassed. "I've been meaning to renew it, but you know how busy it's been lately. I just haven't had the time. I'll take care of it before I leave today. Thank you."

"No problem, Ms. Smith." Ed handed me the badge and tipped his hat. "You have a good morning." He pressed a button and waved me through.

I hurried around a corner and collapsed against the wall before I started hyperventilating.

"None of that, Princess," Puck said, pulling me to my feet just as a group of businessmen turned the corner, talking about reports and staff meetings and firing a junior executive. I avoided eye contact as they swept by, but they paid me no attention.

"By the way, you did great back there," Puck went on as we made our way down the brightly lit corridor. "I thought you would lose it, but you kept it together. Nice job, Princess."

I grinned.

"First hurdle cleared," Puck continued cheerfully. "Now, all we have to do is find floor twenty-nine point five, grab the scepter, and get out again. We're halfway home."

Easy for him to say. My heart had gone into overdrive, and a cold sweat was still dripping down the backs of my knees. I was just about to say so, when I noticed we had another problem. "Um, where's Grimalkin?"

We glanced around hastily, but the cat had disappeared. Maybe his faith in the plan had been shaken by the little scene at the gate, or maybe he'd just decided "the hell with this," and had taken off. It wouldn't be the first time.

"WHY WOULD HE ABANDON US?" Ironhorse questioned, making me wince as his voice echoed down the hall. Thank goodness humans couldn't hear faeries, either. "I THOUGHT THE CAITH SITH HAD HONORABLE INTENTIONS. I WOULD NOT HAVE PEGGED HIM A COWARD."

Puck snorted. "You don't know Grimalkin very well, then," he commented, but I wasn't sure I agreed. Grimalkin had always come through for us, even when he disappeared with no explanation. Though Ironhorse looked stunned, I wasn't worried; Grimalkin would most assuredly pop up again when least expected.

"Never mind." I turned and continued walking. Ironhorse still looked confused, almost hurt that an ally could betray him like this. I gave him what I hoped was a reassuring smile. "It's okay, Ironhorse. Grim can take care of himself, and he'll show up if we need him. We should keep looking for the scepter."

"IF YOU SAY SO, PRINCESS."

At the end of the corridor, we came to a pair of elevators.

"Floor twenty-nine point five," I mused, pressing the up button. A few seconds passed before the doors opened with a *ding* and two women exited, passing us without a second glance. Peeking inside, I scanned the wall but, as I expected, there was no button 29.5.

I stepped over the threshold into the box, Ironhorse following at my heels. Cheerful orchestra music played at a muted volume over the speakers, and the floor was carpeted in red. Puck rushed inside and stood in the middle of the floor, away from the walls, arms crossed tightly to his chest. Ironhorse turned and blinked at him.

"ARE YOU ALL RIGHT, GOODFELLOW?" he asked, his voice nearly bringing tears to my eyes as it echoed within the box. Puck gave him a fearsome smile.

"Me? I'm fine. Big metal box in a big metal tube? Not a problem. Hurry and get us to the right floor, Princess."

I nodded and unfolded a piece of paper from my suit pocket, holding it up to the light. "Well, here goes nothing," I murmured, and started punching in the code on the elevator buttons. 1-1-1-3-1-2-2-1-1-3. The numbers lit up as they were punched, singing out a little tune like the buttons on a cell phone.

I hit the last 3 and stepped back, waiting and holding my breath. For a moment, nothing happened. Ironhorse's raspy breathing echoed off the metal walls, filling the box with the smell of smoke. Puck coughed and muttered something under his breath. I started to punch the code in again, thinking I'd pressed a wrong button, when the doors swooshed shut. The lights dimmed, the music ceased, and a large white button shimmered into existence, marked with a bold 29.5.

I shared a glance with my companions, who nodded.

"Floor twenty-nine point five," I whispered, and hit the button with my thumb. "Going up."

THE ELEVATOR STOPPED, and the doors opened with a cheerful ding.

We peered out at a long, brightly lit hallway with numerous doors lining its walls and gray tiles leading to single door at the very end. I knew we were in the right place. I could feel it in the air, a faint buzz, a sharp tingle just below my skin. It made my neck hairs stand on end, and was oddly familiar. Glancing at Puck and Ironhorse, I knew they could feel it, too.

We inched down the corridor, Puck in front and Ironhorse bringing up the rear. Around us, our footsteps echoed in the silence. We passed doors without hesitation, knowing they were the wrong ones. I could feel the buzzing getting louder the closer we got to the end of the hall.

Then, we were at the last door, and Puck leaned against it, putting his ear to the wood. *I don't hear anything,* he mouthed at us, and pointed to the handle. *Shall we?*

Ironhorse nodded, clenching his massive fists. Puck reached down and freed his daggers, gesturing to me with a point. Biting my lip, I reached out and carefully turned the handle.

The door swung forward with a creak, and a waft of frigid air hit me in the face. I shivered, resisting the impulse to rub my arms as my breath clouded the air before me. Someone had cranked the AC down to like zero degrees; the room was a freezer box as we stepped inside.

A dozen or so humans in expensive business suits sat around a long, U-shaped table in the center of the floor. From the looks of it, we had interrupted a business meeting, for they all turned and stared at me with various degrees of annoyance and confusion. At the end of the table, a swivel chair sat with its back to us, hiding the speaker or CEO or whoever was in charge. I suddenly remembered all the times I'd snuck into class late and had to scurry down the aisles to my desk while everyone watched. My face burned, and for a moment, you could hear a pin drop.

"Um, sorry," I muttered, backing away. The business suits continued to stare at me. "Sorry. Wrong room. We'll just…go."

"Oh, why don't you stick around, my dear." The buzzing, high-pitched voice made my skin crawl. At the front of the table, the figure swiveled the chair around to face us, smiling. She wore a neon-green business suit, radioactive-blue lipstick, and bright yellow glasses above a thin, sneering face. Her hair, a myriad of computer cables, was bound atop her head in a colorful mockery of a bun. She held the scepter in green-nailed hands, like a queen observing her subjects, and my stomach gave a jolt of recognition.

"VIRUS!" Ironhorse boomed.

"No need to shout, old man. I'm right here." Virus put her heels on the table and regarded us smugly. "I've been waiting for you, girl. Looking for this, are you?" She lifted her arm, and I gasped. The Scepter of the Seasons pulsed a strange, sickly green light through her fingers. Virus bared her teeth in a smile. "I was expecting the girl and her clown to come sniffing after it, but I never expected the honorable Ironhorse to turn on us. Tsk-tsk." She shook her head. "Loyalty is so overrated these days. How the mighty have fallen."

"YOU DARE ACCUSE ME?" Ironhorse stalked forward, smoke drifting from his mouth and nostrils. We hurried after him. "YOU ARE THE BETRAYER, WHO FOLLOWS THE COMMANDS OF THE FALSE KING. YOU ARE THE ONE WHO HAS FALLEN."

"Don't be so melodramatic," Virus sighed. "As usual, you have no idea what is really going on. You think I want to follow the wheezings of an obsolete monarch? I want that even less than you. When he put me in charge of stealing the scepter, I knew that was the last command I would ever follow. Poor Tertius, believing I was still loyal to his false king. The gullible fool handed me the scepter without a second thought." She smiled at us, fierce and terrible. "Now, *I* have the Scepter of the Seasons. I have the power. And if the false king wants it, he'll have to take it from me by force."

"I see," I said, coming to a stop a few feet from her. Around us, the men in business suits continued to stare. "*You* want to become the next ruler. You had no intention of giving it to the Iron King."

"Can you blame me?" Virus swung her feet off the table to smile at me. "How often have you disobeyed your king because his commands were rubbish? Goodfellow—" she pointed the scepter at Puck "—how often has the thought of rebelling crossed *your* mind? Don't tell me you've been a faithful little monkey, catering to Oberon's every desire, in all the years you've known him."

"That's different," I said.

"Really?" Virus sneered at me. "I can tell you, it wasn't difficult to convince Rowan. That boy's hatred and jealousy are inspiring. All he needed was a little push, a tiny promise of power, and he betrayed everything he knew. He was the one who told me you were coming for the scepter, you know." She snorted. "Of course, the claims of becoming immune to iron are completely false. As if thousands of years of history can be rewritten or erased. Iron and technology have been and will always be lethal to the traditional fey. That's why we're so inherently superior to you oldbloods. That's why you're going to fall so easily after the war."

Ironhorse growled, the furious rumble of an oncoming train. "I WILL TAKE THAT SCEPTER AND PLACE THE TRUE MONARCH OF THE IRON FEY ON THE THRONE," he vowed, taking a threatening step forward. "YOU WILL GIVE IT TO ME NOW, TRAITOR. YOUR HUMAN PUPPETS WILL NOT BE ENOUGH TO PROTECT YOU."

"Ah ah ah." Virus waggled a finger at him. "Not so fast. I didn't want my drones up here because they are delicate and rather squishy, but I'm not quite so stupid as to be unguarded." She smiled and gazed around the table. "All right, gentlemen. Meeting adjourned."

At that, all the humans sitting at the tables stood, shedding glamour like discarded jackets, filling the air with fraying strands of illusion. Human facades dropped away, to reveal a dozen faeries in spiky black armor, their faces sickly and pale beneath their helms. As one, the Thornguards drew their serrated black swords and pointed them at us, trapping us in a ring of faery steel.

My stomach twisted violently, wanting to crawl up my throat and make a break for the door. I heard Puck's exhalation of breath and Ironhorse's dismayed snort as he pressed closer to me. Virus snickered, leaning back in her chair.

"I'm afraid you've walked nose first into a trap, m'dears," she gloated as we tensed, ready to run or fight. "Oh, but you don't want to rush off now. I have one last little surprise for you." She giggled and snapped her fingers.

The door behind her creaked, and a dark figure stepped into the room, coming to stand behind the chair. This time, my heart dropped to my toes and stayed there.

"I'm sure you four know each other," Virus said, as my world shrank down to a narrow tunnel, blocking everything else out. "My greatest creation so far, I think. It took six Thornguards and nearly two dozen drones to bring him down, but it was *so* worth it. Ironic, isn't it? He nearly got away with the scepter the first time, and now he'll do anything to keep it here."

*No,* my mind whispered. *This isn't happening. No no no no no.*

"Ash," Virus purred as the figure came into the light, "say hello to our guests."

# CHAPTER SIXTEEN

*Traitor*

I stared at Ash in a daze, torn between relief that he was alive and an acute, sickening despair. This couldn't be real, what was happening. I had stepped into a nightmare world, where everything I loved was twisted into something monstrous and horrible. My legs felt weak, and I had to lean against Puck or I would've fallen.

Ironhorse snorted. "AN ILLUSION," he mocked, staring at Ash in contempt. "A SIMPLE GLAMOUR, NOTHING MORE. I HAVE SEEN WHAT HAPPENS TO THE OLD-BLOODS YOU IMPLANT WITH YOUR FOUL BUGS. THEY GO MAD, AND THEN THEY DIE. THAT IS NOT THE WINTER PRINCE, ANY MORE THAN THESE GUARDS."

"You think?" Virus's grin was frighteningly smug. "Well, if you're so sure, old man, you're welcome to try to stop him. It should be easy to defeat one simple guard, although I think you'll find the task harder than you ever expected." She turned a purely sadistic smile on me. "The princess knows, don't you, my dear?"

Ironhorse turned, a question in his eyes, but I couldn't take my gaze off Virus's bodyguard. "It's not an illusion," I whispered. "It really is him." The way my heart fluttered around my chest proved this was real. I stepped forward, ignoring the bristling Thornguard weapons, and the prince's gaze sharpened, cutting me like a knife. "Ash," I whispered, "it's me. Are you hurt? Say something."

Ash regarded me blankly, no glint of recognition in his silver eyes: no anger, sorrow, nothing. "All of you," he said in a quiet voice, "will die."

Shock and horror lanced through me, holding me immobile. Virus giggled her hateful, buzzing laugh. "It's no use," she taunted. "He hears you, he even recognizes you, but he remembers nothing of his old life. He's been completely reprogrammed, thanks to my bug. And now, he listens only to me."

I looked closer, and my heart twisted even more. In the shadows of the room, the prince's face was ashen, the skin pulled so tight across his bones it had split in places, showing open wounds beneath. His cheeks were hollow, and his eyes, though blank and empty, were bright with unspoken pain. I recognized that look; it was the same look Edgebriar had turned on us in the cave, teetering on the edge of madness. "It's killing him," I whispered.

"Well, only a little."

"Stop it," I hissed, and Virus arched a sardonic eyebrow. My heart pounded, but I set my jaw and plunged on. "Please," I begged, stepping forward. "Let him go. Let me take his place. I'll sign a contract, make a bargain, anything, if that's what you want. But take the bug out of his head and let him go."

"Meghan!" Puck snapped, and Ironhorse stared at me in

horror. I didn't care. I couldn't let Ash fade away into nothing, as if he had never existed at all. I imagined myself in a field of white flowers, watching a ghostly Ash and Ariella dance together in the moonlight, together at last. Except it would be a lie. Ash wouldn't be with his true love, even in death. He wouldn't be anything.

Virus chuckled. "Such devotion," she murmured, rising from the chair. "I'm terribly moved. Come here, Ash." Ash immediately stepped up beside her, and Virus laid a hand on his chest. "You should congratulate me," Virus continued, regarding the prince like a student with a winning science project. "I've finally discovered a way to implant my bugs in the fey system without killing them outright, or driving them mad within the first few hours. Instead of rewriting his brain—" she stroked Ash's hair, and I clenched my shaking fists, fighting the urge to leap across the table and rip out her eyes "—I had it take over his cervical nervous system, here." Her fingers dropped to the base of his skull, caressing it. "You're welcome to try to carve it out, I suppose, but I'm afraid that will be quite fatal for him. Only *I* can order my bugs to willingly release their hosts. As for your offer…" She threw me an indulgent smile. "You have only one thing I want, and I will take that from you momentarily. No, I find that I prefer my bodyguard as he is, for however long he has left."

My heart pounded. He was so close. I could reach over the table, grab his hand and pull him to safety. "Ash!" I cried, holding out my hand. "Jump, now! Come on, you can fight it. Please…" My voice dropped to a whisper. "Don't do this. Don't make us fight you…"

Ash gazed straight ahead, not moving a muscle, and a sob tore free from my throat. I couldn't reach him. Ash was lost to us. The cold stranger across the table had taken his place.

"Well." Virus took a step back. "This has grown tiresome.

I think it's time I took what I want from you, my dear. Ash."
She placed a hand on his shoulder. "Kill the princess. Kill them
all."

With a flash of blue light, Ash drew his sword and slashed
it across the table. It happened so quickly, I didn't even have
time to scream before the icy blade streaked down at my face.

Puck lunged in front of me and caught the blade with his
own, deflecting it with a screech and a flurry of sparks. I
stumbled back and Puck grabbed my wrist, dragging me away
even as I protested. "Retreat!" he yelled as the Thornguards
leaped across the tables with a roar. I looked back and saw Ash
jump gracefully onto the table, his terrible blank gaze fastened
on me. "Ironhorse, fall back, there are too many of them!"

With a bellow and a blast of flame, Ironhorse reared up into
his true form, breathing fire and lashing out with his hooves.
The guards fell back in shock and Ironhorse charged, knocking
several aside and clearing a path to the door. As the huge Iron
fey thundered past, Puck shoved me toward the exit. "Go!" he
shouted, and whirled to block Ash's sword, slicing down at his
back.

"Ash, stop this!" I cried, but the Winter prince paid me no
attention. As the Thornguards closed on us again, Puck snarled
a curse and threw a fuzzy black ball into their midst.

It burst into a maddened grizzly, which reared up with a
booming roar, startling everything in the room. As the Thornguards and Ash turned toward this new threat, Puck grabbed
my hand and yanked me out of the room.

"Been saving that, just in case," he panted, as Ironhorse
snorted with appreciation. "Now let's get out of here."

We ran for the elevator. The hallway seemed longer now,
the steel doors deliberately keeping their distance. I looked back
once and saw Ash stalking toward us, his sword radiating blue
light through the corridor. The icy calm on his face sent a bolt
of raw fear through me, and I wrenched my eyes from him.

Ahead of us, the elevator dinged. A second later, the doors slid open, and a squadron of Thornguards stepped into the hall.

"Oh, you gotta be kidding me," Puck exclaimed as we skidded to a halt. As one, the knights drew their swords and marched forward in unison, filling the corridor with the ring of their boots.

I looked behind us. Ash was advancing steadily as well, his eyes glassy and terrifying.

A click echoed through the hall and miraculously, one of the side doors swung open.

"How predictable," Grimalkin sighed, appearing in the doorway. We gaped at him, and he regarded us with amusement. "I thought you might need a second way out. Why is it always up to me to think of these things?"

"I would kiss you, cat," Puck said as we crowded through the doorway, "if we weren't in such a hurry. Also, the hairballs could be unpleasant."

I slammed the door and leaned against it, gasping as we took in our newest surroundings. A vast white room stretched before us, filled with hundreds upon hundreds of cubicles, creating a labyrinth of aisles. A low hum vibrated in the air, accompanied by the rhythmic sound of tapping keys. Humans sat at desks within each cubicle, dressed in identical white shirts and gray pants, staring glassy-eyed at the monitors as they typed away.

"Whoa," Puck muttered, looking around. "Cubicle hell."

Simultaneously, the tapping stopped. Chairs shifted and groaned as every single human in the room stood up and, as one, turned in our direction. And, as one, they opened their mouths and spoke.

*"We see you, Meghan Chase. You will not escape."*

If I hadn't been filled with a hollow, bone-numbing despair, I would've been terrified. Puck cursed and pulled out his dagger just as a *boom* shook the door behind us. "Looks like we're going straight through," he muttered, narrowing his eyes. "Grimalkin, get moving! Rusty, clear us a path!"

Grimalkin bounded into the maze, dodging feet and weaving through legs as the hordes of zombie-drones shuffled toward us. Ironhorse pawed the tile, put his head down and charged with a roar. Drones flung themselves at him, punching and clawing, but they bounced off or were thrown aside as the angry Iron fey stampeded through the hall. Puck and I followed in his wake, leaping over downed bodies, dodging the hands that grabbed for us. Someone latched on to my ankle once, but I let out a shriek and kicked him in the face, knocking him back. He fell away clutching my shoe, and I quickly shook the other off, running barefoot through the hall.

The maze of aisles and cubicles seemed to go on forever. I glanced over my shoulder and saw the mob of zombie heads bobbing above the cubicle walls, following us.

"Dammit," Puck snarled, following my gaze, "they're coming fast. How much farther, cat?"

"Here," Grimalkin said, darting around a cubicle. The room finally ended with a stark white wall and a door in the corner, marked with an Exit sign. "The emergency stairs," he explained as we rushed forward in relief. "This will take us to the street level. Hurry!"

As we charged the door, Ash stepped out of an aisle next to us, appearing from nowhere. There was no time to think or scream a warning. I threw myself to the side, hitting the wall with a jolt that knocked the wind from my lungs.

Time seemed to slow. Puck and Ironhorse bellowed something from far away. A blinding stab of pain shot up my arm. When I grabbed for it, my palm came away slick and wet. For a second, I stared at my fingers, not understanding.

*What happened? Did Ash...do this? Ash cut me?*

Stunned, I looked up into the glassy eyes of the Unseelie prince, his sword raised for the killing blow.

For just a moment, he hesitated. I saw the sword waver as his arm trembled, a flicker of torment crossing his face. Just a moment, before the blade came flashing down, but it was enough time for Ironhorse to lunge between us, shoving Ash away. I heard the hideous screech of metal as the blade ripped into Ironhorse's side and he staggered, almost going to his knees. Then Puck was pulling me to my feet, yelling at Ironhorse to get moving, and I was being dragged through the door, screaming at Puck to let me go. Ironhorse lurched to his feet and followed, dripping a thick black substance behind him, his wheezing breaths echoing down the stairwell. As we escaped SciCorp and fled into the streets, the last thing I remembered was watching the door close behind me on the stairs and seeing Ash's face through the window, a single tear frozen on his cheek.

PART THREE

# CHAPTER SEVENTEEN

*Choices*

In my dream, he was kneeling in the dead grass beneath a great iron tree, head bent, dark hair hiding his face. Around us, a swirling gray fog blanketed everything beyond a few feet, but I could sense another presence here, a cold, hostile being, watching me with cruel intelligence. I tried to ignore it as I approached the figure beneath the tree. He was shirtless, his pale skin covered in tiny red wounds, like punctures, down his spine and across his shoulders.

I blinked. For a moment, I could see the glistening strings of wire sunk into his body, coiling up and vanishing into the fog. I quickened my pace, but with every step I took, the body under the tree moved farther away. I started to run, stumbling and panting, but the fog was drawing him back into its possessive embrace, claiming him for its own.

Desperately, I called to him. He raised his head, and the look on his face was beyond despair. It was utter defeat, hopelessness and pain. His lips moved wordlessly, then the fog coiled around him and he was lost.

I stood there shivering as the mist grew dark, and the other presence hovered at the edge of my consciousness. As the dream faded and I sank into oblivion, I could still see his final words, mouthed to me in desperation, and they chilled me like nothing else.

*Kill me.*

CONSCIOUSNESS RETURNED slowly. I clawed myself up from sleep, feeling dizzy and confused as the world came into focus. Thankfully, I recognized my surroundings almost immediately. Leanansidhe's mansion: the foyer, if the huge fireplace was any indication. I lay on one of her comfortable sofas, dressed in slacks and a loose-collared shirt. Someone had taken off the slinky business suit, and of course I'd left my heels back in SciCorp.

"What happened?" I murmured, struggling to sit up. A blinding flare of pain stabbed up my arm and shoulder, and I gasped.

"Easy, Princess." Suddenly Puck was there, pushing me back down. "You lost a nice amount of blood—it made you woozy. You passed out on our way here. Just sit still for a minute."

I looked at the thick gauze wrapped around my arm and shoulder, a faint pink stain coming through the bandage. It hadn't even hurt until now.

A knot tightened in my stomach as hazy memories pushed their way to the surface. My throat closed up, and I suddenly felt like crying. Pushing those feelings away, I took a shaky breath and focused on the present.

"Where's Ironhorse?" I demanded. "And Grim? Did everyone get out okay?"

"I AM FINE, PRINCESS." Ironhorse, back in his more

human form, peered over the couch at me. "A LITTLE LESS THAN WHEN WE STARTED, BUT I WILL LIVE. MY ONLY REGRET IS THAT I COULD NOT PROTECT YOU FULLY."

"Really?" The door opened and Leanansidhe entered the room, followed by Grim and two brownies bearing a tray with mugs. "I would have a few more regrets than that, darling. Meghan, dove, try to drink this. It should help."

I struggled to sit up, gritting my teeth against the pain. Puck knelt beside the couch and eased me into a sitting position, then handed me the mug the brownies offered. The hot liquid smelled strongly of herbs, making my eyes water. I took a cautious sip, made a face, and swallowed it down.

"Kimi and Nelson?" I asked, forcing down more of the stuff. Gah, it was like drinking potpourri in hot water, but I could feel it working as it slid down my throat—a warm drowsiness stealing through my system. "Are they here, too?"

Leanansidhe swept around the couch, trailing smoke from her cigarette holder. "Haven't checked in yet, darling, but I'm sure they're fine. They're smart kids." With a flourish, she sat in the opposite chair and crossed her legs, watching me over her cigarette. "So, before that kicks in, dove, why don't you tell me what happened in there? Grimalkin told me some of it, but he wasn't there for the whole operation, and I can't get a cohesive story from this pair—" she waved her cigarette at Ironhorse and Puck "—because they're too busy worrying over you. Why couldn't you get the scepter, darling? What happened in SciCorp?"

The memories flooded in, and the despair I'd been hiding from descended like a heavy blanket. "Ash," I whispered, feeling tears prick my eyes. "It was Ash. She has him."

"The prince?"

"Virus has him," I continued in a daze. "She put one of her

mind-control bugs inside him, and he attacked us. He tried… tried to kill us."

"He's the one guarding the scepter," Puck added, collapsing in a chair. "Him and about two dozen nasty Thornguards, and a whole building of Virus's little human drones." He shook his head. "I've fought Ash before, but not like this. Whenever we dueled, there was always a small part of him, deep down, that wasn't serious. I know his royal iciness, and I knew he really didn't want to kill me, no matter how much he boasted otherwise. That's why our little feud has lasted so long." Puck snorted and crossed his arms, looking grave. "The thing I fought today wasn't the frosty Ice prince we all know and love. There's nothing there anymore. No anger, no hate, no fear. He's more dangerous now than he ever was before, because he doesn't care if he lives or dies."

Silence fell. All I could hear was the faint sound of Grimalkin sharpening his claws on the sofa. I wanted to lie down and cry, but the herbs were kicking in, and my depression was giving way to a numbing exhaustion. "So," Leanansidhe ventured at last, "what will you do now?"

I stirred, fighting the drowsiness. "We go back," I murmured, looking at Puck and Ironhorse, hoping they would back me up. "We have to. We have to get the scepter and stop the war. There's no other way around it." Both nodded gravely, and I relaxed, grateful and relieved that they would follow me on this. "At least we know what we're up against now," I continued, grabbing for a faint ray of hope. "We might have a better chance the second time around."

"And the Winter prince?" Leanansidhe asked softly. "What will you do with him?"

I glanced at her sharply, about to tell her that we would save Ash and I didn't like what she was implying, but Puck beat me to it.

"We have to kill him."

The world screeched to a halt. Slowly, I turned my head to stare at Puck, unable to believe what I just heard. "How could you?" I whispered. "He was your friend. You fought side by side. And now you want to cut him down like it was nothing!"

"You saw what he did." Puck met my eyes, beseeching. "You saw what he *is* now. I don't think I can fight him without holding back. If he attacks you again—"

"You don't want to save him," I accused, leaning forward. My arm throbbed, but I was too angry to care. "You don't even want to try! You're jealous, and you've always wanted him out of the way!"

"I never said that!"

"You don't have to! I can see it on your face!"

"HE'S DYING, PRINCESS."

Words froze in my throat. I stared at Ironhorse, silently pleading with him to be wrong. He gazed back with a sorrowful expression. "No." I shook my head, fighting the persistent tears that stung my eyes. "I won't believe that. There has to be a way to save him."

"I AM SORRY, PRINCESS." Ironhorse bowed his head. "I KNOW YOUR FEELINGS FOR THE WINTER PRINCE, AND I WISH I COULD GIVE YOU BETTER NEWS. BUT THERE IS NO WAY TO FORCEFULLY REMOVE THE BUGS ONCE THEY HAVE BEEN IM-PLANTED. NOT WITHOUT KILLING THE HOST." He sighed, and his tone softened, though the volume did not. "GOODFELLOW IS RIGHT. THE WINTER PRINCE IS FAR TOO DANGEROUS. IF HE ATTACKS AGAIN, WE CANNOT HOLD BACK."

"What about Virus?" I pressed, unwilling to give up. "She's the one controlling the bugs. If we take her out, maybe her hold on him will—"

"Even if that were the case," Puck interrupted, "the bug would still be inside him. And with no way to get it out, he'll either go mad, or be in so much torment that he would be better off dead. Ash is strong, Princess, but that thing inside him is killing him. You saw it, you heard what Virus said." His brow furrowed, and his voice went very soft. "I don't think he has much time left."

The tears pressing behind my eyes finally spilled over, and I buried my face in the pillow, biting the fabric to keep from screaming. God, it wasn't fair! What did they want from me? Hadn't I given enough already? I'd sacrificed everything—family, home, a normal life—for the stupid greater good. I had worked so hard; I was trying to be brave and mature about everything, but now I had to watch while the thing I loved most was killed in front of me?

I couldn't. Even if it was impossible, even if Ash killed me himself, I would still try to save him.

The room had grown very quiet. I peeked up and saw that everyone except Puck had left, slipping from the room to let me come to terms with myself, and the decision looming over my head, in peace.

Seeing me glance up, Puck tried catching my gaze. "Meghan…"

I turned away, pressing my face into the cushions. Anger and resentment boiled; Puck was the last person I wanted to see, much less talk to. Right now, I hated him. "Go away, Puck."

He sighed and rose from the chair, coming to perch on the sofa next to me. "Well, you know that never works."

The silence stretched between us. I sensed that Puck wanted to say something but couldn't seem to find the right words. Which was odd; I'd never known him to hesitate about anything.

"I won't let you kill him," I finally muttered after a few minutes of quiet.

There was a lengthy pause before he answered. "Would you ask me to watch you die?" he murmured slowly. "Stand by while he puts a sword through your heart? Or, maybe you want me to die instead. You could just tell me to stand still while Ash chops off my head. Would that make you happy, Princess?"

"Don't be stupid!" I bit my lip in frustration and sat up, wincing as the room spun for a moment. "I don't want anyone to die. But I can't lose him, Puck." My anger abruptly drained away, leaving only a hollow despair. "I can't lose you, either."

Puck put his arms around me and pulled me close, gently so as to not jolt my wounded arm. I laid my head on his chest and closed my eyes, wishing I were normal, that I didn't have to make these impossible decisions, that everything would be all right again. If wishes were horses…

"What do want me to do, Princess?" Puck whispered into my hair.

"If there's any way we can save him…"

He nodded. "I'll try very hard not to kill his royal iciness if we meet again. Believe it or not, Princess, I don't want Ash dead, any more than you do." He sniffed. "Well, maybe a little more than you. But…" And he pulled back to look me in the eye. "If he puts you in danger, I won't hold back. That's my promise. I won't risk losing *you,* either, understand?"

"Yeah," I whispered, closing my eyes. That was all I could ask. *I'll save you,* I thought, as drowsiness stole over me and my mind drifted. *No matter what, I'll find a way to bring you back. I promise.*

I was nearly asleep, surrendering to the exhaustion stealing all my coherent thoughts, when a slamming door jerked me awake and Puck's arms tightened around me.

"Meghan Chase." Kimi's voice cut across the room, clipped, flat and mechanical. I looked up and my stomach dropped away.

Kimi and Nelson stood beside the door like soldiers at attention, a posture so strange for both of them that I didn't recognize them at first. As one, their heads turned, and they gave me an empty stare. The same look Ash had turned on me back in SciCorp.

"Oh, no," I whispered. Puck went stiff with shock.

"Our Mistress has a message for you, Meghan Chase." Kimi took a short step forward, moving like a robot. "'Congratulations for breaking into SciCorp and, more impressive, breaking out again. You have my admiration. Unfortunately, I cannot have you running amok, making plans to return for the scepter, as I know you will. I'll be moving it tonight to a safer location. If you come back to SciCorp, I'm afraid you'll find it quite empty. Oh, and by the way, I'm also sending Ash to kill your family. They're in Louisiana, right?'"

I sucked in a breath, and the blood drained from my face. Kimi's expression didn't change, but her voice turned mocking. "'So you have a choice now, my dear. Come back for the scepter, or run home and try to stop Ash. You'd better hurry. He's probably halfway to the bayou by now.

"'One more thing!'" she added as I leaped to my feet, drowsiness forgotten. Heart pounding, I glared at her. Robot Kimi gave me an empty smile. "'I want you to remember, this is not a game, Meghan Chase. If you think you can waltz into my lair and try to take what is mine without repercussions, you'd best think again. People will get hurt because of you.'" Kimi stepped forward and narrowed her eyes. "'Do not screw with me, child. Let this be a little reminder of what can happen when you play with the big girls.'"

Kimi spasmed, spine arching back, mouth open in a silent scream as she twitched and thrashed. A moment later, Nelson did the same, limbs jerking wildly, before they both collapsed to the floor.

Puck was beside Kimi instantly, rolling her over. The little half-phouka's eyes were open, gazing sightlessly at the ceiling, and she didn't move a muscle. I bit my lip, my heart pounding. "Are they…dead?"

He paused a moment before rising to his feet. "No. At least, I don't think so. They're still breathing, but…" He frowned, squinting at Kimi's slack expression. "I think their brains have short-circuited. Or the bugs are keeping them in some sort of coma." He shook his head, looking up at me. "Sorry, Princess. I can't do anything for them."

"Of course you can't, darling." Leanansidhe breezed through the doorway, her face a porcelain mask, eyes glowing green. "Fortunately, I know a mortal doctor who might be able to help. If he cannot revive the streetrats, then there is no hope for them." She turned to me, and I tried not to cringe under that unearthly gaze. "You are leaving, I presume?"

I nodded. "Ash is out there," I said. "He's going after my family. I have to stop him." I narrowed my eyes, staring her down. "Don't try to keep me here."

She sighed. "I could, darling, but then you would be a complete mess and of no use to us. If there is one thing I've learned about humans, it's that they become absolutely unreasonable when it comes to family." She sniffed and waved her hand. "So go, darling. Rescue your mother and father and brother and get it over with. My door will still be open when you come back. If we're still alive, that is."

"PRINCESS!" Ironhorse bashed the door open, skidding to a halt in the middle of the room, breathing hard. "ARE YOU HURT? WHAT HAS HAPPENED?"

I gazed around for my sneakers, wincing as a bright talon of pain clawed up my arm. "Virus sent Ash to kill my family," I said, dropping to my knees to peer under the couch. "I'm going to stop him."

"WHAT ABOUT THE SCEPTER?" he continued, as I pulled out my sneakers and stuffed my feet into them, gritting my teeth as my arm throbbed with every movement. "WE MUST RETRIEVE IT BEFORE VIRUS HAS IT MOVED. SHE IS VULNURABLE NOW AND WILL NOT BE EXPECTING US. NOW IS THE TIME TO ATTACK."

"No." I felt pulled in several directions at once, and tried to stay calm. "I'm sorry, Ironhorse. I know we have to get the scepter, but my family comes first. Always. I don't expect you to understand."

"VERY WELL," Ironhorse said, surprising me. "THEN I WILL COME WITH YOU."

Startled, I looked up at him, but before I could reply, Grimalkin interrupted me.

"A quaint idea," the cat mused, leaping onto the table, "and exactly what Virus is hoping for. We must have scared her quite a bit for her to react so dramatically. If we abandon the mission now, we might never find her again."

"He's right." I nodded, ignoring Ironhorse's scowl. "We have to split up. Ironhorse, you stay here with Grim. Keep looking for the scepter and Virus. Puck and I will go after Ash. We'll be back as soon as we can."

"I DO NOT LIKE LEAVING YOU ALONE, PRINCESS." Ironhorse raised his head in a proud, stubborn manner. "I SWORE I WOULD PROTECT YOU."

"While we were looking for the scepter, you did. But this is different." I stood up and met his burning red eyes. "This is personal, Ironhorse. And your mission has always been the scepter. I want you to stay behind with Grim. Keep looking for Virus." He opened his mouth to argue, and I spit out the last words. "That's an order."

He blew smoke from his nostrils like a furious bull and turned away. "AS YOU WISH, PRINCESS."

His voice was stiff, but there was no time to dwell on feelings of guilt. I turned to Puck. "We have to get to Louisiana fast. How do we get out of here?"

He glanced at Leanansidhe. "Don't suppose you have any trods to Louisiana from here, do you, Lea?"

"There's one to New Orleans," Leanansidhe replied, looking thoughtful. "I just adore Mardi Gras, darling, though Mab tends to hog the spotlight every year. Typical of her."

"That's too far away." I took a deep breath, feeling time slip away from me. "Isn't there a trod that's closer? I need to get home *now*."

"The Briars." Puck snapped his fingers. "We can go through the Briars. That will take us there quickly."

Leanansidhe blinked. "What makes you think there is a trod to the girl's house through the Briars, dove?"

Puck snorted. "Lea, I know you. You can't stand to be out of the loop, remember? You must have a trod that goes to Meghan's house from the Briars, even though you can't use it. I know you'd want keep an eye on Oberon's daughter. What kind of gossip would you miss out on, otherwise?"

Leanansidhe pursed her lips as if she'd swallowed something sour. "You caught me there, darling. Though you don't hesitate to rub salt in the wound, do you? I *suppose* I can let you use that trod, but you owe me a favor later, darling." Leanansidhe sniffed and puffed her cigarette. "I feel I should charge *something* for letting you in on my greatest secret. Especially since I have no interest in the girl's family. Such a boring lot, except the little boy—he has potential."

"Done," I said. "You have your favor. At least from me. Now, will you let us use it or not?"

Leanansidhe snapped her fingers, and Skrae the piskie fluttered down from the ceiling. "Take them to the basement trod," she ordered, "and guide them to the right door. Go." Skrae bobbed once and zipped to my shoulder, hiding in my hair. "I will continue to have my spies monitor SciCorp," Leanansidhe said. "See if they can discern where Virus is moving it to. You should get going, darling."

I straightened and glanced at Puck, who nodded. "All right, let's go. Grim, keep an eye on Ironhorse, would you? Make sure he doesn't go charging the army by himself. We'll be back soon." I shook my hair, dislodging the piskie huddled against my neck. "All right, Skrae, take us out of here."

# CHAPTER EIGHTEEN

*Close to Ice*

Our trip back through the Briars was less exciting than our trip in. We saw no dragons, spiders or killer-wasp fey, though truthfully I could've wandered straight into their hive without noticing. My mind was consumed with Ash and my family. Would he really…kill them? Cut them down in cold blood, invisible and unheard? What would I do then?

I pressed a palm to my face, trying in vain to stop the tears. I would kill him. If he hurt Ethan or Mom in any way, I would put a knife through his heart myself, even if I was sobbing my eyes out while I did it. Even if I still loved him more than life itself.

Sick with worry, fighting the despair that threatened to drown me, I didn't see Puck stop until I ran into him, and he steadied me without a word. We had reached the end of the tunnel, where a simple wooden door waited in the thorns a few feet away. Even in the tangled darkness of the Briars, I recognized it. This was the gate that had led me into Faery, all those months ago. This was where it all began, at Ethan's closet door.

Ahead of us, Skrae gave a last buzz and flew back down the tunnel, back to Leanansidhe to give his report, I assumed. There was no going back for me. I reached for the door handle.

"Wait," Puck ordered. I turned back, impatient and annoyed, when I saw the grim severity in his eyes. "Are you ready for this, Princess?" he asked softly. "Whatever lies beyond that door isn't Ash any longer. If we're going to save your family, we can't hold back now. We might have to—"

"I know," I interrupted, not wanting to hear it. My chest tightened, and my eyes started to tear, but I dashed them away. "I know. Let's…let's just do this, all right? I'll figure something out when I see him." And before Puck could say anything else, I wrenched the door open and walked through.

The cold hit me immediately, taking my breath away. It hung in the air as I shivered, gazing around in horror, my stomach twisting so painfully that I felt nauseous. Ethan's bedroom was completely encased in ice. The walls, the dresser, the bookshelf; all covered in a layer of crystal nearly two inches thick, but so clear so I could see everything trapped within. Outside the window, a cold, clear night shone through the glass, the moonlight sparkling lifelessly off the ice.

"Oh, man," I heard Puck whisper behind me.

"Where's Ethan?" I gasped, rushing to his bed. The horrific vision of him trapped in ice, unable to breathe, made me virtually ill, and I nearly threw up at the thought. But Ethan's bed was empty, the quilts flat and still beneath the frozen layer.

"Where is he?" I whispered, near panic. Then I heard a faint noise from beneath the bed, a soft, breathy whimper. Dropping to my knees, I peered into the crack, wary of monsters and bogeys and the things that lurked under the bed. A small, shivering lump stirred in the far corner, and a pale face looked up at mine.

"Meggie?"

"Ethan!" Relieved beyond words, I reached under the bed and pulled him out, hugging him close. He was so cold; he clung to me with frozen hands, his four-year-old body shaking like a leaf.

"You c–came back," he whispered, as Puck crossed the room and shut the door without a sound. "Quick! You have to s–save Mommy and Daddy."

My blood ran cold. "What happened?" I asked, holding him with one arm while pulling open the door we came through. Now it was just a normal closet. I yanked out a quilt that wasn't covered in ice and wrapped Ethan in it, sitting him on the frozen bed.

"*He* came," Ethan whispered, pulling the folds tighter around himself. "The dark person. S-Spider told me he was coming. He told me t-to hide."

"Spider? Who's Spider?"

"The m-man under the b-bed."

"I see." I frowned and rubbed his numb fingers between mine. Why would a bogey be helping Ethan? "What happened then?"

"I hid, and everything turned to ice." Ethan gripped my hand, big blue eyes beseeching mine. "Meggie, Mommy and Daddy are still out there, with him! You have to save them. Make him go away!"

"We will," I promised. My heart started an irregular thud in my chest. "We'll make this right, Ethan, I promise."

"He should stay here," Puck murmured, peering through a crack in the door. "Man, it looks like the whole house is iced over. Ash is here, all right."

I nodded. I hated to leave Ethan, but there was no way I wanted my brother to see what came next. "You wait here," I told him, smoothing down his curly hair. "Stay in your room until I come get you. Close the door and don't come out, no matter what, okay?"

He sniffled and huddled deeper into the quilt. With my heart in my throat, I turned to Puck. "All right," I whispered. "Let's find Ash."

We crept down the stairs, Puck in front, me clinging to the railing because the stairs were slick and treacherous. The house was eerily silent, an unfamiliar palace of sparkling crystal, the cold so sharp that it cut into my lungs and burned my fingers as they gripped the railing.

We reached the living room, cloaked in shadow except for the light that came from the open door and the flickering static of the television. Silhouetted against the screen, Mom's and Luke's heads were visible over the top of the couch. Leaning together, as if asleep, they were frozen solid, encased in ice like everything else. My heart stood still.

"Mom!"

I rushed forward, but Puck grabbed my arm, holding me back. Snarling, I turned on him, trying to shake him off, until I saw his face. His eyes were hard, his jaw set as he pulled me behind him, a dagger appearing in his hand.

Trembling, I looked into the living room again just as Ash melted out of the shadows on the far wall, drawing his sword as he did. In the harsh blue light, he looked awful, his skin split open along his cheekbones and his eyes sunk into his face. There were new wounds over his arms and hands, where the skin had blackened along the openings, looking burned and dead. His silver eyes were bright with pain and madness as he stared at us, every inch a killer, but I couldn't be afraid of him. There was only grief now, a horrible, soul-wrenching pain knowing that, no matter what happened, I had to let him die. If I wanted to save my family, Puck would have to kill Ash. Tonight. Right here in my living room. I forced down a sob and stepped forward, ignoring Puck as he grabbed for me, my eyes only for the dark prince standing across the room.

"Ash," I whispered as his eyes flicked to my face, following my every move. "Can you hear me at all? Please, give us something. Otherwise, Puck is going to…" I swallowed hard, as he continued to regard me blankly. "Ash, I can't let you hurt my family. But…I don't want to lose you, either." The tears spilled over, and I faced him desperately. "Please, tell me you can fight this. Please—"

"Kill me."

I sucked in a breath, staring at him. He stood rock still, the muscles working in his jaw, as if he was struggling to speak. "I…can't fight this," he gritted out, closing his eyes in concentration. His arms shook, and his grip on the sword tightened. "You have to…kill me, Meghan. I…can't stop myself…"

"Ash—"

His eyes opened, glazed over once more. "Get away from me, now!"

Puck shoved me away as Ash leaped across the room, his sword coming down in a sapphire blur. I hit the floor, wincing as the ice scraped my palms and bruised my knees. With my back against the wall, I watched Puck and Ash battle in the middle of the living room, feeling dead inside and out. I couldn't save him. Ash was lost to me now, and worse, one of them was going to die. If Puck won, Ash would be killed. But if Ash emerged victorious, I would lose everything, including my own life. I guess I should've been rooting for Puck, but the cold despair in my heart kept me from feeling anything.

As Ash whirled away from a vicious upward slash, something glittered beneath his hair at the base of his skull. Scrambling to my feet, I narrowed my eyes and my senses, staring at it intently. A tiny spark of cold, iron glamour glimmered at the top of Ash's spine and I gasped. That was it! The bug, the thing that was controlling him and, ultimately, killing him.

As if it could sense my thoughts, Ash whirled, his eyes narrowing in my direction. As Puck's knife came down at his back, he spun, knocking it aside, and stabbed forward with his weapon. Puck twisted desperately, but it wasn't enough, and the icy blade plunged deep into his shoulder. I cried out, and Puck stumbled back, dark blood blossoming over his shirt, his face tight with pain.

Ash lunged at me, and I tensed, my heart hammering in my chest. All those times watching him fight gave me an inkling of what was coming. As the sword came slashing down at my head, I dove forward, hearing the savage *chink* of the blade against the ice. Rolling away, I glanced back, saw the sword coming and threw myself aside, barely avoiding the second swing that bit into the floor, pelting me with ice shards. I hit the wall and turned back to see Ash standing over me, weapon raised high. There was nowhere to go. I looked into his face, saw his jaw tighten and his arm tremble as he met my gaze. For a split second, the sword wavered, and he closed his eyes…

Just as Puck rose up from nowhere with a snarl and slammed the dagger into his chest.

Time stood still. A scream lodged in my throat as Puck and Ash stared at each other, Puck's shoulders heaving with breaths or sobs, I couldn't tell. For a moment, they stood there, locked in a morbid embrace, until Puck let out a strangled noise and wrenched himself away, yanking out the dagger in a spray of crimson. The sword fell from Ash's hand, hitting the ground with a ringing clang that echoed through the house.

Ash staggered back, managing to stay on his feet for a moment, arms curled around his stomach. He swayed, putting his back to the wall, as dark blood began to drip to the ice, pooling beneath him. As I finally found my voice and screamed his name, Ash raised his head and gave me a weary smile. Then those silver eyes dimmed, like the sun vanishing behind a cloud, and he crumpled to the ground.

# CHAPTER NINETEEN

*Sickness*

"Ash!"

I rushed forward, shoving Puck out of the way. Puck stumbled aside, moving like a sleepwalker. The bloody dagger dropped limply from his hand. Ignoring him, I lunged toward Ash.

"Stay back!"

His voice brought me up short, sharp and desperate. Ash struggled to his knees, arms around his stomach, shaking with agonized gasps. Blood pooled around him as he raised his head, eyes bright with anguish. "Stay back, Meghan," he gritted out, a line of red trickling from his mouth. "I could...still kill you. Let me be." He grimaced, closing his eyes, one hand clutching at his skull. "I can still...feel it," he rasped, shuddering. "It's in...shock now, but...it's getting strong again." He gasped, clenching his teeth in pain. "Dammit, Goodfellow. You could've...made it clean. Hurry and get it over with."

"No!" I cried, flinging myself down beside him. He flinched away from me, and I caught his shoulder.

It was like touching an electric fence, without the shock. I felt a rush of sharp, metallic glamour coming from Ash, buzzing in my ears and vibrating my senses. I felt something inside me respond, like a current beneath my skin, rushing up to my fingertips, and suddenly everything was much clearer. If glamour was raw emotion and passion, this was the absence of it: logical, calculating, impassive. I felt all my fear, panic and desperation drain away, and I looked at Ash with a new curiosity. This was a problem, but how was I going to fix it? How would I solve this equation?

"Meghan, run." Ash's voice was strangled, and that was all the warning I had before his eyes went glassy and his hands fastened around my throat, cutting off my air. I gasped and clawed at his fingers, staring into his blank eyes as a sharp, droning voice echoed through my head.

*Kill you.*

I gasped airlessly, fighting to stay calm, to stay connected to that cold, impassive glamour buzzing under my skin. As I stared into his eyes, I could *see* the bug, its hateful glare peering back at me. I could see its round, ticklike body, clamped to the top of Ash's spine, the metal parasite that was killing him. I could hear it, and I knew it could hear me, too.

"Meghan!" Puck snatched the ice sword from where it lay, forgotten, and raised it over his head.

"Puck, don't." My voice came out raspy, but calm. I fought for air and felt Ash's grip loosen the tiniest bit. He closed his eyes, breaking my connection with the bug, but I could still feel the iron glamour, buzzing all around me. He was fighting its commands, his face tight with concentration, sweat running down his skin.

"Do it," he rasped, and I realized he spoke to Puck, not me.

"No!" I met Puck's conflicted gaze, saw the sword waver as he swept it toward Ash. "Puck, don't! Trust me!"

My vision was getting fuzzy. I didn't have much time. Praying Puck would hesitate a little longer, I turned back to Ash, laying my palm against his cheek. "Ash," I said, hoping my mangled voice would get through to him, "look at me, please."

He didn't respond at first, his fingers shaking as he fought the compulsion to crush my throat. When he did look up, the raw anguish, horror and torment on his face was agonizing. But, beyond his pain-filled eyes, I could see the parasite as it tightened its hold on him. My will rose up to meet it, iron glamour swirling around us. I shaped that glamour into a command, and sent it lancing into the metal bug.

*Let go,* I told it, putting as much force into the words as I could.

It buzzed furiously and clamped down hard, and Ash cried out in agony. His fingers on my throat tightened, crushing my windpipe and turning my world red with pain. I sagged, fighting to stay conscious, seeing darkness crawling along the edge of my vision. *No!* I told it. *I will not lose to you. I will not give him up! Let go!*

The bug hissed again…and loosened its hold, still fighting me all the way. I put my shaking hand against Ash's chest, over his heart, feeling it crash against his ribs. Ash's grip tightened once more, and the world started to go black. *Get out,* I snarled with the last of my strength. *Get out of him, now!*

A crackle and a flash of light, and Ash convulsed, shoving me away. I fell against the cold floor, striking my head against the ice, blackness momentarily blinding me. Fighting for consciousness, I saw a glint of light, of something tiny and metallic, fly up toward the ceiling, and Ash staring at his hands in horror. The metal spark hovered in the air a moment, than zipped toward me with a furious buzz.

Puck's hand shot out, snatching the bug from the air, hurling it to the floor. For a split second, it lay there glinting coldly against the ice. Then his boot smashed down and ground the bug into oblivion.

I struggled upright, breathing hard, waiting for the room to stop spinning. Puck knelt in front of me, one shoulder covered in blood, his whole body tense with concern.

"Meghan." One of his hands smoothed my cheek, rough and urgent. "Talk to me. Are you all right?"

I nodded. "I think so." My voice came out harsh and raspy, and my throat burned like I'd been gargling with razor blades. Something cold and wet dripped onto my knee. I glanced up and saw that the ceiling was beginning to crack and melt. "Where's Ash?"

Puck moved aside, looking grave. Ash was slumped against the wall in the corner, head down, one hand covering his still bleeding ribs. His eyes were open, staring at the floor, at nothing. Heart in my throat, I gingerly approached and knelt beside him, saw him shift, very slightly, away from me.

"Ash." My worry for him, for Ethan, for my family, was a painful knot in my stomach. I longed to help him, but the image of my mom and Luke, frozen on the couch, filled me with dread and fear. If Ash had hurt them, if they were…I could never forgive him. "My mom," I asked, staring into his face. "My stepdad. Did…did you…?"

He gave his head a small shake, a tiny movement in the shadows. "No," he whispered without looking at me, his voice flat and dead. "They're just…asleep. When the ice melts, they should be fine, with no memory of what happened."

Relief bloomed through me, although short-lived. I reached out to touch his arm, and he flinched as if my touch was poison.

"What will you do with me now?" he whispered.

Puck's shadow fell over us. I looked back and saw him holding Ash's sword, a grim, frightening look on his face. For a second, I was afraid Puck would stab him right there, but he tossed the blade at Ash's feet and turned away. "Think you can walk, Prince?"

Ash nodded without looking up. Puck pulled me reluctantly to my feet and drew me aside. "I'll deal with Ash, Princess," he murmured, holding up a hand to interrupt my protest. "Why don't you check on your brother before we go?"

"Go? Where?"

"I'd say Ash needs a healer, Princess." Puck glanced back at the prince and made a face. "I know I would, if I'd had a metal bug stuck inside my head. Probably screwed him up pretty bad. Luckily, I know a healer not far from here, but we should go *now*."

I looked back at Mom and Luke, at the water slowly dripping from their frozen silhouettes, and yearning twisted my stomach. I missed them, and who knew when I'd see them again. "We can't stay, just a little while?"

"What would you tell them, Princess?" Puck gave me a look that was sympathetic and exasperated at the same time. "The truth? That a faery prince froze the inside of the house in order to draw you here and kill you?" He shook his head, making sense even as I hated him and his logic at that point. "Besides, we need to get his royal iciness to a healer, and soon. Trust me, it's better if your folks never knew you were here."

I gave my parents one last look and nodded slowly. "Right," I sighed. "I was never here. Let me say goodbye to Ethan, at least."

Feeling old inside and out, I retreated up the steps, pausing once to look back. Puck was crouched in front of the Unseelie prince, his lips moving soundlessly, but Ash was looking straight at me, his eyes glimmering slits in the gloom. Biting my lips, I continued on to Ethan's bedroom.

I found him in the hallway, peering out between the railings, the blanket still draped over his shoulders. "Ethan!" I hissed, and he glanced up with big blue eyes. "What are you doing out here? I told you to stay in your room."

"Where's Mommy and Daddy?" he asked as I picked him up, carrying him back to his room. "Did you tell the bad person to go away?"

"They'll be all right," I told him with my own sense of relief. "Ash didn't hurt them, and as soon as the ice melts, they'll be back to normal." Though they would probably wonder why the whole house was wet. The ice was melting rapidly; I stepped around several puddles as I crossed the hall into his room.

Ethan nodded, gazing at me solemnly as I set him on his bed. "You're going away again, aren't you?" he asked matter-of-factly, though his lip trembled and he sniffled, trying to hold back tears. "You didn't come back to stay with me."

I sighed, sitting beside him on the frozen bed. "Not yet," I murmured, smoothing down his hair. "I wish I could. I really do, but..." Ethan sniffled, and I pulled him close. "I'm sorry," I whispered. "There are still some things I have to take care of."

"No!" Ethan clung to me, burying his face in my side. "You can't leave again. They won't take you again. I won't let them."

"Ethan—"

"Princesss." From the darkness under the bed, something latched on to my ankle, claws digging into my skin. I yelped, swinging my feet up onto the mattress, and Ethan gave a startled cry.

"Dammit, bogey!" My sore throat blazed with pain at the outburst, making me even angrier. I leaped off the bed and stalked to Ethan's dresser, grabbing the flashlight still kept on top. Bogeys hated light, and the white beam of a flashlight could make them flee in terror. "I am so not in the mood for this," I rasped, flicking on the beam. "You have three seconds to get out of here before I make you leave."

"Meggie." Ethan hopped off the bed and padded up, taking my hand. "It's okay. It's only Spider. He's my friend."

I looked at him, aghast. Since when did bogeys make friends with the kids they terrorized? I didn't believe it, but a soft slithering sound came from under the bed, and two yellow eyes peered up at me.

"Fear not, Princesss," it whispered, keeping a wary eye on the flashlight in my hand. "I am here under ordersss. Prince Asssh told usss to watch thisss housssse. It isss under the protection of the Unsssseelie Court."

"*Ash* ordered this? When?"

"Before he came to collect your bargain, Princesss. Before you went back with him to Tir Na Nog." The thing slithered to the edge of the crack, staying just out of the light. "The child isss in no danger," it rasped, "and neither are hisss parentsss, though they do not know we are here. Protect thisss housssse and work no missschief on thosssse who live here, those are our ordersss."

"He tells me stories every night," Ethan said, looking up at me. "Most of them are pretty scary, but I don't mind. And sometimes there's a black pony in the front yard, and little man in the basement. Mommy and Daddy don't see them, either."

I closed my eyes. The thought of so many Unseelie fey hanging around my house did nothing to ease my nervousness, even if they were claiming to protect my family. "How did you know about Ash?" I finally asked.

"I sssmelled an Iron fey coming, and knew I musssst protect the boy, at leasssst," Spider went on, oblivious to my conflicted feelings. "I pulled him under the bed, where I could hide him better. Imagine my sssurprissse when I dissscovered it wasss Prince Asssh himssself, attacking thisss housssе. He musssst have been posssesssed, or perhapsss it wasss an Iron fey disssguisssed asss the prince. But, I followed my ordersss, and kept the boy sssafe."

"Well, I'm grateful for that," I muttered. And then a thought occurred to me, one that I almost didn't ask about, but couldn't leave alone. "Have…have my parents…mentioned me? Do they talk about me at all, or wonder where I am?"

"I know nothing of the adultsss, Princesss."

It didn't really matter now, but I suddenly wanted to know. Was I still a part of this family, or just a long-forgotten memory? How could I find out without asking Mom and Luke? I snapped my fingers. My bedroom. I had deliberately avoided it until now, unsure if I could handle seeing it turned into an office, or a guest room, proof that Mom had forgotten me. But with Ethan clutching my hand, his blanket trailing behind us, I walked down the hall to my room and pushed the door open.

It was exactly as I remembered it, frozen in ice, familiar and strange at the same time. A lump caught in my throat as I walked inside. Nothing had changed. There was my old stuffed bear sitting on my bed, a birthday present from long ago. My *Naruto* and *Escaflowne* posters were still on the wall. I ran my fingers over my dresser, scanning the photographs between my scattered collection of CDs, now probably ruined. Photos of me, Mom and Ethan. One family picture with Luke. One of me and Beau, our old German shepherd, as a puppy. And a small, single framed picture on my nightstand that I didn't recognize.

Frowning, I snapped it away from the ice and held it up, staring at the photograph. It was a picture of me as a little kid, no older than Ethan, being held by an unfamiliar man with short brown hair and a lopsided smile.

"Oh, my God," I whispered.

My knees crumpled, and I sat down on the bed, slush and frigid water seeping through my clothes. I barely felt it. Ethan stood on tiptoes to stare at the frame. "Who's that?" he whispered.

Puck appeared in the doorway, his shirt and hands smeared with blood. "Princess? We should get going. Ash says there's a tatter-colt outside who can give us a ride to the healer." He stopped when he saw my face. "What's wrong?"

I held up the frame. "Recognize him?"

Puck squinted at the photo, then his eyes got wide. "Hell," he muttered. "It's Charles."

I nodded faintly. "Charles," I whispered, pulling the frame back. "I didn't even know him. I don't know how I didn't recognize…" I stopped, remembering an old woman shifting through my mind, scattering memories like leaves, searching for the one she wanted. When we were first searching for Ethan and the Iron King, we'd asked an ancient Oracle, living in New Orleans, to help us find Machina's lair. The Oracle agreed to help us…in exchange for one of my memories. I hadn't given it any thought until now. "That was the exchange, wasn't it?" I asked bitterly, looking at Puck. "The Oracle's payment for helping us. This was the memory she took."

Puck didn't say anything. I sighed, staring at the frame, then shook my head. "Who is he?" I asked.

"He was your father," Puck murmured. "Or, at least, the man you thought was your father. Before you came here, and your mom met Luke. He disappeared when you were six."

I couldn't take my eyes off the strange photo, at the man holding me so easily, both of us smiling at the camera. "You knew who he was," I murmured without looking away. "You knew who Charles was, didn't you? All that time we were at Leanansidhe's, you knew." Puck didn't answer, and I finally tore my gaze from the photo, glaring up at him. "Why didn't you tell me?"

"And what would you have done, Princess?" Puck crossed his arms and stared back, unrepentant. "Made a bargain with Leanansidhe? Dragged him home again, like nothing happened? Do you think your mom would take him back without a second thought?"

Of course she wouldn't. She had Luke now, and Ethan. Nothing would change, even if I did manage to bring Charles home. And the worst part was, I couldn't remember why I'd wanted to.

My mind spun. I was drowning in a torrent of confusing emotions, feeling my world turned upside down. The shock of discovery. Guilt that I didn't recognize my mother's first husband, the man who'd raised me as a child, and worse, couldn't remember anything about him. He was like a stranger on the street. Anger at Puck. He had known all along, and deliberately kept me in the dark. Anger at Leanansidhe. What the hell was she doing with my dad? How did he even get there? And how was I going to get him out?

Did I even want to get him out?

"Princess." Puck's voice broke through my numb trance. I glared poisoned daggers at him and he gave me a weak smile. "Scary. You can rip me to pieces later. His royal iciness isn't looking so good. We have to get him to a healer, now."

Ethan sniffed and clamped himself to my leg, his small body tight with determination. "No!" he wailed. "No, she's not leaving! No!"

I looked at Puck helplessly, torn in several directions and feeling I could scream. "I can't leave him here alone."

"He will not be alone, Princesss," came Spider's voice from under my bed. "We will defend him with our livesss, asss ordered."

"Can you promise me that?"

A soft hiss. "Asss you wisssh. We three of the Unssseelie Court, bogey, tatter-colt, and cluricaun, promissse to look after the Chassse boy until we are told otherwisssse by Hisss Highnesss Prince Asssh or Queen Mab herssself."

I still didn't like it, but it was all I could do for now. Once a faery says the word *promise,* it is an ironclad contract. Ethan, however, wailed and clung tighter to my leg. "No!" he cried again, on his way to a rare but intense temper tantrum. "You're not leaving! You're not!"

Puck sighed and placed his palm gently on Ethan's head, murmuring something under his breath. I saw a shimmer of glamour go through the air, and Ethan slumped against my leg, going silent mid-scream. Alarmed, I scooped him up, but a soft snore came from his open mouth, and Puck grinned.

"Did you really have to do that?" I said, bundling Ethan in the blanket and carrying him back to his room.

"Well, it was either that or turn him into a rabbit for a few hours." Puck was infuriatingly unrepentant as he followed me down the hall. "And I don't think your parents would've appreciated that."

Icy water dripped from the ceiling and ran rivulets down the walls, soaking his toys and stuffed animals. "This isn't going to work," I groaned. "Even if he is asleep, I can't leave him in here. He'll freeze!"

As if on command, the closet door swung open, warm and dark and, most important, dry.

"Come on, Princess," Puck urged as I hesitated. "Make a decision here. We're running out of time."

Reluctantly, I set Ethan's small body in the closet, pulling down several more blankets to make a nest around him. He remained deeply asleep, breathing easily through his nose and mouth, and didn't even stir as I piled the quilts around him.

"You'd better take good care of him," I whispered to the shadows around me, knowing they were listening. After smoothing his hair back one last time, pulling the covers over his shoulders, I finally rose and followed Puck down the stairs.

"I hope Ash doesn't object to us dragging his carcass outside," Puck muttered as we made our way down the steps, getting dripped on every few feet. "I patched him up as best I could, but I don't think he can walk very…" He trailed off as we reached the frozen living room. The front door creaked softly on its hinges, spilling a bar of moonlight across the floor, and Ash was nowhere to be seen.

I flung myself across the room, slipping on slush and ice, and burst onto the porch. Ash's lean silhouette was moving silently across the yard, stumbling every few feet, one arm around his middle. At the edge of the trees, barely visible within the shadows, a small black horse with glowing crimson eyes waited for him.

I leaped down the steps and raced across the yard, my heart pounding in my ears. "Ash!" I cried, and lunged, catching hold of his arm. He flinched and tried shrugging me off, but nearly fell with the effort. "Wait! Where are you going?"

"Back for the scepter." His voice was dull, and he tried pulling away again, but I clung to him desperately. "Let me go, Meghan. I have to do this."

"No, you don't! Not like this." Despair rose up like a black tide, and I choked back tears. "What are you thinking? You can't face them all alone. You'll be killed." He didn't move, either to disagree or to shake me off, and my desperation grew. "Why are you doing this?" I whispered. "Why won't you let us help you?"

"Meghan, please." Ash sounded as if he was desperately clinging to the last shreds of his composure. "Let me go. I can't stay here. Not after…" He shuddered and took a ragged breath. "Not after what I did."

"That wasn't you." Releasing his arm, I stepped in front of him, blocking his path. He wouldn't meet my eyes. Steeling myself, I stepped closer, finding the courage to gently turn his face to mine. "Ash, that wasn't you. Don't go blaming yourself—you had no control over this. This is no one's fault but *hers.*"

His silver eyes were haunted. "It doesn't excuse what I did."

"No." He flinched and tried drawing back, but I held firm. "But that doesn't mean you should throw your life away because you feel guilty. What would that accomplish?" He regarded me solemnly, his expression unreadable, and my throat ached with longing. I yearned to fling my arms around him and hug him close, but I knew he wouldn't allow it. "Virus is still out there," I continued, holding his gaze, "and now we have a real chance to get the scepter back. But we have to do it together this time. Deal?"

He regarded me solemnly. "Is this another contract?"

"No," I whispered, appalled. "I wouldn't do that to you again." He remained silent, staring at me, and I reluctantly let him go, raw desperation tearing at my stomach. "Ash, if you really want to leave, I can't stop you. But—"

"I accept."

I blinked at him. "Accept? What—?"

"The terms of our contract." He bowed his head, his voice somber and grim. "I will aid you until we get the scepter back and return it to the Winter Court. I will stay with you until these terms are fulfilled, this I promise."

"Is that all it is to you? A bargain?"

"Meghan." He glanced at me, eyes pleading. "Let me do this. It's the only way I can think of to repay you."

"But—"

"So, are we done here?" Puck sauntered up beside me, putting an arm around my shoulders before I could stop him. Ash stiffened, drawing back, and his eyes went cold. Puck looked past him to the tatter-colt, standing in the trees, and raised an eyebrow. "I guess that's our ride, then."

The black horse pinned its ears and curled back its lips in a very unhorselike snarl, baring flat yellow teeth at us. Puck snickered. "Huh, I don't think your friend likes me very much, Your Highness. Looks like you'll be riding to the healer's solo."

"I'll go with him," I said quickly, stepping out of Puck's casual embrace. He blinked at me and scowled as I pulled him aside. "Ash can barely keep his feet," I whispered, matching his glare. "Someone has to stay with him. I just want to make sure he doesn't go off on his own."

He gave me that infuriating smirk. "Sure, Princess. Whatever you say."

I resisted the urge to punch him. "Just get us to the healer, Puck." He rolled his eyes and stalked off, glaring at Ash as he swept by. Ash watched him leave without comment, his expression strangely dead.

Turning away, he stumbled over to the tatter-colt, which bent its forelegs and knelt for him so that he could pull himself onto its back with a barely noticeable grimace. A little nervously, I approached the equine fey, which tossed its head and swished its ragged tail but thankfully didn't lunge or bite. It didn't kneel for me, however, and I had to scramble onto its back the hard way, settling behind Ash and wrapping my arms around his waist. For a moment, I closed my eyes and laid my cheek against his back, content just to hold him without fear. I heard his heartbeat quicken, and felt a little shiver go through him, but he remained tense in my arms, rigid and uncomfortable. A heaviness settled in my chest, and I swallowed the lump in my throat.

A harsh cry made me glance up. A huge raven swooped overhead, so close that I felt the wind from its passing ruffle my hair. It perched on a branch and looked back at us, eyes glowing green in the darkness, before barking another caw and flapping away into the trees. Ash gave a quiet word to follow, and the tatter-colt started after it, slipping into the woods as silently as a ghost. I turned and watched my house getting smaller and smaller through the branches, until the forest closed in and the trees obscured it completely.

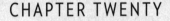

# CHAPTER TWENTY

*The Healer*

We rode for a couple hours while the sky above us turned from pitch black to navy blue to the faintest tinge of pink. Puck kept well ahead of us, flitting from branch to branch until we caught up, then swooping away again. He led us deep into the swamps, through bogs where the tatter-colt sloshed through waist-deep pools of murky water, past huge, moss-covered trees dripping with vines. Ash said nothing as we traveled, but his head hung lower and lower the farther we went, until it was all I could do to hold him upright.

Finally, as the last of the stars faded from the sky, the tatter-colt pushed its way through a cluster of vine-covered trees to find the raven perched atop a rustic-looking shack in the middle of the swamp.

Before the tatter-colt stopped moving, Ash was sliding off its back, crumpling to the misty ground. As soon as he was off, the tatter-colt began tossing its head and bucking, until I half slid, half fell off its back into the mud. Snorting, the colt trotted into the bushes with its head held high and disappeared.

I knelt by Ash, and my heart clenched at how pallid he looked, the abrasions on his face standing out angrily against his pale skin. I touched his cheek and he groaned, but he didn't open his eyes.

Puck was there suddenly, dragging Ash to his feet, grimacing at the pain of his own wound. "Princess," he gritted out, taking the prince's weight, "go wake up the healer. Tell her we've got an iron-sickened prince on our hands. But be careful." He grinned, his normal self once more. "She can be a little cranky before she's had her coffee."

I climbed the rickety wooden steps onto the porch, which creaked under my feet. A cluster of toadstools, growing right out of the wall near the door, pulsed with a soft orange light, and the shack itself was covered in various moss, lichens and mushrooms of different colors. I took a deep breath and knocked on the door.

No one answered right away, so I banged again, louder this time. "Hello?" I called, peering through a dusty, curtained window. My raw throat ached, bringing tears to my eyes, but I raised my voice and called out again. "Is anyone there? We need your help! Hello?"

"Do you have any idea what time it is?" yelled an irritable voice on the other side. "Do you people think healers don't have to sleep, is that it?" Shuffling footsteps made their way to the door while the voice still continued to mutter. "Up all night with a sick catoblepas, but do I get any rest? Of course not, healers don't need rest. They can just drink one of their special potions and stay up all night, for days on end, ready to jump at every emergency that comes banging on their door at five in the morning!" The door whooshed open, and I found myself staring at empty air.

"What?" snapped the voice near my feet. I looked down.

An ancient gnome stared up at me, her face wrinkled and shriveled like a walnut under a frayed clump of white hair. Barely two feet tall, dressed in a once-white robe with tiny gold glasses on the end of her nose, she glared at me like a furious midget bear, black eyes snapping with irritation.

I felt a stab of recognition. "Ms....Ms. Stacy?" I blurted out, seeing, for just a moment, my old school nurse. The gnome blinked up at me, then pulled her glasses off and began cleaning them.

"Well now, Ms. Chase," she said, cementing my hunch. "It has been a while. Last I saw you, you were hiding in my office after that cruel trick that boy played on you in the cafeteria."

I winced at the memory. That had been the most embarrassing day of my life, and I didn't want to think about it. "What are you doing here?" I asked, amazed. The nurse snorted and shoved her glasses back atop her nose.

"Your father, Lord Oberon, bade me keep an eye on you with Mr. Goodfellow," she replied, looking up at me primly. "If you were hurt, I was supposed to heal you. If you saw anything strange, I was to help you forget. I provided Goodfellow with the necessary herbs and potions he needed to keep you from seeing us." She sighed. "But then, you went traipsing off to the Nevernever to find your brother, and everything unraveled. Fortunately, Oberon allowed me to keep my job as school nurse, in case you ever came back."

I felt a small prick of anger that this woman had blinded me for so long, but I couldn't think about that now. "We need your help," I said, turning so she could see Puck and Ash coming toward the porch. "My friend has been stabbed, but not only that, he's iron-sick and getting weaker. Please, can you help him?"

"Iron-sick? Oh dear." The gnome peered past me, staring

at the two fey boys in the yard, and her eyes got wide behind her glasses. "That…is that…Prince Ash?" she gasped, as the blood drained from her face. "*Mab's* son? You expect me to help a prince of Winter? Have you gone mad? I…no!" She backed through the door, shaking her head. "No, absolutely not!"

The door started to slam, but I stuck my foot in the frame, wincing as it banged my knee. "Please," I begged, shouldering my way through the gap. The nurse glared at me, pursing her lips, as I crowded through the frame. "Please, he could be dying, and we have nowhere else to go."

"I don't make a habit of aiding the Unseelie, Ms. Chase." The nurse sniffed and struggled to close the door, but I wasn't budging. "Let his own take care of him. I'm sure the Winter Court has its share of healers."

"We don't have time!" Anger flared. Ash was getting weaker. He could be dying, and with every second, the scepter got farther away. I bashed my shoulder into the door, and it flew open. The nurse stumbled back, hand going to her chest, as I stepped into the room. "I'm sorry," I told her in my best firm voice, "but I'm not giving you a choice. You *will* help Ash, or things will get very unpleasant in a very short time."

"I won't be bullied by a half-human brat!"

I straightened and towered over her, my head just touching the ceiling. "Oberon *is* my father, you said so yourself. Consider this an order from your princess." When she scowled, her eyes nearly sinking into the creases of her face, I crossed my arms and glared imperiously. "Or, should I inform my father that you refused to help me? That I came to you for aid, and you turned me away? I don't think he'd be too pleased about that."

"All right, all right!" She raised her hands. "I'll get no peace otherwise, I see that now. Bring in the Winter prince. But your father will hear of this, young lady." She turned and shook a finger at me. "He will hear of this, and then we will see who will be the target of his ire."

I felt a small pang of guilt that I had to pull the daddy card like some spoiled rich kid, but it faded as Puck dragged Ash up the stairs. The prince seemed more wraith than flesh now, his skin a sickly gray except for the angry red wounds on his face and arms, where the skin seemed to be peeling off the bones. I shuddered and my heart twisted with worry.

"Put him in here," the nurse ordered, directing Puck to a small side room with a low-lying bed. Puck complied, laying Ash down on the sheets before collapsing into a chair that looked like an enormous mushroom.

The nurse sniffed. "I see the princess has you in on this, too, Robin."

"Don't look at me." Puck smirked and wiped a hand across his face. "I did my best to kill the guy, but when the princess wants something, there's no changing her mind."

I scowled at him. He shrugged and offered a helpless grin, and I turned back to Ash.

"Ugh, he doesn't just smell of iron, he reeks of it," the nurse muttered, examining the wounds on his face and arms. "These burns aren't normal—they've erupted from the inside out. It's almost like he had something metal inside him."

"He did," I said quietly, and the nurse shuddered, wiping her hands. She pulled up Ash's shirt, revealing a layer of gauze that was just beginning to seep blood onto the mattress. "At least the bandaging was done properly," she mused. "Very nice, clean work. Your handiwork, I presume, Goodfellow?"

"Which one?"

"The bandage, Robin."

"Yeah, that was mine, too."

The nurse sighed, bending over Ash, studying the cuts on his face, peeling away the gauze to see the stab wound. Her brow furrowed. "So, let me get this straight," she continued, looking at Puck. "You stabbed Ash, prince of the Winter Court."

"Guilty as charged."

"And, judging by both of your conditions—" her eyes flickered to my throat and Puck's bloody shoulder "—I'm guessing the Winter prince did that to you, as well."

"Right again."

"Which means you were fighting each other." The nurse's eyes narrowed. "Which means he was probably trying to kill you, yes?"

"Well…" I stammered.

"So, why in the name of all that's sacred do you want me to heal him? Not that I won't," she added, holding up her hand, "but what's to stop him from attacking you again? Or me, for that matter?"

"He won't," I said quickly. "I promise, he won't."

"Are you planning to use him as a hostage, is that it?"

"No! It's just—" I sighed. "It's a long story."

"Well, you will have to tell me later," the nurse sighed, standing up. "Your friend is very lucky," she continued, crossing the room to take a porcelain jar off the shelf. "I don't know how he didn't die, but he is strong, to survive as long as he did. He must've been in terrible pain." She returned to his side, shaking her head as she knelt beside him. "I can heal his surface wounds, but I don't know what I can do about the iron sickness. He must recover from that himself. It is better if he returns to Tir Na Nog after this. His body will throw off the sickness faster in his own land."

"That's not really an option," I ventured. The nurse snorted.

"Then I'm afraid he will be quite weak for a long, long time." She straightened and turned around, staring at us with her hands on her hips. "Now I need to work. Both of you, out. If you're tired, use the extra bed in the adjoining room, but don't disturb my other patient. The prince will be fine, but I can't be tripping over you every few seconds. Go on, now. Get."

Making shooing motions with her hands, she chased us from the room and slammed the door behind us.

EVEN EXHAUSTED, I was too worried to sleep. I wandered the healer's small cabin like a restless cat, checking the door every ten seconds, waiting for it to open. Ash was on the other side, and I didn't know what was happening to him. I drove Puck and the satyr with the broken leg crazy, drifting from one room to the next, until Puck threatened, only half jokingly, to put a sleeping spell on me if I didn't relax. To which I threatened, only half jokingly, that I would kill him if he did.

Finally, the door creaked open and the nurse stepped out, bloodstained and weary-eyed, her hair in disarray.

"He's fine," she told me as I rushed up, the question on the tip of my tongue. "Like I said before, he's still weak from the iron-sickness, but he's no longer in any danger. Though I must say—" and she glared at me fiercely, "—the boy almost snapped my wrist when I tried sewing his wounds shut. Wretched Unseelie, the only thing they know is violence."

"Can I see him?"

She eyed me over her gold-rimmed glasses, and sighed. "I should tell you no, he needs his rest, but you wouldn't listen to me, anyway. So yes, you can see him, but keep it short. Oh, and Robin," she said, crooking a finger at Puck, "a word."

Puck gave me a grimace of mock terror and followed the nurse from the room. I watched them leave, then slipped quietly into the darkened room, closing the door behind me.

Easing over to his bed, I sat beside him and studied his face. The cuts were still there, but they were faded now, less severe. His shirt was off, and clean bandages wrapped his stomach and torso. His breathing was slow and deep, his chest rising and falling with each breath. I reached down and gently placed a hand over his heart, wanting to touch him, to feel his heartbeat under my fingers. His face was peaceful, free of harsh lines or worries, but even in sleep, he looked a little sad.

Preoccupied with watching his face, I didn't see his arm move until strong fingers curled gently over mine. My stomach leaped as I looked down, seeing my hand trapped within his, and glanced back at his face. His silver eyes were open now, staring at me, his expression unreadable in the darkness. My breath caught in my throat.

"Hi," I whispered, for lack of anything to say. He continued to watch me, unmoving, and I rattled on. "Um, the nurse says you're going to be fine now. You'll be a little sick from the iron, but that should fade with time." He remained silent, his eyes never leaving my face, and my cheeks started to burn. Maybe he just had a nightmare, and I'd startled him by creeping into his room like a stalker. I was lucky he hadn't snapped my wrist like he almost did with the nurse. "Sorry if I woke you," I muttered, attempting to pull back. "I'll let you sleep now."

His grip tightened, stopping me. "Stay."

My heart soared. I looked down at him, wishing I could just melt into him, feel his arms around me. He sighed, and his eyes closed. "You were right," he murmured, his voice nearly lost in the darkness. "I couldn't do it alone. I should have listened to you back in Tir Na Nog."

"Yes, you should have," I whispered. "Remember that, so that next time you can just agree with whatever I say and we'll be fine."

Though he didn't open his eyes, one corner of his mouth curled, ever so slightly. It was what I was hoping for. For a moment, the barriers had crumbled and we were all right again. I squeezed his hand. "I missed you," I whispered.

I waited for him to say *I missed you, too,* but he grew very still under my hand, and my heart plummeted. "Meghan," he began, sounding uncomfortable. "I…I still don't know if…" He stopped, opening his eyes. "We're still on opposite sides," he murmured, his voice tinged with regret. "Nothing changes that, even now. Contract aside, you're still considered my enemy. Besides, I thought you and Goodfellow—"

I shook my head. "Puck is…" I began, and stopped. What was he? Thinking about him, I suddenly realized I couldn't say he was just a friend. "Just friends" didn't kiss each other in an empty bedroom. "Just a friend" wouldn't make my stomach squirm in weird, fluttery ways when he came through a door. Was this love, this strange, confusing swirl of emotion? I didn't have the same intense feelings for Puck that I did for Ash, but I did feel something for him. I couldn't deny that anymore.

I swallowed. "Puck is…" I tried again.

"Is what?"

I spun around. Puck stood in the doorway, a rather dangerous smile on his face, watching us with narrowed green eyes.

"…talking to the nurse," I said faintly, as Ash released my hand and turned his face away. Puck stared at me, hard and uncomfortable, as if he knew what I was thinking.

"Nurse wants to talk to you," he said at last, turning away. "Says to leave his royal iciness alone so he can sleep. Better go see what she has to say, Princess, before she starts throwing her coffee mug."

I glanced down at Ash, but his eyes were closed and he wasn't looking at me.

A little apprehensive, I approached the kitchen, where the nurse sat at the table with a steaming mug of what was probably coffee, since the whole room smelled like it. The nurse glanced up and waved me to the opposite chair.

"Sit down, Miss Chase."

I did. Puck joined us, plunking into the seat beside me, munching an apple he'd gotten from who knew where.

"Robin tells me you're going on a dangerous mission after this," she began, cupping her withered hands around the mug, staring into the coffee. "He wouldn't give me details, but that's why you need the Winter prince healthy, so he can help you. Is that right?"

I nodded.

"The problem is, if you go through with this plan, you'll almost certainly kill him."

I jerked up. "What are you talking about?"

"He is very sick, Miss Chase." She glared at me over the rim of her mug, steam writhing off her glasses. "I wasn't joking when I said he'll be weak. The iron was in his system too long."

"Isn't there anything else you can do?"

"Me? No. He needs the glamour of his own realm to heal, so his body can throw off the sickness. Barring that—" she took a sip of coffee "—if you could find a great influx of human emotion, in large quantities, that might help him. At the very least, he could begin to recover."

"Lots of glamour?" I thought a moment. Where would there be a lot of crazy, unrestrained human emotion? A concert or a club would be perfect, but we had no tickets, and I was underage for most clubs. But, as Grimalkin had taught me, that wasn't a problem when you could conjure money from leaves and a valid license from a Blockbuster card. "Puck—think you can sneak us into a club tonight?"

He snorted. "I can sneak us into anything, Princess. Who do you think you're talking to?" He snapped his fingers, grinning. "We can pay a visit to Blue Chaos again, that'll be fun."

The nurse blinked. "Blue Chaos is owned by a Winter sidhe who employs redcaps and is rumored to have an ogre in the basement." She sighed. "Wait. If you insist on doing this, I've a better idea, one not so…insane." She looked caught between reluctance and resignation as she turned to me. "The Winter Formal is tonight at your old school, Miss Chase. If there is one place that is sure to have an overabundance of emotionally charged, hormonal teenagers, that would be it."

"The Winter Formal? Tonight?" My stomach fluttered. Going back to my school would mean facing my former classmates, and all the gossip, rumors and stories that followed. I would have to wear a fancy dress in front of everyone, maybe even dance, and they would all snicker and laugh and whisper behind my back. *Think of an excuse, Meghan, quick.* "How will we get in? I haven't been to school in forever, and they're likely to be monitoring the tickets to make sure only students attend."

Puck snorted. "Please. How many of these things do you think I've crashed? Tickets?" He sneered. "We don't need no stinkin' tickets."

The nurse shot Puck an annoyed look and turned to me. "Your parents called off the investigation for you a few months ago, Miss Chase," she said solemnly. "I believe the excuse your mother used was that you had come home and that they sent you away to a boarding school out of state. I'm not sure what she told your father—"

"Stepfather," I muttered automatically.

"—but no one has been looking for you for a while," the nurse finished, as if I hadn't said anything. "Your appearance might seem odd at first, but I'm sure Robin can fix it so you aren't conspicuous. Either way, I doubt anyone will remember you."

I wasn't sure about that. "What about a dress?" I argued, still determined to find a loophole. "I don't have anything to wear."

This time, I received scornful looks from both the nurse and Puck. "We can get you a dress, Princess," Puck scoffed. "Hell,

I can glamour you a dress made of diamonds and butterflies, if you want."

"That's a little extravagant, don't you think, Robin?" The nurse shook her head at him. "Do not worry, Miss Chase," she told me. "I have friends who can help us in that regard. You will have a beautiful dress for the formal, I promise you that."

Well, that would be a nice sentiment, if I wasn't absolutely terrified. I tried again. "The school is forty-five minutes away," I pointed out, "and I don't have a license. How will we get there?"

"I have a trod that leads directly to my office in the school," the nurse replied, crushing that hope. "We can be there in seconds, and you won't miss a thing."

Damn. I was fast running out of excuses. Desperately, I played my last card.

"What about Ash? Should we move him this soon? What if he doesn't want to go?"

"I'll go."

We all whirled around. Ash stood in the doorway, leaning against the frame, looking exhausted but a little better than before. His skin had lost the gray pallor, and the wounds across his face and arms were not as striking. He didn't look good, by any means, but at least he wasn't at death's door.

Ash clenched a fist in front of his face, then let it drop. "I can't fight like this," he said. "I'd be a liability, and our chances of getting the scepter will diminish. If there's a chance for me to shake this off, I'll take it."

"Are you sure?"

He looked at me, and that faint, familiar smile crossed his lips. "I have to be on top of my game if I'm going to kill things for you, right?"

"What you need," the nurse replied, stalking toward him with a steely glint in her eye, "is to go back to bed. I did not spend the last few hours stitching you back together for you to fall apart because you refused to stay down. Go on, now. Back to bed!"

He looked vaguely amused, but let himself be herded back into the room, and the nurse shut the door firmly behind him. "Bullheaded youngsters," she sighed. "Think they're damned invincible." Puck snickered, which was the wrong thing to do.

She whirled around. "Oh, you think it's funny, do you, Goodfellow?" she snapped, and Puck winced. "I happened to notice your shoulder doesn't look well at all. In fact, it's bleeding all over my clean floor. I believe it needs stitches. Follow me, please."

"It's only a flesh wound," Puck said, and the nurse's gaze darkened. Stalking back across the floor, she grabbed him by one long ear and pulled him out of the chair. "Ow! Hey! Ow! Okay, okay, I'm coming! Jeez."

"Miss Chase," the nurse snapped, and I jerked to attention. "While I'm fixing up this idiot, I want you to get some sleep. You look exhausted. Use the empty cot in the patient room, and tell Amano that if he bothers you, I'll break his other leg. After I'm done with Robin, I'll come by with something for your throat."

Doubts still nagged at me, but I nodded. Finding the empty cot, I lay down, ignoring the satyr who invited me to share his "much softer bed." *I'll just lie down for a minute,* I thought, turning my back on Amano. *Just for a minute, and then I'll check on Ash.*

"COME ON, you sleeping beauty. We've got a ball to attend."

I woke up, embarrassed and confused, staring around blearily. The room was dark; candles flickered erratically, and mushrooms on the walls glowed with a soft yellow luminance. Puck stood over me, grinning as usual, the light casting weird, fluttering shadows over his face.

"Come on, Princess. You slept all day and missed the fun. Our lovely nurse got a few of her friends together to make you a dress. They refuse to show it to me, of course, so you have to march in there and come out wearing it."

"What are you talking about?" I muttered, before I remembered. The Winter Formal! I was supposed to show up at my old school after being gone for so long, and face all my former classmates. There would be pointing and rumors and whispers behind my back, and my stomach clenched at the thought.

But there was no going back now. If we were going to get the scepter, Ash needed to heal, which meant I had to endure the humiliation and just get on with it.

I trailed Puck out of the room, where the nurse was waiting for me in the hall, a small, pleased smile on her lips. "Ah, there you are, Miss Chase."

"How's Ash?" I asked before she could say anything else. With a snort, the nurse turned and beckoned me to follow.

"The same," she replied, leading me down the hall. We passed Ash's room, the door tightly closed, and continued without pausing. "The stubborn fool is walking now, and even challenged Robin to a sparring match this afternoon. I stopped them, of course, though Robin was only too happy to fight him, the idiot."

"Hey," Puck said behind us. "I'm not the one who offered. I was just doing the guy a favor."

The nurse whirled and fixed him with a gimlet eye. "You—" she began, then threw her hands up. "Go get ready, idiot. You've been hovering at the door like a lost puppy all day. Tell the prince we'll be leaving as soon as Miss Chase is ready. Now, get."

Puck retreated, grinning, and the nurse sighed. "Those two," she muttered. "They're either best friends or darkest enemies, I can't tell which. Come with me, Miss Chase."

She pushed open another door and stepped through, and I followed, ducking my head. We entered a small room with shelves and potted plants encircling the walls, and a sharp, almost medicinal tang filled the room, as if I had wandered into someone's herb garden. Which, I guess, I had. Two other gnomes, as shriveled and wrinkly as the nurse, looked up from three-legged stools and waved cheerfully.

My breath caught. They were working on a dress so gorgeous my mind stumbled to a halt for a moment. A floor-length, blue satin gown hung from a mannequin in the center of the room, rippling like water in the sun. The bodice was embroidered with silvery designs and glittering ribbons of pure light, and a gauzy blue shawl had been draped over the naked shoulders, so sheer that it was almost invisible. A sparkling diamond choker encircled the mannequin's neck, sending prisms of fragmented light across the walls. The entire outfit was dazzling.

I swallowed. "Is that…for me?"

One of the other gnomes, a short man with a nose like a potato, laughed. "Well, the prince certainly isn't going to wear it."

"It's beautiful."

The gnomes preened. "Our ancestors were shoemakers, but we've learned to sew a few other things, as well. This weave is stronger than normal glamour, and won't fray if you happen to touch anything made of iron. Now, come try it on."

It fit perfectly, sliding over my skin as if made for me. I caught a shimmer of glamour out of the corner of my eye as I pulled it on, and deliberately ignored it. If this dress was put together with leaves, moss and spider silk, I didn't want to know.

When I was done, I raised my arms and turned around for

inspection. The tailor gnomes clapped like happy seals, and the nurse nodded approvingly.

"Take a look at yourself," she murmured, making a spinning motion with her finger. I turned to see myself in the floor-length mirror that appeared out of nowhere, and blinked in surprise.

Not only was the dress perfect, but my hair was styled into complex curls, my face lightly touched with makeup, making me look older than before. And, whether it was part of the dress's glamour or the nurse's doing, I looked *human* again, without the pointed ears and huge, unnatural eyes. I looked like a normal teenager, ready for prom. Illusion, I knew, but it still startled me a moment, this tall, elegant stranger in the mirror.

"The boys won't be able to keep their eyes off her," a gnome sighed, and all my fears came rushing back. Fancy dress or no, I was still me, the invisible Swamp Girl of Albany High. Nothing would change that.

"Come," the nurse said, putting a shriveled hand on mine. "It's almost time."

Back we went, through the door into the central room, where a handsome boy in a classic black tuxedo waited for us. I gasped when I saw it was Puck. His crimson hair had been spiked up so it didn't look quite as disheveled, and his shoulders filled out the jacket he wore. I hadn't realized how fit he was. His green eyes raked me up and down, very, very briefly before returning to my face, and he smiled. Not teasing or sarcastic, but a pure, genuine smile.

"Humph," said the nurse, not nearly as shocked as me. "I guess you can clean up when you want to, Robin."

"I try." Puck, looking very human now, crossed the room and reached for my hand, slipping a white corsage onto my wrist. "You look gorgeous, Princess."

"Thanks," I whispered. "You look nice, yourself."

"Nervous?" he asked.

I nodded. "A little. What will I say if someone asks me where I've been? How will I explain what I've done all year, especially after I come waltzing in like nothing has happened? What about you?" I looked up at him. "Won't they wonder where you've been all this time?"

"Not me." Puck's normal grin came flashing back. "I've been gone too long—long enough for anyone to forget that I ever went to high school. The most I'll get is a vague recollection, like déjà vu, but no one will really recognize me." He shrugged. "One of the perks of being me."

"Lucky you," I muttered.

"Are we ready?" the nurse asked, suddenly appearing in her human mien, a short, stout woman in a white lab coat, with lined brown skin and the same gold glasses on the end of her nose. "And if you're wondering, yes, I am coming with you," she announced, peering at us over her glasses, "just to make sure my patient doesn't push himself so hard he collapses. So, are we done here?"

"We're still waiting for Ash."

"Not anymore," she replied, gazing over my shoulder. I turned slowly, heart pounding against my ribs, not knowing what to expect. For a moment, my mind went completely blank.

I'd daydreamed about Ash in a tuxedo, silly fantasies that crossed my mind every so often, but the image in my head was as far removed as a house cat was to a jaguar. His tuxedo wasn't black, but a dazzling, spotless white, the open jacket showing a white vest and an icy blue tie beneath. His cuff links, the silk handkerchief in his breast pocket, and the glittering stud in his ear were the same icy color. Everything else was white, even his shoes, but instead of appearing ghostly or faded, he filled the room with presence, a royal among commoners. He stood in the doorway with his hands in his pockets, the picture of nonchalance, and even as a human, he was too gorgeous for words. His dark hair had been combed back, falling softly around his face, and his mercury eyes, though they should've seemed pale against all the white, glimmered more brightly than anything.

And they were fixed solely on me.

I was unable to move or make a sound. If my knees hadn't already been locked, I would've been a satiny blue puddle on the floor. Ash's gaze held mine; his eyes didn't stray from my face, but I felt him looking at all of me, taking me in as surely as Puck had scanned the length of my dress in a glance. I couldn't stop staring back. Everything around me—noise, colors, people—faded into the ether, losing all relevance and meaning, until it was only me and Ash in the entire world.

Then someone took my elbow, and my heart jolted back to normal.

"Okay," Puck said a little too loudly, steering me away, "the gang's all here. Are we going to this party, or not?"

Ash walked up beside me. He made no noise, but I could feel his presence as surely as my own. He didn't offer his arm or make any move to touch me, but my nerves buzzed and my skin tingled, just with him standing there. I caught a hint of frost and the strange, sharp smell that was uniquely him, and the memory of our first dance together came rushing back.

I didn't miss the subtle look that passed between Ash and Puck, either. Ash kept his expression carefully blank, but Puck's mouth twitched in a faint smirk—one of his dangerous ones— and his eyes narrowed a fraction.

The nurse must've seen it, too, for she clapped her hands briskly, and I jumped about three feet in the air. "May I remind you three," she stated in a no-nonsense voice, "that even though this is a party, we are there for a specific reason. We are not there to spike the punch, seduce the humans, glamour the food, challenge the males to a fight, or do anything pertaining to mischief. Is that understood?" She shot a piercing glare at Puck when she said this, and he pointed to himself with wide-eyed, *who, me?* look. It did not amuse her. "I will be watching you," she warned, and even though she was barely four feet tall, white-haired, and shriveled like a prune, she made the threat sound ominous. "Do try to behave yourselves."

# CHAPTER TWENTY-ONE

*The Winter Formal*

It was an eerie feeling, walking the hallways of my school after being gone for so long. Dozens of memories floated through my head as we passed once-familiar landmarks: Mr. Delany's classroom where I'd sat behind Scott Waldron in Classic Lit, the bathrooms I'd spent a lot of time in, crying, the cafeteria where Robbie and I had always eaten together at the last table in the corner. So much had changed since then. The school seemed different somehow, less real than before. Or maybe I was the one who had changed.

Clusters of blue and white balloons led the way to the gym, light and music pouring out from the double doors and windows. My stomach started turning nervous backflips the closer we got, especially when the doors swung open and two students walked out, holding hands and giggling. The boy pulled his date to him for a long, tongue-swabbing kiss, before they broke apart and began creeping behind the building.

"Mmm, smell the lust," Puck muttered beside me. The nurse snorted.

"They're not supposed to leave the gym without supervision," she growled, putting her hands on her hips. "Where are the chaperones? I suppose I'll have to deal with this. You three, behave." She stalked away, virtually bristling with indignation, following the pair around the gym and into the shadows.

The coast was clear. Swallowing my nervousness, I looked back at the boys to see if they were ready. Puck grinned at me, eager as always, mischief written plainly on his face. Ash regarded me with a solemn expression. He looked stronger already, his eyes bright, the cuts healed to just faint, thin scars across his cheeks. Our gazes met, and the depth of emotion smoldering within left me breathless.

"How do you feel?" I asked, to hide the longing I knew must show on my face. "Is this helping at all? Are you getting better?"

He smiled, very faintly. "Save me a dance," he murmured.

And then we were moving toward the gym. The music grew louder and the din of voices echoed beyond the walls. Puck and Ash each pushed open a door, and we swept through into another world.

The gym had been decorated with more blue and white balloons, crepe paper, and glittering foam snowflakes, though we never saw snow in Louisiana. We passed the ticket booth with a group of teens clustered around it, either buying tickets or waiting in line. No one seemed to notice us as we swept by, but my stomach lurched as I caught sight of a familiar figure, smiling as she handed tickets to another well-dressed couple. Angie the ex-cheerleader stood behind the table, minus the huge pig nose Puck had given her last year in a vengeful prank. She seemed perfectly happy, smiling and nodding as if she did this kind of work every day. I tried to catch her eye as we passed, but her attention was on the line in front of her and the moment was gone.

Beyond the ticket booth, blue and white tables lined one side of the room; only a few people sat there, the unfortunate ones who couldn't get a date but didn't want to miss the formal just because they were single.

*Where I would be,* I thought, *if I hadn't been pulled into Faery. Or, more than likely, I wouldn't have been here in the first place. I'd have been home, with a movie and a half-pint of ice cream.*

The room's other half was a sea of swirling gowns and tuxedos. Couples swayed to the music, some dancing casually with their partners, some so welded together you'd need a crowbar to pry them apart. Scott Waldron, my old crush, had his arms around a stick-thin blonde I recognized as one of the cheerleaders, his hands sliding below her waist to fondle her rear. I watched them dance, their hands roaming all over each other, and felt nothing.

And then the murmurs began, starting from the table where the Dateless sat, spreading to the dance floor and the corners of the room. People were staring at us, shooting furtive glances over their dates' shoulders, heads bent low to whisper to each other. My face burned and my steps faltered, wanting to beat a hasty retreat from the room to the nearest bathroom stall. Mr. Delany, my old English teacher, looked up from where he stood guard over the punch bowl and frowned. Breaking away from the table, he strode toward us, squinting through his thick glasses. My heart pounded, and I turned to Puck in a panic.

"Mr. Delany is coming toward us!" I hissed. Puck blinked and looked over my shoulder.

"Huh, it is old Delany. Jeez, he's gotten fat. Hey, remember the time I put itching powder in his toupee?" He sighed dreamily. "That was a good day."

"Puck!" I glared at him. "Help me out here! What do I say? He knows I haven't been in school for months!"

"Excuse me," Mr. Delany said, right behind me, and my heart nearly stopped. "Is that...Meghan Chase?" I turned to him with a sickly smile. "It *is* you. I thought so." He gaped at me. "What are you doing here? Your mother told us you were at a boarding school in Maine."

*So that's where I've been all this time. Nice cover, Mom.* "I'm...uh...home for Christmas vacation," I answered, saying the first thing that came to mind. "And I wanted to see my old school one more time before I went back."

Mr. Delany frowned. "But, Christmas vacation was several..." He trailed off suddenly, a glazed look coming over his face. "Christmas vacation," he murmured. "Of course. How lovely for you. Will you be coming back next year?"

"Um." I blinked at his sudden change of mood. "I don't know. Maybe? There's still a lot of things to work out."

"I see. Well, it was nice to see you, Meghan. Enjoy the dance."

"See you, Mr. Delany."

As he wandered back toward the punch bowl, I breathed a sigh of relief. "That was a close one. Nice save, Puck."

"Huh?" Puck frowned at me. "What do you mean?"

"The charm spell?" I lowered my voice to a whisper. "Come on, you didn't cast that?"

"Not me, Princess. I was about to turn his wig into a ferret, but then he went all sleepy-eyed before I could pull it off." Puck sighed, gazing at the retreating English teacher in disappointment. "Pity, really. That would've livened up the party. There's so much glamour here, it's a shame not to use it."

I looked over his shoulder. "Ash?"

The Winter prince gave me a faint smile. "Subtlety has never been Goodfellow's forte," he murmured, ignoring Puck's scowl. "We're not here to cause a riot. And human emotions have always been easy to manipulate."

*Like mine were?* I wondered as we continued across the gym floor. *Did you just cast a charm spell to manipulate my emotions, like Rowan tried to do? Are my feelings for you real, or some sort of fabricated glamour? And do I even care if they are?*

At the tables, Puck stepped in front of me and bowed. "Princess," he said formally, though his eyes were twinkling as he held out a hand. "May I have the honor of the first dance?"

"Um." For a moment, I balked at the idea, on the verge of telling Puck that I couldn't dance. But then I felt Ash's gaze, reminding me of a moonlit grove and swirling around the dance floor with the Unseelie prince as scores of faeries looked on. *You're Oberon's blood,* his deep voice murmured in my head. *Of course you can dance.*

Besides, Puck wasn't exactly giving me a choice. Taking my hand, he led me toward the floor. I glanced at Ash in apology, but the prince had moved to a dark corner and was leaning against the wall, looking out over the sea of faces.

And then we were dancing.

Puck danced very well, though I don't know why this surprised me. He probably had loads of experience. I stumbled a few times at first, then closed my eyes and imagined my first dance with Ash. *Stop thinking,* Ash had told me that night as we swirled across the floor in front of several dozen fey. *The audience doesn't matter. The steps don't matter. Just close your eyes and listen to the music.* I remembered that dance, the way I'd felt with him, and the steps came easily once more.

Puck gave a soft chuckle. "Okaaaay," he murmured as we spun around the room, "I seem to remember a certain someone swearing that she couldn't dance at all. Obviously I must've been with her twin sister, because I was expecting you to step on my toes all night. Been taking lessons, Princess?"

"Oh…um. I sort of picked it up while I was in the Nevernever." *Not entirely a lie.*

As we moved around the dance floor, I caught glimpses of Ash, standing alone in the corner with his hands in his pockets. It was too dark to see the emotion on his face, but his gaze never left us. Then Puck pulled me into a twirl, and I lost sight of him for a moment.

The next time I glanced in Ash's direction, he wasn't alone. Three girls, one of them the skinny blonde who had been melded to Scott a few minutes ago, had trapped him and were very obviously flirting. Smiling coyly, they oozed close, flipping their hair and giving him sultry looks from beneath their lashes. My hand fisted on Puck's lapel. It took all my willpower not to stomp over and tell them to back the hell off, but what right did I have? Ash wasn't mine. I didn't have any claim to him.

Besides, he would probably just ignore them, or tell them to go away. But when I peeked at the corner again, I saw Ash smiling at the girls, achingly handsome and charming, and my stomach roiled. He was *flirting* with them.

The song came to an end and Puck drew back, frowning slightly, as though he knew my heart wasn't in it anymore. I fanned myself with both hands, feigning breathlessness, but really drying the tears that stung my eyes. Ash was still there in the corner, chuckling at something one of the girls had said. My throat closed up, and my chest felt tight.

"You okay, Princess?"

I wrenched my gaze from Ash and the girls, swallowing hard. "A little hot," I confessed, smiling as we edged our way off the dance floor, back to the tables. "And maybe a little dizzy." Puck chuckled, his old self again, and pulled out a chair for me.

"Sorry. I just have that effect on people." I smacked his

stomach with the back of my hand as I sat down, and he grinned. "Hang on. I'll get you something to drink." He vanished into the crowd, making his way toward the refreshment table at the far wall. I hoped he wouldn't spike the punch with something that would turn everyone into frogs. Sighing at the thought, I let my gaze wander around the gym, deliberately keeping it from straying to the far corner.

"Hey." A body moved across my vision, blocking my view. A wide-shouldered body, in a perfectly tailored black tux. I glanced up past the vest and lapels and bow tie, and met Scott Waldron's smiling gaze.

"Hi," he greeted cheerfully, as my stomach did a backflip. Was I seeing this right? Was *Scott Waldron,* football jock extraordinaire, talking to me? Or was this another of his tricks, meant to embarrass and humiliate me, just like last time? I had to admit, he was still really cute—wide shoulders, wavy blond hair, adorable smile—but the memory of the entire cafeteria, roaring with laughter at my expense dampened my enthusiasm a bit. He wouldn't play me like that, ever again.

"Uh, hi," I returned cautiously.

"I'm Scott," he went on in the confident, self-assured way of someone who was used to being admired. "I haven't seen you around school before. You must go somewhere else, right? I'm the varsity quarterback for Albany High."

He didn't even recognize me. I didn't know whether to be relieved or annoyed. Would he be talking to me now if he knew who I was? Would he remember the shy, geeky Swamp Girl who'd crushed on him for two years and waited by his locker every day just to watch him pass her in the hall? Did he ever regret the horrible prank he'd pulled all those months ago?

"You wanna dance?" he asked, holding out his big, football-callused hand.

I glanced toward the drinks table to see that Puck had been

cornered by the nurse, who, from his half annoyed, half contrite expression, appeared to have caught him doing some kind of mischief. Probably spiking the punch, exactly as I'd feared.

A high-pitched giggle came from the corner I wasn't looking at, and my stomach turned.

"Sure," I answered, putting my hand in his. If he heard the bitterness in my voice, he didn't let on as we swept out to the dance floor.

Scott put his hands very low on my waist as we swayed to the music, standing closer than I was really comfortable with, but I didn't protest. Here I was, me, Meghan Chase, dancing with the esteemed Golden Boy of Albany High. I tried to be excited; a year ago, I would've given *anything* for Scott to look at me and smile. Had he asked me to dance, I probably would have fainted. But now, feeling his hands on my hips, seeing his face not six inches from mine, I thought only that Scott seemed very young. Still handsome and charming, there was no mistaking that, but the intense fluttery feeling I used to get whenever I looked at him was gone.

"So," Scott murmured, running his hands up my back. I shifted uncomfortably, but at least they didn't slide in the opposite direction. "Did I mention I'm the varsity quarterback already?"

"You did." I smiled at him.

"Oh, right." He grinned back, wrapping a curl of my hair around his finger. "Well, have you ever been to any of my games?"

"A few."

"Yeah? Pretty impressive, huh? Think we have a chance to make Nationals this year?"

"I really don't know much about football," I admitted, hoping he would drop the subject. Apparently, it was the wrong thing to say. He immediately launched into a full explanation of the sport, citing all the games he'd won, his teammate's flaws and shortcomings, and all the years he'd carried the team to victory. That led to his plans for college, how he'd gotten a scholarship to Louisiana State, how he'd been voted Most Likely to Succeed, and the brand-new Mustang his dad bought him just because he was so proud. I plastered a smile to my face, made appropriate noises of appreciation, and tried not to let my eyes glaze over.

"Hey," he said at last, as I secretly hoped he was wrapping up, "you wanna get out of here? I'm meeting a bunch of people at Brody's house later—his old man is out of town, and there's gonna be a party after the dance. Wanna come?"

Another shock. Scott was inviting me to a cool kids' party, where there would be drinking, drugs and other activities parents frowned upon. For just a moment, I felt a twinge of regret. The one night I got invited to a party would be the one night I couldn't go.

"I can't," I told him. "I'm sorry, I have other plans tonight."

He pouted. "Really?" he said, and his hands slid past my hips, definitely farther than I was comfortable with. "You can't break them, even for me?"

I stiffened, and he actually seemed to get the hint, sliding them back into neutral territory. "I'm sorry," I said again. "But I really can't. Not tonight."

He sighed in genuine regret. "All right, mystery girl, break my heart." Taking my hand, he pressed it to his chest and gave me a coy, little-boy smile. "But at least let me call you this weekend. What's your name?"

And there it was.

I could tell him. I could tell him, and watch the smile fade from his lips as he realized whom he'd been seducing so earnestly. Watch that cocky grin turn to horror and disbelief, and maybe just a little regret. I wanted to see regret. He deserved it, after what he'd done to me. I just had to say two words, two simple words, *Meghan Chase,* and the Golden Boy of Albany High would be laid lower than the bottom of my heels.

All I had to do was say my name.

I sighed, softly patted his chest, and whispered, "Let's keep it a mystery, okay?"

"Uh…" The grin faltered, and he blinked, looking so confused that I almost laughed out loud. "Okay. But…how will I get in touch with you? How will I know who to call?"

"Excuse me."

My stomach fluttered. I felt the smile stretching my face even before we turned around, though I tried to look severe and angry. It was no use. Ash stood there under the dim lights, solemn and beautiful as he extended his hand to me. "May I cut in?"

Knowing Scott, I expected him to refuse, to tell the competition to back off. But perhaps he was still off balance, or maybe it was something in the prince's steady gaze that made him take a step back. Still looking a bit confused, like he didn't know what had just happened, he wandered off the dance floor and into the crowd. And I suddenly had the feeling that would be the last time I ever saw Scott Waldron.

I suppose I should've been happy, but all I felt was relief that he was gone. Ash smiled at me, and I forgot to be angry, forgot to be distant and coy and aloof as I'd planned. Instead, I took his hand and let him draw me close, breathed in the frosty scent of him, and was whisked away to our first dance under the stars, the first time I held his hand, looked into his eyes, and was completely lost.

Dancing with Ash was exactly how I remembered it.

The song was slow and sweet, so we swayed back and forth,

barely moving, but the look on his face, the feel of his hand on mine, was all heart-achingly familiar. I laid my head on his chest and closed my eyes, content to touch him, to listen to his heartbeat. He sighed and rested his chin atop my head, and for a moment, neither of us spoke; we just swayed to the music.

Until I decided to be an idiot and open my mouth.

"So, you seemed to be enjoying yourself back there." I couldn't keep the accusation from my voice, even though I hated myself for sounding like a freaky-possessive girlfriend. "Those girls found you very interesting, I suppose. What were you talking about?"

He chuckled, sending a tingle down my spine. He laughed so infrequently, and it was a deep, marvelous sound when he did. "They invited me to a party after the dance," he murmured, pulling back to look at me directly. "I told them I was already with someone, so they spent the next few minutes trying to convince me to…ditch?…whomever I was with and join them. It was a rather interesting conversation."

"You could've just told them to go away." I'd seen that cold, *don't-bother-me-or-I'll-kill-you* glare. No one in their right mind would continue pestering the Ice prince once that chilling gaze was turned on them.

"That wouldn't have been very gentlemanly." Ash sounded amused. "And it was advantageous for me to have them stay. There was enough glamour in that one corner to choke a dragon. Isn't that why we're here?"

"Oh." Relief and embarrassment colored my face. "Right. It is. I just thought…never mind. I'll shut up now."

Ash looked down at me, cocking his head with a puzzled frown. "What exactly are you accusing me of, Meghan Chase?"

"I wasn't accusing." I hid my face in his shirt, mumbling through the cool fabric. "I just thought…with how easy it is to manipulate human emotions…that you, I don't know. Might find something more interesting than me."

Wow, that had come out stupid and psycho possessive. My face burned even more. I kept my head down so he wouldn't see my crimson cheeks, and I wouldn't have to see his reaction either.

"Ah." Ash brushed my cheek with the back of his hand, catching a loose strand of hair between his fingers. "I've seen thousands of mortal girls," he said softly, "more than you could ever count, from all corners of your world. To me, they're all the same." His finger slid below my chin, tilting my head up. "They see only this outer shell, not who I really am, beneath. You have. You've seen me without the glamour and the illusions, even the ones I show my family, the farce I maintain just to survive. You've seen who I really am, and yet, you're still here." He brushed his thumb over my skin, leaving a trail of icy heat. "You're here, and the only dance I want is this one."

My heart skipped a beat. His nearness was overwhelming, his face and lips just inches away. We stared at each other, and I could see the hunger in his eyes. I trembled in anticipation, my lips aching to touch his, but a flicker of regret crossed his face and he silently drew back, ending the moment. Sighing, I laid my head against his shirt, my entire being buzzing with thwarted hope, a heavy disappointment settling in my chest. I heard his heart thudding against my cheek, and felt him tremble, too.

"Since we're on the subject," Ash murmured after a few minutes of silent dancing, as our hearts and minds composed themselves, "you never answered my question."

He sounded uncharacteristically unsure. I shifted in his arms and looked up, meeting his gaze. "What question?"

His eyes were deep gray in the dim light. Glamour shimmered around him, heavy in the air and in the dreams of those around us. For just a moment, the illusion of the human boy dancing with me wavered, revealing an unearthly faery with silver eyes, glamour pouring off of him in waves. Compared to the suddenly plain human dancers surrounding us, his beauty was almost painful.

"Do you love him?"

My breath caught. For the barest of seconds, I thought he meant Scott, but of course that wasn't right. There was only one person he could mean. Almost against my will, I glanced behind me, through the swaying crowd of dancers, to where Puck stood at the edge of the light. His arms were crossed, and he was watching us with narrowed green eyes.

My heart skipped a beat. I turned back, feeling Ash's gaze on me, my mind spinning several directions at once. *Tell him no,* it whispered. *Tell him Puck is just a friend. That you don't feel anything for him.*

"I don't know," I whispered miserably.

Ash didn't say anything. I heard him sigh, and his arms tightened around me, pulling us closer together. We fell silent again, lost in our own thoughts. I closed my eyes, wanting time to freeze, wanting to forget about the scepter and the faery courts and make this night last forever.

But of course, it ended much too soon.

As the last strains of music shivered across the gym floor, Ash lowered his head, his lips grazing my ear. "We have company," he murmured, his breath cool on my skin. I opened my eyes and looked around, peering through the heavy glamour for invisible enemies.

A pair of slitted golden orbs stared at me from a table, floating in midair above the flowery centerpiece. I blinked, and Grimalkin appeared, bushy tail curled around himself, watching me. No one else in the room seemed to notice a large gray cat sitting in the middle of the table; they moved around and past him without a single glance.

Puck met us at the edge of the dance floor, indicating he'd seen Grimalkin too. Casually, we walked up to the table, where Grimalkin had moved on to grooming a hind leg. He glanced up lazily as we approached.

"Hello, Prince," he purred, regarding Ash through half-lidded eyes. "Nice to see you are not evil…well…you know. I assume you are here for the scepter, as well?"

"Among other things." Ash's voice was cold; fury rippled below the surface, and the air around him turned chilly. I shivered. He didn't just want the scepter; he was out for revenge.

"Did you find anything, Grim?" I asked, hoping the other students wouldn't notice the sudden drop in temperature. Grimalkin sneezed once and stood, waving his tail. His gold eyes were suddenly serious.

"I think you had best see this for yourself," he replied. Leaping off the table, he slipped through the crowds and out the door. I took one last look around the gym, at my old classmates and teachers, feeling a twinge of sadness. I'd probably never see them again. Then Puck caught my gaze with his encouraging smile, and we followed Grimalkin out the doors into the night.

Outside, it was bitingly cold. I shivered in my thin gown, wondering if Ash's mood could spread to the entire district. Ahead of us, Grimalkin slipped around a corner like a furry ghost, barely visible in the shadows. We followed him down the corridors, past numerous classrooms, and into the parking lot, where he stopped at the edge of the sidewalk, gazing out over the blacktop.

"Oh, my God," I whispered. The entire lot—pavement,

cars, the old yellow bus in the distance—was covered with a fine sheeting of white powder that sparkled under the moonlight. "No way. Is that...*snow?*" I bent and scooped up a handful of the white drifts. Wet, cold and crumbly. It couldn't be anything else. "What's going on? It never snows here."

"The balance is off," Ash said grimly, gazing around the alien landscape. "Winter is supposed to hold the power right now, but with the scepter gone, the natural cycle is thrown off. So you get events like this." He gestured to the snowy parking lot. "It will only get worse, unfortunately."

"We have to get the scepter back now," I said, looking down at Grimalkin. He gazed back calmly, as if snow in Louisiana was perfectly normal. "Grim, did you and Ironhorse find anything yet?"

The cat made a great show of licking his front paw. "Perhaps."

I wondered if Ash and Puck ever felt the urge to strangle him. Apparently, I wasn't asking the right questions. "What did you find?" Puck asked, and Grimalkin finally looked up.

"Maybe the scepter. Maybe nothing." He flicked his paw several times before continuing. "But...there is a rumor on the streets of a great gathering of Iron fey in a factory in downtown San Jose. We located it, and it looks abandoned, so perhaps Virus has not gathered her army yet."

"Where's Ironhorse?" I asked.

Ash narrowed his eyes.

"I left him at the factory," Grimalkin said. "He was ready to charge in, but I convinced him I would return with you and Goodfellow. He is still there, for all I know."

"You left him *alone?*"

"Is that not what I just said, human?" Grimalkin narrowed his eyes at me, and I gave the boys a panicked look. "I suggest you hurry," he purred, looking out over the parking lot. "Not only is Virus gathering a great army of Iron fey, but I do not think Ironhorse will wait very long. He seemed rather eager to charge in by himself."

"Let's go," I said, glancing at Ash and Puck. "Ash, are you all right for this? Will you be able to fight?"

He regarded me solemnly and made a quick gesture with his hand. The glamour fell away, the tuxedo dissolving into mist, as the human boy disappeared and the Unseelie prince took his place, his black coat swirling around him.

I looked back at Puck and saw his tux replaced with his normal green hoodie. He gave me a once-over and grinned. "Not exactly dressed for battle, are you, Princess?"

I looked down at my gorgeous dress, feeling a pang of regret that it would probably be ruined before the night was out. "I don't suppose I have time to change," I sighed.

"No." Grimalkin twitched an ear. "You do not." He shook his head and glanced skyward. "What time is it?"

"Um…I don't know." I'd long given up wearing a watch. "Almost midnight, I think. Why?"

He appeared to smile, which was rather eerie. "Just sit tight, human. They will be here soon."

"What are you talking…," I trailed off as a cold wind whipped across the parking lot, swirling the snow into eddies, making them dance and sparkle over the drifts. The branches rattled, an unearthly wailing rising over the wind and trees. I shivered, and saw Ash close his eyes.

"You called *Them,* caith sith?"

"They owed me a favor," Grimalkin purred, as Puck glanced nervously at the sky. "We do not have the time to locate a trod, and this is the fastest way to travel from here. Deal with it."

"What's going on?" I asked, as both Ash and Puck moved closer, tense and protective. "Who'd he call? What's coming?"

"The Host," Ash murmured darkly.

"What…" But at that moment I heard a great rushing noise, like thousands of leaves rustling in the wind. I looked up and saw a ragged cloud moving toward us at a frightening speed, blotting out the sky and stars.

"Hang on," Puck said, and grabbed my hand.

The black mass rushed toward us, screaming with a hundred voices. I saw dozens of faces, eyes, open mouths, before it was upon us, and I cringed back in fear. Cold, cold fingers snatched at me, bearing me up. My feet left the ground in a rush, and I was hurtling skyward, a shriek lodging in my throat. Icy wind surrounded me, tearing at my hair and clothes, numbing me to all feeling except a small spot of warmth where Puck still held my hand. I closed my eyes, tightening my grip as the Host bore us away into the night.

# CHAPTER TWENTY-TWO

*Ironhorse's Choice*

I don't know how long the Host carried us through the sky, screeching and wailing in their unearthly voices. I don't know if they had trods that let them move between worlds, if they could bend space and time, or if they just flew really, really fast. But what should have been hours felt like only minutes before my feet hit solid ground and I was falling forward.

Puck's grip on me tightened, jerking me to a halt before I could fall over. I clutched his arm to regain my balance, looking around dizzily.

We stood on the outskirts of an enormous factory. Across a bright parking lot, lit with neat rows of glowing streetlamps, a huge glass, steel and cement monstrosity loomed at the edge of the pavement. Though the lot was empty, the building itself didn't look damaged in any way: no smashed windows, no graffiti streaking the sides. I caught glimpses of things moving along the walls, flashes of blue light, like erratic fireflies. A moment later, I realized they were gremlins—hundreds, if not thousands of them—scuttling over the factory like ants. The blue lights were the glow of their fangs, hissing, shrieking and baring teeth at each other. A chill ran through me, and I shivered.

"A gremlin nest," Grimalkin mused, watching the swarm curiously. "Leanansidhe said the gremlins congregate in places that have a lot of technology. It makes sense Virus would come here, too."

"I know this place," Ash said suddenly, and we all looked at him. He was gazing at the plant with a small frown on his face. "I remember Virus talking about it when I…when I was with her." The frown grew deeper, and a shadow crept over his face. He shook it off. "There's supposed to be a trod to the Iron Kingdom inside."

Puck nudged my arm and pointed. "Look at that."

I followed his finger to a sign at the front of the building, one of those big marble slabs with giant glowing words carved into it. "SciCorp Enterprises," I muttered, shaking my head.

"Coincidence?" Puck waggled his eyebrows. "I think not."

"Where's Ironhorse?" I asked, looking around.

"This way," Grimalkin said, trotting along the edge of the parking lot. We followed, the boys slightly blurred at the edges, telling me they were invisible to humans, and me in my very conspicuous prom dress and heels that were so not useful for raiding a giant factory, or even walking down a sidewalk. To my right, cars zoomed past us on the street; a few slowed down to honk at me or whistle, and my cheeks burned. I wished I could glamour myself invisible, or at least have had time to change into something less cumbersome.

Grimalkin led us around the factory, skirting the edges of the sidewalk, to a drainage ditch that separated one lot from the other. At the bottom of the ditch, oily black water pooled from a massive storm drain, trickling through the weeds and grass. Bottles and cans littered the ground, glinting in the moonlight, but there was no sign of Ironhorse.

"I left him right here," Grimalkin said. Looking around briefly, he leaped to a dry rock and began shaking his paws, one by one. "We appear to be too late. It seems our impatient friend has already gone inside."

A deep snort cut through the air before I could panic. "HOW FOOLISH DO YOU THINK I AM?" Ironhorse rumbled, bending low to clear the rim of the pipe. He was in his more human form, as there was no way he could have fit his real body inside. "THERE WAS A PATROL COMING, AND I WAS FORCED TO HIDE. I DO NOT BREAK THE PROMISES I GIVE." He glared at Grimalkin, but the cat only yawned and started washing his tail.

Ash stiffened, and his hand went casually to his sword hilt. I didn't blame him. Barring his brief stint with Virus, the last Ash had seen of Ironhorse, he was dragging us to Machina in chains. Of course, Ironhorse was wearing a different form now, but you had only to look closely to see the huge, black iron monster that lurked beneath the surface.

I switched to the problem at hand, not oblivious to the dark look he was receiving from Ash. "We're sure Virus is in there?" I asked, subtly moving between them. "So, how are we going to get inside, especially with the gremlins crawling all over the building?"

Ironhorse snorted. "THE GREMLINS WILL NOT BOTHER US, PRINCESS. THEY ARE SIMPLE CREA-TURES. THEY LIVE FOR CHAOS AND DESTRUC-TION, BUT THEY ARE COWARDLY AND WILL NOT ATTACK A POWERFUL OPPONENT."

"I'm afraid I have to disagree," Ash said, a dangerous edge to his voice now. "You yourself lead an army of gremlins in

Machina's realm, or have you forgotten? They don't attack powerful opponents? I seem to recall a wave of them trying to tear me apart in the mines."

"That's right," I echoed, frowning. "And what about the time the gremlins kidnapped me and hauled me off to meet you? Don't tell me the gremlins aren't dangerous."

"NO." Ironhorse shook his head. "LET ME CLARIFY. BOTH TIMES, THE GREMLINS WERE UNDER MACHINA'S COMMAND. LORD MACHINA WAS THE ONLY ONE WHO COULD CONTROL THEM, THE ONLY ONE THEY EVER LISTENED TO. WHEN HE DIED, THEY REVERTED TO THEIR NORMAL, FERAL STATE. THEY ARE NO THREAT TO US, NOW."

"What about Virus?" Puck asked.

"VIRUS SEES THEM AS VERMIN. EVEN IF SHE COULD CONTROL THEM, SHE WOULD RATHER LET HER DRONES DO THE WORK THAN STOOP TO DEALING WITH ANIMALS."

"Well, this should be easy, then." Puck smirked. "We'll just stroll in the front door, waltz up to Virus, grab the scepter, have some tea and save the world before breakfast. Silly me, thinking it would be hard."

"What I think Puck is trying to say," I said, shooting Puck a frown, "is—what will we do about Virus when we find her? She's got the scepter. Isn't it supposed to be powerful?"

"Don't worry about that." Ash's voice raised the hairs on my neck. "I'll take care of Virus."

Puck rolled his eyes. "Very nice, Prince Cheerful, but there is one problem. We have to get inside first. How do you propose we do that?"

"You're the expert." Ash glanced at Puck, and his mouth twitched into a smirk of his own. "You tell me."

Grimalkin sighed and rose, his tail lashing his flanks. "The hope of the Nevernever," he said, eyeing each of us disdainfully. "Wait here. I will check the place out."

HE HADN'T BEEN GONE LONG when Puck stiffened and Ash jerked up, his hand going to his sword. "Someone's coming," he warned, and we scrambled into the ditch, my gown catching on weeds and jagged pieces of glass. Sloshing into the pipe, I grimaced as the cold, filthy water soaked my shoes and dress. At this rate, it wouldn't survive the night.

Two figures marched past our hiding spot, dressed in familiar black armor with spines growing from the shoulders and back. The faint smell of rot and putrefying flesh drifted into the tube at their passing. I stifled a cough and put my hand over my nose.

"Rowan's Thornguards," Ash murmured grimly as the pair moved on. Frowning, Puck peeked over his shoulder.

"Wonder how many are in there?"

"I'd guess a few squads at least," Ash replied. "I imagine Rowan wanted to send his best to take over the realm."

"You are right," Grimalkin said, suddenly materializing beside us. He perched on a cinder block so as not to touch the water, keeping his tail straight up. "There are many Thornguards inside, along with several Iron fey and a few dozen human drones. And gremlins, of course. The factory is crawling with them, but no one seems to pay them much attention."

"Did you see Virus or the scepter?" I asked.

"No." Grimalkin sat down, curling his tail tightly around his feet. "However, there are two Thornguards stationed at a back door who will not let anyone past."

At Virus's name, Ash narrowed his eyes. "Can we fight our way through?"

"I would not advise it," Grimalkin replied. "It appears some of them are using iron weapons—steel swords and crossbows with iron bolts and such. It would only take one well-placed shot to kill you."

Puck frowned. "Fey using iron weapons? You think Virus has them all bugged?"

"Something far worse, I'm afraid." Ash's face was like stone as he stared at the factory. "I was forced into service. Virus didn't give me a choice. The Thornguards are acting on their own. Like Rowan. They want to destroy the Nevernever and give it to the Iron fey."

Puck's eyebrows shot up. "*The hell?* Why?"

"Because they think they can become like Virus," I replied, thinking back to what Edgebriar had said, remembering the crazed, doomed look in his eye. "They believe it's only a matter of time before Faery fades away entirely. So the only way to survive is to become like the Iron fey. They wear a metal ring beneath their gloves to prove their loyalty, and because they think it will make them immune to the effects. But it's just killing them slowly."

"Huh. Well, that's...absolutely horrifying." Puck shook his head in disbelief. "Still, we have to get in there somehow, iron weapons or no. Can we glamour ourselves to look like them?"

"It won't hold up against all the iron," Ash muttered, deep in thought.

"I might have a better idea," Grimalkin said. "There are several glass skylights on the roof of the factory. You could map the layout of the building from there, maybe even see where Virus is."

That sounded like a good idea. But... "How do we get up there?" I asked, staring at the looming glass-and-metal wall of the factory. "Puck can fly, and I'm sure Ash can get up there, but Ironhorse and I are a little more earthbound."

Grimalkin nodded sagely. "Normally, I would agree. But tonight, it seems the Fates are on our side. There is a window cleaner's platform on the far side of the building."

EVEN WITH Ironhorse's assurance that the gremlins wouldn't bother us, we approached with extreme caution. The memory of being kidnapped by the gremlins, their sharp claws digging into my skin, their freaky, maniacal laughter and buzzing voices, still burned hot in my mind. One had even lived in my iPod before it was broken, and Machina had used it to communicate with me even within the borders of Arcadia. Gremlins were sneaky, evil, little monsters, and I didn't trust them one bit.

Fortunately, our luck seemed to hold as we made our way around the back of the factory. A small platform hovered over the ground, attached to a pulley system that climbed all the way up to the roof. The wall was dark, and the gremlins were absent, at least for now.

Grimalkin hopped lightly onto the wooden platform, followed by Ash and Puck, being careful not to touch the iron railings. Ash pulled me up after him, and then Ironhorse clambered aboard. The wooden planks creaked horribly and bent in the middle, but thankfully held firm. I prayed the entire thing wouldn't snap like a matchstick when we were three stories in the air.

Puck and Ironhorse each grabbed a rope and began drawing the platform up the side of the building. The dark, mirrored walls reflected a strange party back at us: a cat, two elf-boys, a girl in a slightly tattered gown, and a monstrous black man with glowing red eyes. I contemplated how strange my life had become, but was interrupted by a soft hiss overhead.

A gremlin crouched on the pulleys near the top of the roof,

slanted eyes glowing in the dark. Spindly and long limbed, with huge batlike ears, it flashed me its razor-blue grin and let out a buzzing cry.

Instantly, gremlins started appearing from everywhere, crawling out of windows, scuttling along the walls, swarming over the roof to peer at us. A few even clung to the pulley ropes or perched on the railings, staring at us with their eerie green gaze. Ash pulled me close, his sword bared to slash at any gremlin who ventured near, but the tiny Iron fey didn't make any move to attack. Their buzzing voices filled the air, like radio static, and their vivid grins surrounded us with a blue glow as we continued to inch up the wall, unhindered.

"What are they doing?" I whispered, pressing closer to Ash. He held me protectively with one arm, his sword between us and the gremlins. "Why are they just staring at us? What do they want? Ironhorse?"

The lieutenant shook his head. "I DO NOT KNOW, PRINCESS," he replied, sounding as mystified as I felt. "I HAVE NEVER SEEN THEM ACT IN THIS MANNER BEFORE."

"Well, tell them to go away. They're creeping me out."

A buzz went through the gremlins surrounding us, and the swarm began to clear. Crawling back along the walls, they disappeared through the windows, squeezed into the cracks or scrambled back over the roof. As suddenly as they'd appeared, the gremlins vanished, and the wall was dark and silent again.

"Okay." Puck cast wary looks all around us. "That was…weird. Did someone release gremlin repellant? Did they just get bored?"

Ash sheathed his sword and released me. "Maybe we scared them off."

"Maybe," I said, but Ironhorse was staring at me, his crimson eyes unfathomable.

Grimalkin reappeared, scratching his ear as if nothing had happened. "It does not matter now," he said, as the platform scraped up against the roof. "They are gone, and the scepter is close." He yawned and blinked up at us. "Well? Are you just going to stand there and hope it flies into your hands?"

We crowded off the platform onto the roof of the factory. The wind was stronger here, tugging at my hair and making my gown snap like a sail. I held on to Ash as we made our way across the roof. Far below and all around us, the city sprawled out like a glittering carpet of stars.

Several raised glass skylights sat in the middle of the roof, emitting a fluorescent green glow. Cautiously, I edged up to one and peered down.

"There," Ash muttered, pointing to a mezzanine twenty or so feet above the floor, and maybe thirty feet below us. Through the glass, I could pick out a blur of poison-green amid the stark grays and whites, surrounded by several faeries in black armor. Virus walked to the edge of the overhang and gazed out over a crowd of assembled fey, ready to give a speech, I supposed. I saw Thornguards and wiremen and a few green-skinned men in business suits, along with several fey I didn't recognize. The scepter pulsed yellow-green in Virus's hands as she swept it over her head, and a muffled roar went through the crowd.

"Okay, so we found her," Puck mused, pressing his nose against the glass. "And it looks like she hasn't gathered her whole army quite yet, which is nice. So, how do we get to her?"

Ash made a quiet noise and drew back.

"You don't," he muttered. "I will." He turned to face me. "For all she knows, I'm still under her control. If I can get close enough to grab the scepter before she figures out what happened—"

"Ash, no. That's way too dangerous."

He gave me a patient look. "Anything we try will be dangerous. I'm willing to take that risk." His hand came up, fingers brushing the spot where Puck had stabbed him. "I'm still not completely recovered. I won't be able to fight as well as I normally do. Hopefully, I can fool Virus long enough to get the scepter from her."

"And then what?" I demanded. "Fight your way out? Against those masses? And Virus? What if she knows you don't have the bug anymore? You can't expect to—" I stopped, staring at him, as something clicked in my head. "This isn't about getting the scepter, is it?" I murmured, and he looked away. "This is about killing Virus. You're hoping to get close enough to stab her or cut off her head or whatever, and you don't care what happens next."

"What she did to me was bad enough." Ash's silver eyes glittered as he turned back, cold as the moon overhead. "What she made me do, I will never forgive. If I am discovered, I will at least create a big enough distraction for you to slip in and grab the scepter."

"You could die!"

"It doesn't matter now."

"It does to me." I stared at him in horror. He really meant it. "Ash, you can't go down there alone. I don't know where this fatalistic crap is coming from, but you can stop it right now. I'm not going to lose you again."

"SHE IS RIGHT."

We looked up. Ironhorse stood on the other side of the glass, watching us. His eyes glowed red in the darkness. "IT *IS* TOO DANGEROUS. FOR YOU."

I frowned. "What are you talking—"

"PRINCESS." Abruptly, he bowed. "IT HAS BEEN AN HONOR. WERE THINGS DIFFERENT, I WOULD

GLADLY SERVE YOU UNTIL THE END OF TIME." He looked to Ash and nodded, as it suddenly dawned on me what he was implying. "SHE THINKS THE WORLD OF YOU, PRINCE. PROTECT HER WITH YOUR LIFE."

"Ironhorse, don't you dare!"

He whirled and took off, oblivious to my cries for him to stop. My heart clenched as he approached the second skylight, and I watched helplessly as he gathered himself and jumped...

The glass exploded as he crashed into it, shattering into a million sparkling pieces. Gasping, I looked through the skylight to see the glittering shards rain down on the crowd below. Screaming and snarling, they looked up, covering their eyes and faces as the massive iron horse smashed into their midst with a *boom* that shook the building. Roaring, Ironhorse reared up, blasting flame from his nostrils, steel hooves flailing in deadly arcs.

The room erupted into chaos. Once they recovered from their shock, Thornguards and wiremen surged forward to attack, flinging themselves at Ironhorse, ripping and clawing.

"We have to get down there!" I cried, rushing toward the broken skylight only to have Ash catch my arm.

"Not that way," he said, pulling me back to the unbroken window. "The distraction has already been launched. We cannot help him now. Our target is Virus and the scepter. You should stay here, Meghan. You have no magic and—"

I yanked my arm from his grip. "You did *not* just bring that excuse up again!" I snarled, and he blinked in surprise. I glared at him. "Remember what happened the last time you went off without me? Get this through your stubborn head, Ash. I'm not staying behind and that's final."

One corner of his mouth twitched, just a little. "As you wish, Princess" he said, and glanced at Puck, who was leering at us both. "Goodfellow, are you ready?"

Puck nodded and leaped onto the skylight. I scowled at them both and clambered onto the glass, ignoring Puck's hand to help me up. "How do you expect us to get down there?" I demanded as I clawed myself upright. "Go right through the window?"

Puck snickered. "Glass is a funny thing, Princess. Why do you think ancient people put salt along windowsills to keep us out?" I looked down and saw Virus directly below us, shouting and waving the scepter above her head, her attention riveted on the battle and Ironhorse.

Ash leaped onto the skylight, drawing his sword as he did. "Look after Meghan," he said, as glamour began shimmering around both him and Puck. "I'll take care of Virus."

"What—?" I started, but Puck suddenly swept me into his arms. I was so surprised I didn't have time to protest.

"Hold on tight, Princess," he murmured, as a shimmer went through the air around us, and we dropped straight through the glass like it wasn't there.

We plummeted toward the overhang, a shriek escaping my throat, but it was swallowed up in the chaos between Ironhorse and the rest of the fey. Ash dropped toward Virus like an avenging angel, his coat flapping in the wind, sword bared and gleaming as he raised it over his head.

At the last moment, one of the Thornguards surrounding Virus glanced up, and his eyes got huge. Drawing his sword, he gave a shout of warning, and amazingly, Virus whirled and looked up. Ash's blade slashed down in a streak of blue and met the Scepter of the Seasons as Virus swept it up to block him.

There was a flash of blue and green light and a hideous screech that echoed through the room and caused every eye to turn to the pair on the overhang. Sparks flew between the ice blade and the scepter, bathing the combatants' faces in flickering lights. Virus looked rather shocked to be facing her former soldier; Ash's mouth was tight with concentration as he bore down on her with his sword.

Puck set me down—I didn't even remember landing—and leaped between the Thornguards as they rushed up with drawn swords. Grinning, he threw himself at the guards, daggers flashing in the hellish light coming from Ash's blade and the scepter.

Then Virus started to laugh.

I felt a surge of cold iron glamour, and she shoved Ash away, pushing him back in a flash of green. He recovered immediately, but before he could rush her again, Virus retreated, stepping off the mezzanine to float several feet in the air. Her poisonous green eyes found me and she smiled.

"Well." She sniffed and cast bemused glances at the chaos spread at her feet. Ironhorse, surrounded by Iron fey, still kicked and raged at them, though his struggles were growing weaker. More Thornguards came rushing up the steps, but these held crossbows with iron bolts, pointed right at us. Ash and Puck drew back so that they were standing between me and the guards, who had us surrounded in a bristly black ring.

"Meghan Chase. You are full of surprises, aren't you?" Virus smiled at me. "I've no idea how you managed to free the Winter prince from my bug, but it doesn't matter now. The armies of the false king are ready to march on Summer and Winter. Once they have taken the Nevernever and killed off the oldblood rulers, it will be our turn. We will overrun their armies and kill the false king before he has a chance to savor his victory. Then, the Nevernever will belong to m—"

She didn't have a chance to finish. Ash drew back and hurled a flurry of ice daggers at her face, taking her by surprise. She flinched, holding up the scepter; there was a flash of green light and a surge of power. The icicles shattered, bursting apart before they reached her. With angry shouts, the crossbow men released their quarrels even as Virus screamed at them to stop.

The deadly storm of iron bolts flew toward us. I could *feel* them sailing through the air, *Matrix* style, leaving distorted ripples in their wake. Without thinking, I turned and flung out my hand. I didn't think how crazy it was, that at such close range the bolts would rip right through me like I was paper. That we would all most certainly die, peppered by lethal darts that could kill even if they weren't made of iron. I wasn't thinking of anything as I spun and gestured sharply, feeling a surge of electricity beneath my skin.

A ripple went through the air. The bolts flew to either side of us, thunking into the walls and pinging off metal beams to clatter to the floor. I heard Iron fey shriek as they were hit, but not one of the half-dozen bolts touched us.

The Thornguards gaped. Ash and Puck stared at me as if I had grown another head. I shivered violently, trembling from the strange cold glamour that writhed under my skin and buzzed in my ears.

"Impossible." Virus spun slowly to face me, her face draining of color. She shook her head, as if trying to convince herself. "You cannot be the one. A weakling human girl? You're not even one of us. It's a mistake, it must be!"

I had no idea what she was talking about, but it didn't seem to matter. Virus started to giggle, sticking a green-tinted nail in her mouth, her laughter growing louder and more hysterical, until she stopped and glared at me with wide, crazy eyes. "No!" she screamed, making even the Thornguards flinch. "It isn't right! I was his second! His power should have been mine!"

Her mouth opened, gaping impossibly wide, and the Thornguards backed away. Heart pounding, I pressed close to Ash and Puck, feeling their grim determination, their resolve to go down fighting no matter what. The air started to vibrate, a terrible buzzing filling the air, and Virus threw her head back. With the droning of a million bees, a huge swarm of metal bugs spiraled up from Virus's mouth, swirling around her in a frantic glittering cloud.

Her smile was savage as she looked down at us, extending a hand from the center of the buzzing tornado. "Now, my dears," she said, barely audible over the droning of a thousand bugs, "we will end this little game once and for all. I should have done this when I first saw you, but I had no idea you were the one I was searching for all along."

Everything grew very still. The cold glamour still buzzed beneath my skin, and I could taste metal on the air. I looked at the swarm and saw thousands of individual bugs, but also a single creature sharing one mind, one goal, one purpose.

*A hive mind,* I thought impassively, not knowing why I felt so calm. *Control one, and you control them all.*

Vaguely, I was aware that Virus was speaking, her voice seeming to come from very far away.

"Go," she screamed, sweeping her arm toward us. "Crawl down their throats and nostrils, into their eyes and ears and every open pore. Burrow into their brains and make them tear out their own hearts!"

The Swarm flew toward us, a furious, buzzing cloud. Ash and Puck pressed close; I felt one of them shaking but couldn't tell who. A droning filled my ears as the Swarm approached, glowing bright with iron glamour, melded into a single massive entity.

*One mind. One creature.*

I threw up both my hands as the Swarm dove forward to attack,

*Stop!*

The Swarm broke apart, swirling around us, filling the air

with their deafening buzz. But they didn't attack. We stood in the middle of the screaming hurricane, metal bugs zipping around us frantically but moving no closer.

I felt the Swarm straining against my will, fighting to get past it. I saw Virus's face, first slack with disbelief, then white with fury. She made a violent gesture, and the Swarm buzzed angrily in response. I strengthened my hold, pouring magic into the invisible barrier, drawing glamour from the factory. My head pounded, and sweat ran into my eyes, but I couldn't break my concentration or we'd be torn apart.

Virus smiled nastily. "I have underestimated you, Meghan Chase," she said, rising higher into the air. "I did not think you would force me to use the scepter, but there you go. Do you know what this does, my dear?" she asked, holding it out before her. Ash looked up sharply. "It took me forever to puzzle it out, but I finally got it." She grinned, triumphant. "It enhances the power of the one who holds it. Isn't that interesting? So, for instance, I could make my darling bugs do this…"

The scepter glowed a sickly green, and in that light, the Swarm started to change. They swelled like ticks full of blood, becoming sharp and spiky, with long stingers and huge curved jaws. Now they were the size of my fist, a horrible cross between a wasp and a scorpion, and their wings scraped against each other like a million knives. And their *minds* changed, to something more savage, more visceral and predatory. I nearly lost my hold on them, and the whirlwind tightened, pressing closer to us, before I regained control and pushed them back.

Buzzing furiously, they turned on whatever living thing they could reach, including the guards surrounding us. The Thorn-guards screamed, reeling back and clawing at themselves as the metal bugs swarmed over them, biting and stinging, burrowing into their armor.

Virus giggled madly overhead. "Kill them!" she cried, as several bugs chewed their way into their victims, who fell thrashing and screaming to the ground. My stomach heaved, but I couldn't look away for fear of losing control of the Swarm. I didn't know what Virus thought she was doing until a moment later, when the Thornguards lurched to their feet again, crazed gleams in their eyes.

Raising their swords, they staggered toward us, blood pouring from their wounds and the holes in their armor, their eyes empty of reason. Ash and Puck met them at the edge of the whirlwind, and the clash of weapons joined the metallic drone of the Swarm.

We were lost. I couldn't keep this up forever. My head throbbed so much that I felt nauseous, and my arms were shaking violently. I could feel my strength draining with the amount of glamour I was using to keep the Swarm at bay.

Out of the corner of my eye, I saw a Thornguard, covered in bugs, stagger to the edge of the platform and pick up a crossbow. Raising it up, he loaded an iron bolt and swung it around at me. I couldn't move. If I dodged, the Swarm would break free and kill us. Puck and Ash were busy fighting off the other guards and couldn't help. I couldn't even shout a warning. In slow motion, I watched him raise the crossbow, unhindered, and take aim.

Later, I remembered the clanging footsteps charging up the steps only because they seemed so out of place. I saw Puck whirl around, saw his dagger whip out and soar end over end toward the Thornguard, just as he pulled the trigger. The dagger thunked into the guard's chest, hurling him off the mezzanine, but it was too late. The bolt was coming toward me, and I couldn't do anything about it.

Something huge and black lunged across my vision a split second before the bolt hit home. Ironhorse, covered in bugs and shedding chunks of iron everywhere, stumbled, fighting desperately to stay on his feet. He staggered toward the edge of the overhang, shaking his head as bugs swarmed him viciously. A hoof slipped off the edge, and he lurched sideways.

"No!" I screamed.

With a last defiant bellow and blast of flame, Ironhorse toppled from the edge, vanishing from sight. I heard his body strike the cement with a resounding boom that echoed through the building, and my vision went white with rage.

I arched my back, clenching my fists, and glamour rushed through me, exploding out in a wave. *"GET BACK!"* I roared at the Swarm, at Virus, at every Iron faery in the room. *"Damn you all! Back off, NOW!"*

The Swarm flew in every direction, scattering to all four corners of the room. The Thornguards flinched and stumbled backward; some even fell off the edge of the railing. Even Virus jerked in midair, reeling back like she had been sucker punched, her hands falling limply at her sides.

I slumped to the floor, all the strength going out of me. As the Swarm began coalescing again, buzzing angrily as they swarmed back together, and the Thornguards regained their senses, Virus put a hand to her temple and looked down at me, a smug grin stretching her blue lips.

"Well, Meghan Chase. Congratulations, you've managed to give me a pounding headache. But it is not enough to— aaaahhhhhh!"

She jerked, throwing up her hands as Ash launched himself off the edge of the railing and leaped at her, sword raised high. Still screaming, she tried to bring up the scepter, too late. The ice blade sliced down, through her collarbone and out the other side, cutting her clean in two.

If I wasn't so dizzy, I might've puked. Virus's halves fell

away, wires and oily goo spilling from her severed body as both she and Ash dropped out of sight.

The Thornguards spasmed, then collapsed like puppets with cut strings. As I sat there, dazed by what had just happened, Puck hauled me upright and dragged me under a beam. Then it started raining insects.

The clatter of metal bugs brought me back to my senses. "Ash," I muttered, struggling to free myself. Puck wrapped his arms around me and held me to his chest. "I have to go to him…see if he's all right."

"He's fine, Princess," Puck snapped, tightening his grip. "Relax. He knows enough to get out of the rain."

I relented. Closing my eyes, I leaned into him, resting my head on his chest as the bugs clattered around us like glittering hail. He hugged me close, muttering something about Egyptian plagues, but I wasn't listening. My head hurt, and I was still trying to process everything that had just happened. I was so tired, but at least it was over. And we had survived.

Or, most of us had.

"Ironhorse," I whispered as the rain of bugs finally came to an end. I felt Puck tense. Freeing myself from his arms, I stumbled across the mezzanine, taking care to avoid the dead bugs and Thornguards, and groped my way down the stairs. I didn't know what I'd find, but I was hopeful. Ironhorse couldn't be dead. He was the strongest of us all. He might be terribly hurt, and we'd have to find someone to put him back together, but Ironhorse was near invincible. He had to have survived. He had to.

I'd almost convinced myself not to worry when Ash stepped out from beneath the overhang and stood at the foot of the stairs, gazing up at me. His sword was sheathed, and in one hand, the Scepter of the Seasons pulsed with a clean blue light.

For a long moment, we stared at each other, unwilling to

break the silence, to voice what we both were thinking. I wondered if Ash would take the scepter and leave. Our contract was done. He had what he came for; there was no reason for him to stick around any longer.

"So." I broke the silence first, trying to quell the tremor in my voice, the stupid tears that pressed behind my eyes once more. "Are you leaving now?"

"Soon." His voice was calm but tired. "I'll be returning to Winter, but I thought I would pay my respects to the fallen before I go."

My stomach dropped. I looked behind him and saw, for the first time, the pile of mangled iron in the shadows of the mezzanine. With a gasp, I lurched down the rest of the stairs, pushed past Ash, and half ran, half stumbled to where Ironhorse lay surrounded by dead bugs and the smoking remains of Virus.

"Ironhorse?" For a split second, I thought I saw Grimalkin there, sitting at his head. But I blinked back tears and the image was gone. Ironhorse lay on his side, heaving with great raspy breaths, the fires in his belly burning low. One of his legs was shattered, and huge chunks of his body had been ripped away. Pistons and gears were scattered around him like broken clockwork.

I knelt beside his head, putting a shaking hand on his neck. It was cold, and his once burning red eyes were dim, flickering erratically. At my touch, he stirred, but didn't raise his head or look at me. I had a horrid suspicion he couldn't see any of us.

"Princess?"

Hearing his voice, so small and breathy, almost made me burst into tears. "I'm so sorry," I whispered, feeling Puck and Ash press behind me, gazing over my shoulder.

"No." The red in his eyes dimmed to tiny pinpricks, and his

voice dropped to a whisper. I had to strain to hear him. "It was…an honor…" He sighed one last time, as the tiny spots of light flickered once, twice. "…my queen." And he was gone.

I closed my eyes and let the tears come. For Ironhorse, who had never wavered, never once compromised his beliefs or convictions. Who had been an enemy, but chose to become an ally, a guardian and, ultimately, a friend. I knelt on the cold tile and sobbed, unembarrassed, as Puck and Ash looked on gravely, until the faint rays of dawn began seeping through the broken skylights.

"Meghan." Ash's quiet voice broke through my grieving. "We should go." His tone was gentle but unrelenting. "The Iron King's army is ready to march. We have to return the scepter. There's not much time left."

I sat up and wiped my eyes, cursing the damned faeries and their eternal war. It seemed there was never enough time. Time to dance, or talk, or laugh, or even mourn the passing of a friend. Slipping off my corsage, I laid it on Ironhorse's cold metal shoulder, wanting him to have something natural and beautiful in this lifeless place. *Goodbye, Ironhorse.* Ash held out a hand, and I let him pull me to my feet.

"Where to now?" I sniffled.

"The Reaping Fields," answered a familiar voice, and Grimalkin appeared, perched several feet away on a cardboard box. He gingerly batted a metal bug off the surface, where it pinged to the floor, before continuing. "All the major battles between the courts have been fought on those plains. If I were looking for the armies of Summer and Winter, that is where I would go."

"Are you sure?" I asked.

"I did not say I was sure, human." Grimalkin twitched his

whiskers at me. "I only said that is where I would look. Also, I am not coming with you."

Somehow, this didn't surprise me. "Why not? Where are you going this time?"

"Back to Leanansidhe's." Grimalkin yawned and stretched, arching his tail over his back. "Now that we are done here, I will inform her that Virus is dead, and that the scepter is on its way back to the Winter Court. I am sure she will want to hear about your success." The cat turned, waving his tail in farewell. "Until next time, human."

"Grim, wait."

He paused, looking back with unblinking golden eyes.

"What did Ironhorse promise you, that made you come along?"

He flicked his tail. "It is not for you to know, human," he replied, his voice low and solemn. "Perhaps you will find out, someday. Oh, and if you do make it to Reaping Field, look for a friend of mine. He still owes me a favor. I believe you have met him before." And with that cryptic message, he leaped off the box and wove gracefully through the scattered hordes of fey and metal bugs. Trotting behind a beam, he disappeared.

I looked at the boys. "How will we get to Reaping Field?"

Ash held up the scepter. It throbbed with icy blue light, sparkling like it was made of crystal, as I'd first seen it back in Tir Na Nog. "I'll use the scepter to open a trod," he murmured, turning away. "Stand back."

The scepter flared, filling the room with cold, making my breath steam. The air around us shimmered, as though a veil had been dropped over everything. A hazy circle opened up in front of Ash; beyond it, I saw trees and earth and the foggy twilight of the wyldwood.

"Go," Ash told us, his voice slightly strained.

"Come on, Princess. This is our stop." Puck gestured at the portal, waiting for me to go through. I turned and cast one final look at Ironhorse's body, lying cold on the cement, and blinked back tears.

*Thank you,* I told him silently, and stepped through the circle.

# CHAPTER TWENTY-THREE

*Reaping Fields*

The wyldwood was in chaos. Wind and hail whipped around me as I stumbled off the trod, screaming through the branches and pelting me with shards of ice. Green lightning streaked overhead, slashing through massive clouds that roiled and churned above us, shaking branches and stirring debris into violent whirlwinds. Gouts of snow intermingled with the rain, gathering in mounds and drifts and then scattered by the wind. A violet-skinned piskie went hurtling by, caught in a savage tailspin, until she vanished into the trees.

"Dammit." Puck appeared behind me, crimson hair flying in all directions. He had to shout to be heard. "They started the war without us. I had an invitation, too."

Ash stepped through the circle, and it closed behind him. "Reaping Field is close." He raised his head to the wind, closing his eyes, and his brow furrowed. "The fighting is well underway. I can smell the blood. Follow me."

We hurried through the forest, Ash in front leading the way, the scepter a bright blue glow against the dark of the wyldwood. Around us, the storm raged and howled, and thunder boomed overhead, shaking the ground. My shoes sank into the mud, and my gown snagged on a dozen thorns and branches that tore through the fabric and ripped what remained to shreds.

Finally, the trees fell away, leaving us staring over a vast, icy gulley flanked by rugged hills, their tops disappearing into the clouds. A frozen river snaked its way through the boulder-studded valley, coiling lazily around the ruins of an ancient castle in the center of the plains.

From here, the armies of Summer and Winter looked like swarming ants, a huge, chaotic blur of motion and color. Roars and screams filled the air, rising above the howl of the wind. Ranks of soldiers clashed against one another in a somewhat disciplined fashion, while other groups bounded across the field, ricocheting from one fight to the next, joyfully hurling themselves into the fray. Giant shapes lumbered through the masses, swinging and crushing, and swarms of flying creatures attacked from the air. It was a colossal, violent, crazy free-for-all that would be suicide to go through.

I gulped and looked to Ash and Puck. "We're going through that, aren't we?"

Ash nodded. "Look for Oberon or Mab," he said grimly, scanning the battlefield. "They'll likely be on opposite sides of the river. Try not to engage anything, Goodfellow. We don't want a fight—we just want to get the scepter to the queen."

"Don't kid yourself, Prince." Puck grinned and drew his daggers, pointing to Ash with the tip. "You're a traitor, Meghan's the Summer princess, and I'm Robin Goodfellow. I'm sure the ranks of Unseelie will just let us waltz right through."

And then, a shadow fell over us, and a blast of wind nearly knocked me down. Ash shoved me away as a huge, winged lizard landed where I'd stood in an explosion of snow and rock. The creature hissed and shrieked, beating tattered wings and churning the ground with two clawed forelegs. Its scales were a dusty brown, its yellow eyes vicious and stupid. A long, muscular tail whipped the air behind it, a wicked, gleaming barb on the end. Hissing, it stepped between me, Ash and Puck, separating us with its body, coiling its tail over its back like a massive scorpion.

A rider sat between the creature's shoulder blades, his white armor pristine and shining, not a drop of blood on him.

"Rowan!" I gasped.

"Well, well." The older prince sneered at me from the back of his lizard mount. "Here you are again. The wayward princess and our traitor prince. Don't move, Ash," he warned, shooting his brother a dark look. "One tiny move, and Thraxa will snap up your beloved half-breed faster than you can blink. You don't want to lose *another* girl to wyvern poison, do you?"

Ash already had his sword out, but at Rowan's threat he paled and shot me a haunted look. I saw the desperation in his eyes before he lowered his blade and stepped back.

"Good boy. This will be over soon, don't worry." Rowan raised his fist, and a dozen Thornguards emerged from the trees, weapons drawn, trapping us between them and Rowan. "It shouldn't be long now," the older prince smiled. "Once the courts are done tearing each other to pieces, the Iron King's armies will sweep in, and everything will be over.

"But first," he continued, turning to glare at Ash, "I'll need that scepter. Hand it over, little brother."

Ash tensed, but before he could do anything, Puck stepped between us, an evil grin stretching his face. "Come and get it," he challenged. Rowan looked over and sneered.

"Robin Goodfellow," he smiled. "I've heard so much about you. You're the reason Ariella is dead, aren't you?" Puck frowned, but Rowan went on without pause. "A pity Ash won't ever take his revenge, but believe me when I say this will be a pleasure. Thraxa," he ordered, sweeping his arm contemptuously toward Puck. "Kill."

The wyvern hissed and snaked its head down, baring needle sharp fangs. It was frighteningly quick, like a viper, and its jaws snapped shut over Puck's head.

I gasped, but Puck exploded in a swirl of leaves, leaving the wyvern blinking and confused. As it drew back, huffing and scanning the ground for its victim, a huge black raven swooped out of the trees, aiming right for its face. With a screeching caw, the bird sank its talons into the side of the wyvern's head and plunged its sharp beak into the slitted yellow eye.

The wyvern reared back with a scream, beating its wings and shaking its head, trying to dislodge the bird that clung to it. Rowan, nearly thrown from the saddle, cursed and yanked at the reins, trying to regain control, but the wyvern was panicked now, screeching and thrashing about in anguish. I ducked beneath the monster and ran to Ash, who caught me in an almost desperate hug, even as he kept his eyes on Rowan. I felt his heart racing beneath his coat.

The raven hung on, jabbing and clawing, until black ichor spattered the wyvern's face and the eye was a popped, useless mess. With a caw of triumph, it broke away and swooped back to us, changing to Puck in an explosion of feathers. He was still laughing as he rose to his feet, drawing his weapons with a flourish.

"Kill them!" Rowan screamed, as his mount decided it had had enough, and leaped skyward. "Kill them all and get that scepter! Don't let them ruin everything!"

"Stay back," Ash told me as the Thornguards started forward, closing their deadly half circle. There were a lot of them, seeming to melt out of the trees and bramble, more than I first thought. My eyes fell on Ash, holding both the scepter and his sword in a double-weapon stance. Could I just take the scepter and run? I shot a quick glance down the slope, into the valley, and my heart went cold with fear. No way. There was no way I'd get through that churning mass alive.

Lightning flickered, bright and eerie, and between one flash and the next, a white creature appeared at the edge of the slope. At first, I thought it was a horse. Only it was smaller and more graceful than any I'd seen before, more deer than equine, with a lion's tail and cloven hooves that barely touched the ground. Its horn spiraled up between its ears, beautiful and terrible at the same time, destroying any preconceived notions I had of the word *unicorn*. It regarded me with eyes as ancient as the forest, and I felt a shiver of recognition, like a memory from a dream, but then it was gone.

*Grimalkin sent me.* The voice whispered in my head, soft as a feather's passing. *Hurry, Meghan Chase.* With a toss of its head, the unicorn turned and vanished down the slope. In that moment, I knew what I had to do.

That whole encounter seemed to have taken place in an instant. When I turned back to the boys, they were still waiting for the Thornguards, who approached slowly, as if they knew we weren't going anywhere. "Ash," I murmured, placing a hand on his arm. "Give me the scepter."

He shot me a look over his shoulder. "What?"

"I'll get it to Mab. Just hold them off until I can get across the field." Ash stared at me, his expression torn. I closed my hand over the scepter, gritting my teeth as the cold burned like fire. "I can do this."

"Hey, Prince," Puck called over his shoulder, "uh, you can join in anytime, now. Whenever you're ready."

A shriek echoed over the valley, and a dark shape wheeled toward us on leathery wings. Rowan was coming back.

"Ash!" The Thornguards were almost upon us, and Ash still held the scepter tightly. Desperately, I met his eyes, saw the indecision there, the doubt, and the fear that he was sending me to my death. "Ash," I whispered, and put my other hand over his, "you have to trust me."

He shivered, nodded once, and released his grip. Clutching the scepter, I backed away, holding his worried gaze as the Thornguards got closer and the wail of the wyvern echoed over the trees. "Be careful," he said, a storm of emotion in those two simple words. I nodded breathlessly.

"I won't fail," I promised.

The Thornguards charged with a roar. Ash spun toward them, blade flashing, as Puck gave a whooping battle cry and plunged into their midst. Feeling the scepter burn in my hands, I turned and fled down the slope.

The unicorn waited at the bottom of the hill, almost invisible in the mist, its horn more real than the rest of it. My heart pounded as I approached. Even though the unicorn stood perfectly still, watching me, it was akin to walking up to a tiger that was tame and friendly, but still a tiger. It could either kneel and lay its head in my lap, or explode into violence and skewer me with that glimmering horn. Thankfully it did neither, standing motionless as a statue as I walked up close enough to see my reflection in its dark eyes. *What do I say? Do I have to ask permission to get on its back?*

A piercing wail rent the air above us, and the shadow of the wyvern passed overhead. The unicorn jumped, flattening its ears, trembling with the effort not to bolt. *Screw it, I don't have time!* As the wyvern's howl rang out again, I heaved myself awkwardly onto the unicorn's back and grabbed its mane.

As soon as I was settled, the unicorn made a fantastic leap

over the rocks and landed at the edge of the icy field, making my stomach lodge in my throat. For a moment, it hesitated, looking this way and that, trying to find an easier way in. A red-eyed hound sprang at us with a snarl, tongue lolling. The unicorn leaped nimbly aside, lashing out with its hooves. I heard a crack and a yelp, and the hound fled into the mist on three legs.

"There's no time to go around!" I yelled, hoping the unicorn could understand me. "Mab is on the far side of the river! We have to go straight through!"

A bellow sounded behind us. I glanced back to see the wyvern dive from the slope and glide toward the ground, straight for us. I saw Rowan on the wyvern's back, sword drawn, his furious gaze fixed on me, and my stomach clenched in terror. "Go!" I shrieked, and with a desperate whinny, we plunged into the heart of the battle.

The unicorn bounded through the chaos, dodging weapons, leaping over obstacles, moving with terrifying speed. My hand gripped the mane so hard that my arms shook; the other hand burned with the scepter. Around us, Summer and Winter fey tore and slashed at each other, screaming in fury, pain and pure, joyful bloodlust. I caught flashes of the battle as we sped through. A pair of trolls pounded stone clubs into a swarm of goblins, their shoulders and backs bristling with spears. A trio of redcaps dragged a wailing sylph from the air, ignoring the razor edge of her dragonfly wings, and buried her under their stabbing knives. Seelie knights in green and gold armor clashed swords with Unseelie warriors, their movements so graceful it looked like they were dancing, but their unearthly beauty was twisted with hate.

The roar of the wyvern sounded directly above us, and the unicorn leaped aside so quickly I nearly lost my seat. I saw the wyvern's hooked, grasping talons slam into a dwarf, and the bearded man screamed as he was torn away and lifted into the air, struggling weakly. The wyvern soared upward, and I watched in horror as it dropped the still struggling dwarf to the rocks below. Wheeling in a lazy circle, it came for us again.

My mount started weaving, a frantic, zigzag pattern that jostled me from side to side and made me sick with fear. I pressed my knees into the unicorn's sides so hard that I felt its ribs through my gown. The wyvern wavered in the air, confused, then dove with another chilling wail. My nimble steed dodged once more, but this time the wyvern passed so close I could've slapped its claws with the back of my hand.

We were in the middle of the field, still nowhere near the river, when the unicorn went down.

The fighting was thicker in the center of the battleground, where soldiers from both sides clashed together over the dead and the dying. The unicorn darted between the crowds, seeming to know exactly when a hole would open up, slipping through without slowing down. But Rowan was still on our tail. As the unicorn dodged the wyvern's pass for the third time, a huge, rocklike monster reared up from beneath the snow, swiping at us with a massive club. It clipped the unicorn's front legs, and the graceful animal collapsed with a shrill whinny. I went flying off its back and hit a snowbank with a landing that drove the air from my lungs.

Dazed, I lay there as the world spun like a carousel, flickering in and out of view. Blurred, shadowy figures raged around me, screaming, but the sounds were muffled and distorted, coming from a great distance away.

Then the white shape of the unicorn reared up, pawing the air, slashing with its horn, before it was pulled under the black mass. I pushed myself to my knees, calling out to it, but my arms shook, and I collapsed, sobbing in frustration. Once more, the unicorn reared up, its white coat streaked with crimson, several dark things clinging to its back. I cried out, crawling forward desperately, but with a shrill cry, the unicorn disappeared into the churning mass once more. This time, it didn't resurface.

As I gasped for breath, fighting tears, something wet and slimy dripped onto my arm. I looked up into the warty face of a goblin, its crooked teeth slick with drool as it grinned at me, flicking a pale tongue over its lips.

"Tasty girl dead yet?" it asked, poking my arm with the butt of its spear.

I lurched upright. Nausea surged through me and the ground twirled. I concentrated on not passing out. The goblin scuttled back with a hiss, then edged forward again. I frantically gazed around for a weapon, and saw the scepter, lying in the snow a few feet away.

The goblin grinned, raising its spear, then vanished under several tons of wyvern as the monstrous lizard landed on it with a boom that shook the ground, sending snow flying. Roaring, it reared back to strike, and I lunged for the scepter.

My hand closed over the rod, and a jolt of electricity shot up my arm. I felt the wyvern's hot breath on my neck and rolled back, bringing up the scepter. In that split second, I saw the gaping, tooth-filled maw of the wyvern fill my whole vision, and the scepter in my hand glowing, not blue or gold or green, but a pure, blinding white.

Lightning shot from the rod, slamming into the wyvern's open mouth. The blast flung the lizard's head back, filling the air with the stench of charred flesh. At the same time, I felt something inside me break, like a hammer striking glass, shattering into a million pieces. Sound, color and emotion flooded my mind, a bottled-up wave of glamour pouring outward, and I screamed.

A pulse ripped through the air, flying outward. It knocked the nearest fighters off their feet and continued, spreading across the field. Fighting a wave of dizziness, I staggered to my feet, swaying like a drunk sailor in a torn and filthy gown. I couldn't see Mab or Oberon through the indistinct shadows around me, but I did see hundreds of glowing eyes, shining blades and bared teeth, ready to tear me apart. I certainly had everyone's attention now.

The scepter pulsed in my hand. Gripping the handle, I raised it over my head. A flickering light spilled over the crowd, making them mutter and draw back.

"Where is Queen Mab?" I called, my voice reedy and faint, barely rising above the howl of the wind. No one answered, so I tried again. "My name is Meghan Chase, daughter of Lord Oberon. I am here to return the Scepter of the Seasons." I hoped someone told Mab quickly; I didn't know how much longer I could stay conscious, much less speak in coherent sentences in front of the queen.

Slowly, the crowd parted, and the air around us dropped several degrees, making my breath steam before my face. Mab came through the crowd on a huge white warhorse, her gown trailing behind her, her hair unbound and flowing down her back. The horse's hooves didn't quite touch the ground, and great gouts of steam billowed from its nostrils, wreathing the Winter Queen in a ghostly halo of fog. Her lips and nails were blue, her eyes as black as a starless night as she peered down at me.

"Meghan Chase." The queen's voice was a hiss, her perfect features terrifyingly blank. Her gaze flicked to the rod in my hand, and she smiled, cold and dangerous. "I see you have my scepter. So, is the Summer Court finally admitting their mistake?"

"No," came a strong voice before I could answer. "The Summer Court had nothing to do with stealing the scepter. You are the one who jumped to conclusions, Lady Mab."

And Oberon was there, sweeping through the crowd on a golden-bay stallion, flanked by a squad of elven knights. His faery mail glittered emerald and gold, bright links woven around protrusions of bark and bone, and an antlered helm rose above his head.

I felt a surge of relief at seeing him, but it shriveled when the Erlking looked at me, his green eyes cold and remote. "I told you before, Queen Mab," he said, speaking to Mab but still glaring at me, "I knew nothing of this, nor did I send my people to steal the scepter from you. You have started a war with us over a false pretense."

"So you say." Mab gave me a predatory smile, making me feel like a trapped rabbit. "But, it seems the Summer Court is still at fault, Erlking. You might have known nothing of the scepter, but your daughter admits her guilt by trying to return what is mine, hoping perhaps, that I will be merciful. Is that not correct, Meghan Chase?"

I noticed crowds of both Winter and Summer fey edging back from the rulers, and wished I could do the same. "No," I blurted out, feeling the glare of both rulers burning holes through my skull. "I mean…no, I didn't steal it."

"Lies!" Mab leaped from her warhorse and stalking toward me. The mad gleam was back, and my stomach contracted in fear. "You are a filthy human, and all you speak is lies. You turned Ash against me. You made him fight his own brother. You fled Tir Na Nog and sought sanctuary with the exile Leanansidhe. Is this not true, Meghan Chase?"

"Yes, but—"

"You were in the throne room when my son was murdered.

Why did they let you live? How did you survive, if it was not the Summer Court behind it all?"

"I told you—"

"If you did not steal the Scepter of the Seasons, who did?"

"The Iron fey!" I shouted, as my temper finally snapped. Not the smartest move, but I was hurt, dizzy, exhausted, and could still see the body of Ironhorse, sprawled lifelessly on the cement, the unicorn torn apart before my eyes. After everything we'd done, everything we'd gone through, to have some faery bitch accuse me of lying was the last straw. "I'm not lying, dammit!" I screamed at her. "Stop talking and just listen to me! The Iron fey stole the scepter and killed Sage! I was right there when it happened! There's an army of them out there, and they're getting ready to attack! That's why they stole the scepter! They wanted you to kill each other before they came in and wiped out everything!"

Mab's eyes went glassy and terrifying, and she raised her hand. I figured I was dead. You don't shout at a faery queen and expect to walk away scot-free. But Oberon finally stepped forward, interrupting Mab before she could turn me into a Popsicle. "Hold, Lady Mab," he said in a low voice. The Winter Queen turned her mad, killing glare on him, but he faced her calmly. "Just a moment, please. She is my daughter, after all." He gave me a measuring look. "Meghan Chase, please return the scepter to Lady Mab, and let us be done with this."

*Gladly.* I approached Mab and held out the scepter in both hands, anxious to be rid of the stupid thing. For all its power, it seemed such a small, trivial item, to cause so much hate and confusion and death. For a moment, the Winter Queen stared at me, her features cold and blank, letting me sweat. Finally, and with great dignity, she reached out and took the scepter, and a great sigh of relief spread across the battlefield. It was done. The Scepter of the Seasons was back where it belonged, and the war was over.

"Now, Meghan Chase," Oberon said as the ripple died down, "why don't you tell us everything that happened?"

So I did, summarizing as best I could. I told them about Tertius stealing the scepter and killing Sage. I told them about the Thornguards, and how they wanted to become Iron fey themselves. I described Grimalkin leading us through the Briars, and how we met Leanansidhe, who agreed to help us. And finally, I told them about Virus, her plans to invade the Nevernever, and how we were able to track her down and get the scepter back.

I left out the parts with Ironhorse. Despite his help and noble sacrifice, they would only see him as the enemy, and I didn't want to be accused of guilt by association. When I was done, an incredulous silence hung in the air, and for a moment only the wind could be heard, howling over the plains.

"Impossible." Mab's voice was chilly, but it had lost the crazy edge, at least. My handing over the scepter seemed to placate her for now. "How did they get into the palace, and out again, without anyone seeing them?"

"Ask Rowan," I shot back, and a mutter went through the ranks of surrounding fey. "He's working with them."

Mab went absolutely still. Goose bumps rose along my arms as ice began creeping over the ground, snapping and crinkling, spreading out from the feet of the Winter Queen. When she spoke, her voice was soft, almost a whisper, but it scared me more than when she was crazy and shouting. "What did you say, half-breed?"

I glanced at Oberon, but he looked disbelieving, as well. I could feel his patience and support wearing thin; if I was going to accuse a son of Mab's of treason, I'd better be able to prove it. Else he wouldn't be able to protect me much longer.

"Rowan is working with the Iron fey," I repeated, as the ice spread around me, sparkling in the snow. "Him and the Thornguards. They...they want to become like them, immune to iron. They think—"

*"Enough!"* Mab's shriek made everyone but Oberon flinch. "Where is your proof, half-breed? Do not expect me to accept these blasphemous claims without proof—you are a human and can lie so easily! You say my son has betrayed his court and kin, to side with these iron abominations that none have seen? Very well! Show me proof!" She pointed a finger at me, eyes narrowed in triumph. "If you have none, you are guilty of slandering the royal family, and I will punish you as I see fit!"

"I don't—" But the sounds of a struggle interrupted us. The crowds shifted, looking around, then stepped out of the way as a trio of faeries came through. Ash and Puck, bleeding, grim faced and dirty, dragging the spiky frame of a Thornguard between them. Staggering into the circle, they threw the faery at Mab's feet.

Panting, Puck straightened, wiping blood from his mouth with the back of his hand. "There's your proof."

Oberon raised an eyebrow. "Goodfellow," he said, and that one word sent shivers down my spine and made Puck wince. "What is the meaning of this?"

Mab smiled. "Ash," she purred, but it wasn't a friendly greeting. "What a surprise to find you here, in the company of the Summer girl and Robin Goodfellow. Would you care to add anything more to your list of crimes?"

"My queen." Ash stood before Mab, breathing heavily, his expression bleak and resigned. "The princess speaks the truth. Rowan is a traitor to us. He sent his elite guard to bolster the armies of the Iron fey, he allowed them access into the palace, and he is responsible for the death of Prince Sage. Were it not for Robin Goodfellow and the Summer princess, the scepter would be lost, and the armies of the Iron King would overwhelm us." Mab narrowed her eyes, and Ash stepped back, nodding to the moaning Thornguard. "If you doubt my word, my queen, just ask him for the truth. I'm sure he would be happy to tell you everything."

"Screw it," Puck snapped, stalking past me. "Or you could just do this."

He pounced on the guard, driving his knee into the faery's armored chest. The Thornguard's arms came up to protect himself, and Puck grabbed one of his gauntlets, ripping the glove away and holding up his wrist.

The sharp tang of metal filled the air, and the circle of curious onlookers leaped back with cries of horror. The Thornguard's entire hand was blackened and shriveled, the skin flaking off like ash. And on his long, gnarled finger, the iron ring gleamed brightly against the withered flesh.

"There!" Puck snapped, throwing the arm down and stepping away. "That proof enough for you? Every one of these bastards has one of those rings on, and it's not a fashion statement. If you want more proof, check the brambles at the top of the hill. We left this one alive to explain his little coup ambitions to his queen."

Mab turned her cold, cold gaze on the Thornguard, who cringed and started babbling.

"My queen, I can explain. Rowan ordered us to. I was acting on his command. He said it was the only way to save us. Please, I never wanted to…please, no!"

Mab gestured. There was a flash of blue light, and ice covered the guard, encasing him in frozen crystal. He drew a breath for one last scream, but the ice closed over his face and smothered it. I shivered and looked away.

"He will tell me everything later." Mab smiled coldly, speaking more to herself than to us. "Oh, yes. He will be begging to tell me." She looked up, her eyes as terrible as her voice. "Where is Rowan?"

As the crowds began muttering and looking around, I glanced over at the dead wyvern lying several yards away, smoke still curling from its open mouth. I shivered and turned away, already knowing the answer. Rowan was gone. They wouldn't find him in the Nevernever; he would flee to the Iron fey, continuing his quest to become like them.

After a long moment, it became clear that Rowan was no longer on the field. "Lady Mab," Oberon said, drawing himself up. "In light of this newest revelation, I propose a temporary truce. If the Iron King does plan to attack us, I'd prefer to meet him with my forces strong and ready. We will speak on this later, but for now I will be taking my people back to Arcadia. Meghan, Goodfellow." He nodded to us stiffly. "Come."

I looked at Ash, and he gave me a faint smile. I saw the relief on his face. But Mab wasn't about to let me go just yet. "Not so fast, my dear Oberon," she purred, and the smug satisfaction in her voice made my skin crawl. "I believe you are forgetting something. The laws of our people apply to your daughter, as well. She must answer for turning my son against me." Mab pointed the scepter at me as angry murmurs went through the crowd. "She must be punished for tricking him into helping her escape Tir Na Nog."

"That wasn't Meghan's decision." Ash's deep voice cut through the muttering. I looked at him sharply and shook my head, but he ignored me. "It was mine. I made the choice. She had nothing to do with it."

Mab turned to him, and her gaze softened. Smiling, she crooked a finger, and he approached at once, never wavering, though his hands were clenched at his sides. "Ash," Mab crooned as he drew near. "My poor boy. Rowan told me what happened between the two of you, but I know you had your reasons. Why would you betray me?"

"I love her."

Softly, and without hesitation, as if he'd already made up his mind. My heart turned over and I gasped, but it was lost in the ripple of horror and disbelief that went through the crowd. Whispers and muttering filled the air; some faeries snarled and hissed, baring their teeth, as if they wanted to mob Ash, but kept their distance from the queen.

Mab didn't look surprised, though the smile curling her lips was as cold and cruel as a blade. "You love her. The half-breed daughter of the Summer lord."

"Yes."

I ached for him, my stomach twisting painfully. He looked so desolate standing there alone, facing a mad queen and several thousand angry fey. His voice was flat and resigned, as if he'd been pushed into a corner and had given up, not caring what happened next. I started to go to him, but Puck grabbed my arm, his green eyes solemn as he shook his head.

"Ash." Mab placed a palm on his cheek. "You're confused. I can see it in your eyes. You didn't want this, did you? Not after Ariella." Ash didn't reply, and Mab drew back, regarding him intently. "You know what comes next, don't you?"

Ash nodded once. "I swear an oath," he whispered, "never to see her again, never to speak to her again, to sever all relationships and return to the Winter Court."

"Yes," Mab whispered back, and a sick despair tore at my heart. If Ash spoke those words, it would be over. A faery *couldn't* break a promise, even if he wanted to. "Swear the oath," Mab continued, "and all is forgiven. You can come back to Tir Na Nog. Return to the palace, and take your place as heir to the throne. Sage is gone, and Rowan is dead to me." Mab placed a kiss on Ash's cheek and stepped back. "You are the last prince of Winter. It is time to come home."

"I..." For the first time, Ash hesitated. His gaze met mine, bright and anguished, begging forgiveness. I choked on a sob and turned away, my throat aching with misery, not wanting to hear the words that would take him from me forever.

"I can't."

Silence fell over the field. Puck stiffened; I could feel his shock. Biting my lip, I turned back, hardly daring to believe. Ash faced Mab calmly, the queen staring at him with a terrible, blank expression on her face. "Forgive me," Ash murmured, and I heard the faintest of tremors beneath his voice. "But I can't...I won't...give her up. Not now, when I've just found her."

I couldn't take it anymore. Breaking away from Puck, I started toward Ash. I couldn't let him do this alone. But Oberon stepped in front of me, holding out his arm, as unmovable as a mountain. "Do not interfere, daughter," Oberon said in a voice meant only for me. "This is between the Winter prince and his queen. Let the song play to its conclusion."

Distraught, I looked back to Ash. Mab had gone very still, a beautiful, deadly statue, the ground beneath her coated with ice. Only her lips moved as she stared at her son, the air around them growing colder by the second. "You know what will happen, if you refuse."

If Ash was afraid, he didn't show it. "I know," he said in a weary voice.

"Their world will eat at you," Mab said. "Strip you away bit by bit. Cut off from the Nevernever, you will not survive. Whether it takes one mortal year or a thousand, you will gradually fade away, until you simply cease to exist." Mab stepped closer, pointing at me with the scepter. "She will die, Ash. She is only human. She will grow old, wither and die, and her soul will flee to a place you cannot follow. And then, you will be left to wander the mortal world alone, until you yourself are only a memory. And after that—" the queen opened her empty fist "—nothing. Forever."

Ash didn't react, but I felt the queen's words punch me in the stomach. Bile rose in my throat. How could I be so blind and stupid? Grimalkin had told me once that faeries banished from the Nevernever would die, that they would fade away until nothing was left. Tiaothin had told me that in the Winter palace, when I was trying to ignore her. I'd known all along, but refused to believe. Or perhaps I just hadn't wanted to remember.

"This is your final chance, Prince." Mab stepped back, her voice stiff and icy, like she was talking to a stranger. "Give me your solemn vow, or be damned to the mortal world forever. Make your choice."

Ash looked at me. I saw pain in his eyes, and a little regret, but they shone with such emotion I felt breathless. "I already have."

"So be it." If Mab's voice was cold before, it was in the sub-zero range now. She waved the scepter and, with a sharp crack, a rip appeared in the air. Like ink spreading over paper, it widened into a jagged archway. Beyond the arch, a flickering streetlamp glimmered, and rain pounded the road, hissing. The smell of tar and wet asphalt drifted through the opening. "From this day forth," Mab boomed, her voice carrying over the field, "Prince Ash is considered a traitor and an exile. All trods will be closed to him, all safe holds are barred, and if he is seen anywhere within the Nevernever, he is to be hunted down and killed immediately." She looked at Ash, fury and contempt curling her lips. "You are not my son. Get out of my sight."

Ash stepped back. Without a word, he turned and walked toward the archway, shoulders back and head high. At the edge of the trod, he hesitated, and I saw a shadow of fear cross his face. But then his expression hardened, and he swept through the door without looking back.

"Ash, wait!"

Darting around Oberon, I rushed for the trod. Faeries hissed and snarled, and Puck yelled for me to stop, but I ignored them all. As I approached Mab, her lips curled in a cruel smile and she stepped back, giving me a clear shot at the open trod.

"Meghan Chase!"

Oberon's voice cracked like a whip, and a roar of thunder shook the ground. I stumbled to a halt a few feet from the doorway, so close that I could see the road and darkened street, the blurry outline of houses through the rain.

The Erlking's voice was ominously quiet, and his eyes glowed amber through the gently falling snow. "The laws of our people are absolute," Oberon warned. "Summer and Winter share many things, but love is not one of them. If you make this choice, daughter, the trods will never open for you again."

My stomach dropped. There it was. Oberon would banish me from the Nevernever, as well. For a split second, I almost laughed in his face. This wasn't my home. I hadn't asked to be half-fey. I'd never wanted to be caught up in their problems, or their world. Let him exile me; what did I care?

*Don't kid yourself,* I thought with a sudden sick feeling in my gut. *You love this world. You risked everything to save it. Are you really going to walk away and forget it ever existed?*

"Meghan." Puck stepped forward, pleading. "Don't do this. I can't follow you this time. Stay here. With me."

"I can't," I whispered. "I'm sorry, Puck. I do love you, but I have to do this." His face clouded with pain, and he turned away. Guilt stabbed at me, but in the end, the choice had always been clear.

"I'm sorry," I whispered again to Puck, to Oberon, to everyone, and turned back to the doorway. *I don't belong here. Not really. Time to wake up and go home for real.*

"Are you sure, Meghan Chase?" Oberon's voce was cold, remorseless. "Walk out of Faery with him now, and you're never coming back."

Somehow, the ultimatum made it that much easier.

"Then I'm never coming back," I said softly, and went through the arch, leaving Faery behind me forever.

# EPILOGUE

*Second Homecoming*

As I stumbled through the trod and onto the sidewalk, the rain hit me like a hammer, cold, wet and comfortingly unpleasant. Like normal rain. Lightning flickered overhead; regular, white lightning that didn't respond to the whims of a faery king's mood. My gown clung to my body; the drenching would be the finishing touch to ruining it completely, but I didn't care. My time in Faery was over. No more faery glamour, faery food or faery tricks. I was done.

With one exception, of course.

"Ash!" I called, squinting through the rain and darkness, through the glow of the streetlamps that made it impossible to see more than a few feet. "Ash, I'm here! Where are you?"

The empty road mocked me. Didn't he think I'd come after him? Was he already gone, fading into the rain without a backward glance, believing himself alone in the world? Tears muffled my voice. "Ash!" I yelled, taking a few steps down the sidewalk. "Ash!"

"You'll wake everyone up if you keep shouting like that."

I whirled around. He stood where the portal had been, hands in his pockets, the rain drumming his shoulders and making his hair run into his eyes. Lamplight fell around him, shining off his slick coat, surrounding him with a faint nimbus of light. But to me, he'd never looked so real.

"You came after me," he murmured, sounding awed, incredulous, and relieved at the same time. I walked up to him, smiling through my tears.

"You didn't think I'd let you go off alone, did you?"

"I was hoping." Ash stepped forward and hugged me, pulling me close with desperate relief. I slid my arms beneath his coat and held him tight, closing my eyes. The rain pounded us, and a lone car passed us on the road, spraying us with gutter water, but I felt no urge to move. As long as Ash held me, I could stay here forever.

He finally pulled back but didn't release me from the circle of his arms. "So," he murmured, his silver eyes boring into mine. "What do we do now?"

"I don't know," I said, shivering as he brushed a strand of wet hair from my cheek. "I think…I should go home soon. Mom and Luke are probably going nuts. What about you?"

He shrugged, a casual lift of one shoulder. "You tell me. When I left the Nevernever, I didn't have any plans other than being with you. If you want me around, just say the word."

My eyes watered. I thought of Rowan, of Ironhorse, and the armies of the false king, still on the move. I thought of Leanansidhe and Charles, trapped in the Between. I would have to get him out someday, and confront Leanansidhe about stealing my dad so long ago. But for now, the only thing I wanted was standing right here, looking at me with an expression so open and unguarded that I thought my heart would burst out of my chest. "Don't leave," I whispered, tightening my hold. "Never leave me again. Stay with me. Forever."

The Winter prince smiled, a small, easy smile, and lowered his lips to mine. "I promise."

★ ★ ★ ★ ★

# ACKNOWLEDGMENTS

One would think the second book in a series would be easy to write, now that you've finished the first one and gotten all the hard stuff out of the way. Ha ha ha! No. The second book is just as difficult, if not more so, as the first, and so the list of people I have to thank has not diminished in the slightest. My family, of course, for being so supportive and always believing I could do the impossible. My newfound friends online: Khy and Sharon and Kristi and Liyana, and all the wonderful YA book bloggers of the blogosphere, whose excitement and love of this genre makes me grateful and humbled at the same time. I cannot begin to express my thanks for all they have done. My agent, Laurie McLean, who always has time to answer my questions even though I spell her name wrong sometimes. Natashya Wilson and Adam Wilson, the perfect tag team of Super Editors, and all the wonderful, hardworking folks at Harlequin Teen. I cannot thank you all enough.

And again, I must express my deepest, heartfelt gratitude to my husband, Nick, the greatest listener of all time. I still couldn't have done it without him.

# JULIE KAGAWA

JULIE KAGAWA

*"The Iron King is a must read!"*
— NEW YORK TIMES BESTSELLING
AUTHOR GENA SHOWALTER

## THE IRON KING

IRON. ICE.
A LOVE DOOMED
FROM THE START.
THE IRON FEY

Humanity's obsession with progress and technology has produced something terrible: the Iron Fey. And their presence is slowly destroying the Nevernever, home of the original faeries. It is up to Meghan Chase, half-human daughter of the Summer King, to stop them, and somehow find a way for both species to survive.

Look for the first book in The Iron Fey series!

JULIE KAGAWA

## THE IRON DAUGHTER

LOVE & BETRAYAL.
A FAERY WORLD
GONE MAD.
THE IRON FEY

Book two in The Iron Fey series on sale now!

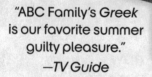